Anne Baker trained as a nurse at Birkenhead General Hospital, but after her marriage went to live first in Libya and then in Nigeria. She eventually returned to her native Birkenhead where she worked as a Health Visitor for over ten years before taking up writing. She now lives with her husband in Merseyside. Anne Baker's other Merseyside sagas are all available from Headline and have been highly praised:

'A fast-moving and entertaining novel, with a fascinating location and warm, friendly characters' *Bradford Telegraph and Argus*

'A wartime Merseyside saga so full of Scouse wit and warmth that it is bound to melt the hardest heart' *Northern Echo*

'Baker's understanding and compassion for very human dilemmas makes her one of romantic fiction's most popular authors' *Lancashire Evening Post*

'A gentle tale with all the right ingredients for a heartwarming novel' *Huddersfield Daily Examiner*

'A well-written enjoyable book that legions of saga fans will love' *Historical Novels Review*

Anne Baker

Daughters of the Mersey

headline

First published in 2012
by HEADLINE PUBLISHING GROUP

First published in paperback in 2013
by HEADLINE PUBLISHING GROUP

4

Cataloguing in Publication Data is available from the British Library

ISBN 978 0 7553 9109 7

Typeset in Baskerville by Avon DataSet Ltd, Bidford-on-Avon, Warwickshire

Printed and bound in Great Britain by
Clays Ltd, Elcograf S.p.A

Headline's policy is to use papers that are natural, renewable and recyclable
products and made from wood grown in sustainable forests. The logging
and manufacturing processes are expected to conform to the
environmental regulations of the country of origin.

HEADLINE PUBLISHING GROUP
An Hachette UK Company
338 Euston Road
London NW1 3BH

www.headline.co.uk
www.hachette.co.uk

DAUGHTERS OF
THE MERSEY

CHAPTER ONE

Summer 1929

L EONIE DRANSFIELD HAD UNDRESSED for bed. Feeling
confused and worried, she was sitting in front of her
dressing table watching Steve, her husband, in her mirror. His
movements were slow and awkward and it took him a long
time to unstrap his false leg and take it off.

Without it, he needed his crutches to move about and he
kept them propped against the side of their bed. He let his false
leg clatter to the floor and heaved himself between the sheets;
even now she had to look away from that bare stump.

During the war, Steve had fought in the trenches and been
horribly injured in the winter of 1917. His left leg had had to
be amputated above the knee, and though his other wounds
had eventually healed, scars had been left not only on his body
but on his mind.

She'd noticed he'd been upset and grumpy over the last few
days. He'd said he wasn't well, that he was plagued by one of
his migraines, but now he'd admitted that he'd had this bad
news and hadn't been able to tell her. That made it sound very
bad indeed.

She felt anxiety stir within her. 'What d'you mean, bad news?'

'You know I've sold two shops.' Steve had inherited a leading antiques business from his family. 'You know the business went down in the war and that it's never really recovered.'

'Of course I know the shops have been sold.' Leonie was impatient, afraid something terrible had happened. 'You said the money would be a nice little nest egg, it would provide a cushion in bad times and a comfort in our old age, but really we need it now to put food on the table and fuel in the grate. What have you done with it? I thought you intended to hand it over to Hawkes and Harmsworth to invest.'

The stockbrokers Hawkes and Harmsworth had served the Dransfield family well over the last fifty years. They still looked after the remnants of the wealth they'd made in antiques.

'I tried something new. I went to a different firm.'

'For heaven's sake! What on earth made you do that?' Leonie's heart plummeted. They were desperate for more income. That was why he'd sold the shops in the first place. Surely he hadn't lost all that money? She could hardly sit still.

Steve groaned. 'William Hawkes is so old-fashioned. He puts me into companies that don't earn much interest.'

She leapt up to open the bedroom window. 'He's honest, Steve. Yes, he may be conservative, but he's always been mindful of your interests and doesn't take unnecessary risks with your money.'

'I did it for you and the children.'

'What?' Leonie could no longer bite back her anger. 'The last thing I wanted was for you to take risks. You must know that.'

'I'm sorry. We needed more money. I thought I could get it. You know I've lost my health and strength, I can't work like a normal man.'

Leonie seethed, everything always came back to that.

She couldn't help bursting out at him, 'You were greedy. So not only is there no interest, but the capital has gone too?'

'It wasn't my fault. It was out-and-out fraud. They were gangsters, out to do me. I've been worried stiff this past week.'

'Steve, surely you knew there were fraudsters out there who would cheat you if you gave them half a chance? You knew you could trust William Hawkes. I can't believe you've done this.'

Steve looked contrite.

'Have you reported it to the police?'

'Yes, but I don't think anything will come of it. They didn't hold out much hope of my getting it back.'

'What's done is done,' she said with the resignation she'd learned from married life.

He was only forty-six but he was gauntly thin with rounded shoulders and sparse mouse-brown hair that was greying. Pain and disappointment had dogged him since the last war. He looked old for his years and she felt full of pity for him, but he didn't want pity. There was nothing he resented more.

'I'm sorry,' he said. 'Don't go on at me, Leonie, I can't stand that. I know I made a mistake and I truly wish I'd stayed with William Hawkes.'

She could see tears welling in his eyes and looked away. She mustn't say any more, he was given to bouts of depression and she didn't want to make matters worse. He knew well enough he'd been a fool. 'If it's gone, it's better to put it out of your mind.'

'But I can't. What are we going to do for money? Our income is going down all the time and we've got two children to bring up.'

'We'll manage somehow,' Leonie said, giving her dark-blond hair a perfunctory brushing – a token of her normal routine. 'We'll manage,' she repeated. 'We always have.'

She glanced at herself in the mirror and sighed. Worried eyes stared back at her.

Was her fringe and shoulder-length bob getting a bit girlish for her at thirty-six? She wished she had lustrous curls like her children but they'd inherited those from Steve, though his brown hair was anything but lustrous now. Her hair was almost straight with just enough bend in it to frame her face. At one time, Steve used to say it suited her like this.

Leonie got into bed beside him but she couldn't get to sleep. To be defrauded out of the money they'd been relying on brought them to crisis point.

Leonie had been orphaned at seven years of age and brought up by her Great-Aunt Felicity, who had managed on a small income through thrift and self-sufficiency and using her common sense. Leonie had been brought up to do the same and it was these skills that had helped them survive so far. Steve, on the other hand, had been born to a family that had never gone short. He'd been used to spending money freely and having the best of everything.

When Leonie had become engaged to Steven Dransfield, her Aunt Felicity had said, 'How fortunate you are, to be marrying into a family like the Dransfields. You'll never want for anything.' Leonie had been of the same opinion and had enjoyed every comfort money could buy during the first few years of her marriage. But the war had changed everything and Aunt Felicity had been proved very wrong.

Leonie knew well enough how they'd managed so far. Steve's only brother Raymond had been killed at Mons and Steve had inherited all his family's wealth. First and foremost was the house they lived in, it had been the Dransfield family home and very comfortable in its day. In addition, he'd received the business that had earned a good living for the family over several generations. As they'd been antique dealers, they'd kept the pieces they'd admired most to furnish it, so he'd inherited many valuable objects too. Most of these he'd already sold into the trade because he owned the shops where the value of antiques and fine art could easily be realised.

Steve had been a boarder at a public school and though his children weren't having that luxury, they were at fee-paying day schools. His mother's jewellery was the first thing he'd sold to meet that expense.

When they'd had a plumbing problem, Steve had taken an eighteenth-century French ormolu mantel clock to the shop. When a tree had blown down in a gale and taken a few slates off the roof, he'd taken the George III silver tea and coffee service to pay the bill.

Leonie tossed and turned in bed, wondering how on earth they would manage now.

CHAPTER TWO

LEONIE AND STEVE HAD been married just before the Great War began. At that time his parents had been alive and so had his brother. Leonie felt full of love for Steve and knew he felt the same way about her. She expected marriage to transform her life. She'd looked forward to being a good wife and taking care of Steve and the home he'd rented for them. They'd both hoped that, in time, they'd have a family of their own.

Steve had been working for his father in the family antiques business which had been started by his great-grandfather in the last century. At the time, they'd been running an auction house and they owned four shops. The flagship of the business was in central Liverpool.

The family lived in some style on the Esplanade at New Ferry, in a spacious single-storey house they called Mersey Reach, built to their own specifications about the middle of Queen Victoria's reign. It had been designed with many Georgian features, and had six bedrooms, a music room, a garden of two acres and accommodation for live-in staff in the cellar. It was in a very convenient position being within easy walking distance of the ferry terminus to Liverpool.

At the beginning of the war Steve hadn't wanted to join up,

he'd just wanted to get on with his life and stay with Leonie, their future had looked rosy. He'd had to struggle with his conscience, believing he should do his bit but his father had persuaded him not to, saying he needed him in the business. When the avalanche of volunteers dried up in 1916, conscription came in and he'd had to go.

The war had marred everything and brought unexpected hardships. Leonie felt it had torn them apart. Left on her own, she gave up the tenancy of the house Steve had rented on their marriage and returned to live with her Aunt Felicity because she was now in her eighties and in failing health. There was little food to be had in the shops and it was rising rapidly in price. By the time Miles, their first child, was born in 1917, Steve was fighting in the trenches in France.

Miles was a Dransfield family name and Steve's choice. He was a lovely strong baby with a lot of dark hair that had a reddish tinge. His face was round and rarely without a smile and he slept all night from an early age.

Leonie was kept busy caring for her baby and her aunt and looking after the house. Every evening when both were settled for the night she wrote to Steve, and his regular letters gave point to her day.

Then suddenly his letters stopped coming. Leonie tried to believe it was a problem with the post and that several would come together. The empty days stretched on until she was almost out of her mind with worry.

It was over a month before she heard that he'd been injured on the Somme and repatriated to a hospital near London. Her first feelings were of utter relief. He was alive and that was all that mattered.

When she went down to see him, she was shocked to find him in pain and looking so ill. He had been caught in shellfire which had killed three men and injured two others. He had abdominal injuries caused by flying debris, as well as major injuries to his leg which had meant amputation.

His doctors told Leonie they saw no reason why he shouldn't make a good recovery and cope with his disability. He spent almost a year in different hospitals before being sent to Woodley Grange, a mansion near Chester that had been converted to provide rehabilitation and convalescence for injured soldiers. He was near enough for Leonie to visit him often, and though his doctors continued to talk hopefully of his recovery, he'd begun to lose heart.

Steve's parents, Edward and Isobel, were worried about him too and they did their best to help her. Edward hired a carriage to drive Leonie to and from the train station and Isobel liked to have charge of the baby. But only a few months later she began to complain of feeling unwell. Nothing seemed to help and eventually she was diagnosed with stomach cancer. It was a terrible shock to them all.

There were other problems too. The Dransfields had always employed a cook and a housemaid, but they both gave notice in the same month. The war had resulted in a dearth of domestic help as munitions factories were advertising for workers and paying higher wages for shorter hours. Leonie found them a woman who would come on three mornings a week to do the rough work but it wasn't enough. Edward did what he could but Leonie had to go in every day to help with the cooking. With Miles and Aunt Felicity to take care of too, they were both finding it exhausting.

One day Edward and Isobel suggested she move in with them and take over the running of the family home. It seemed the only logical course. Leonie was fond of her in-laws and they got on well together.

Great-Aunt Felicity was moved into a room with a lovely view over the river, but she survived there for only another six weeks. Leonie cared for her and sat with her when she was dying and found it emotionally exhausting. Steve's mother was failing too. She spent the last months of her life when the weather was fine on a day bed in the summer house.

When Isobel passed away in her sleep one night, Leonie was grief-stricken and she and her father-in-law comforted each other as best they could.

Edward was coming up to retirement age but carried on working because a lot of his staff had joined up, but in truth, there was less work to do, the business was suffering.

Leonie longed for the end of the war but focused her mind on visiting Steve in Woodley Grange, her daily chores and caring for Edward and her little son. Miles was thriving, a happy little boy who brought great pleasure to them both and made them hope for a better future.

When the war ended, the War Office granted Steve a pension of £1. 10/- per week and Leonie brought him home to Mersey Reach to join the family. By the end of 1919 he'd recovered enough to return to work to become one of their buyers. It entailed a lot of travelling and attending auctions to buy good-quality antiques to stock their shops and both Leonie and Edward noticed he found the work tiring.

The only good thing that happened in the family in the aftermath of war was that Leonie gave birth to a daughter.

They called her June and she brought comfort to Steve and his father. She was a pretty baby with fair hair and big round blue eyes and both Edward and Steve loved to sit and hold her in their arms. Leonie blessed the fact that there was a family business to support them and devoted herself to the children and the running of the house.

They'd always held their auctions in a hall that was lease-hold and in 1924 the lease came up for renewal. Edward deliberated for a long time about whether he should renew it and in the end decided not to because the rent was being put up to what he considered was an exorbitant level. It upset him to see the family business going downhill.

One lunchtime, Steve argued with his father about the value of a grandfather clock he'd bought at auction. Edward said he'd paid too much for it and Steve blamed him for the deteriorating profits in the business. The argument developed into a huge row. When the shouting died down, Leonie took a tea tray into the conservatory where she knew Edward was reading. It shocked her to see his eyes swimming with tears and she sank down in the chair beside him.

'He doesn't mean to upset you, Edward. Deep down Steve probably knows you are right, but he can't control these terrible moods he has.'

'He certainly can't. He said some terrible things.'

'You must forgive him. There are times when he hardly knows what he's saying. I think it's frustration that he can't pull his weight. He wants to take his rightful place in the business but he can't. He can't get over what the war did to him.'

Edward took her hand in his and squeezed it. 'He's lucky to have married a strong woman like you.'

'I don't feel strong, just sorry that things have turned out like this for us all.'

'You are strong, Leonie, and very patient too, and you're going to need all the strength you have. I find Steve hard to cope with now and I'm afraid that in time you may too.'

'No.' She smiled. 'He's my husband.'

His hand, distorted with the swollen joints of old age, patted hers. 'He's not the husband you married. Steve needs you. If ever you left him—'

'I won't, I love him.'

'I love him too but . . . Promise me, Leonie,' he said, 'that you'll never give up on him. Promise me you'll never leave him.'

'I won't, Edward. I promise.'

He patted her hand again. 'Thank you.'

'I won't give up on you either. What about having this tea now?'

For the first time in three generations the family felt short of money.

Steve had been brought up to believe that when his father retired, the job of running the family business would be his, but he was worried that his father thought he was not up to it. Edward knew the time had come for him to make a decision, and he finally concluded that for the sake of the business, his wisest choice would be to promote George Courtney as manager. George was a distant relative, considerably older than Steve, and had been working in the business for ten years in a senior position.

Steve was expecting it, Edward had talked it over with him, but it made him resentful and more frustrated than ever.

Without the daily trip to the shop, Edward seemed to lose all purpose in life and began to fade away. One morning when Steve looked in on his father before going to work he found him asleep. He was still in bed at lunchtime. Leonie heated some soup and took it up for him but she couldn't persuade him to eat much of it. She'd thought he was dozing again when suddenly he jerked into a sitting position. 'Open the gates,' he commanded in a more imperious voice than she'd ever heard him use before. He closed his eyes and dropped back against his pillows. It took her a long moment to realise he was dead.

Leonie could hardly get her breath. She'd failed to understand how close to death Edward had been and that shocked and upset her. With shaking fingers she covered Edward's face with his sheet, pulled herself upright and went to phone for the doctor, blessing the fact one had been recently installed. She was still trembling when Steve came home.

She didn't realise how deeply affected Steve was by the death of his father and neither did his doctor. He became completely wrapped up in his own difficulties and left the day-to-day running of the family and the home to her, and the responsibilities of the business to others.

He'd missed several opportunities to buy stock for the shops and George had felt compelled to find somebody else to do his job. After that, Steve only went near the business when he felt like it.

As the years went by he seemed to withdraw from Leonie and no longer wanted to join in family activities. He had good days and bad, but his black moods made him flare up at everybody and the children got on his nerves. She blessed the fact that their bungalow was large and substantially built, so the children's noise didn't carry to his study, but all the same it became a struggle to cope.

The children were growing up and finding their own friends. She'd always thought the name Miles a bit formal for a small boy and when he started school and she heard his friends calling him Milo, she thought it suited him better. Only his father persisted in calling him Miles.

Routine maintenance on the house had long since ceased. It had not been repainted for eleven years and was beginning to look shabby. There was a Victorian conservatory between the large drawing room and the music room. The roof was a dome of glass but the walls were brick and windowless. It caught the afternoon sun and Edward had grown hothouse flowers there, but now the glass panes leaked.

The garden was no longer magnificent. Once there had been a full-time gardener and a boy to look after it, now they had an old man who came for a few hours a week in the summer to cut the grass nearest to the house. The children played in the summer house and Leonie occasionally sat there if she had time on a sunny afternoon. She'd dug over a plot and was growing vegetables to save money. That still left a large area that had reverted to field where Milo played football.

Recently, George had suggested they sell two of the shops as they were finding it hard to buy in enough good-quality antiques to stock four outlets. The business was still turning over a small profit but it was largely being eaten up by running expenses. Fewer shops would increase the profitability of the remaining, and as they owned the freehold to all them, it would release capital for them to live on.

It had seemed a good idea at the time, but now the knowledge that Steve had been defrauded of the money made Leonie toss and turn for hours. There was nothing else for it, she'd have to earn money to add to their income. She would have to learn to stand on her own feet. If she didn't, life was going to be desperately hard for them all.

CHAPTER THREE

B Y THE TIME THE ALARM went the next morning, Leonie was in a heavy sleep, but she had to get the children up for school and make them breakfast. Steve didn't get up with them on school mornings because the noise and the rushing about gave him a headache.

Today, she made boiled eggs with toast and a pot of tea for the children and herself. She was pleased to see them come silently to the table dressed in their school uniforms.

They went to different schools although both caught the same bus. Milo's school was further on than June's and he'd been going on his own for some time before she started. In order to save the cost of her own bus fare, Leonie soon gave him the responsibility of seeing June got off at the right stop.

Steve's daily copy of *The Times* was delivered to a box at the back gate. June had taken on the job of collecting it and running back with it for her father, before she went to catch the bus.

When Leonie waved them off at the back door and there was peace in the house again, she poured herself a second cup of tea and set about preparing the same breakfast for Steve. She set his breakfast tray and took it to the bedroom. As always, he'd put on his bedside light to read his newspaper. Usually he was still half asleep but this morning he looked agitated.

'This is terrible,' he told her. 'I told you last night we'd lost a lot of money but this is an absolute calamity. This on top of everything else will ruin me.' He was sitting bolt upright. When she tried to settle his breakfast tray across his knees he waved it away.

'Look at this.' He pushed the newspaper across the bed towards her.

With sinking heart she asked, 'What's happened?'

'There's been a financial slump in America.' He spoke rapidly. 'People are throwing themselves out of skyscrapers in New York because they've lost all their money on the stock market.'

Leonie wasn't sure how that affected them. New York seemed a long way away. 'You might as well eat your breakfast while it's hot.'

'Don't you understand what I'm saying? The London stock market has crashed too. Last night's prices are printed here and it looks as though I've lost a packet. I must get up and phone William Hawkes.'

'He won't be at his desk this early. Eat your breakfast.'

'He'll probably have been in his office all night.' He swung away on his crutches to do it.

Leonie picked up the newspaper and sat down to read.

Steve soon came back and slumped on the bed. 'You're right, he's not in his office.' Leonie lifted his breakfast tray across his legs. He looked fraught. 'What are we going to do now? As if we haven't got enough trouble without this. I've probably lost the last few pounds Dad left me.'

Leonie sighed. 'I wouldn't worry about losing all the money. You'll still have the shares, they'll just be worth less and you'll still get the same dividends.'

'I doubt that when shareholders are committing suicide in New York.'

'Yes, but it says in the paper that those people were borrowing money to buy shares because the market was going up and up. They were greedy, expecting to make a fortune, but instead the market has collapsed and their shares are worth less than the amount they borrowed to buy them. You haven't done anything like that.'

'But they'll certainly be worth less than they were last week.'

'Yes.' She frowned. 'I couldn't get to sleep last night. I spent the time pondering what I could do to earn some money. We aren't going to have enough to live on.'

He was irritable. 'You don't need to tell me that!'

'I thought I might set myself up as a dressmaker.'

'What d'you mean?' He was full of suspicion. In Steve's family the women didn't work.

'I could make clothes for other people – anybody who'll pay me for doing it.'

'I can't let you do that.' He was horrified.

'I enjoy sewing, you know I do, and I've always made my own clothes and those for the children. It seems sensible to use the skills I have. I already have a large sewing room to work in and Aunt Felicity's treadle machine, and there's plenty more space in the house if I should need it.'

'You'll never earn enough to make it worthwhile.' He screwed up his face, showing his abhorrence.

'It'll take me time to build it up but I love fashion and Aunt Felicity earned her living that way.' Steve had rather looked down on her for doing that. 'She taught me a lot about the trade. I think it's my best bet.'

'Leonie, nobody has much money to spend on clothes these days. You'll hardly earn anything. I could try going back to work. George will find me a job in the office if I ask him.'

Leonie turned to stare out through the big Victorian bay window and across the Mersey estuary. This morning it looked grey and misty but it was always busy with small coasters bustling up and down, each with thick black smoke pouring from its funnel. And of course there were the ferry boats criss-crossing the river, but unfortunately for Steve, the service no longer came to New Ferry.

In 1922, the same severe gale that had blown down a tree in their garden had caused a steamer to run into the end of the pier. It did so much damage that the pier had had to be demolished and the ferry service closed, thus bringing to an end the pleasant and convenient way of travelling to Liverpool that Steve's forebears had enjoyed.

The parade of shops leading down to the pier lost much of their custom and the post office closed, turning the district into an increasingly shabby backwater. The middle-class merchants who had once occupied the neighbouring large houses had moved to other districts. Some of the houses had been split up and were now occupied by more than one family.

That and the coming of the motor car had put out of business the commercial stable that had once plied for trade almost at their back gate. Steve had never owned a car or learned to drive. There was a good bus service into town but it was an eight- or ten-minute walk to the bus stop on the New Chester Road and Steve could not walk far. It was hardly practical for him to think of going back to work, especially as it was some years since he'd done so. Leonie was afraid he'd do again what he'd done so often in the past. He'd take on a job with good intentions but a morning would come when he'd feel unwell and just stay in bed.

Leonie made up her mind. Whatever Steve thought of the idea, she intended to try dressmaking. She would advertise in the local paper, put cards in nearby newsagents' windows and put a notice on the back gate inviting would-be customers to the door to ring the bell.

She set about reorganising her sewing room and found it exciting to have something different in her life. She went out and bought a new oil heater because it would be cold to sew in there in the winter. They were reduced to one coal fire in the dining room which had come to be used as a general living room.

Steve couldn't eat his breakfast. He slid the tray over to Leonie's side of the bed and stared out of the window at the view he'd known since childhood. Those had been sunlit years for him and his family, but the war had changed all that.

He was fated. No matter how hard he tried, everything went wrong. Everybody gave up on him. Dad had decided George Courtney was a better man to run the firm, and now Leonie was going to take over as the family breadwinner. He felt reduced to nothing. He was superfluous here; he wished he'd been killed in France, at least they'd remember him as a hero.

His eye was caught by a coaster chugging upriver, leaving a trail of smoke. The Mersey tide was full in and slapping against the wall of the Esplanade; he never tired of watching life out there. He craned his neck to see the two old ships moored permanently in the Sloyne, an area of deep water just to the right of their window.

The *Conway* was a handsome nineteenth-century black and white wooden ship that had started life as HMS *Nile* and was now a school for training officers for the merchant navy. The other, the *Indefatigable*, was an iron ship, now a school for training the orphans of seamen for a life before the mast. Nothing much seemed to be happening on either of them at the moment.

As Steve saw it, life was hell and set to get worse, they were going to be as poor as church mice. He should be thankful he still had Leonie. At least she still loved him, even though everybody else had given up on him.

Over supper that evening, it brought him more pain to hear her talk of plans to add to the family income. He thought it highly unlikely she'd earn much, particularly as she'd started by buying a new oil heater.

'That's an unnecessary expense,' he told her. 'There's an oil heater in the old servants' quarters in the cellar that you could have used.'

Milo looked up from his mutton chop. 'Is there? If Mum doesn't need it, I'd like to take it to the summer house. Can I have it, Pa?'

'No,' Steve retorted. 'It's too dangerous. You'll set the place on fire and burn it down.'

At twelve, Milo was growing up and becoming more independent. Steve had objected to his friends coming to the house, saying they were too noisy and he couldn't get his rest. Some of the boys were scared of him because he would burst into the playroom and scold them when their noise level lifted high enough for him to hear it. Milo had argued with him, saying it was just good-humoured chatting. As a result, he'd asked his mother if he could take over the old summer house that nobody used now.

'A good idea,' she'd said. She'd thought they wouldn't annoy Steve out there in the fresh air.

Milo and his friends had begun to use it as a club room, but it did annoy Steve, he'd see the boys coming and going through the window of his study. 'They disturb me,' he'd complained.

'Dad, can we move it further from the house?'

'No, it's far too old. It was my mother's, your grandmother's. She liked to sit out there on sunny days.'

'It was meant to move, wasn't it?'

'No, only round to catch the sun.'

'I could ask Duggie's father to come and see if he thinks it's possible to move it. If we set it against the wall by the back gate, Pa, you wouldn't see or hear anything.'

'You'll never manage it,' he said contemptuously and returned to his study.

Leonie believed in letting children attempt what they thought they could achieve, and as Steve hadn't actually forbidden it, when Milo had appealed to her for permission she said, 'You can try if you wish, but you mustn't churn up the garden and there must be nothing left on the lawn near the house.'

Milo brought two adults, a father and an older brother to give their opinion. They thought moving it would be possible, the wood had been treated with ship's varnish and was still in good condition, but they would need to take it apart into manageable pieces. Leonie persuaded Steve to give his permission and it took three weekends. Milo rounded up almost every boy in the neighbourhood to help and they all seemed to enjoy doing it.

Somewhere along the line it was decided that the open front of the summer house should be turned against the eight-foot garden wall and bonded to it. There were windows on both sides, one of which was turned into a half-glassed door that became the entrance. The boys loved it. Milo reckoned it was better than the scout hut and it was marvellous to have the use of it for himself and his friends.

They had played there throughout the summer and Steve had not been disturbed. The weather was getting cooler now and when Milo asked to use the oil heater, Leonie said to Steve, 'I think we should allow it, providing Milo promises to abide by certain rules.'

'Oh, I do, Mum. I promise I'll take great care. Being able to use the heater will be marvellous over the winter. The last thing I want is to burn the summer house down.'

The next morning, Milo carried the heater up to the summer house and Leonie positioned it against the brick wall. She impressed on Milo that he alone must be responsible for lighting it and turning it out every night.

She showed him how to manage it and checked that he could. 'This old summer house will go up like a tinder box if it catches fire but I think you're old enough to take responsibility for your own safety and that of your friends.'

'I am, Mum. I promise I'll be very careful.'

'Don't forget,' she warned, 'at the first sign of fire, get everybody out as fast as you can.'

* * *

Customers started to come in response to Leonie's advertisements. She enjoyed sewing for them. It brought purpose to her life.

She was sewing one day when she heard the phone ring. 'My name is Elaine Clifford,' an attractive, husky voice told her. 'I've designed three summer dresses and made paper patterns so that a home dressmaker could make them. I need to test my work by having them made up in some cheap material. It's sort of experimental. Would you be interested in doing that for me?'

'That sounds intriguing,' Leonie said. 'Yes, I'm very interested.'

'Good. When can I come round to see you?'

'This afternoon or tomorrow. What time would suit you?'

Elaine Clifford gave a hoot of pleasure. 'This afternoon, say three o'clock. Is that all right?'

'That would be excellent,' Leonie replied and spent the intervening time wondering about her. She sounded young and enthusiastic.

When Leonie answered the ring of the doorbell shortly after three, she found a smartly dressed young lady on the step. Elaine Clifford looked elegant in navy blue and white. Her clothes looked expensive. Leonie knew she could not reproduce clothes like that.

'Come to my sewing room,' she said, leading the way.

Leonie had rearranged her room and put a chair each side of a table where she could spread out her patterns and fabrics to show customers. 'Take a seat,' she said.

Elaine took off her coat and hat, and Leonie hung it on the peg on the door and hooked her hat on top. Elaine had thick, dark shiny hair and friendly dark eyes. She sat down and opened her case to spread her sketches and paper patterns across the table for Leonie to see.

'Before I was married,' she said, 'I worked in the fashion department of George Henry Lee's and I loved it.' Leonie nodded. It was one of Liverpool's more expensive department stores, too expensive for her.

'I gave up to get married and that's long enough ago for me to feel the need for more to fill my days. They sell lovely clothes. Very fashionable clothes.'

Leonie could see she was ambitious. 'The height of fashion.'

'Yes, well, I'm hoping to make a new career designing clothes and selling paper patterns of them to the trade. There are several large firms who sell patterns for dressmakers.'

'Yes, I sent for those three heavy pattern catalogues so my customers can choose what they want.' Leonie pointed them out on a shelf.

'I'm hoping to sell my designs to one of them,' Elaine said. 'I understand some of their designers are freelance. And I've noticed magazines quite often give away free paper patterns.'

'They probably get them from the big companies.'

'Well, what I want to do is to check my designs. I want you to cut out the garments and run them up in cheap material. I have to be sure my patterns work and that they are simple enough for the home dressmaker to follow.'

'I'll be glad to do that.' She'd enjoy doing it, it was something different. Leonie pulled the first of Elaine's designs towards her and studied it. 'This is quite complicated – a sophisticated design. It would take some degree of skill to make it up.'

'Could you do it?'

'Yes.' She looked up and smiled. 'I could but I've always done a lot of sewing. What sort of material would you recommend it be made up in?'

'Something soft like chiffon, delicate, sheer and filmy silk.'

'There's no cheap cloth like that. Muslin might work. You need a material that would drape.'

'Do you think it's too complicated? That I'm wasting my time?'

'No, I like it. There's one company that specialises in sophisticated patterns so they might like it too. What size have you made the patterns?' She unfolded the tissue paper to see the shapes.

'Thirty-four bust, twenty-six waist. I want my dresses to look their best, so I think of fairly slim women.' Elaine was tall and slimmer than that but Leonie could see she was at least a decade younger than her. 'I'll have to work out the measurements for every size but I thought I'd find out if any adjustments to the basic shape were needed first. I've got a simpler design here and it would look good in cotton.'

'Yes, I could make this one up in cheap cotton for you.' She got up to find a dress length in the pile of fabrics she was building up. 'Do you see it in this?'

'Yes, it would look good in that.'

'Then I'll start with these two. The size is right for me and I could make them fit me. I need some summer dresses. I'll pay for the cloth if you'll let me keep them.'

'That's kind of you. If these look as good as I hope when they're made up,' Elaine said, 'I'll start measuring out patterns in every size.'

She had a friendly, outgoing personality, and they shared a keen interest in the latest fashions. Leone felt she might have found a friend. Running the dressmaking business gave her a life of her own and it made her feel better, more confident and less affected by Steve's low moods.

CHAPTER FOUR

LEONIE HAD BEEN DOING her dressmaking for more than a year and was delighted at her growing list of clients and the money it brought in. But she found Steve was beginning to follow her round the house, often coming to her sewing room to demand her attention. He didn't like her having a fuller and more interesting life in which he could play no part. In particular he seemed to resent her growing friendship with Elaine. She had sold several of her designs and had seen one bought specially to give away with a magazine. 'That woman's here by the minute,' Steve complained, though Elaine was always friendly and polite towards him.

One evening, a client arrived late for a fitting and Leonie was late getting their supper on the table. Steve ate in cold, brooding silence so that even the children noticed he was in a bad mood. Milo tried to help his mother but he heaped too much praise on the rather ordinary casserole that had been cooking all afternoon.

After they'd eaten, the children washed up and Milo made coffee for them. Steve began to grumble about women coming to the house for fittings.

'You know I'm not well,' he complained. 'How do you expect me to rest when there are strange women ringing the doorbell and tramping through the house at all times of the day?'

'I always answer the door,' Leonie replied quickly. But her sewing room was further from the front door than his study and they had to walk past his door to reach it. She'd known for months that he found that an irritation.

Things came to a head one afternoon when Elaine was with her. She was full of enthusiasm and had come with two new designs for summer dresses, together with their paper patterns.

'I love these,' Leonie said. 'They've really got a modern look.'

'I'm dying to know if they'll work out.'

Leonie got out a well-tried stock pattern of her own for comparison and frowned. 'I think this one may need further adjustment on the shoulders.' Concentrating hard, they worked together on the measurements until the middle of the afternoon, by which time Leonie felt she was flagging. 'What about a cup of tea?' she suggested.

Elaine was still bubbling with energy. 'I'm thrilled with what we've done, and yes, I'd love a cuppa.'

Together they went to the kitchen to make it. Steve had had a bad headache that morning and stayed in bed until lunchtime. Leonie took a cup of tea and a slice of cake along to his study for him.

The kitchen was a vast bare room, a place for hired staff to work. It had changed little since the bungalow had been built and wasn't a comfortable place. As their work was spread over her sewing-room table, she took the tea tray into what had once been a formal dining room, but since they'd lost the live-in servants it was used as their living room.

'Gosh,' Elaine said. 'I've never seen so many large pictures in one room. I can hardly see the wallpaper.' They were all of early steamships and most were pictured at the height of a great storm. They were darkened with age, all in ornate gilt frames.

'Does Steve collect them?'

'No, his father collected them, but Steve's fond of them. They're all over the house. Unfortunately they aren't popular these days and Steve doesn't think they're worth much.' He'd talked of getting George down to give his opinion but had never got round to it. 'Grandpa loved his pictures and maritime history was one of his hobbies.'

They were drinking their tea at the huge mahogany dining table and laughing over a story Elaine was recounting when Steve stormed in, his face flushed with anger.

'Leonie, do you have to make so much noise? It's bad enough when your customers are ringing the doorbell and tramping to your sewing room, but now you're spreading them all over the house.'

'Elaine isn't a customer,' she said sharply. 'She's my friend.' She was angry with him for pretending not to recognise her. She'd taken Elaine to his study to introduce her and he'd seen her about the place several times since.

'You knew I was having a bad turn,' he complained, 'and I can't stand noise when I'm not well. You woke me up.'

'You were awake when I took your tea in.'

There was an awkward silence.

'I'm sorry.' Elaine stood up abruptly. 'I'll go.'

'There's little point in rushing away now I'm awake. The damage has been done.'

'I need to go anyway,' Elaine said mildly. 'My husband will be home soon.'

'I'll see you out.' Leonie got to her feet. She was angry and felt she had to get away from Steve for a few minutes to calm down. It was always a mistake to take offence at what he said or did. It could put him in a bad mood for the rest of the day.

'He'd try the patience of a saint,' Elaine sympathised once they were out of earshot. 'It must make things very hard for you.'

'Let's go for a little walk,' Leonie said, leading her out through the front door. They set off along the Esplanade. 'Steve resents me having anybody to the house,' she explained. 'I've been thinking for some time that I'll have to rent a workroom and keep my customers out of his way. The business is thriving and I love the work. Everything is fine but that. He knows we need the money but it's as though if he can't work, he doesn't want me to.'

Elaine squeezed her arm. 'That's the answer, isn't it, a workroom quite separate from your home. Are you making enough to afford the rent?'

'I am,' Leonie said, 'but I'd rather work at home and spend it on things we need. It isn't as though there's any shortage of space.'

'Bite the bullet and go as soon as you can,' Elaine advised, 'if that's the only way to stop Steve griping at you.' She pondered for a moment. 'Look, I need your practical experience if I'm ever to get my designs off the ground. We could do this together, couldn't we? Let me help you find a workroom.'

That comforted Leonie. It would be easier if she could talk things through first and have Elaine's opinion. 'That makes sense,' she said, 'though I have other clients on my books and other sewing to do.'

'Of course you have. And if we choose the right place to rent, you might find more customers. Your home isn't easy to find, it's away from the bus routes. Really, you're not in a convenient place to run a business.'

'I'd love to expand, who wouldn't? But we're in the middle of a depression. Will I get enough new customers to make it pay?'

'There are always women who have money to spend on clothes,' Elaine told her. 'George Henry Lee's has advertisements that say things like, "We can provide ladies with smart clothes for every occasion at prices well within the average dress allowance." You should aim for that market.'

Leonie was excited at the idea. 'All right, let's do it, let's start looking for a place.'

A few days later, Elaine came to see her again. 'I've been round the local estate agents to see what is available to rent, and I've picked up particulars of several places I think might suit you. How about this – it's a couple of rooms to rent in a house on Kennet Road. You'd have pretty much the same set-up as you have here and it would be more central for your clients. But have you thought about renting a shop? There are a lot of empty shops at the moment because of the depression. If you took one on a busy road, with people passing the window all the time, wouldn't that attract more customers?'

'Yes,' Leonie agreed, 'it probably would.' She read the brochures Elaine had brought her. 'This shop on the New Chester Road sounds ideal, but I had in mind to pay a weekly rent and the offer here is for a long lease.'

'That seems to be usual for a shop.'

'But I don't want to sign a ten-year lease, I can't think that far ahead, not yet, and I don't know what leasing entails.'

'Neither do I, but I know somebody who does. He's a solicitor, a friend of Tom's, and he's coming round for supper tonight. I'll ask him about leases and rental agreements.'

Elaine reported back to Leonie the next morning. 'It's quite complicated. He told me to bring you to his office to meet him. He thinks you might find it easier to understand if he spoke directly to you.'

That lunchtime, Elaine took her to see the shop that had impressed her on New Chester Road. There was a flat upstairs and another room behind the shop. Leonie could see great possibilities in the premises and began to feel quite excited. She went to look at one or two other shops but they were not on such a busy street, nor within such easy walking distance from her home.

A few days later, Elaine took her to a solicitor's office in Hamilton Square where her friend worked. As soon as they entered his room, he got up from his desk and came forward to greet them with his hand outstretched.

Elaine introduced him. 'Nicholas Bailey, he's a very good friend of ours. He lived with Tom for years.'

He smiled at Leonie. 'Please sit down. I'd better start by looking at the documents you've been given,' he said. 'You've brought them with you?'

She studied him while he did so and liked what she saw. He was good-looking and in his early forties, of medium build with neatly trimmed dark hair. His eyes were a very dark blue and he had a habit of screwing them up against the light. There were a lot of fine lines round them. He was wearing the formal dark suit, white shirt and quiet tie she'd expect of a solicitor.

He outlined all the advantages and disadvantages of a lease to her. 'If you sign a long lease like this,' he told her, 'you are agreeing to pay the rent for the whole of the ten years. This could be a problem if the business doesn't do as well as you hope. Legally you'd have to continue paying even if your business failed and you closed the shop.'

'I was afraid that might be the case.' Leonie was getting cold feet.

'The shop has been empty quite some time,' Elaine said. 'About a year, I think. The estate agent told me it used to be a camera shop.'

'In the present financial depression, many businesses have failed and people are understandably reluctant to sign up to a long-term lease like this.' He looked up and smiled again. 'But with so many empty shops on the high street, some landlords are willing to settle for a weekly rent. Would you like me to see if I can negotiate something with this landlord? I'll be happy to act for you as a friend.'

It took Leonie a moment to realise what he meant. 'You mean for free?' She met the gaze of his intense blue eyes and he nodded. 'That's very kind of you,' she faltered.

On the way home, Elaine told her that Nicholas and Tom were close friends and had been brought up together after Nick's mother had died. 'Nick has always come regularly to our house but three years ago he lost his wife and baby in childbirth.'

'How dreadful for him.'

'Yes, it took him a long time to get over that,' she said. 'Tom and I feel sorry for him, so now he has a regular invitation to

Sunday lunch to get him through the weekend and on Wednesday evenings we either go out to the theatre or cinema or he has a quiet supper with us at home.'

Leonie thought about him a good deal over the next few days. He had an aura of sadness about him and seemed a quiet and gentle person.

He was as good as his word. He negotiated a tenancy at an affordable rent for a period of six months, which afterwards could be terminated with a month's notice.

Leonie went alone to his office to sign the agreement and chatted to him for half an hour over coffee and biscuits. She warmed to him; he seemed interested in what she was doing. 'Your problem now,' he said, 'is that after six months the landlord can give you a month's notice to leave, but in the present climate it isn't very likely. He's probably glad to get some income from his property.'

When Leonie left his second-floor office, Nicholas Bailey went to the window to watch her cross Hamilton Square. She walked with a spring in her step and held her head high.

Elaine had told him all about her, had spoken at length about how much she liked and admired Leonie. He'd gathered that her husband was a bad-tempered invalid who demanded his family's full attention and kept Leonie running in circles trying to keep him happy. Elaine said the only reason Leonie wanted to move her little business away from her home was because her husband complained if customers came to the house. He was a positive tyrant and even complained about her asking her friends in. He was too ill to work but he hated to see her trying to earn a little money.

From Elaine's account, Nick had envisaged a subservient woman in need of help, and he'd been surprised to find Leonie very different. She had an air of calm composure and gentle patience but she was quick to understand his reasoning. Her hair was thick, dark blond and cut into a fringe; she had wide-spaced greenish eyes and a short straight nose. He thought her quite beautiful. She looked younger than her years, no older than Elaine.

He was fond of Elaine, she and Tom had the sort of marriage he'd aspired to. They seemed very happy together and he envied that. Tom had grown up in a close family and had been able to establish the same happy relationship for himself when he married.

Nick felt he hadn't been so lucky. His own father had been killed in the trenches in the Great War and he had only dim memories of him. His mother Grace had brought him up single-handed. She had been cushioned from the economic woes of the time because she'd inherited a small house from her husband and had been trained in her youth as a primary school teacher.

Grace and Tom's mother, Bernice, had been fellow teachers and colleagues at one time, and had remained close friends throughout their lives. In those days, marriage meant they could no longer be employed as teachers, but although Bernice went to live with her solicitor husband in Mollington just outside Chester, and Grace stayed in Birkenhead, they'd remained in touch and met frequently.

They had their first babies at almost the same time; Tom was just one month older than Nick. Bernice went on to have a daughter called Olive but by that time Grace was widowed and had returned to her career. At Christmas, she and Nick were invited to spend a week with Bernice and her family. In the summer they usually all went to the seaside for a holiday. Then Grace would take Tom and Olive home with her for another week so their parents could go away on their own. Both thought they gained from these arrangements.

Nick had been eleven years old when his mother had had to go into hospital to have her appendix removed. Bernice volunteered to take care of Nick until she recovered and a camp bed was set up in Tom's bedroom for him.

They all had the shock of their lives when Grace died suddenly following what was considered a routine operation. Somehow, she developed a blood clot which travelled to her heart and killed her two days later. Nick had been heart-broken.

The Clifford family told him he'd have a home with them for as long as he needed it. 'From now on,' Bernice told him, 'you're one of the family, another son for us and a brother for Olive and Tom.'

Tom and Olive called their father Pops and Nick had no trouble doing the same, but he couldn't bring himself to call Bernice Mum. Grace had been his mum and no one could take her place. The Clifford family understood and suggested he call her Aunt Bernie.

Nick was entered in the school Tom went to, and placed in the same class. For the first few months he relied heavily on Tom but eventually he found his feet and began to settle. The Cliffords talked to him about adopting him legally but as things were working out satisfactorily as they were, nothing was ever done about that.

Tom's father decided that Grace's home should be sold and the money invested in Nick's name. He looked after Nick's investments for the rest of his life. When the time came for the boys to decide on their careers, it pleased George Clifford that Nick wanted to be a solicitor like him. He arranged for him to take up an apprenticeship with the Liverpool firm that had trained him. Tom wanted to become an accountant and they lodged together during their apprenticeships. Nick saw Tom as both his brother and his closest friend.

Tom fell in love and married Elaine soon after he qualified, and they set up home near his job in Birkenhead. Nick was invited round frequently but once again he was the outsider looking in. What he wanted more than anything else was to get married, have a family of his own and settle down. But love evaded him for almost a decade and he was afraid he'd be left a permanent bachelor.

Then at Olive's thirtieth birthday party, she introduced him to a friend, and he fell in love with Marianne Mathews and a year later they married.

Nick longed to have a family of his own and planned to make it as much like the Clifford family as he could. Within eighteen months Marianne was pregnant and he was over-joyed. But her pregnancy did not go smoothly, at thirty weeks her ankles began to swell and her blood pressure went up. At thirty-four weeks she was admitted to hospital and told she had pre-eclampsia.

Nick had never heard of such a condition but the doctors told him it could be very serious. He spent as much time as possible at her bedside, but Marianne didn't improve and her blood pressure continued to rise. Two weeks later, they decided to induce labour. After that Nick wasn't allowed in, in case it tired Marianne. The process took thirty-six hours.

He was worried sick and the outcome was even more terrible than he'd imagined in his worst nightmare. The baby was stillborn and Marianne faded into unconsciousness and died the following day.

Nick stayed in his bed feeling bereft and raw. He didn't want to see anybody, not even Tom. He blamed himself. If he hadn't wanted children, if he hadn't got her pregnant, she'd be well and with him still. If he'd had the faintest inkling that Marianne might die, he wouldn't have risked it, but now it was too late.

CHAPTER FIVE

WHEN LEONIE TOLD STEVE she'd taken a lease on shop premises, he told her she was foolhardy to do so in the present dire financial climate. He predicted she'd increase the cost of her business and get no more customers. But Elaine was full of enthusiasm and came to help redecorate the shop inside and out before Leonie moved in. As Milo was on his half-term holiday, she roped him in too.

They spent a morning painting all the ceilings on the ground floor in readiness for the paper hanger who was due to start work the next morning. Elaine rushed off to get lunch for Tom because they were going to Chester, and Milo had had enough, so Leonie sent him home. She was tidying round and wiping away the few spots of white paint they'd dropped on the shop window when she looked up and saw a smiling Nick Bailey outside on the pavement watching her. Her heart jolted but she laughed and ran to door.

'Hello,' she said. 'I'm so glad you've come to see my new premises, I'm delighted with them. Do come in, you're my first visitor though I'm not straight yet. In fact, the place is a tip.' She laughed and he laughed with her as he came in to look round.

'You've moved some furniture in already.'

'No, I'm miles off that. These things were here.'

'Of course – they're the shop fittings mentioned in the agreement.'

'I shall keep most of them. It's a substantial counter and I can use it as a cutting-out table. I'll put my sewing machine over in that corner and these glass-fronted cupboards are just right for my threads and patterns.' She led him through to the room behind. 'I've ordered plenty of mirrors and some artificial flowers to decorate this room and I'll make a big brocade curtain to hang across that part to provide privacy for my clients to undress and try on the clothes I make for them.'

He bumped into two dummies Leonie had bought from a clothes shop that was closing down, making them rock. She smiled. 'Those two models will decorate the shop window. Elaine is going to help me dress them in fashionable outfits and we can change them as the seasons change.'

He seemed a little embarrassed. 'I'm not stopping you working, am I?'

'No, I'm too tired now to do any more here. I shall go home and sew this afternoon. I could do with a cup of tea. Will you have one with me?' Leonie had brought a sandwich with her for her lunch but she'd eat that when he'd gone. She was grateful for the help he'd given her and the gaze of his blue eyes kept meeting hers. She liked him more and more.

She shot into the lobby that partitioned off the stairs leading up to the flat. There was a row of pegs for outdoor clothes and a small table supporting a kettle and a tray of cups. Beyond this was a cramped cloakroom. Leonie filled the kettle from the wash bowl and put it to boil.

'This won't do, of course. I'm going to move the tea-making upstairs. Come and see what's up there.' It was a two-bedroom flat with bathroom, living room and kitchen.

'You could sublet this if you don't want to use these rooms,' Nicholas said.

'I couldn't really because the only way in and out is through the shop. I couldn't lock my things away. Anyway, it's a noisy place on this busy road. Let's go down and have that tea.'

'It's lunchtime, Leonie. Elaine told me she was coming here this morning. I thought I'd take you both out for a bite to eat, to celebrate getting your shop. Would you come on your own?'

That took Leonie's breath away. She was excited just having him here with her, but to be taken out to lunch would be marvellous except . . .

'I'm a total mess, I've been painting all morning in my oldest clothes.' She'd taken off her overall and the scarf that had covered her hair.

'You look very nice.' His eyes assessed her face and then her clothes and she could see he approved of what he saw. 'We needn't go anywhere fancy. I passed a little café only a hundred yards down the road.'

Leonie was tempted. She could see he was as much drawn to her as she was to him, the tension, the attraction sparked between them, but she was afraid he didn't understand her circumstances. She didn't want him to think this could lead anywhere.

'I'm married,' she choked awkwardly. 'Have been for years and I have two growing children.' She couldn't look at him.

'I know,' he said with equal awkwardness. 'Elaine has

explained all about your family. Are you going home to make lunch for them?'

'No, it's half-term so the children are off school at the moment and I've made arrangements for them to be looked after.' In order to give herself more time to sew, Leonie employed Mrs Killen to clean three mornings a week and she had agreed to work more hours in the school holidays to keep an eye on the children.

'Then please come. A one-off to mark your new venture.' His blue eyes smiled down into hers. 'No strings attached.'

How could she refuse such an invitation? In any case, she was thrilled to accept. Nicholas made her feel young again, a girl instead of a humdrum married woman of almost thirty-seven. He made her feel alive and on top of the world.

Leonie continued to spruce up her shop. She had the outside painted bright red and organised a sign-writer to paint her name above it, describing her as a high-class dressmaker. He also painted a board she could display in the shop to advertise Elaine's services as a designer who could arrange for clients to have clothes individually styled for them.

She found herself thinking about Nick all the time. He was free to search for a soul mate, but for her it was forbidden. The lunch they'd shared had been a great success, they'd both enjoyed it, but they'd made no plans to do it again.

It had been Elaine who had unintentionally moved the relationship on. One afternoon, she brought her husband Tom and Nicholas to the shop to see the improvements they were making. Leonie had been daydreaming about Nick and to have him unexpectedly in her shop made her tingle all over and feel as though her cheeks were on fire.

She told herself she must concentrate on Tom and Elaine.

Inside, the shop was beginning to look smart. Tom praised their work until in the back room he paused at the window which looked out over the yard. 'What are you going to do here?' he asked.

'I haven't given the yard much thought,' Leonie said. 'What do you suggest?'

He took another look. It was raining hard outside. 'Keep the curtains drawn. It looks pretty dismal out there.'

They all laughed. 'I'd have to keep the lights on if I did that,' she said.

Nick was holding himself back, he wouldn't look at her but he took a long look through the window and said, 'There's some rubbish there that could be cleared away. Then I'd white-wash the walls and have a few tubs of flowers. That would make all the difference.'

Leonie took them to see the flat upstairs, where Elaine said excitedly, 'I've just had a marvellous idea. Leonie, I hope you agree. I'd like to take over one of these bedrooms and turn it into a workroom. I could make my patterns here instead of trying to find space to do it at home. I'd be here with you and more part of the business.'

'Of course,' Leonie said, 'an excellent idea. Any client who can't make up her mind from the set patterns I have I can send upstairs to you.'

'You could sublet and charge her rent,' Nick suggested.

'No need for anything like that,' Leonie assured Elaine. 'We have an understanding, don't we?'

'We do, or we did have, but if I'm to use one of the bedrooms then I want to pay part of the rent.'

'That's only fair,' Nicholas agreed. 'We must work out how much. Do you want a formal agreement?'

'No,' Leone said.

But Elaine said yes. 'It's a business, after all. We must be businesslike.'

Tom arranged for all the rubbish to be taken away and Nick knew of a boy called Roy who would come and hose down the yard and whitewash the walls. When Roy had finished that, he painted the back gate scarlet and as they'd need to keep the bin, he painted that too.

She knew Nick intended to buy the tubs and plant them up for her. He brought them in one afternoon while she and Elaine were working on one of her patterns.

'I've put in mostly shrubs,' he said, carrying them through to the yard, 'because you'll need some greenery out there through the winter.'

'The yard looks so much better.' Elaine was enthusiastic. 'But there's one more thing needed and that's a garden seat. Then we can have our tea out here in good weather.'

As Leonie had several benches in the garden at home, she asked Steve if she might take one. She had to get a carrier to move it but she was able to have her treadle sewing machine, pattern books and samples of material taken to the shop at the same time.

Several of the firms she dealt with sent her a greater selection of materials when she told them she was taking on new premises and she sent postcards to all her current customers giving them her new address and phone number. Elaine brought two of her own outfits to dress the models for the shop window and laid out the materials and pattern books tastefully throughout the shop. Leonie declared the shop ready to open two days before the target date.

Elaine said they must go out to celebrate and Tom booked a table for dinner at the Central Hotel. Leonie was worried about Steve, so he was invited too. As she had suspected, he neither wanted to go himself nor let her go without him.

He had been more depressed than usual over recent weeks and told her that, after all, he preferred her to work from home, that he didn't want her out all day and he didn't like being alone in the house when he wasn't well. Eventually he grudgingly agreed to accompany her to the celebration dinner and Tom picked them up in his car.

Steve seemed quiet and withdrawn compared with the others while Elaine was the life and soul of the party, bubbling over with high spirits because another of the big firms had bought her latest patterns.

The next day in the shop, Leonie and Elaine decided to have the whole of the upstairs repainted, because now compared with downstairs it looked shabby. They decided to have it mainly white because the rooms were quite dark, and as Roy, the lad who had painted the yard, had done a good job, they agreed to ask him to come back and do it.

Leonie had to ring Nick to find out how to get in touch with Roy and he brought him round two days later. Roy estimated how much paint the job would need and as it was Saturday afternoon and the shops were all round them, Nick offered to go with Leonie to help her buy it.

All the time they were with other people, Leonie knew that

both she and Nick were acting. They had become expert in the role of friendly acquaintance. She had been keeping a tight control on her actions, on her facial expressions, and on what she said to hide her true feelings for Nick from the others, and she knew he was doing the same.

When they got back with the paint, Leonie was tired and put the kettle on to make tea. Today they were alone and she was very conscious of Nick's presence. She knew the moment the invitation crossed her lips that she should not have asked him to stay for a cup of tea. As it was a warm and sunny afternoon, she led him out to the yard to sit on the garden seat to drink it.

She stretched back on the seat with the sun warm on her face to sip her tea, her left hand resting beside her on the seat.

She felt him stir. He covered her hand with his own, 'Leonie . . .'

His touch made a thrill run up her arm. Instantly she jerked upright, snatched her hand away and spilled some of her tea on her blouse. Nick looked shocked, he hadn't expected that.

'I'm sorry,' they said at the same moment. She put her cup and saucer down on the ground and mopped at her blouse with her handkerchief.

'I'm sorry,' he repeated and his eyes searched hers. As though at some signal they moved closer together and the next moment Leonie felt his arms tighten round her. She lifted her lips to his and knew there was no going back. She could not go on fighting against her love for him.

Leonie did not see herself as a woman who would have an extramarital affair. That had not been her intention any more than it had been Nick's intention to draw her into one. They'd made that clear to each other right at the beginning. She had been struggling with her conscience for weeks. She'd tried not to think of him. She hadn't wanted to admit to herself that she was falling in love but it hadn't helped. What she felt for him had grown stronger.

She knew Nick was a lonely man and her seventeen years of marriage to Steve had not been exactly happy. What could be more natural than that they should fall in love?

A few days later, he came to the shop just before closing time. As soon as Leonie locked up, he took her into his arms and kissed her. She took him up to the flat and they made love for the first time. Leonie felt she'd been swept away on a wave of delight. It had been wonderful but afterwards she felt guilty about it and confused too, because she was happy at the same time.

Over the following weeks Nick became a part of her life that she kept hidden, but her feelings of guilt grew. She rubbed along with Steve as she always had. Most of the time he expected her to run around after him seeing to his every comfort, though when he was depressed he didn't want her near him. But there were other times when he was filled with rage and frustration at what life had dealt out to him, and then he'd get worked up and be hungry for sex. She found it impossible to refuse his sudden demands. He called it passion, but Leonie felt it had nothing to do with love.

Nick was very different, he was loving and caring and they were growing more serious. Leonie was deeply in love with him. They could meet only at lunchtime or during working hours. Sometimes she went to his house and sometimes he came to the shop. Elaine had furnished the flat above. As well as a workroom, she'd made a comfortable sitting room with big sofas where they could relax.

One day she remarked, 'Nick looks very much better. Being included in doing up the shop has given him something else to think about. He seems happier.'

It was true. He was standing up straighter and had enthusiasm and energy for everything.

Elaine had been right about the position of the shop. People walked past the window all day. Many paused to look inside where Leonie could be seen sewing. Some came in to talk to her, and soon she had more work than she could manage and had to advertise for an experienced seamstress to work part-time.

They were swamped with applicants. Elaine helped her sort through them and interview the four they thought most likely to suit them. They both took to Ida, a woman in late middle age, now a widow who had worked all her life in a clothing factory and wanted a job nearer to her home.

She was buxom and outgoing and tended to mother them. Within weeks, Leonie found her invaluable as she could turn her hand to anything and could be left in charge of the shop which meant Leonie didn't feel pinned down by the long hours it had to be kept open.

Nick came often. Sometimes he took her out to lunch but more often than not they sat up in the flat drinking tea. They just wanted to be together.

One afternoon Elaine returned to the shop unexpectedly having forgotten something and walked into the sitting room to catch Leonie in Nick's arms. Leonie felt the blood run up her cheeks and couldn't look at her.

Elaine recovered first. 'Sorry, sorry, sorry.'

'Not your fault,' Nick managed. 'It's just . . .'

'To be honest, I have wondered.' Elaine smiled. 'Tom has too. We thought it almost inevitable that you'd fall in love. I'm too closely involved with both of you not to see it happening. You needed each other. But don't worry, I won't tell anybody.'

'Except Tom,' Nick said.

'Yes, but he won't spread the news around.'

Later, when Nick had gone back to work and they were alone, Elaine said, 'My advice to you is to grab what happiness you can. We only have one life. Leave Steve, he's always going to wallow in his misery. I know he lost a leg in the war but lots of other men fared no better. There's a man in Tom's office who lost part of his arm as well as his leg and he's making a go of it. He works hard and plays hard.'

'It's not that easy,' Leonie said. 'I have two children as well.'

'They're growing up.' Elaine pretended to be harder than she really was. 'You should think of yourself now. How old is June?'

'She's eight. I can't take the kids away from Steve as well. He'd be left by himself. It would deprive him of everything, but neither can I leave them with him and walk away.'

So although Elaine knew about her and Nick, it changed nothing. If anything it made it easier, because she stayed out of the way at lunchtime and at any other time if she knew Nick was coming. For Leonie, life was hectically busy but the time she spent with Nick was pure bliss. They discussed everything in his life and hers. She thought she was closer to him than she'd ever been to any other person.

CHAPTER SIX

LEONIE'S RELATIONSHIP WITH NICK developed and strengthened; she began to think it would go on for ever, but at the same time her feelings of guilt grew. She felt she was living a lie with Steve.

One Saturday Leonie got up feeling sick. During the day, the suspicion that she might be pregnant took hold and wouldn't go away. She was shocked and horrified. Another baby was the last thing she wanted, she loved her children but her family was complete. Another baby now would change everything.

She made up her mind to say nothing to anybody until she was sure, but she found it impossible not to tell Nick at lunchtime the next day.

'I can't believe it,' she said. 'The baby is yours but it's the last thing I want. I thought we were taking steps to prevent it.'

'We were.' He was contrite. 'I thought I was being careful. This is my fault, I'm so sorry. What can we do about it?' He took her into his arms. 'What do you want to do about it?'

'I want to find out I'm wrong.' She put her head down on his shoulder, almost in tears. 'If I'm not, I don't know what I can do.'

She saw Nick swallow hard before he asked, 'Might Steve believe this baby is his?'

Leonie had wondered the same thing. A few weeks ago Steve had had one of his episodes of anger and frustration and demanded sex. She'd given him what he asked for, what else could she do? To refuse made him boil over with rage, turn nasty and it prolonged the conflict. To resolve it, she'd always had to give in. But the dates didn't fit. The baby was Nick's.

'Perhaps – I don't know,' she said. 'I don't know how to deal with this. I need to think about it. Try to work out what would be best.'

His arms tightened round her. 'You're not thinking . . . There are ways. It could be aborted. Not that I know the first thing about how to do it.'

She straightened up with a jerk. 'Is that what you want?'

'No.' His voice was agonised. 'It's the last thing I want, Leonie. It's illegal and I'd be terrified for you.'

She wiped her eyes with the back of her hand. 'I know it would solve the problem but I couldn't. I wouldn't.' They talked it through backwards and forwards many times, while Leonie worried about what she should say to Steve.

'I've always longed for children,' Nick said slowly. 'But it couldn't have come at a worst moment for you.'

'The sensible thing is to calm down and wait,' Leonie said, trying to smile. 'In a week or so I'll know for certain one way or the other.'

The days passed and for Leonie each one confirmed her worst fears. Nick came to see her almost every day but inevitably it brought their relationship to crisis point.

Nick kept saying, 'I'll always love you, Leonie. I want you to come and live with me on a permanent basis. I know we can't be married just yet but perhaps one day, and in the meantime I shall treat you as my wife. I want you to think of that as a promise.'

Leonie trusted him. 'I know you'll keep it.'

'Bring Milo and June. I know that's what you want. I'll love them, make them welcome, because they're part of you. Together we'll be the family I've always wanted.'

She wanted desperately to move in with him, she knew that was where she'd find happiness, but she also knew she had to decide this herself. Her business was thriving, she could afford to provide for herself and her children but that would leave Steve on his own. She fretted and worried about what she should do for over a week before deciding that she couldn't walk out on Steve, she owed him more than that. None of this was his fault. It was entirely hers.

Leonie tried to tell Nick of the decision she'd made but he found it hard to accept and kept trying to persuade her to change her mind. She was scared of how Steve would react when she told him about this baby but felt she couldn't go on keeping secrets from him. If she was to stay with him, he would have to know the truth. She didn't like to think of herself as deceitful and she'd found the tension of keeping a large part of her life from him incredibly stressful.

She would have to let him know exactly how things stood, but the thought of actually doing it terrified her. For days it gnawed at her while she thought about how she would say it. She rehearsed it in her mind and had to steel herself to get the words out.

That night when they were getting ready for bed, she said, 'Steve, I'm pregnant.'

'What?' He sat down on his side of the bed to unstrap his false leg. 'Pregnant, eh? Well, I'll be blowed! So there's life in the old dog yet.' He rolled on to his back and looked at her. 'And when is the happy event to be? Not that I see much pleasure in having a screaming baby in the house again.'

'It will be born in July.' She held her breath. If he told her to get out she knew where to go. Feeling sick and nerve-wracked, she forced herself to go on. 'This baby isn't yours.'

His face crumbled. 'What? Don't be silly!' He stared at her for a long moment. 'Whose is it then?'

'The father is Nicholas Bailey.' She reminded him who he was and how she'd met him.

He exploded. 'Good God, woman. That's adultery!'

'Yes, I know it is. Steve, I know this must be hurtful—'

'Hurtful! You've got the face to tell me that straight out?' he raged at the top of his voice. 'I knew no good would come of you having that shop. If you'd run your business from home this wouldn't have happened.'

'Please don't shout. Do you want the children to hear you?'

That made him rant even louder. He swore and screamed and called her some terrible names and at the same time he thumped his fist on his bed table, knocking over the glass of water Leonie always brought for him. Sweat was running off him and his cheeks were crimson.

Leonie pulled on her dressing gown and went to the door. 'I'm not staying to listen to this. It's getting us nowhere. I'll go until you calm down.'

He struggled to get up from the bed to follow her, but feeling for his crutches he over-reached himself and crashed to the floor. He lay there sobbing, pounding the floor with his fist.

Leonie turned back. 'Get up,' she said quietly. 'I know you can. Get back into bed.'

'You bitch,' he sobbed. 'Damn you, I can't get up! You can see I can't.'

He was almost twice her weight and she couldn't lift him, but with a little help from her he managed to claw his way back on to the mattress.

'Why can't you be satisfied?' he raged. 'I've given you everything I could. I've tried as hard as I could for you and the kids. I'm sorry I ever set eyes on you.'

She knew she had to keep her temper. 'Do you want me to leave?' she asked quietly. 'If I go, I want to take the children.'

'No, I'm not having that. My children stay with me. I'll divorce you,' he grated. 'Adultery is grounds for divorce and you're the guilty one. No court would give you custody of the children.'

'Steve, I am the guilty one but I think they might give me custody. Would a court of law think you were capable of looking after them? You can't look after yourself. You couldn't cook a meal for yourself. You've never done a hand's turn about the house.'

'Mrs Killen does most of that. She can carry on.'

'For how long d'you think she'd put up with your bad temper? I'm always making excuses for you. Anyway, without my earnings you couldn't afford her.'

'I'd find more money from somewhere.'

'You'd need to buy the food and give her some guidance as to what you want done with it. You've always shut yourself away in your study and expected to have everything ready when you want it. That wouldn't work if I wasn't here.'

'Stop going on at me, how d'you expect me to get to sleep after this?' He turned over and pulled the bedclothes up round him.

'I don't want you to go to sleep just yet,' she said softly. 'Please stay awake and think about the future. I've told you what the position is. Now I want to know how you feel about it.'

'I'm bloody shocked,' he burst out. 'I can't believe you'd do this to me.'

'I know I did wrong and I'm very sorry, but what do you want to do now?' Leonie was shaking.

She could see he needed a few minutes by himself to think. 'I'm going to make us a cup of tea,' she said. 'We're both in need of it.'

She went to the kitchen feeling agitated but at the same time relieved to have it all out in the open. She hoped Steve would decide on divorce because that would mean she could marry Nick.

When she returned with the tea, she found he'd put his lamp out and pulled the bedclothes over his head. She could hear him snuffling.

'Steve, have you decided?' She put his tea on his bedside table, took off her dressing gown and got into bed. Only then did she realise he was weeping.

'Don't leave me, Leonie,' he sobbed. 'Please don't leave me. I'll forgive you. I'll be a father to this baby, just as I am to June and Miles. Don't take them away. I want us to stay together, nothing need change. I know I've made things hard for you at times and I'm sorry for that. I'll try to be better tempered, and take you and the children out sometimes. I don't want a divorce. You know I'm not well. I need you here.' He blew his nose hard. 'I want us to stay together.'

Leonie's heart sank. That brought back to her the promise she'd made to his father years ago. 'Promise me, Leonie,' he'd said, 'that you'll never give up on him. Promise me you'll never leave him.'

'I won't, Edward. I promise,' she'd said. She'd meant it too. She put out her light and sank back on her pillows.

'You're my wife,' Steve said still tearful. 'You promised before God that we'd stay together until death do us part.'

'Yes,' she admitted. 'I did.'

Steve felt he was touching bottom, caught up in despair so deep there was no way out. He felt unloved, unwanted and useless. Leonie had told him as bold as brass that she'd betrayed him and taken a lover. That hurt like hell, he hadn't expected it of her. He'd trusted her but even Leonie didn't love him any more.

He'd had setbacks before. In fact, things had rarely gone well for him. He spent a lot of time alone in his study so as not to make a mess in the living room and be thought a nuisance, and he'd come to believe that if he opted out of making decisions and left the action to others, less could go wrong.

That had made him adopt a safe routine like a transparent capsule through which he could look out at life. For years he'd visited George Courtney in the shop on Friday afternoons to discuss progress, but business methods were changing and he didn't really understand what was going on there. He went no more than once a month now, it had become a social visit; he got there early and George took him out for lunch.

Today, like most weekdays, he stayed in bed until eleven and then he strapped on his false leg and struggled as far as a pub nearby called the Great Eastern, to have a glass of beer. It had been named after Isambard Kingdom Brunel's ill-fated ship which had been broken up on the beach not far away.

During the break-up, the remains of a body believed to be of a workman was found walled up in the hold. It was thought to have been there since the ship was built in 1858. Some of the ship's fittings, the doors, panelling and the fancy glass from the main saloon had been used to furnish the pub. Steve liked the place, it had been touched by history and it had survived. But his marriage had not. He'd felt sick with shock since Leonie had told him she was pregnant. She'd had no shame, yet he'd had to plead with her not to leave him. He wasn't sure he could trust her to stay.

The Great Eastern opened at half past eleven and the regulars were gathering when he arrived. They all passed the time of day with him. Usually, he quite enjoyed the company of Alfred Williams, a retired tug master, and Walter Duggan who'd spent his working life on a dredger. They called him Mr Dransfield while they were Williams and Duggan to him. As far as Steve was concerned, the pub was the only place where people paid him respect these days.

They tried to make him feel welcome. Duggan got up to buy him a drink as soon as he walked in. Williams indicated the seat next to him. Steve was always careful to return the hospitality when their glasses were empty, though he had to ignore the fact that they drank pints of bitter while his was only a half. Today, their chatter bored him. They had nothing new to talk about, it had become too much of a habit.

When the one o'clock gun boomed across the Mersey, they drained their glasses, said goodbye and went home to a hot dinner cooked by their wives. Steve toyed with the thought of another glass of beer but his stomach was turning sour. He limped home to an empty house. It wasn't Mrs Killen's day to come so he'd have to forage for something to eat.

If Leonie went he wouldn't be able to manage. He felt despairing. Life seemed so hopeless, so futile.

Leonie saw the future as bleak. She felt very much in love with Nick and was going to miss him terribly, but she'd known all along that staying with Steve was the right thing, he was her husband. To see him weep and plead with her to stay had prodded her conscience. It would be impossible to go to Nick, take Milo and June with her and leave him on his own.

Steve said several times in the days that followed, 'Please stop seeing that man. You'll never settle down until you show him the door.'

He heaped blame on Nick. He'd seduced her, dragged her into an affair, and he said some nasty things about him. Steve was jealous, but she'd given him reason to be.

She found Steve's words and his manner painful but knew he was right. She couldn't carry on a double life as she had. It had been exhausting and there had been times when her neck had crawled with guilt.

One afternoon after Elaine had gone home and Ida was sewing downstairs and looking after the shop, Nick came in and Leonie took him up to the sitting room and poured all her grief out to him. He put his arms round her and she wept.

'It isn't what I want,' he said, 'and it isn't what you want either. Don't stop me coming to see you. You're having my child . . . Leonie, I want to stay near you. You might need my help over the coming months. I love you and I want to see this child safely born. Please don't send me away until it is.'

'Steve wants to believe it's his.'

'The truth is,' Nick said sadly, 'a child by me is not only your disaster but mine too. I wanted us to go on as we were, to be happy . . .'

'We were happy, we were in love.'

He shook his head. 'But I've brought you nothing but trouble.'

She said sadly, 'Giving me a baby – it tells the world we're in love. We've been caught out, haven't we? It's embarrassing for us and for Steve.'

Nick's arms tightened round her. 'It's happened,' he said. 'We're bringing another person into this world and there's no way out of that.'

'I wonder if it's a boy or a girl. Odd to think it's already decided.'

'If it's a girl,' Nick said, 'I'd like her to have your name. What could be prettier than Leonora?'

She tried to smile. 'It's too much of a mouthful and gets shortened to Leonie or Nora. It would be all right as a second name.'

'What about Amy Leonora then?'

She pulled a face. 'Sounds better the other way round, Leonora Amy.'

'That's it then.'

'What I'd really like would be to name her Nicola after you but I can't, and if it's a boy, I can't give him your name. For Steve, that would be like a red rag to a bull.'

'I do understand, love.' Nick paused. 'Things have gone too far, haven't they? We love each other too much to part now, especially when soon we'll be a family.'

'You mustn't say that.' Leonie shook her head. 'Once this is over, when the baby is born and we are both well, you and I must stop seeing each other. You must forget about me and the baby.'

'If that's what you want, then I'll try,' Nick said quietly, 'but I don't know how I'm going to do it. I'll always love you. You can change your mind at any time and come and live with me.'

CHAPTER SEVEN

WITH SUPPORT FROM THE Cliffords, Nick had started his own practice in an office in Chester and had taken one or two clients with him. He was painstakingly trying to attract more. He'd bought a house in the suburbs some months ago and Elaine had helped him furnish it. But over the next weeks he found it impossible to get on with his work, his mind kept churning. What problems he'd created for himself and Leonie!

He opened the file in front of him on his desk and tried to concentrate but yet again he was reading the same paragraph over and over and couldn't make sense of it.

Tom's family had brought him up to do what was morally right but in starting an affair with Leonie, he'd fallen from the high standards they'd set for him and he felt ashamed. He'd seen Leonie struggling with a difficult marriage. She'd seemed so vulnerable and he couldn't stop his love for her growing. It had very soon been out of control but for her to bear his child now was a disaster for them all. When she decided the right thing to do was to stay with Steve, he couldn't argue against it.

Elaine had told him openly that Leonie's happiness lay with him. 'Steve doesn't appreciate her,' she said. 'She has a terrible life with him. Don't let her do this.'

He couldn't stop her.

He had so wanted what most other men achieve with ease, a wife and children of his own, but for him it was not to be. He'd lived through bereavement and loss once and it had been raw and agonising. In some ways this felt worse because he knew Marianne and her baby would be with him if they could, but Leonie had chosen not to be.

Leonie knew her future without Nick would be bleak, and the first months were indeed very painful. She was overwhelmed by a sense of loss and grief. She told herself she had to stop thinking about him and the best way to achieve that was to keep so busy that she had little time for herself.

After the baby, a girl, was born, she went back to work at the shop and took Amy with her. That way, she could look after both her child and her business. In fact Amy was not difficult to look after during the first six months. She slept a lot in her pram and Ida was more than happy to pick her up and play with her if she cried.

Life with Steve never did settle back to the way it had been. She knew she'd destroyed the relationship she'd had with him for ever. He remained angry and suspicious and couldn't forgive her. If she was late coming home, he'd remind her that she'd promised never to leave him. He tried to ignore the baby, but Leonie could see him watching closely while she fed her. She knew Steve no longer trusted her, but eventually, they seemed to achieve an uneasy truce.

Leonie told herself life wasn't all bad, and if she could put her grief behind her there were compensations. She had her children, she had her business, she had her friend Elaine and most of all she had baby Amy. She mustn't forget that Amy was part of Nick and if she couldn't have him, then his child was the next best thing and a great comfort to her.

She knew Nick still regularly visited Tom and Elaine. Elaine said, 'He can get you a divorce, Leonie, if that's what you want. He'd do anything to have you as his wife. Being together would sort you both out.'

Leonie shook her head. 'I know but I can't walk out on my two older children and I can't strip Steve of everything.'

Elaine had been more interested in furthering her career in the fashion world when she was first married but Leonie knew she and Tom were now trying for a baby, so when a few months later, Elaine told her she was pregnant, she was delighted for her. Elaine sought her advice about pregnancy, childbirth and childcare and she was glad to help where she could.

Three months before the birth, Elaine's pregnancy was diagnosed as twins and to start with that made her anxious, but when Dulcie and Lucas were born, she was over the moon that she had a boy and a girl.

'We've got our family now,' she told Leonie. 'We wanted two children and I feel lucky I don't have to go through another pregnancy to get them.'

But she found looking after two babies very hard work and had to find a live-in nanny to help her. Nanny Bridge was a capable middle-aged spinster who had built her life round caring for other people's children. Elaine continued to spend a good deal of her time working in her room above the shop and she couldn't help but notice that as Amy grew older and slept less, it was not so easy for Leonie to care for her there.

One lunchtime, as they were having a cup of tea and a

sandwich on the sofa in the living room, Amy was learning to walk and kept pushing her dog on wheels into their legs.

'Do you think it would be a good idea to let Nanny Bridge look after her as well as the twins?' Elaine suggested.

Leonie's sandwich was suspended halfway to her mouth while she thought about it. 'An excellent idea,' she said, 'but would she not find three children too much for her?'

'I don't think so. The twins sleep most of the time. I think she'd probably enjoy having a toddler to look after too.'

'We could share the cost,' Leonie said. 'I'd get a lot more work done while I was here, and it would be better for Amy. She needs to be able to run about more.' Leonie was relieved because Amy had reached the stage when she was active and needed a lot of attention. Her fingers were into everything. Instead of getting on with their work, everybody spent time talking to her and playing with her, even the customers did, and it took longer to produce the finished work.

Leonie found it a long walk to take Amy to Elaine's house on her way to work, but it was worth it and sometimes the nanny took the children out for a walk and delivered her back to the shop late in the afternoon.

A week or two later, Elaine told her that Nick was insisting on paying her share of the nanny's salary. She said he felt he should do more to help with the support of his child.

'Has he seen her while she's been there?'

'No, he comes for dinner when work is over for the day. Except sometimes he comes on Sundays, but Amy isn't with us then.'

Despite her efforts, Leonie had not been able to stop thinking of Nick and often wondered how he was getting on.

She'd had to school herself not to ask Elaine about him. Occasionally, though, Elaine dropped snippets of information about Nick. He was well and had settled down in Chester. He'd bought a new car.

On Amy's first birthday Leonie wrote Nick a long letter about her health and how she was growing. She had Amy's photograph taken to send to him. He replied to thank her and said he'd like to send Amy cards and little gifts but thought it wiser not to, that Steve would not want her to know of him. It would be better for Amy if he left the fathering to Steve for the time being. Perhaps when she was grown up and able to understand, she could be told about him. Leonie thought that very unselfish of him.

The years began to pass, at Christmas she sent him a card and wrote a few sentences about Amy's progress on it. On her birthdays she always wrote him long letters about Amy's development and tried to remember all the funny things she said and did. Nick always replied to thank her; he told her his practice was proving successful and that he still loved her and would welcome her if she changed her mind about staying with Steve.

Leonie's business was also growing and she needed to take on another seamstress. Ida introduced Maggie, a younger woman she'd worked with for many years, who would work in the afternoons after Ida had gone home. Leonie enjoyed what she was doing and she was earning more than enough to cope with the household expenses.

Steve continued to have bad moods and at times he railed at both her and the children. Her relationship with him did not improve and that drove her closer to her children. They were growing up. Milo was very like Edward his grandfather; he was outgoing and had lots of friends, the sort of person who needed people around him. He enjoyed company and in this way he was the very opposite to Steve.

The family likeness was evident in the features of her older children but they had very different colouring. June was the beauty of the family with a perfect fair complexion and pink cheeks. Leonie envied her long curly hair. It was the colour of manuka honey and developed golden highlights in the summer. Milo's hair had a reddish tinge, but a dark red, not ginger or carroty; it must be a family throwback because she'd not seen it in any living family member.

Milo was open about what was going on in his life, while June was not. In that way she was more like Steve, who rarely spoke of his interests. Leonie tried to get her to talk about her school and her friends but she revealed very little.

Amy was an altogether sturdier build than her half-siblings but she had lovely rounded limbs and a pretty face. Leonie couldn't stop herself searching for a resemblance to Nick. Amy had inherited her own straight hair, and it was not a beguiling colour like June's, but then Nick had straight hair too. Amy had dimples in her cheeks and they must have come from Nick. Leone knew she hugged her more than she had her two older children. Amy was her love child.

Most people found her delightful because she would smile up at them and talk to them; she'd even edge up to sit on their knees. Leonie had been half afraid Steve would take against Amy, but she watched her do that to him and he treated her with as much affection as he'd given Milo and June when they were very young.

Nurse Bridge and Mrs Killen were equally enamoured of her and very happy to take charge of her. She shared her sweets and toys with other children and expected them to share theirs.

From an early age, the children played outside and ran wild with their friends. Milo had always known there was a sailing dinghy in one of the two sheds in the two-acre garden.

'I'd like to use it, Pa,' he said one night over supper. 'It's called *Dido* and the sails seem fine, all they need is new ropes. They're all there, Duggie Jenkins and I spread them out to see.'

'It'll be no use to man nor beast now,' Steve said shortly. 'It's been lying there far too long.'

'Duggie's dad came to look at it and he says it can be repaired.'

'What business has he got coming into our garden and what does he know about boats?'

'Did it belong to Edward?' Leonie asked to deflect his ire.

'No, it was Raymond's'

'Your Uncle Raymond was killed in the Great War, love,' Leonie told their son.

'There are times when I wish I'd been killed too,' Steve said irritably. 'It would be better than this.'

'No, Pa, you don't. Nobody wants to be dead,' Milo said in disbelief. He put down his knife and fork. 'Does that mean I can take over the dinghy?'

'Miles, don't you listen to what I say? If you put *Dido* in the river, it would sink. The wood must be rotten by now.'

'Mr Jenkins says it is clinker built and all it needs is a couple of planks replacing and he could show us how to do it.'

'Don't expect me to pay him for that. It's not safe, Miles,

you could drown yourself and those boys. It would be better to leave it alone.'

'But Pa, please look at the boat. If you talk to Duggie's dad you'll see he knows all about—'

'No I will not. Your mother and I would be very worried if we thought you were out on the river in that. There are huge tides and strong currents, quite apart from the big ships out there.'

'I want to learn, Pa. I want to learn everything about boats. Can I ask Mum to have a word with Mr Jenkins?'

His father flared. 'No, I said. Don't argue. We need to eat our meals in peace. You're giving me indigestion.'

Leonie turned to her son and surreptitiously put her finger across her lips.

'Sorry, Pa,' Milo said. 'I didn't mean to upset you.'

When the meal was over, the children helped Leonie to clear the table, while Steve went off to his study.

In the kitchen, Milo said, 'Mum, we really want to try to put that boat in order. Duggie's dad is a boatbuilder, he knows what he's talking about. He thinks it would be a great project for us boys. He doesn't want to be paid. He says it'll be good for us all and we'll learn a lot.'

'But you'll need wood,' Leonie said, 'and money for paint and things.'

'Yes, and I'm going to get a job to pay for them.'

'Milo,' she cautioned. 'You're only fourteen.'

'Lots of boys start work at fourteen.'

'But not you, you have to stay at school.'

'Mum, John's auntie runs a fish and chip shop near Rock Ferry Station. They need a Saturday boy, I can get that job.'

Leonie pulled a face. 'What would Pa say? You working in a fish and chip shop?'

'He won't like it.'

'I'm not sure I like it, Milo.'

'The work is cleaning up and potato-peeling. I only get to cook and serve when I've been there a while and they've shown me how. What harm is there in that, Mum?'

Leonie pursed her lips. Milo knew it wasn't the sort of job a boy at a private school was expected to take. 'But you go to school on some Saturday mornings.'

'Only to play games and I don't have to. When I get to serve, it'll teach me to add up quickly and all that and I'll be earning money to buy stuff to mend the boat.'

'All right,' Leonie said, drying her hands. 'Perhaps I'd better take a look at this boat. I knew there was one there but I haven't been near it for years.'

It was covered with thick dust but didn't look too bad. Milo pointed out the planks that needed to be replaced. 'Mr Jenkins says it would be quite easy and then the whole boat will need to be recaulked and it'll be as good as new.'

Leonie couldn't see any harm in letting the boys do that.

After supper the following evening, Milo came running back from the shed while Leonie was preparing a meal for the next day.

'Mr Jenkins is in our shed, Mum. Come and talk to him. He's quite keen for us to do the boat.'

Leonie found two men waiting for her by the shed. One came forward, he was heavily built and wore rimless glasses.

'Good evening, Mrs Dransfield, I'm Henry Jenkins, Duggie's father.' He put out his hand. 'It's very good of you to let the boys have the freedom of your premises. Duggie treats it like a club and loves to come and meet his friends here.'

'I'm not giving them much freedom,' she smiled, 'only of this shed and a bit of the garden. Anyway, it's a long way from the house and keeps Milo out of earshot.' She learned for the first time that Duggie was in Milo's class at school.

Mr Jenkins introduced the tall and slender man with him. 'This is Oswald Hemmings, Gerald's father. He has a sailing boat called *Seagull* and belongs to the Rock Ferry Yacht Club.'

'I'll teach them the rudiments of sailing, Mrs Dransfield, and how to stay safe.'

'*Dido* is old,' Mr Jenkins said, 'and at sixteen feet, a bit heavy for the boys but it's a classic design. Repairing it and putting it in the water is a practical proposition. Thank you for letting them do it.'

'Milo couldn't do this on his own,' Leonie said. 'It needs to be a shared project, so I should be thanking you. If you are willing to help them and teach them what they need to know, I'm sure the boys will learn a lot and have a lot of fun.'

Leonie could see only good in what Milo wanted to do. When he was going to bed that night, she said, 'I'll have a word with Pa but you must promise that your schoolwork won't suffer because of the time you'll spend on the boat.'

'You let that boy do exactly as he likes,' Steve said later. 'I hope he doesn't drown himself.'

'Better that he learns the skills now while he's young,' she said. 'Getting *Dido* in the river is still some time off.'

CHAPTER EIGHT

W HEN AMY WAS FOUR years old, Leonie put her into nursery school. June was able to take her there in the mornings but in the afternoons Amy was released an hour before June so Leonie usually went to fetch her.

Amy soon made a little friend in the same class. Her name was Pat Greenway and they usually came out together. Pat was a few months older than Amy but she appeared younger because she was a small and skinny child. She had rather sharp features and skimpy pale-brown pigtails of little more than shoulder length.

Leonie knew her mother by sight but they'd rarely spoken. Amy pulled at her skirt and told her that the Greenways lived at Beechwood only four houses further along the Esplanade. Colleen Greenway drove her own Austin Seven and offered them a lift home. The same thing happened the following afternoon and as they got to know each other, Colleen realised that Leonie's shop made it difficult for her to collect Amy from school. She offered to pick her up with Pat and take her home to Steve. More often than not Amy walked back along the Esplanade to play with Pat for an hour or so before June and Milo came home, but as time went on Leonie often failed to find her when she got home and had to send June or Milo out to look for her at mealtimes. Though Steve knew when Amy came home from school, he took little notice of what she did or where she went. Leonie began to worry that the child had too much freedom.

Amy didn't always see having a brother and sister so much older than her as an advantage. It was like having two mothers and two fathers, there was always somebody on hand bossing her around.

Amy knew Pa had taken a dislike to Pat, he said she was cheeky. 'You mustn't go off with her,' he said, 'unless you first ask permission. Your mother is worried about what you get up to.'

'That isn't fair.' Amy was indignant. 'Me and Pat are both six years old and she is told to go out and play by herself.'

'Well, I'm telling you to stay at home now and play with June.'

'June doesn't want to play with me,' she fumed. 'Pat has three older sisters and not one of them wants to play with her. Can I ask her in to play here? We want to be together.'

'No, you'll make too much noise.'

'Pa, I want to—'

'I won't say it again. Do as you're told, go and play with June.'

With bad grace Amy gave up. June was doing her homework and took no notice of her. She went to Milo's room. He was sucking a humbug. 'Can I have one?' she asked.

'Sorry, I haven't any more,' Milo said. 'Duggie gave me this one in school.'

It took Amy some time to accept he was telling the truth. 'I'd like some sweets.'

'Go and ask Pa for a penny then.'

'He's cross with me – in a bad mood.'

'He won't eat you, go and try.'

'Why don't you ask him?'

'He won't give me anything. You're the youngest and his favourite, he'll give you money.'

Amy doubted she was his favourite. June was in the next room and heard them. She came in.

'He likes you best, June,' Amy said. 'You're his favourite.'

June shook her head. 'He gave me twopence yesterday, it's your turn. Come on.'

June's hand pressed into her back, propelling her to the door of Pa's study, 'Go on,' she whispered and pushed the door open for her. Pa was deep in his newspaper again.

'Please, Pa,' she asked, 'will you give me a penny for sweets?' With his attention still on his paper, Amy was pleased to see his hand go absent-mindedly to his trouser pocket, but there was only a halfpenny on his palm when it came out.

'Please, a penny,' she wheedled.

He seemed to have forgotten their earlier exchange. 'Sweets will rot your teeth.'

'Please, Pa. June wants sweets too.'

Another halfpenny came out. 'Thank you Pa,' Amy grabbed it and ran for the door where her half-siblings were waiting.

June smiled as she took the coins from her. 'I'll look after them for you.'

Milo and June each took one of Amy's hands and swung her between them as they ran to the nearest sweet shop. All three paused to glory at the mouth-watering display in the window.

'What d'you want to buy, Amy?' June asked.

She chose carefully. 'A stick of liquorice and a halfpenny bottle of red pop.'

They shook their heads. Amy knew Mum would do that too, she didn't allow soft drinks other than orange squash and thought all sweets except caramels and boiled sweets were rubbish.

'It would be better to choose something else.' Milo was always diplomatic. 'I fancy sherbet bombs.'

'I'd like aniseed balls,' June said and they all went inside to buy them. Once out on the pavement again they counted out the sweets, dividing them carefully into three.

'That's fair, isn't it, Amy?' Milo asked and slid her share straight into her pocket, so they could each keep a paper bag.

'I wanted a bottle of pop.'

'Mum says the gas isn't good for you,' June reminded her. 'You can find your own way home, can't you?'

'I want to go with you.'

'Another time, Amy.'

'Milo, please?'

He shook his head. 'I'll have a game of Ludo with you after supper.'

Amy watched them go their separate ways and then went to see if her friend Pat would play with her.

In the spring of 1937 Leonie told June she could come straight from school to the shop to be measured for a couple of new summer dresses. June was delighted and quickened her step. She looked forward to examining Mum's catalogues and swathes of material and choosing what she wanted.

But the shop seemed unusually full and the staff hectically

busy. Elaine, her mother's friend, was conferring with a customer over a pile of pattern books, while her twins were causing havoc. Now they were at school, Nanny Bridge had moved on to another full-time job and Elaine was relying on a part-time mother's help. Amy was at home, she'd been off school that day because she had a cold.

Mum was flushed. 'Sorry, love,' she whispered to June. 'We'll have to leave it. Would you mind coming again tomorrow?'

'Mum!'

'We're getting a big order to make clothes for a wedding, and not only the bride and bridesmaids. Elaine has been asked to design something special for the bride's mother.'

June could see she'd get no attention today. 'I suppose so,' she said grudgingly.

'There's something else,' Leonie said. 'Elaine picked up Dulcie and Lucas from school and we can't cope with them here just now. Would you mind taking them home?'

June eyed them with distaste. She'd heard even their mother say she wished they were better behaved.

'I'd be very grateful,' Elaine said, holding one twin's sticky hand away from her sketches. 'I know Tom is home now, I've just spoken to him on the phone.'

June nodded. 'All right.' She was not only disappointed but fed up. She'd been looking forward all day to this and she really needed some new dresses. All her old things were so childish. Now she was sixteen she needed a whole wardrobe of new clothes. Mum said she was shooting up but the hems of her dresses could be let down. June felt the problem was much greater than that.

'I'll bring the pattern books home with me,' her mother promised, to placate her. 'You can look through them tonight.'

'You know where we live, don't you?' Elaine asked.

'Yes, didn't I bring Amy to the twins' birthday party?'

'Of course you did, and you came back to take her home.' Elaine slid some coins into her hand. 'For the bus,' she said. 'Thanks, I do appreciate this.'

Mum raised her brows. 'They could walk quite easily. It's not that far.'

'The bus, the bus,' the twins clamoured. June thought they were pests, noisy and never still, far worse than Amy, though she was less than a year older.

'Don't take your eyes off them,' her mother cautioned as she saw them out.

June hitched her school satchel on her back and took a firm grasp on one hand of each twin. She'd have to take care, these two could be little imps, but the bus came almost immediately and the twins had calmed down. When she had them settled in a seat and was able to examine the coins Elaine had given her, she found she'd been given an extra shilling. A tip like that made her see this trip in a very different light.

As they walked down the road towards Elaine's house, June saw a smart red two-sweater car parked in their drive. Her gaze lingered on it as she edged the children past, it was gorgeous. When she released one hand to ring their front doorbell, Dulcie shot off round the back.

'We always go the back way,' Lucas told her. So June followed, dragging him with her to the back garden. She was in time to see Dulcie shoot into the house leaving the back door open, and when she reached the step she could see a man with her in the hall. June hesitated, nervous about entering the house of near strangers.

'Uncle Ralph,' Lucas yelled, hurling himself at him.

'Hello,' June said. 'I've brought them home.'

'So I see.' He was staring at her.

June found herself examining him. He was tall and had an athletic build, dark wavy hair and lustrous brown eyes that wouldn't leave her face.

'It's Uncle Ralph,' Dulcie screamed again, swinging on his arm.

By now they'd reached the conservatory and Mr Clifford, Elaine's husband and the twins' father, was lolling back on a sofa, with a cup of tea at his elbow. He rustled his newspaper down when he saw her and stood up. 'Hello, June. Do you know Ralph? Ralph Harvey, Elaine's brother.' He had Dulcie in his arms.

'It's Daddy's birthday,' Lucas told her. 'We've got presents for him and Mummy's made a cake.'

June explained about the sudden influx of customers in her mother's shop, and why Elaine wanted peace to concentrate on the customers' needs.

'I might have guessed,' he said. 'Just the day she wanted to be back early. Thank you for bringing the babies home.' He collapsed back on the sofa. 'Would you like a cup of tea?'

'No thanks.' It was only then June noticed the chocolate biscuits on the tea tray, she'd have loved a couple of those. 'No, I need to get home.'

Dulcie was trying to climb on her father's knee from one side and Lucas from the other. He pushed them off, causing Dulcie to let out an angry cry and upset his teacup.

June backed away. Her pa would have walloped her backside for doing that.

'I'll see you out,' Ralph said, leading the way to the front door. There he paused. There was something about the way he looked at her that made June feel grown up, almost as though she was as old as he was. She knew he liked her. His eyes were playing with hers and making that obvious. He was a lookalike for Gary Cooper and not really old at all. He was exuding charm. She felt her heart begin to race.

'Can I offer you a lift home?' he asked. 'After all, you must have come out of your way to bring the kids here.' He was moving towards the red two-seater. 'It's starting to rain too.'

'Is that your car?' June couldn't believe her luck. She'd been disappointed not to be measured up for new dresses today, but this was far better, she wouldn't have missed this for the world. 'Thank you,' she said. 'I'd love a lift home in that.'

She was thrilled to see him fish his car keys from the pocket of his Harris Tweed sports jacket and hold the door open for her. She got in, putting her feet on her satchel to hide it and fingering the hem of her gymslip. Why did she have to be wearing her school uniform? She glanced at him and he turned to smile at her. It was fantastic to sit beside him in this gorgeous car and direct him to her home.

'Are you really in a hurry?' he asked.

'No.' She wanted this to go on forever but she couldn't say that. He didn't take her straight home but drove instead to the disused ferry terminal in New Ferry where there was a wide parking area overlooking the river, which as usual was deserted. He stretched back in his seat and turned to look at her. 'Tell me about yourself,' he said.

She smiled. 'I'd rather hear about you.'

He laughed. 'I work in a bank. I'm a lonely bachelor, uncle to those twins and I don't know why I let them crawl over me. I'm an old man of thirty-one and prefer more grown-up company. How old are you?'

June's heart was thudding. 'Eighteen,' she dared, stretching it a little.

'Good, a lovely age to be, on the threshold, so to speak, with all your life before you.' He leaned across and kissed her on her lips. 'I think you're very beautiful.'

June glowed. She'd never been kissed before, not by a grown man. The girls at school chased callow youths, but Ralph was altogether different. And he thought she was grown up!

His arms went round her and he pulled her close. Thank goodness, there was nobody about to witness her first adult kiss, or see how much it thrilled her. The rain drummed on the canvas roof of the car and drew a curtain of mist round them. June gave herself up to his kisses. There was nothing she wanted more.

Ralph Harvey felt a tinge of guilt as he drove back to his sister's house. He'd been invited to celebrate Tom's birthday and he'd absented himself to chase after June. He'd never seen a more beautiful girl in his life, slim as a wand with wide-set eyes full of innocence. Everything about her was fresh and virginal. He didn't believe she was eighteen; she'd blushed when she'd told him that. What if she was only fourteen?

Whatever age she was, he knew she was too young for him and he should not have kissed her in that way. He had this penchant for very young girls. He'd married Maureen when she was barely seventeen, but that didn't really count because he'd been very young himself. Unfortunately it hadn't worked out; she'd grown up and told him she'd had enough of him seven years later. There had been other young girls, Sylvia for one and Janet for another. Elaine had wagged a warning finger at him and called him the black sheep of their family, though she only knew the half of it.

He just had to see June move her long bare legs to be totally immersed in emotion. He wanted her, he felt drawn to her. He'd told her she was a beautiful dryad. He smiled at the recollection. June bewitched him.

He'd asked her if she'd come out with him on Saturday night, and suggested a visit to the Argyle Theatre where George Formby was heading the list in a variety show. She'd jumped at the chance – a girl after his own heart. He thought she was a risk-taker, a girl who wanted everything life had to offer and she wanted it now.

He would need to keep his interest in June well away from Elaine's ears. For the last couple of years, he'd lived alone in a couple of rented rooms in one of those mansions overlooking Birkenhead Park, so that shouldn't be too difficult. He'd never do anything to hurt June.

When he got back he found Tom boiling eggs for the twins' tea and the birthday cake already set out on the playroom table for afters. Ralph knew Elaine would put the children to bed and then serve a slap-up dinner for the adults. Tonight, there'd be other guests.

Elaine came in and took charge. She lit the candles on the cake and they all sang Happy Birthday for Tom. He opened his presents and whooped with delight to find Dulcie had given him a box of liquorice allsorts and Lucas a key ring. He thanked them with numerous hugs and kisses.

Ralph envied Tom, he had a wife and family, it was what he wanted for himself but so far he'd not achieved it. He thought again of June.

Elaine started to tell them why she was late coming home. He'd heard her talk about her friend Leonie Dransfield many times, her shop and their joint ambitions. Suddenly Ralph froze. He hadn't until that moment registered that June was Leonie's daughter.

Elaine would accuse him of leading the girl astray and be absolutely furious if any harm came to her and he'd have her mother after his guts too. He'd given no thought as to who she might be. To keep on seeing her would be more dangerous than he'd first supposed.

When the dinner guests started to arrive, Nicholas Bailey amongst them, Ralph realised June was doubly connected to people he already knew. He'd known Nicholas Bailey for many years and knew the sad story of his first marriage. Elaine had been inviting them both for supper on a regular basis. No doubt it was her way of providing support and friendship for Nick and working off her sisterly duty towards a younger sibling. He remembered something else now, over the years he'd heard something of Nick's attraction to Leonie Dransfield.

Ralph decided June could prove something of a hot potato, but he couldn't stand her up. She was the most beautiful girl he'd ever seen and something drew him to her.

CHAPTER NINE

JUNE WAS WALKING ON air, she couldn't wait for Saturday night, she couldn't she get Ralph out of her mind. She'd told nobody about him, not even Peggy Bryce, her friend at school. She didn't need to be told that Pa would have a fit if she said a man like Ralph was taking her to the Argyle Theatre.

When some boys she knew invited her to a party, Pa had demanded she brought them in and introduced them to him and Mum before she went out. They'd wanted to know what sort of a party and the address where it was being held. Pa would take one look at Ralph and he'd say no, he's too old for you.

She'd have to say she was going out with Peggy and it would be safer not to mention the Argyle. Even then, he wanted to know which cinema they were going to, and insisted she be home by ten o'clock.

June gave a lot of thought about what she should wear. Everything she had was so childish. In the end she borrowed a red dress from her mother's wardrobe without her knowing, and covered it with her best camel coat which was a recent purchase and quite nice.

Ralph had said he'd pick her up at the ferry terminal, and she saw him sitting in his car as she ran down. He got out to greet her and give her a box of chocolates. He really knew how to treat a woman. She had to tell him about her ten o'clock curfew or she wouldn't be allowed to do this again. He didn't seem surprised.

'Would it be easier to meet me during the day?' he asked.

'Yes, much easier.'

'Then what about tomorrow afternoon?'

Of course she jumped at the chance.

For years Leonie had been telling herself that renting the shop had been the right thing to do, her business was growing and Elaine was achieving her ambition. It had been a success for them both, but what of her children? She didn't think it had been good for them. She'd never had enough time to care for them properly and left far too much to Mrs Killen and sometimes to Steve.

Leonie didn't know why the relationship between Milo and Steve had gone so wrong. Milo had not been happy throughout his teens and there'd been constant conflict between them. He'd been inclined to stand up to his father and answer back and Steve had always been a very strict parent, stricter with Milo than he'd been with the girls.

Milo had not been academic; he'd not done well at school. What he enjoyed was messing about in boats. He'd wanted to join the merchant navy when he was sixteen and asked his father if he could train on the *Conway* which was moored in front of their house. Often they heard whistles blowing on board and saw the boys rowing towards Rock Ferry pier.

When the *Dido* was eventually launched on the Mersey, Milo was in his element. He spent long hours out on the river or at the Yacht Club. In spite of his promise, he put less effort into his schoolwork and it showed. After some very bad exam results Steve told him he was wasting his time and would be better off working in the business.

Despite Leonie's misgivings, George Courtney was asked to find him a place in the firm and Milo duly started. Leonie knew Milo loved his dinghy and was saving every penny he could from his wages to buy a bigger boat. Almost a year later, she took George aside to ask how Milo was getting on and whether he was enjoying the job.

'I think he is,' George said. 'He's popular with the girls he works with, and he's trying hard and coping. He'll be fine, Leonie, you don't need to worry about him.'

She was relieved to hear that and thought he was settling at last.

Leonie found June quite difficult too. She'd wanted to leave school when she was sixteen and had talked about getting a job. Leonie told her she'd be better staying on at school, and Steve fully agreed with that, but her school work was going down too. She was taking little interest in it.

Steve thought she wanted to start work in the business and asked George to find her a job in the Liverpool shop, but she refused that vehemently. It seemed she wanted to do things her way.

Leonie told her she wouldn't get a decent job unless she had some skill to offer. Steve thought they'd be able to employ her in a secretarial capacity in the business and eventually it was agreed that she could leave school if she went to secretarial college.

June went out by herself a good deal and often arranged to

absent herself from meals. She said she was with her old school friend Peggy or the other girls on her commercial course. At one time, she'd been keen on coming to Leonie's shop, but she rarely came these days. June had definitely made a life for herself and she wanted to be allowed to get on with it.

She found, too, that Milo had not settled as she'd hoped. He sold *Dido* to buy a second-hand fishing boat called the *Vera May* and admitted that his ambition was to cut loose from the antiques business and earn his living as a fisherman. It was thirty-eight feet long and had a cuddy instead of a cabin. He spent his next summer holiday trying to do just that.

'You're a fool,' Steve told him, 'you'll never be able to earn enough.'

'I can't argue with Pa,' he told his mother, 'but I need to try. It's what I want to do.'

Milo found that the fishing industry was well organised on Merseyside. There were larger, more efficient boats in the fishing fleet and the only reason Milo had been able to afford the *Vera May* was that it was too small for the job. There was a fish market where the fish Milo caught could be sold, but they dealt with large amounts. He tried it but his catch looked puny by comparison with the rest and brought him little money.

Also, he'd found that he had to go out into the Irish Sea to fish because there were few fish in the tidal estuary of the Mersey that could survive the ever-changing mix of salt and fresh water, and that increased the cost of each trip. He tried selling his catch direct to the retail fish stalls in the market, but the owners were in the habit of getting out of bed at five o'clock to buy their stock in the wholesale market. Unless Milo could guarantee a regular supply, they weren't interested.

Leonie knew Milo had had his dream for the future shattered. Commercial fishing on such a small scale was not an economic proposition. It was an added hurt that his father had been right.

One evening, while the family were round the table eating supper, June said, 'I want to go out with the girls straight from college tomorrow night, so I won't be home until late.' Mum gave her a rather suspicious look and Pa started the usual grilling about where they planned to go, but June had expected that and had the answers to soothe him.

She had to listen to the usual fussing about too many late nights and be sure to be home by ten. She pleaded for an extension and it was grudgingly given when she pointed out that it was difficult for her to come out of the cinema before the big picture finished when her friends would want to see the end. She breathed a sigh of relief when it was over. At least she was now free to spend all tomorrow evening with Ralph.

She was head over heels in love with him and believed he felt the same about her. She got into bed and snuggled down, still thinking about all he meant to her. June was managing to keep her love affair a secret. She wasn't finding it easy, but only Milo had found out and she'd sworn him to secrecy. He said, 'I hope you know what you're doing. Pa will crucify you if he finds out.'

She'd had a very close escape last Saturday. Amy had been bored with her own company and after supper when she was changing to go out, Amy had nagged to go with her. She'd fobbed her off to run down to the old ferry terminal where Ralph had arranged to pick her up.

Amy had followed her out of the house without her knowing. Fortunately, Ralph had walked up to the sweet shop to buy cigarettes. As he'd waited to be served he'd stood watching for her just inside the door. He attracted June's attention and had turned back to the counter when Amy caught up with June inside the shop.

June almost jumped out of her skin, but realised in time that Amy thought she was waiting to be served too. Without a word, she grabbed her hand and ran her back home. Milo was in the old summerhouse near the garden gate with a couple of friends. He'd banned Amy from going near it and normally June stayed clear, but that night Milo grasped the problem and let Amy stay for an hour.

June still felt shaky when she went back to the sweet shop to find Ralph waiting for her outside. 'That was a close one.' He smiled.

'Luck was on our side.' She took a deep steadying breath. 'A split second earlier and she'd have seen I was meeting you.'

He tucked June's arm through his and they ran down to his car, laughing. But she was beginning to feel guilty about hiding this most important part of her life from Pa and Mum. She should never have started doing this.

Chapter Ten

Amy loved school but she also loved the freedom of school holidays when she could play all day. She knew her mother did her best to take time off so that she could be at home with her during the holidays.

'But with the business to run, love,' she said, 'I'm afraid there are days when it isn't possible.'

Amy didn't mind Mum not being there. Pa always was, but he stayed in his room and didn't interfere with her. Mum asked Elaine to invite her to her house to play with the twins. Amy wasn't keen on them, they were babies and they always had someone looking after them who bossed her around as though she was their age.

Amy wanted to play with Pat. Her mother didn't go to work and said she was happy to have Amy at Beechwood House as Pat needed somebody to play with in the school holidays, and who better than Amy. She liked going to Beechwood, there was always something going on there because Pat had three older sisters. They didn't always let her and Pat play with them and tended to push them out of their circle, but at lunchtime they always included Amy if she was there.

She and Pat liked to drift from one house to the other and play in the gardens or on the shore. Mum was always telling her to be good. She was allowed to go to the sweet shop, but she mustn't go far by herself.

'And don't get into mischief. June will be at home too, her holidays almost coincide, don't they? She's going to keep an eye on you.'

But Mum didn't know June was always going out and often couldn't be bothered with them.

In the Easter holidays, Amy and Pat broke one of Mum's firmest rules. They took off their shoes and socks and walked out half a mile across the Mersey mud to Milo's boat, paddling the last few yards through the tide to reach it. It was easy to climb on board because the *Vera May* was beached on her side with her deck on a slant.

To be so far out from the shore was a lovely change and great fun; the breeze was brisk and smelled of the sea and brought the sound of a pipe band from the deck of the *Conway* which was at its mooring close by. Curiosity led Amy and Pat to search through Milo's possessions in the cabin. They found tea in a jar, two tins of condensed milk and a biscuit tin with ginger biscuits inside. They ate them all.

Amy had given no thought to the state of the tide until she felt the *Vera May* level up and begin to float on the deepening water. The tide had come in without either of them noticing and water was swirling round the boat and already looked too deep to paddle through. The mud, still showing their footprints, seemed tantalisingly far away.

Amy could feel her heart pounding, she was scared stiff, but she put on a brave front. 'We'll have to swim. It isn't far.'

'You know I can't swim,' Pat wailed and grabbed her arm. 'Don't leave me here.'

Amy hesitated. 'The longer we stay, the deeper it'll get.'

The safety of the shore suddenly seemed far away. She could see her house, the end one of a short row with their gardens sloping down to the Esplanade. Several children were playing on the sand below.

'That's Peter Jones,' Pat gulped, 'and Betty Waters. She lives next door to me.' She cupped her hands round her mouth and yelled, 'Betty! Help, we're marooned. Tell my mum.' The breeze whipped her words away and the children on the shore went on digging.

Amy fetched some towels from the cabin. 'Wave this,' she said, pushing one at Pat. 'And shout as loud as you can.'

They shouted and screamed until they were hoarse. Eventually the children noticed them and waved back. 'We're marooned,' they bellowed.

At last they saw Betty swing herself easily up the high wall of the Esplanade using the iron stays. All the children living in those houses could do that, they climbed up and down several times a day. Betty slid through the railings and ran up the path to the front door of Amy's house. Her knock brought June out to the garden; with her hand shading her eyes, she looked towards them.

They waved their towels and shouted louder than ever. Then they saw June go back inside and Betty Waters climb down to the sand.

'What do we do now?' Pat wanted to know.

'We'll have to wait. June knows where we are.'

'Is it twelve hours before the tide goes out again?'

Amy wasn't sure.

'That's all night. We could be waiting that long.'

'No, June knows we're here. She'll do something to get us off.'

The early pleasure they'd had at being on Milo's boat was gone. They were scared and they were cold and there was nothing else to eat on board. Amy looked at the camping stove and wondered if she could light it to make a cup of tea, but although they were surrounded by swirling muddy river water there wasn't a drop of water they could drink.

The sky clouded over and the children left the shore. Amy and Pat huddled together on the narrow berth in the cabin with Milo's wet weather equipment piled on top of them.

It was an hour or so before Amy heard Milo hailing them. She shot out on deck to see him sculling towards them in a dinghy.

'You little pests,' he said when he came alongside. 'Come on, you first, Amy.' Keeping the boats as close as he could on the heaving water, he yanked them down one by one.

'It isn't safe, Amy, for you to come out to my boat without me.'

'You never bring me.'

'Do you blame me? You should have more sense. Stay away from it until you've learned about the tides.' He looked at Pat. 'You're another pest. Your mother rang June up ages ago to ask her to send you home. She wanted to take you shopping for new shoes.' He looked at her bare feet. Amy tried to keep hers out of sight.

'Don't you two have any shoes?'

'We left them on board,' Amy muttered. They'd buckled their sandals together to make them easy to carry.

'We aren't going back for them now,' Milo said grimly. He told them June had telephoned him at work, that he'd come home early and borrowed a friend's dinghy to get them off. 'Why can't you play at home?'

'We were but Pa made us go out. He said we were making too much noise in the house.' They'd been playing with the gramophone, another thing Amy wasn't allowed to do on her own, singing along to it.

Suddenly in the spring of 1939, conscription came and blotted out all their personal problems. Nobody had expected it to come before the war started and it renewed and heightened all their fears. If there was already conscription, who could doubt that war was coming? It took Milo by surprise. He was in the first batch to be called up, and found himself in Aldershot before he had time to think about it.

A few months later, with his basic training behind him, he came home on leave for a weekend. In the middle of Sunday lunch, he said he didn't like all the square-bashing and would have preferred the merchant navy because he knew a lot about boats.

'Why didn't you tell them?' Mum asked

'I did,' he said.

Pa was cross with him. 'You never stop to think about anything. Didn't I tell you they'd start on unmarried men without dependents, and it wouldn't necessarily be the eighteen-year-olds? With a little forethought, you could have made your choice before conscription came in.'

That had made Milo furious. 'I never wanted to work in your stupid business. I wanted to join the merchant navy when I left school and you stopped me.'

Pa was scathing. 'I thought I'd mentioned to you that in the event of war the antiques business would not be considered war work and might not even survive.'

In fact he'd nagged Milo over the last year, but now he held his tardiness up as an example to June because her birthday was just four months away.

'Once you're eighteen,' he'd told her, 'you'll probably find yourself directed into uncongenial war work.'

June's commercial course would finish in July and less had been said recently about her working in the family business.

'If you've any sense, June, you'll make your job choice now in essential work. Building planes or boats, or manufacturing munitions – they all need secretarial workers.'

Leonie worried about her too but in a different way. Steve had told her several times, 'You can leave June to me,' and to a large extent she had. Leonie didn't doubt for a moment that June was his favourite child, he made it rather too obvious, but June seemed secretive, and though she paid lip service to loving her father as much as he did her, she escaped from his company as often as she could. Leonie was afraid June didn't want much of her company either, and blamed herself for not giving her more attention as she grew up.

The preparations for war were making Leonie anxious. Gas attacks were expected and gas masks were distributed to all civilians. They were told bombing raids could occur too and public air-raid shelters were being built, but the advice was that householders with space on their own premises should make private arrangements. Every post brought pages of advice about this.

'I'm not going to a public shelter,' Steve said. 'We have the cellar here, we'll use that.'

'Can you get down those steps?' Leonie asked. 'They're quite steep.'

'I've never tried,' he said sharply. 'Never had reason to until now. But I can't walk far and goodness knows where the nearest shelter will be.'

The next day, Leonie went to look at the cellar steps and open the area up. It was years since the cellars had been used. The steps were grimy and made slippery with green algae. Milo would be coming home on another forty-eight-hour pass at the weekend and Leonie decided she'd ask him to help her clean the place up so they could use it.

There was a row of windows that matched those upstairs, but they were only six feet from a retaining wall holding the soil of the garden in place, and they were so begrimed that very little light penetrated into the rooms. She had to get a torch to explore those away from the windows.

She could remember the time when the servants running the house had lived down here, and was surprised to find how extensive the cellars were. In a room that had been used as a kitchen, there was a dripping tap over an ancient stone sink. She had to take a hammer to turn it on, but yes, there was running water down here. There was also a laundry room with more sinks and pulleys for drying clothes, an open fireplace in a living room, but there was no electricity. She found candles and oil lamps that she thought might be useful. The servants' bedrooms were at the front of the house but below ground level, and clearly that would be the safest place to shelter.

At the weekend, she and the children cleaned the steps and

swept the cellars out. There were four iron bedsteads, some with mattresses filled with straw and some with flock. Together they carried them up to the end of the garden and burned them and carried down others from the house.

Leonie fixed up one room with two beds and made them up for herself and Steve. They might as well have as much comfort as they could during a raid. She put the other two beds in another room for the children to use and thought they could take down an old bed chair for Amy.

For years, all Leonie's attention had been on her personal problems and they had kept her fully stretched but now quite clearly a greater and more general problem was imminent.

The very thought of war terrified her and at nine o'clock every evening, she and Steve made a point of listening to the latest news bulletin. Tonight as the news ended, Leonie snapped off the wireless and collapsed back on her armchair. War seemed only a breath away.

Steve stirred in the armchair on the other side of the empty grate. She could see the dread on his face. 'It won't be long,' he said, 'but I won't be in this one.'

Leonie said, as she had many times to bolster his self-confidence, 'You've done your bit. You fought for your country last time.'

'And paid for it.' His voice shook. 'The war to end wars and it's only twenty years since . . . It's Miles and June who will bear the brunt of it this time.'

That was what frightened Leonie most. It would break her heart if Milo ended up like his father.

She felt Amy tug at her skirt. Just to look at her all ready for bed in her flannelette nightdress tugged at her heart too. Amy was growing up; she was now a pretty nine-year-old with clear skin and straight, light-brown hair that the summer sun had streaked with gold. She had been listening quietly to the news broadcast.

'Mum, who is this man Hitler? His name is always in the news. Why are you afraid of him?'

Leonie squeezed her hand. Amy would need to understand. 'He is the German leader, we think he's about to declare war on us.'

'But you said war was coming when Milo got called up.'

'It's closer now.'

'Hitler will send his army with guns and tanks to invade us,' Steve added bitterly.

'Surely they won't come here?' Amy's blue eyes were wide in horror.

'We're afraid they might.'

'Not necessarily,' Leonie said quickly.

Steve pulled a wry face. 'Hitler has fought and overrun other countries, now it looks as though it's our turn.'

'There's no need to fright—'

'You'll be all right, Amy,' Steve said, 'it's your brother and sister I'm worried about. A war now is going to catch them at the wrong age.'

Leonie was afraid for Amy too. The child was sitting on a stool near her chair and tugging at her again. 'But if the Germans are coming here, surely we could all be shot, even me? And they're going to drop gas on us, aren't they? That's why we've been given gas masks.'

'We don't really know what's going to happen.' Leonie shook her head. 'This war will be different from the last one.'

'When June took me to see *Snow White and the Seven Dwarfs*,' Amy said, 'we saw a newsreel with German tanks and hundreds of goose-stepping soldiers. They all had their guns on their shoulders.'

'It's time you were in bed,' Steve said abruptly. 'Come and say goodnight.'

'I want Mum to—'

'She'll come and tuck you in when you're in bed.'

Slowly and with a great show of reluctance, Amy went. 'Don't be long, Mum.'

When the door had closed behind her, Leonie burst out, 'What are we going to do about her?'

Last week they had received a letter from Amy's school outlining an evacuation plan and inviting them to a meeting to learn more about it. Leonie had wanted Steve to go with her but he'd said he didn't feel well enough so she'd gone alone.

'I thought you'd decided to keep her here with us,' he said.

Actually, Leonie had signed the form giving permission for Amy to be included in the evacuation, but by the time she'd returned home she couldn't bear the thought of parting with her. Goodness knows where they'd send her and Leonie didn't want to have strangers care for her child. What if they weren't kind to Amy?

'I wish I knew what to do for the best,' she said. Steve was no help when it came to making decisions about Amy.

'It's up to you, isn't it?' he said with cold finality.

All evening Leonie felt under pressure. She knew she had to decide one way or the other and prepare the child for what was coming. She'd heard all the arguments a dozen times. Liverpool was the major port for trading with America, an industrial area

97

where munitions were being made. The banks of the Mersey would be a dangerous place to live. Almost certainly the Germans would bomb Liverpool. If she wanted to keep Amy safe, she would have to let her go to the country.

Leonie finally drifted off to sleep but at three o'clock that night the silence was shattered by shrill shrieking and yelling that went on and on. She woke with a pounding heart and it took her a while to realise it was Amy who was screaming.

By the time she reached the bedroom Amy shared with her older sister, June had switched the light on and was sitting on Amy's bed, trying to wrap her arms round the child's shaking body.

'I thought the war had started,' Amy sobbed.

June's face was flushed with sleep. 'She's had a nightmare.'

'No, Amy, the war hasn't started,' Leonie told her. 'There's nothing to be scared of.'

'I saw them, Hitler was in an open car,' Amy sobbed. 'And there were tanks and guns and lots of German soldiers marching along the New Chester Road. Everybody was running, trying to get away from them before they got shot.'

'You're all right, Amy. Nothing like that is happening,' June comforted her. 'It was just a bad dream.'

'You're safe at home in your own bed,' Leonie added. 'Hitler's miles away in Germany.'

Steve crowded into the room on his crutches. 'Now look.' June hugged her more tightly. 'You've woken up the whole family.'

'Pa said the Germans were coming.'

'I said they might come.' Steve patted her back. 'But they aren't here yet so there's nothing to be frightened of. Settle down now and go back to sleep.'

Amy lifted her tear-stained face and stared round defiantly. 'Everybody's frightened of Hitler. Mum said so. It's not just me.'

'Quite,' Steve said. 'But it's the middle of the night and the rest of us need our sleep. Be a good girl and settle down.'

Amy stifled a sob.

'Bad dreams are horrible things,' June said soothingly. 'But they aren't real. Come on.' She turned her sister on her side and lay down beside her. 'I'll stay in your bed for the rest of the night and hold you close like this.' She pulled the blankets round them. 'Are you comfy?'

'Thank you,' Leonie mouthed at her older daughter and switched off the light. Steve had not wanted Amy in their bedroom even as a baby. He'd insisted she slept in a room some distance from theirs in case she woke him with her crying. As a toddler Amy had found the large old house spooky, and had said she was scared to sleep in a room by herself. June had been persuaded to let her share hers and now Amy didn't want to leave although there were other empty rooms.

Back with Steve in their bedroom, Leonie said, 'Amy would be terrified in an air raid, wouldn't she?'

'Panic-stricken.' He yawned. 'Better if she was sent off somewhere safe as soon as possible. Otherwise the rest of us will be deprived of sleep.'

CHAPTER ELEVEN

HALFWAY BETWEEN SLEEP AND wakefulness, June could feel Ralph's arms tightening round her and his lips were settling butterfly kisses light as air on her neck. Then his lips were searching for hers and she gave herself up to them.

But it was broad daylight and it wasn't Ralph but Amy's arms that were round her. June daydreamed about Ralph all the time and could think of little else but that he loved her as much as she loved him. He had taken over her life. More awake now, she realised Amy was lying half on top of her and her arms weren't holding her tight, they were pushing her away.

'Don't,' June groaned. 'Don't push. You'll have me on the floor.'

'Wake up,' Amy said. 'It's time to get up.'

'No it isn't,' June protested. 'You woke us all up in the middle of the night.' Then she sighed, heaved herself up and threw herself across to her own bed.

'I didn't mean you to go,' Amy wailed.

'There's not enough room for two.'

'Don't go to sleep again.'

June turned away from her. What she wanted was to return to that dreamy state where Ralph Harvey was making love to her.

'It's not fair,' Amy said. 'I couldn't help waking you all up. You can't blame me for that. Even Pa is frightened of Hitler and it really scared me to see that. Then I dreamed of him riding in a car ahead of a battalion of storm troopers with rifles at the ready. Just like at the pictures.'

'Shut up,' June said. 'Let me go back to sleep.'

Amy sat up and stared at the mound under the eiderdown on the other bed. June was nearly nine years older, slim and graceful with long, curly, honey-blond hair. Pa had told her she was fat because she ate too many sweets while June was the beauty of the family. Mum said she was strong and sturdy and not to worry, that she'd slim down as she grew up.

June's college course had finished and she'd achieved certificates to prove she had skills in shorthand and typing of an acceptable standard to an employer. Every suppertime now, Pa talked to June about having forethought and making choices. He wanted her to find a suitable a job and settle in before her eighteenth birthday, after which she'd be old enough to be directed into war work.

The whole family missed Milo and felt he'd been whisked into the army before he'd had time to think about what he wanted to do, and to make it worse, the letters he wrote home told them he wasn't happy.

Last night, Pa had nagged June again, but she'd turned on him. 'Pa, leave me alone. I don't know what I want to do.'

Amy couldn't believe that. 'But you must know what you're good at and what you like doing,' she insisted.

June sniffed. 'I've considered a hundred alternatives but Mum persuades me out of them. You do, Mum, you know you do. I'd quite like to join the WRNs. It's a lovely uniform.'

'That's a stupid way to choose a career,' Pa told her heatedly.

'If you've decided against clerical work, June,' Mum said, 'you could train as a nurse. Ida's niece has decided it would be a good choice of war work. You could go to a hospital in a safe area. You don't have to go far. What about Southport or Chester?'

'I don't want to leave home.' June smiled at them. 'I don't want to go far from you and Pa.'

That seemed to please Pa but he was still putting on the pressure, and as usual June delayed making any decision.

Over the next few days Amy couldn't help but notice that her mother was sorting through the drawers in her bedroom, washing and ironing and sewing buttons on her clothes.

'What are you doing?' she asked.

'Pa and I have decided that in the event of war, it would be safer for you to live in the country. This could be a dangerous place, close to the docks and munitions factories. You love the country, don't you? It'll be like a very long holiday.'

Amy's interest was captured. 'Will I be going to the seaside? I like that too.'

'We don't know exactly where you'll be going, pet.'

'Those clothes you're packing are not what I like to wear. I want to take the dress with blue birds on and the green one with poppies.'

'You won't need cotton dresses,' Mum said. 'Summer's nearly over, it's going to get colder. You'll need jumpers and skirts and your winter coat.'

The next day Amy watched her mother pull down a suitcase from the top of a wardrobe and pack her things into it.

'Come and see if you can carry this.' Mum snapped the case shut and slid it to the floor at her feet.

Amy found that scary. 'Why?'

'You'll need to take care of your own things. Be responsible for them.'

'I don't want to go by myself. I want June to come with me.'

'You know I can't,' June said. 'I'm grown up and will have to do war work. This evacuation scheme is to keep children safe. You'll be going with your school.'

'But you need to be kept safe too, Mum said so.'

'Come and lift this case.' Mum's voice was brisk. 'Let's see if you can manage it.'

Amy wanted to refuse but with her family watching, that was impossible. She lifted the case two inches off the floor and thumped it down again. 'It's too heavy,' she announced, hoping that would be reason enough to cancel the whole project.

'Take some of the stuff out,' Pa advised.

'She'll have to take a change of clothes,' Mum worried. 'The case is heavy before anything goes in.'

'Then let her use that smaller black one.'

'I want space to take my teddy.'

'You're too old to play with a teddy,' her family chorused. They'd said that when she'd asked for a new teddy bear for her eighth birthday but she loved the one she'd received. It was really big.

'You won't be able to take toys, not if you can't manage your clothes,' June said.

'I want—'

'Don't be a pain in the neck.'

103

Pa, too, was growing impatient. 'They won't abandon the child's luggage, for heaven's sake. Somebody will help her.'

'It would be better if Amy could manage it herself.' Mum's lips were in a tight, straight line.

'I don't want to go, not by myself.'

'You won't be by yourself. You'll be with your teacher and most of your class.'

'Mum, I want you to take me.'

'I'm sorry, pet, but that isn't possible.'

Amy felt the coming war was messing everybody up, making them do what they didn't want. Now, she could see her mother's smile was slipping.

'You can cope perfectly well on your own, you know you can,' she said. 'You're always going out by yourself. Yesterday, for instance, you didn't tell anybody where you were going and I couldn't find you at suppertime.'

'I wasn't on my own and you knew I'd be with Pat. Pat's family isn't forcing her to go away. They want her to stay here with them.'

'Oh, stop moaning,' June said. 'If there's a war, we'll all have to do things we'd rather not.'

'It's for your own good, pet.' Mum's voice trembled. 'I wish we could all be evacuated with you, but we can't. Don't worry about the suitcase. I know how to fix that so you can carry what you need.'

Amy thought her mother could fix anything, and once her mind was made up nothing would persuade her to change it. The next day Mum made her a haversack from a length of light calico she had amongst her dress lengths. Then she wrote her name on it in block capitals with an indelible pencil.

'If it's a wet day,' Pa said, holding it up to the light, 'all the child's things will get soaked.'

'No they won't,' Leonie said. 'I'll wrap her mac round her clothes before I put them in.'

'Perhaps you're all wrong,' Amy said hopefully, 'and war won't come.'

'Of course it will come,' Pa exclaimed in a burst of irritation. 'It isn't a question of if any more. It's a question of when.'

Amy was told not to talk during the wireless news bulletins these days and each broadcast seemed to darken the gloom. That evening, she heard the newsreader make an announcement about the evacuation of schoolchildren.

Afterwards Mum opened the haversack and said, 'Amy, I'm putting in three stamped addressed envelopes for you.' She pulled them out to show her. 'Look inside and you'll find a sheet of writing paper in each one and here is a stump of pencil. We won't know where you are unless you write to us. We need to know the name of the people who are looking after you and the address where you are staying. You must promise me you'll do that.'

Amy shuddered, it was definitely going to happen. 'Yes, I promise.'

'I want you to get one of these into the post as soon as you can because I'll be worried until I hear from you.'

Mum would be worried! That terrified Amy. 'Mummy, don't send me away. I don't want to go.'

'Of course you want to go,' Mum suddenly sounded very hearty. 'It'll be a great adventure. Once I have your address, I'll be able to send you your teddy bear and some books. Perhaps later on I could come and see you. I want you to write me long letters all about the people you're staying with and about your new school.'

'I don't want to go to a new school,' she wailed. 'I like the old one.'

All day at college June looked forward to her evening with Ralph. She got off the bus near Birkenhead Park and walked the few yards to the lovely old house overlooking it where Ralph lived. She enjoyed nothing better than going to his rooms.

She reached the house and let herself in with the key he'd had cut for her. Ralph had said he couldn't afford a whole house because he was paying alimony to his divorced wife. The rooms were rented out individually and the bathrooms shared. He had the original drawing room which was very grand and two smaller rooms on the ground floor. They were at the front of the house and only a few paces from the front door, so nobody need see her going in and out. Ralph said the other people living here were very friendly but the less they knew about his business the better.

He heard her come in and opened the drawing-room door before she reached it.

'Darling June,' he said. He drew her inside, pushed the door shut and took her into his arms to kiss her. Ralph was very romantic.

His big drawing room looked absolutely gorgeous. He'd redecorated and fitted it out to look very gracious. All his furniture was ultra-modern, he didn't care for the old stuff Pa liked. June had helped him choose the turquoise satin curtains that hung from ceiling to floor at the big windows. He had a tea tray set and the cherry cake she loved all ready for her.

'Don't eat too much of it,' he cautioned. 'I've booked a table for dinner at the Central Hotel.'

He had a little kitchen but he didn't like cooking. Sometimes she cooked a simple meal for them, but Ralph liked taking her out to restaurants and pubs. He let her try wine and cigarettes and gave her money to buy clothes which she couldn't take home or Mum would want to know where she'd got them. She felt sorry for the girls she'd known at school. She'd grown up and left all that girlie stuff behind.

After she'd had her tea she snuggled into his arms on the sofa and kissed him. It hadn't taken her long to let him make love to her, she hadn't been able to help herself. At college the girls spoke of going 'all the way' as though it was a huge divide. All girls were given to understand they must never allow that, not until they were married. Pa would kill her if he knew but having done it once there seemed no point at all in depriving themselves of the thrill of it.

Ralph was raining kisses up and down her neck, on her throat and across her shoulders until she had to satisfy her craving. She took him by the hand and led him to his bedroom. Unfortunately his rooms didn't connect and they had to go out into the hall which was used by other people to reach his bedroom, so it didn't feel very private. It was a nice room too. He kept the heavy curtains closed here and had a black and gold satin eiderdown on his bed and pictures of tigers on the walls. She kept the clothes he bought her in the big wardrobe with his own.

They spent an hour or so under the eiderdown. June loved to feel his body against hers, while he told her how much she meant to him. This was the time she enjoyed most. Then she crept to the cold and ugly shared bathroom while Ralph picked out the outfit he wanted her to wear. She felt very sophisticated in a dress and coat that even Mum would think was high fashion, and most of all she loved her high heels.

Ralph drove into the town centre and parked close to the hotel. She took his arm as they went inside. He told the receptionist they had a reservation for the restaurant. 'We'd like to eat straight away,' he said.

They were being escorted to their table when he stopped. 'Er, no.' He half turned to June and she felt herself being backed out of the restaurant.

'What's the matter?'

He was drawing her towards the reception desk. 'Sorry,' he said to the girl manning it. 'Cancel our reservation for dinner tonight. Something's come up, we can't stay. Sorry.'

He bundled June back into his car. 'Whatever is the matter? You look as though you've seen a ghost.'

'Elaine was there. Tom too.' He mopped his brow with his handkerchief. 'But I don't think they saw me. Anyway, they couldn't have seen you. I turned round and shut off their view. Elaine would give me hell if she knew about us. We'll go to New Brighton and get well away from them. We'll find somewhere to eat there.'

Up till now, June hadn't worried about being seen with Ralph. Her parents didn't go out to eat and most of her old friends couldn't afford to go to the places Ralph chose.

There were several big hotels along the seafront. By the time they'd been shown to a table, Ralph had recovered from his shock and was laughing at their lucky escape. He ordered champagne to celebrate and June had never enjoyed an evening more. She had to go back to Ralph's rooms to change her clothes. She loved his car and it was what made it possible to keep the deadlines Pa set.

It was only a few minutes after ten when Ralph drew up at her garden gate. He was in a more serious mood now. 'I've been a fool,' he told her. 'I earned myself a reputation as a divorced man who preys on young girls, and I set out to do it all over again with you.'

June laughed and pulled him closer to kiss him. 'I can't believe that. You knocked me off my feet the moment I set eyes on you. You're loving and kind and generous and I adore you.'

'I should have had more sense than to let you meet me without your parents knowing. They'll hate me if they find out. I want you to know that what I feel for you is completely different. I've never felt so deeply in love with anyone before.'

June found it very hard to tear herself away from him, but she had to observe Pa's rules. Her parents were in the living room talking about the coming war yet again.

Pa asked for about the hundredth time, 'Have you made up your mind, June, about what you want to do? There's a job advertised in tonight's *Echo* that might—'

'No,' she said. 'I can't think about the war now.' She couldn't stand any more of this tonight. 'Goodnight, Pa, goodnight, Mum.' She rushed to her bedroom.

June knew that Ralph was afraid the war could bring this golden interlude in their lives to an end. It was unsettling, and unfair. She hated the very thought of war, and she knew her parents were even more scared. They'd lived through the last one.

* * *

Later that week Ralph Harvey drove home from the bank looking forward to seeing June again. He'd got through three empty evenings when he'd gone home wondering how to fill them. June couldn't meet him as often as they would both have liked. She touched all his senses, he could think of little else but her beautiful face.

He wanted to end his man-about-town, bachelor life. Searching for girls and having a good time in restaurants and bars was no longer what he wanted. It had never been as much fun as it was cracked up to be. He wanted to settle down and marry June. Perhaps he'd grown up at last; it had certainly taken him longer than most to do it. The odd thing was, June had always seemed more mature than he was.

He let himself into his drawing room and she shot into his arms, radiant and laughing with sheer pleasure at being with him again. The way she greeted him warmed his heart, made him realise how lucky he was to have her.

She'd known what time to expect him and had a tea tray waiting for him set with a chocolate cake which she'd bought on the way because she knew it was his favourite.

Perhaps they didn't go out so often now, perhaps they were spending more time in his rooms where June sometimes cooked a meal, but as usual they enjoyed their tea. Then because he couldn't keep his hands away from her they ended up on his sofa. When they could wait no longer, he took her to his bedroom.

An hour or so later, with all passion spent, Ralph raised himself up on his elbow to look at her. Her lovely fair hair was spread across the pillow. 'You're very beautiful,' he told her, 'and you're the sweetest, loveliest person I've ever known.' She smiled up at him. He collapsed back against his pillow. 'I'm sorry.'

'What for?' He could hear the laugh in her voice. 'I want you to think I'm beautiful and a lovely person.'

'I have a lot to apologise for. I'm no saint, June.'

'You've told me that before. I know I'm not the first girl you've had in your life.'

'I hope you're going to stay with me for ever. Will you marry me?'

'Of course I will. There's nothing I want more, but—'

'I know.' He took her into his arms again and pulled her close. 'I realise now how stupid I was to earn myself the reputation I have.'

'You like young girls, what's wrong with that?'

'Some would say I abused young girls.'

She gave a little laugh. 'You've never abused me.'

'I have. I lusted after you from the moment I set eyes on you. I went all out to get you. I knew it was very wrong to take you to theatres and hotels and keep what we were doing a secret.'

She kissed him and clung closer. 'Was there any other way?'

'I should have found one. If I'd known I was going to fall deeply in love with you, and how important you were going to be to me, I'd have gone about bringing you into my life in a very different way.

'For a start, I should never have allowed you to keep our meetings secret from your family. It meant you had to tell lies to explain where you were going. It reduced our love to a furtive affair and both our families will see it like that.'

She was taking him seriously at last. 'But what can we do about it now?'

'I've asked myself that a hundred times. I've got us into a bit of a predicament, haven't I?'

'It was what I wanted too.'

'I can think of no easy way out now. The fact is, it would be very difficult to pretend to Elaine and your parents that we've only just met without inventing a whole new tissue of lies.'

'We'll have to think of some way.'

'I've really tried.'

'Then we'll have to carry on as we are until I'm twenty-one. We'll get married then.'

'June! That's still three years off,' Ralph said, 'and I'm afraid we'll be at war long before then. I want to look after you forever, but I'm afraid I'll get called up.' He'd explained before that men were being called up in age groups. He was thirty-three now and so far his turn hadn't come, but it would. 'We won't be able to go on like this. I'll be forced to leave you.'

He took her shopping to buy an engagement ring. 'I want you to have something to remind you while I'm away that you are engaged. I want you to trust me.'

'I do, I don't need anything to remind me.'

She chose a sapphire with a small diamond on each side of it, and then he had to buy her a fine gold chain so she could wear it round her neck and her family wouldn't see it.

What a fool he'd been. He'd been taking June out and about for over two years now. If only he'd gone about this in the right way, both their families would have accepted that they were in love and wanted to spend their lives together.

CHAPTER TWELVE

A MY WAS ON HER long summer holiday but one morning, her mother told her she was going to take her to school the next day.

'I've been going by myself for years,' she scoffed but the moment she saw the haversack come out of a cupboard, she knew why. She was scared and wouldn't let go of Mum's hand on the journey. The school was quieter than Amy had ever known it. She was handed over officially to a teacher she didn't know and her name checked off a list.

'I'm Miss Cosgrove.' The teacher smiled brightly at both of them as she tied a label with Amy's name and address to a button on her coat. 'We'll be setting off soon and I'll be coming with you. We'll have a bus ride and then a train ride. Won't that be nice? We've got your luggage, yes. Have you brought your gas mask and a packed lunch?'

'This is my gas mask.' Amy wore it as recommended, swinging from a string round her neck so it bumped against her stomach. Mum had covered the cardboard box with red Rexene to keep it dry. She'd made hundreds of them for other people in the shop. 'And this is my lunch.' She held up the brown paper bag.

'Excellent,' said the teacher. 'Say goodbye to your mother and then wait in the hall until the bus comes.'

With a determined smile on her face, Mum led her by the hand to the doors of the school hall. 'Now I want you to be a good girl,' she said. 'Do as you're told and don't forget to write to me and post it as soon as you can.'

'Yes, Mum.' Amy could feel butterflies in her stomach.

'You'll have an exciting time, you'll see. You'll enjoy it.' She gave her a hug, pecked at her cheek, then pushed her into the hall and walked briskly away.

There were other children there, some from Amy's class. They sat on the floor in subdued groups until another teacher wheeled in a trolley loaded with picture books, slates and chalks and encouraged them to amuse themselves.

Amy picked up a slate and, like many of the others, drew matchstick figures of Hitler. Then she rubbed the slate clean and drew another of herself waving goodbye to her family. She didn't want to say goodbye to them. It wasn't butterflies she had in her stomach now but an aching void.

As the hall filled up, it became more like a normal playtime. Amy watched the other children inspecting their packed lunches and sampling them. She opened hers up and bit into an egg and lettuce sandwich.

They started running about squealing and screaming and some even started sliding on the polished parquet floor, a practice strictly forbidden and punished heavily when caught. Today nobody came to stop them.

They were all bored and impatient before they were herded into coaches and bussed to the railway station. To Amy, the train journey was more of a novelty, though she had her misgivings when she saw the streets she was used to give way to fields and woods and hills. The journey seemed to go on forever and they all grew bored again. With her packed lunch long since eaten, Amy, like most of them, was hungry.

At last the train stopped in a small town, they got off and were counted again and led to a nearby school in a two-by-two crocodile. In the hall there, tables had been arranged as they were for the school Christmas party. Each place was set with a paper cup of lemonade and a paper plate with a currant bun and two biscuits. They all fell on the welcome feast.

After that they were let out into the school yard but by then they were tired and had had enough of the great adventure. Full of trepidation, Amy saw they were being picked out and sorted into groups. Miss Cosgrove took Amy and seven others, checked off their names on yet another list and marched them towards a line of waiting cars. The children were all squashed into the back of a big one. Three adults sat in front.

Moments later they were chugging up a country road along the floor of a wide valley. To Amy, it all seemed very strange. She huddled closer to the other seven girls and one boy; she was subdued now and plagued by worries. She felt she'd been pushed out of the world she knew, parted from her loved ones and could see no way forward into the new safe world Mum had promised. One of the girls started to cry and the boy told her to shut up. Amy wanted to go home, she thought they all did.

The car slowed, pulled off the road and stopped. Amy could see no building for what seemed miles around but a man and a woman were waiting. The adults got out to talk to them, one with his clipboard. Amy could hear them talking but couldn't understand a word. She knew they were speaking Welsh because Wales was where her family went for their holidays.

She sat back to wait as she'd done so many times today, but then she noticed her haversack was being taken from the boot and set down on the grass verge. Suddenly her heart began to pound. A brown paper carrier bag was set down beside it and the back door of the car opened. The man with the clipboard beckoned her to come out.

She cringed back, not wanting to leave the children she'd come with, but was half lifted out and handed over to the strangers. Amy was engulfed in panic as she watched the car drive away, but the woman took her hand in hers. She was small and dumpy with kindly eyes. Amy couldn't take her eyes away from the cherries on her black straw hat that slid about as she moved her head.

'Hello,' she said in English. 'You'll be staying with us and you're very welcome. You can call me Auntie Bessie.' The man with her kept smiling at her and took charge of the carrier bag and her haversack. Amy relaxed a little, Mum needn't have worried, she hadn't had to carry her haversack at all.

'I'm Uncle Jack,' he said, relieving her of her gas mask. 'There is our house.' He pointed upwards and Amy glimpsed a white building high up on the hill, half hidden by a belt of fir trees. 'We have to walk from here.' She found their accent difficult to understand.

Auntie Bessie led the way through a picket gate. 'We call this the cwm,' she said. The path was so narrow they had to walk in single file. A stream rushed down bubbling and frothing and the path climbed steeply away from it up the side of a deep gulley filled with trees, some enormous and some shrubbery sized. After a while, they crossed a wooden bridge over the stream and went into a field.

It was the steepest field Amy had ever seen. 'This is our land, we call it the sideland,' she was told. There were out-croppings of granite and gorse in the short slippery grass. Her hands were taken by Auntie Bessie on one side and Uncle Jack on the other. They asked her questions about herself and her family and about where she lived. In between they spoke in Welsh together, but soon they were puffing and pausing to get their breath.

Sheep moved away as they advanced, two Hereford cows and two calves stared stolidly at them as they passed. Uncle Jack told her that he'd finished the evening milking so Amy knew she'd be staying on a farm. Now the climb was levelling off and they were in another field where there was better grass. They were high up on the side of the valley and Amy could see for miles, the views were magnificent and took her breath away.

A dog started to bark. 'Be quiet, Fly,' Jack shouted and at the sound of his voice the dog stopped barking.

They passed an area of closely planted fir trees and then were in the farmyard. A black and white long-haired sheepdog was leaping about on the end of a long chain and wagging his tail. Amy liked dogs and took a few steps towards him.

'No,' Jack said. 'He's a working farm dog and he'll think he's a pet if you make a fuss of him. I don't want you to play with him.'

They went through another picket gate on to a tiled terrace. The farm buildings were of black weatherboarding and attached to a pretty whitewashed stone cottage. Amy sniffed at the smell of wood smoke.

'Come in, bach,' Bessie told her. Indoors, a fire burned red in a Victorian kitchen grate, with a stool on either side. The polished steel fender reflected the glow and that and a large homemade peg rug were set in a cosy recess.

Jack poked at the fire until it burst into flames and lowered the large black kettle on its chain to swing over the fire. Immediately it began to sing and a pot of tea was set to brew. Amy stared round.

Ancient varnished beams ran across the ceiling, from which were suspended a whole flitch of bacon and two large hams. Half a dozen pots of geraniums were in flower on the wide windowsill. It was nothing like the home Amy had come from and she didn't know quite what to make of it.

Auntie Bessie took her and her haversack upstairs. They crossed one bedroom to reach the other that was to be hers. It was a modern bedroom suite and had a double bed just for her. Her haversack was tossed on to the gold eiderdown and she was asked to open it up. On top were the self-addressed envelopes Mum had given her.

She was reminded of her promise. 'Mum wants me to let her know where I am as soon as I can,' she told Auntie Bessie.

'It's Saturday tomorrow,' she replied, slipping one of the envelopes into her apron pocket, 'so we'll be going to town. We'll write the letter later and you can post it then.'

She helped Amy lay out her nightdress and slippers. Amy could see the big wardrobe was already full of Bessie and Jack's best clothes, but space was made to hang up her best frock and a drawer in a chest was emptied for her other things.

On a tiled washstand, she could see a large pottery jug standing in a washbowl, both decorated with purple flowers, and under the bed was a large matching pot. Amy felt much too grown up to use that sort of thing, but feeling an urgent need she asked for the bathroom.

'The bathroom? We don't have one here, bach.'

Amy was surprised to be led back downstairs and taken outside. 'There's the *ty bach*,' Bessie said, pointing out a stone structure half hidden amongst the fruit trees of the orchard. 'That means little house,' she added and left her.

Amy half slid down the steep path to open the door. The stench made her take a step back. She felt she needed to close the door for privacy and though a line of Vs had been cut into the wood along the top of the door, it was dark but not so dark that she couldn't see the spiders and the webs they'd spun across the corners. She hated it but she had to use it. She made all haste to get out.

Amy wasn't at all sure she liked her new home, it didn't feel safe, quite the opposite. She didn't know these people and though they were trying to be kind, she didn't know what to expect or what they expected of her. She wanted June and she wanted her mum, she wanted to be in her old familiar home with her real family.

But back in the house a cup of tea was put in her hand and she was told to sit by the fire on one of the stools. She found Auntie Bessie and Jack turning out the contents of the carrier bag.

Amy saw a collection of food, mostly tinned, given by the government to help feed an unexpected addition to the household during the first days of their stay. Tins of corned beef, luncheon meat and fruit were approved of, but a tin of evaporated milk caused considerable surprise and laughter. They spoke Welsh together but changed to English when they turned to her.

'Is this the sort of milk you drink back in the town you've come from?'

'Sometimes,' Amy said. 'We have it on tinned fruit. It's like cream.' There was more laughter. It seemed they had plenty of fresh milk and real cream. 'Sometimes my mother makes rice pudding with it,' she added. 'Mum thinks it's good for that.'

'Rice pudding?' Auntie Bessie beamed at her. 'Good, I can use it that way.'

Amy was pleased she knew something that they did not. Perhaps in time, it would all make sense to her.

'I have to go round the hens and shut them in for the night, so the foxes don't get them,' Jack said. 'Do you want to come with me?'

She felt tired but she wanted to see more of this farm so she followed him out. He explained he had three henhouses and each held a flock of hens. The first was in the farmyard and alongside an open barn that was stacked full of hay.

She could see several rows of birds perched on rails three feet off the floor. They jostled and cackled in alarm and edged further away as they entered.

'Won't they fall off when they go to sleep?' Amy asked.

'No, perches are like beds to them.' Jack was checking the nesting boxes and gave her an egg to hold. He carefully closed not only the big door through which they'd entered but dropped the trapdoor over the hole which the hens used.

The dog came out again as far as his chain would let him, wagging his tail. Amy could see he was attached to a kennel pushed under the tightly planted fir trees in the plantation that served as a windbreak for the house.

She wanted to stroke him but Jack was shaking his head. 'Go to bed, Fly,' he ordered and the dog slunk into his kennel. 'Goodnight,' Jack added.

The other two henhouses were purpose-built and out in the fields some distance away so the birds could forage for most of their food. Jack went through the same routine and found more eggs which he put in his pocket. Daylight was fading and the evening air was cool and fresh. Amy put her hand in Jack's; it felt rough and calloused but made her feel safe.

It was getting dark in the kitchen. Bessie was spreading a white cloth on a small table for supper. Jack lit the oil lamp and the light sparkled on a silver tea service inside a display cabinet sitting on top of a sort of sideboard.

Amy watched mesmerised as one of the tins of luncheon meat was opened and shared between three plates. It was eaten with bread and butter and a selection of pickles and chutneys. She wasn't hungry.

'Eat your best,' Aunt Bessie kept saying, but she couldn't. Her eyes were closing in the heat of the fire.

'She needs her bed.' Uncle Jack forked luncheon meat from her plate to his. 'She's had a long day.'

Bed was what Amy wanted. A candle was lit for her. Going to bed at home meant a routine visit to the bathroom first, but the thought of visiting *ty bach* now it was dark made her quake.

'No need.' Auntie Bessie led the way up to her bedroom and yanked the pot from under the bed. 'You use the piss pot during the night,' she said.

Amy was shocked. She wouldn't have dared say the word piss at home. That was considered rude. Milo got into trouble when he said rude words.

'Goodnight, sleep tight,' Bessie said to her. Amy got undressed and put on her nightdress. There was no water in the big jug so it seemed she was excused teeth-cleaning and washing here.

She opened the window and the room filled with the soft fresh air and the strange noises of the night. The bed seemed very high, she had to climb up into it and felt herself sink into the thick overlay of goose feathers. It was supremely comfortable.

Leonie went straight from Amy's school to her shop, her mind racing with worries. She wasn't sure now that she'd done the right thing. Amy's face had told her what she felt about being sent off into the unknown. Leonie already felt lost without her and weighed down with guilt.

She was a little late opening up and she had a customer waiting for her. She snatched up the two letters that had been delivered and slid them on the part of the shop counter she used as a desk. As soon as that little flurry of activity was over she sat down at her sewing machine but she couldn't get Amy out of her mind and for once her work brought no feeling of contentment. She couldn't settle to sew, couldn't settle to anything.

It was mid-morning before she noticed her unopened letters and attended to them. The first was a bill for threads and buttons but the second made her draw in her breath as she recognised Nick's handwriting.

The last letter she'd received from him had been after Amy's ninth birthday. He'd thanked her for news of her progress. The only time he'd ever written to her had been to thank her for news of Amy.

Now she sat down at her machine and ripped open the envelope, full of eager anticipation.

'*I've missed you very much over the years,*' Nicholas had written, '*but now I've found someone else who is free to marry me and after a lot of thought and deliberation I've decided to go ahead.*'

Leonie leapt to her feet, she couldn't read any more. Nick wanted to marry someone else! She felt tears start to her eyes. She pushed the letter into her pocket and set her machine to run furiously up the long seams of a princess-style dress. Ida arrived for work and chatted about her dog being unwell. It was a distraction but Leonie kept touching the letter and telling herself she mustn't let it upset her.

Nick had a right to all the happiness he could get; she couldn't expect lifelong devotion from him when she could give him nothing. She had to admit they were not as close as they had been. How could they be after all this time? But nevertheless she felt he was deserting her.

She went up to the flat to make some tea and read more of his letter. He said that his bride knew about Amy and he hoped Leonie wouldn't stop sending him letters about her progress.

When Elaine came that afternoon, Leonie forced herself to talk about Nick. If she didn't, it would mean she was very upset at his news.

Elaine seemed pleased. 'I didn't know he was planning to marry,' she said. 'He's told you first.'

Elaine had met Heather and was able to tell Leonie she was Nick's secretary and had been working for him for two years. She was pretty, only twenty-seven, and very good company.

Leonie told herself she should feel happy that he'd managed to find someone else. She spent a whole afternoon trailing round the Liverpool shops seeking a wedding gift for him before she chose table linen and a card of good wishes. Elaine and Tom were invited to the wedding and Leonie had the bitter-sweet experience of hearing all about it at second hand.

It left Leonie feeling flat. She had drifted far from Steve, it was loyalty and pity rather than love that kept her with him. Steve hadn't got on with Milo and was largely indifferent to Amy, but June was still at home and he doted on her.

At least Leonie's dressmaking business was now a paying concern which she enjoyed. She had a life of her own. It wasn't everything she'd have chosen but she had to be content with what she had.

CHAPTER THIRTEEN

AMY WAS WOKEN BY cockerels crowing from far and near, and her room was filled with early sun. She slid out of bed, tiptoed to the door and peeped into the adjoining bedroom. The brass bed hadn't yet been made but Bessie and Jack had gone. Amy got dressed and went downstairs.

The house was silent but the small table was set for breakfast and a small fire was burning in the grate, with the kettle singing on its chain. Then she noticed that the stamped addressed envelope to her mother was lying on the big table. Feeling guilty that she hadn't done what she'd promised, she sat down to write to her now.

As she pulled out the sheet of notepaper in the envelope, she found that Bessie had already written a note to her mother.

Amy read it. '*Don't worry about Amy, she is being a very good girl and I'll take good care of her.*' Mum would like that. Bessie had also printed the address of the farm, which was called Coed Cae Bach, in capital letters, so Mum would know where she was and could write to her.

Amy told her it was a funny house with no bathroom, that instead there was a smelly lavatory outside that had a whole army of great big spiders inside. '*I want to come home,*' she wrote. '*I don't like it here.*' Amy tucked the letters in the envelope and stuck it down so Bessie couldn't read what she'd written.

Then she went outside to explore. From the terrace she could look down and across the wide Severn Valley. She saw a pattern of fields and woods and farms. On the other side, the fields gave way to purplish-brown hill land dotted with sheep. She could hear Bessie milking and went to the open door of the cowshed to speak to her.

'Good morning,' Bessie said. 'I hope you slept all right. You can have a wash in the barn next door.'

Amy went to look. The barn was between the house and the cowshed. A large enamel bowl stood on an ancient bench, with a china soap dish beside it and a bucket of cold water stored below.

Bessie's voice drifted in from under the cow next door. 'Uncle Jack has knocked in some nails for your towel and face flannel and I've put an enamel mug there so you can clean your teeth.'

'Thank you,' Amy said and washed her face. She unhooked her towel from the nail on the back of the cow stalls and looked through the feeding rack to where Bessie was swishing milk into her bucket. The cow stared back at her, chewing its cud.

'When you've finished, you can throw the dirty water on to the garden,' Bessie said.

Amy giggled and crossed the terrace to do it. 'Won't the soap hurt the flowers?'

'No, it's good for them.'

Like the cowshed, the barn had a door split like that of a caravan. The top half was left open because the window was small and there was little natural light. Amy could see now that the laundry was also done in the barn, it housed a wringer and a zinc tub where work clothes could be soaked. In addition, there was a large churn and a paraffin stove with an oven on top in which cakes and pastries could be baked. There was no upstairs here and huge cobwebs were looped high up on the inside of the roof.

Amy heard a clatter of chains as the cows were released from their ties and the next moment they were driven out through the back door. Auntie Bessie struggled indoors with a bucket of frothy milk and took it through the kitchen to the pantry. Amy followed her.

The house was built into the side of the hill and the pantry was a cool narrow room that was partly underground with a tiny window set so high only the sky could be seen through it. It was filled with a greenish light like the bottom of the sea.

'You'll be wanting your breakfast,' Bessie said. 'And you can do something for me while I make it.' She tipped the bucket of milk into the top of a machine. 'This is a separator. I want you to turn the handle and when you get it moving fast enough it'll separate the milk from the cream.'

At first, Amy found the handle hard to turn and the machine buzzed noisily but it was satisfying to see the skimmed milk running into an enamel pail on one side and the thick yellow cream coming out into a bowl on the other. It made her feel quite grown up to be doing useful work.

When she'd finished, a boiled egg with bread and butter was waiting on the little table for her breakfast. Bessie joined her on the settle to have tea and a slice of bread and butter.

'Don't you like eggs?' Amy asked.

'Yes, but this is my bait, just a snack to keep me going,' she said. Even when speaking English she used words that were strange to Amy. 'I had my breakfast with Uncle Jack. He's gone to work now.'

'Doesn't he work here on the farm?'

'No, bach, this is a smallholding of seventeen acres. He works full time for the Forestry Commission planting trees. Saturday is his half day but it's market day in town, and the day I do my shopping. I'll take you with me.'

Auntie Bessie never stopped working and didn't stop explaining things to Amy as she did so. As well as the housework, she had to take the separator apart and scald all its parts to prevent the next milk she put into it turning sour.

Bessie had ready a large basket of butter and eggs to take to her customers and told Amy the wet battery needed to be taken in to be recharged and asked her if she'd carry it.

'It's for the wireless,' Bessie told her. 'Because we don't have electricity we have to run it on batteries. It needs that dry battery too.' She pointed it out. It was the size of two house bricks.

The first thing Bessie did in town was deliver the fresh butter and eggs to her customers. Amy trailed behind her carrying the heavy wet battery. It had a carrying handle on top and was made mainly of glass and filled with acid. They went up the street to a shop selling electrical goods where the wet battery was handed in and exchanged for one that had been recharged.

Bessie seemed to know everybody and stopped to talk, sometimes even in English. It was always about the coming war. There was just as much dread of it here although it was said to be a safe place.

In the newsagent's, Bessie bought the *Radio Times* and a local paper. Before Amy had left home, Pa had bought her a copy of the *Children's Newspaper* and told her he'd give her three pence a week to buy it so she could keep up to date with the war news, but Amy thought it pretty much like the newspapers grown-ups bought for themselves. Instead, she bought a copy of Enid Blyton's *Sunny Stories* and spent the penny change on sweets.

Amy had often been taken shopping for food by her mother and sometimes by June and she didn't like it much. Here a shopping trip was a social occasion as well as a necessity. People were isolated in their farms so the weekly visit to the town meant they greeted each other with enthusiasm and torrents of Welsh. Amy was introduced each time and asked about the evacuation but as soon as she'd posted her letter she'd had enough of town.

There was no bus to take them home but Bessie came from a large family and late in the afternoon her sister and brother-in-law gave them a lift to the bottom of the cwm in their Austin Seven. Uncle Jack was at home and had been watching for the car below and came down to meet them to help carry up the week's shopping. It had started to drizzle so he'd brought Bessie an umbrella.

She pulled Amy close. 'Cuddle up to me,' she ordered, 'we mustn't let your nice coat get wet.'

Uncle Jack was a gentle, mild-mannered man, only an inch or so taller than Bessie, but while Bessie was well-padded, he hadn't an ounce of spare flesh on his frame. He wore an old flat cap and a khaki drill milking coat with buttons missing and a torn pocket. His ancient trousers were tied with string at the ankles over his heavy steel-studded boots. He relieved Amy of the wet battery and Bessie of several shopping bags.

The cows were grazing on the sideland. '*Hobe hobe*,' he shouted at them. They knew what that meant even if Amy didn't and turned reluctantly for home.

'Time for milking,' he explained to her and drove them on. If they moved too slowly for Jack he encouraged them up the steep slope with more *hobe hobe*s.

'Don't get too near them,' he advised, and a moment later Amy could see why. Each in turn lifted its tail and huge plop-plops of khaki manure splashed down as they walked.

'Mind that shit,' Bessie commanded. 'Don't get it on your shoes.'

Amy's eyes widened at Bessie's use of the word 'shit'.

The cows went the back way into the farmyard and Jack followed them to open and close the gates. Bessie led Amy through the meadow, where the path was easier. Once indoors, she unwrapped a pound of sausages for tonight's supper and also a joint of beef for tomorrow's Sunday lunch. Both were put straight into the oven beside the fire. Jack pushed the hot coals under it.

'We need to start the joint cooking tonight,' Bessie explained. 'It's a slow oven.'

Jack collected buckets from the pantry and said he was going out to milk. 'Do you want to come with me?' he asked Amy.

Bessie was on the point of going upstairs to change out of her town-going clothes. She stopped and shook her head at Amy's best coat.

'Not in that, you'll spoil it, *fach*,' she said. Amy was immediately divested of it and a drill milking coat provided from a peg behind the front door. It smelled of cows and reached to her

130

ankles. 'And be careful where you put your feet or you'll spoil those shoes.'

Uncle Jack was sitting on a three-legged stool with a bucket between his knees, milking one of the two cows. It was swishing its tail round his head. The tail was encrusted with dried balls of manure and sounded like clattering wooden beads, which clearly hurt as they slapped Jack's head. He gave the cow a smack on the flank and scolded her.

'Take that tin and get her a few nuts,' he said to Amy. 'You'll find them in a cask next door.'

The food store was on the end of the building. There were sacks and several casks, one full of buttermilk for the pigs, with cabbage stalks and potato peelings floating in it. It didn't look appetising. There was Indian corn for the hens and several sorts of dried meal. There was nothing Amy recognised as nuts but one cask held small, hard, biscuit-like pieces that smelled of treacle. She half-filled the tin with those and took them back to Uncle Jack. 'Are these the nuts for cows?'

'That's right,' he said. 'Tip them in this cow's manger. She'll be busy eating and forget about me milking her.' As the nuts rained down, the other cow rattled the chain that tied her up. 'Perhaps you'd better get a few for her too,' Jack said. 'She's easier to milk, but we don't want to upset her.'

'Doesn't your cow like being milked?'

'She knows she has to be or her udder would get too big and heavy, and no cow likes that. She's just grumpy.'

'What are their names?'

'I don't give them names.'

'You could call that one Grumpy.'

He laughed. 'Would you like to learn to milk?'

'No.' She shuddered. Amy was nervous about getting close to such a big animal and scared she'd swish her revolting tail round her head as she had Jack's. All the time his pail was filling with frothy milk.

'Aren't you afraid that cow will kick the bucket over?'

'She knows she'll be in big trouble if she does, I'll give her a wallop. The other cow is younger and better tempered than this, she never kicks.'

'Then you could call her Sunshine. That's a nice name for a cow, isn't it? How old is she?'

'About three. I only bought her last year.'

'How much did she cost?'

'Thirty-two pounds.' he smiled. 'A lot of money.

A ginger cat came in meowing and rubbed himself against Amy's legs. He almost tripped her up as she tried to move. She bent to stroke him, feeling she understood cats better than cows.

'Pass over that old sardine tin.' Uncle Jack pointed to it. 'And you can give the cat her supper.'

Amy saw it against the wall, still with its lid rolled back over the key and none too clean. She knocked out the bits of straw and held it out to Jack. 'Hold it closer so I can fill it with milk,' he said.

But her arms were short and her feet wouldn't move her any closer to those large cloven hooves.

'She won't hurt you.' Jack took the tin from her and filled it with two squirts from a teat before handing it back.

Amy set it down and the cat lapped at it eagerly, licking his tongue round the tin until it shone bright and clean. He started to purr and looked up at her.

'He wants more,' she said.

'No.' Jack was firm. 'If he wants more food he must catch it himself. I want him to keep the mice down so they don't eat the animal feed and he won't do that if his belly is full. One tin at each milking time is plenty for him.'

'What's his name?'

He shrugged and smiled, 'Pusscat.'

'I shall call him Marmaduke because he's a lovely marmalade colour.'

She picked him up; he had a purr as loud as a motorbike and she loved him.

CHAPTER FOURTEEN

THE NEXT MORNING AMY was taken to chapel by her hosts. Jack and Bessie dressed in their smartest clothes and they all carried their best shoes under their arms in paper bags and walked down through the muddy cwm in old ones. At the wicket gate on to the road, they changed and pushed their old shoes into the hedge to await their return.

Now they were ready to attend chapel. Uncle Jack wore a suit with a waistcoat and a bowler hat. It was a walk of some two miles to the hamlet of Llanhafod which consisted of the chapel, the school and a large farm. The farmhouse was big and gracious and built of pink bricks in the Queen Anne style.

Amy's new school was pointed out to her. A plaque built into the wall told her it had opened in June 1875 as a result of the 1870 Education Act that had made councils responsible for providing free education for children up to the age of twelve. It was built of local granite and roofed with purple slates from Bethesda and the house for the teacher was attached to it. To Amy it seemed small and nothing like her school at home.

The chapel had been rebuilt on a grand scale in the early twentieth century. There was a spacious vestry, a manse for the resident minister and a stable that in the early days was used by visiting preachers and members of the congregation arriving on horseback.

Bessie pushed an open hymn book into Amy's hands when the harmonium, played by a lady with fluttering feathers in her hat started to play. She found the Welsh took great delight in singing. The voices of the congregation soared above the harmonium, almost lifting the roof. At home, by comparison, the congregation hardly seemed to open their mouths and had to be dragged along by the organist. Amy enjoyed the singing but she couldn't join in because she couldn't read Welsh.

She understood nothing of the Welsh service but she'd been given to understand that she must sit still for the hour it would last. It seemed light inside, all the woodwork was polished pine and very plain. There was a high pulpit and an enclosure below for the deacons so that they sat a little higher than the rest of the congregation. There were other children there but none of those who had come on the train with her.

Amy watched the clock, swung her legs to ease the hard seat and wondered how her family was faring without her and whether she'd ever see them again. Bessie noticed her restlessness and offered her a mint imperial from a paper bag she kept in her handbag. Amy was glad when the final hymn came.

Outside, people gathered in groups to gossip with their friends and relatives. Amy knew by their dire expressions that they were talking yet again of their dread of another war. She kicked at the gravel, impatient to go.

The congregation had begun to drift away in twos and threes when the minister came rushing out to release a torrent of excited Welsh at those who remained. It clearly stunned them all.

Again, Amy didn't understand his words but she knew he brought the dreaded news that war had been declared on Germany. Bessie took her hand and led her away, explaining that the teacher who had come from Amy's school had heard Neville Chamberlain's broadcast at eleven o'clock while they had been gathering in the chapel.

They hurried home in a subdued frame of mind. Amy was afraid it meant she'd have to stay here for a very long time and that her family at home was now in danger. War must be a truly terrible thing if adults were scared stiff of it like this.

June woke up slowly. The distant sound of church bells reminded her it was Sunday. She'd have a lie-in. The house was quiet – too quiet.

She propped herself up on her elbow to look at Amy's bed. The white candlewick bedspread was pulled up neatly over the pillow – of course, Amy was gone, Milo was gone and Pa was certain the war was about to start. Why did this have to blow up now?

She'd talked Amy into bringing her up a slice of toast and a cup of tea on Sunday mornings but today she wasn't going to get it. She'd have to get up because Mum got tetchy if the breakfast table wasn't cleared by ten o'clock.

As June went along to the bathroom, she could hear the wireless in the dining room below. Pa and Mum were obsessed with the war news. She paused to listen but she couldn't catch the words. When she went downstairs ten minutes later, she found her parents sitting silent and white-faced at the breakfast table.

June said, 'Has something happened?'

'Neville Chamberlain promised the Poles that Britain would help them defend their border,' Pa told her grimly. 'Now it seems Hitler has invaded Poland and Britain has sent an ultimatum to Hitler saying that if he doesn't withdraw his troops by eleven o'clock this morning, then we too will be at war with him.'

June could see the dread on their faces. The news was like a heavy weight hanging over them but it didn't stop Mum getting the joint of beef into the oven to roast.

'Peel a few potatoes for me, love,' she said to June and she found herself chopping cabbage too, while Pa watched the clock and read the Sunday papers.

Mum was worried and making heavy weather of beating batter for the Yorkshire pudding. 'I'll make an apple tart – could you peel and chop a few apples for me too?'

Pa called them into the dining room as eleven o'clock approached and they sat round with great formality as though they were about to hear their own death sentence.

The announcement, made with great solemnity, was exactly what they were expecting to hear. Mum's face went whiter still and Pa clenched his fists. 'So we're about to fight another world war,' he said.

June was afraid this would bring Ralph's call-up papers. It was bad enough to think of Milo in the army, but for Ralph to be sent to the other end of the country or, even worse, to some war zone where he'd be in the thick of the fighting was absolutely awful. She couldn't bear to think of it, couldn't think of life without him.

June watched her mother get up slowly and switch off the wireless. War had been a threat hanging over them for so long, she'd begun to think it never would come. She was shocked.

'Your time is running out, my girl,' Pa said grimly. 'You won't be allowed to sit around at home twiddling your fingers.'

June was afraid he was right. She'd been looking half-heartedly for a job but had seen nothing exciting enough to put in an application. She was more interested in spending as much time with Ralph as she could before they were parted.

He'd arranged to meet her at the ferry terminal at two o'clock this afternoon. They spent part of the afternoon making love on his bed, and then as he was interested in cricket, they walked across the park to see a match. June sat enjoying the warm sun on her face while he explained what was taking place on the field. June had played cricket at school but was not that interested.

It was a fine mellow evening and as they strolled back to Ralph's rooms, they saw a couple of nurses walking up to the nurse's home in the park. She remembered what her mother had said.

Suddenly June laughed and turned to Ralph. 'Why don't I become a nurse at that hospital?' It was visible through the trees. 'I could see you as often as I wanted. Nobody would be grilling me about where I'd been and who I was with.'

His mind was still on the cricket. 'I didn't know you wanted to be a nurse.'

'I don't. Well, not particularly. But I'll have to get a job before I'm eighteen or I could be directed into something worse, stuffing explosives into bombs in a munitions factory or something.'

'What if you don't like it?

'There's a lot I will like.' She laughed again. 'That hospital is so handy. Don't you think that's a good idea?'

'I like the idea of you being just across the park,' he said, drawing her closer, 'and free to come to my place when you're not working, but I could be called up at any time, June. Conscription applies to all men between the ages of eighteen and forty.'

'I know, but thirty-three is getting on a bit for a fighting man.'

'The government decides on what age group they want to conscript and I've no doubt my turn will come. Would you still want to be a nurse then?'

'If you had to go away, I wouldn't care what I did. It might as well be nursing as anything else.'

Over the first few days, Amy followed Bessie around all day as she worked and she hardly ever stopped explaining things to her. She told Amy that she and Jack had bought Coed Cae Bach on a mortgage in 1916, the year they got married, and that it had cost £1,700 but was all paid off now. Uncle Jack had had to find work to do this. To start with he'd worked on the bigger farms nearby, but he'd been with the Forestry Commission for nearly ten years now and liked it better.

Amy soon understood how the different enterprises at Coed Cae Bach dovetailed together. They kept two cows to supply the house with milk, Bessie made butter from the cream and the skimmed milk was fed to the calves which were fattened and sold for beef.

They kept two pigs to fatten on the buttermilk, one of which was sold and one killed and cured for home use. There were flocks of hens and fifty or so sheep. Jack had fenced off half an acre in the little field and a neighbouring farmer ploughed it for him in exchange for his labour at harvest times. Jack planted all the potatoes, carrots, swedes, onions and cabbages they would need.

In the garden in front of the house they grew salad vegetables, lettuce, shallots, radish and a row or two of scarlet runner beans and garden peas. They had gooseberry and blackcurrant bushes, a thriving bed of rhubarb and the orchard produced apples, pears and always a plentiful crop of plums and damsons. For the most part they ate what they produced.

Bessie sold her surplus butter and her eggs, and the money she earned bought the things she couldn't produce, the sugar, soap, candles and paraffin oil.

At mid-morning, less than a week after Amy had arrived, Auntie Bessie pointed out a figure walking up the field towards them. 'That's the postman,' she told her. 'He could be bringing you a letter from your mother.'

Bessie had suggested Amy use another of the stamped addressed envelopes she'd been given and write to her mother again. This time Amy had told her about the cows and about Marmaduke.

'The postman will take your letter,' she said. 'You won't have to wait until Saturday to post it.'

'He's carrying a big parcel,' Amy said. 'Could that be for me?'

'We won't know till he gets here. It might be for someone else on his round,' she warned.

But Amy was fluttering with hope. Mum had said she'd send on some of her toys and more of her clothes. She had a pink party frock with a tulle skirt and a satin bodice that had once belonged to June. Amy wanted to have that and she wanted her teddy bear too. She waited, holding her breath, with hope growing inside her all the time. She met the postman at the gate.

Joy of joys, the parcel was for her. 'It feels like my birthday although it isn't,' she told them excitedly. She couldn't wait to get it open and they crowded round to see what Mum had sent, but she felt a surge of disappointment when she saw the contents. 'It's just my old clothes.'

'Wellingtons.' Auntie Bessie picked them out. 'And warm jumpers and more underwear. These are just what you need.'

'What I'd really like,' Amy said, 'is my teddy bear.'

'Well, you must write and thank her for the parcel so she knows you have received it, and you could ask her for a pair of strong boots to wear to school every day, they'd last much longer than those shoes.'

Amy was thrilled to find books at the bottom of the box and a bag of boiled sweets, a full writing pad and a packet of envelopes with the stamps already on them. There were three letters folded inside, one was for Auntie Bessie but there were two for Amy. One from Mum, folded round a whole shilling.

The other letter was from June who wrote:

You might just as well have stayed at home. There's no sign of any invasion, and no need to worry about German columns marching along the main road to Chester. Nothing at all has happened to show Britain is at war. I am starting my training at the hospital tomorrow and Pa says that without us, life at home will be more peaceful than it ever was before.

Mum and I have decided that at nine years old you should be giving up baby's toys like teddy bears. I'm sending you some of my old books. I enjoyed them and hope you will too.

* * *

It was Sunday and June had been told to report to the General Hospital at five o'clock today. She'd told her parents that the time set was two o'clock so that she could meet Ralph after lunch and spend the afternoon in his rooms with him. But she was on edge and the time crawled.

'Sunday at five o'clock seems a funny time to ask you to start,' Ralph said.

'It's so we can settle in,' June said. 'We'll be allotted our sleeping quarters and collect our uniforms so we're ready to start tomorrow morning.'

At twenty to five, Ralph walked with her across the park to the hospital gates, carrying her suitcase. It was an awkward goodbye and June was nervous because she was leaving all that was familiar. She mounted the front steps and entered through the rather grand front door. In the entrance hall she found a group of girls all about her own age and was able to relax a little and study them. Three were Welsh, three were Irish and four were from the local area. There would be ten in the new class.

The Home Sister led them across to the nurse's home and allotted them their rooms. June thought hers fairly spartan to look at but there were radiators which meant central heating when the cold weather came. She'd been measured for her uniform when she'd come for her medical exam and it was piled on the narrow bed waiting for her.

'Change into your uniforms,' the sister ordered and held up what looked like a large gauze tray cloth. 'This is your cap. Bring one with you to the sitting room and I'll teach you how to fold it.'

They did as they were told. June felt very strange in the stiff striped dress of heavy cotton.

'I see you've all remembered to bring two tiepins to hold up the bibs of your aprons, and I hope you've all brought hair clips or a hat pin for your caps.' Her eyes went round the group, looking at their hair. 'Long hair is to be worn up tucked under your cap. Short hair must be short enough not to touch your collar at the back, and must not be all over your face. A fringe is allowed but only if it is cut an inch above the eyebrows.'

Three of the girls were advised to get a haircut. June had twisted her long honey-coloured curls into a French pleat before coming. They had to concentrate hard to fold their caps correctly and when June clipped it on her head it felt anything but secure.

'You all look like nurses now,' the sister told them, 'and in future,' she looked June in the eye, 'you will be addressed as Nurse Dransfield. You do not address your fellow nurses by their given names on the ward, it is unprofessional.'

The Sister Tutor arrived and took them to see the school. She told them they'd be spending the next six weeks there from nine until four thirty, but they would have breakfast at seven o'clock with the other nurses and work on the wards between seven thirty and nine o'clock.

'It is now half past six and time for the first seating at supper, so I'll take you along to the dining room and wish you goodnight. Do not be late for classes. I'll see you all at nine o'clock sharp.'

The last thing June wanted was food, but she followed the others and held her plate out in front of the serving counter to receive a portion cauliflower cheese. She found herself seated at a long table between two girls, one from Ireland called Mary

CHAPTER FIFTEEN

IT WAS EARLY SEPTEMBER AND time for the new school year to start. On the first day, Amy was on edge. Bessie got her out of bed early, cut a sandwich for her lunch and filled a brown sauce bottle with milk.

'This morning,' she said, 'I'll walk down with you to meet the taxi and see you into it.' The taxi had to come from town, collecting children on its way. It then had to go a further twelve miles or so along the road to pick up the children from farms further up the valley and get them to school for the nine o'clock start.

'You'll be able to find your way home by yourself, won't you?' Amy could see Auntie Bessie was anxious about that.

'Yes,' she said, though she was nervous because everything was so different, except her green gymslip and blazer with green and gold tie. Her familiar old uniform was something of a comfort.

Before long, a large taxi with several children inside drew up in front of them. The driver called the usual friendly greetings in Welsh as Bessie opened the back door, pushed her inside and waved her off.

The children stared at Amy and fingered her gymslip, but they spoke English to her and alternated between English and

Welsh between themselves. Bessie had assured her she'd meet up with the children that had come from her school but these were all strangers.

The taxi emptied outside the school and the children trooped straight inside, drawing Amy with them to the girls' cloakroom where they hung up their coats. It surprised Amy to see that each of the girls wore a pinafore over a jumper and skirt and had heavy workman-type boots of stiff unlined leather with steel studs on sole and heel.

One girl was both friendly and pretty and said her name was Glenys. She thought Amy's sturdy lace-ups were fancy and called them town shoes. She showed her the girls' playground, a bare patch of concrete with railings round, with the girls' lavatories on the far side, which stank even more than the one at Coed Cae Bach.

Amy thought they played around for what seemed an age before school began, but eventually a bell was rung and they all trooped into the main schoolroom. The others began to sit down at their desks but the teacher sent Amy on to another small room divided from the main schoolroom by a partition of wood and glass.

Here she was relieved to see the familiar faces of the other evacuees, seven girls and one boy and all about her own age. They were all from her school and some had been in her class.

Miss Cosgrove came over from her lodgings at the manse carrying a large bag in which a Thermos flask could be seen. She told them that Miss Morris, who taught the youngest age group, those between five and seven, had kindly given up her classroom to accommodate them. Miss Morris now had to teach the small ones on the other side of the partition, which meant there were two classes being taught in the same room.

Miss Cosgrove handed out new pens and exercise books and her lessons were what Amy was used to. She was able to relax.

When school was over, the taxi was waiting outside but it was going up the road and Amy found Glenys and some of the other children walked home rather than wait for the taxi to return. The other children pointed out the wicket gate to her that led up the cwm. Auntie Bessie congratulated her on finding her way home alone. She was setting the table for afternoon tea, but first Amy was sent upstairs to change out of her school clothes. They sat down together to eat bread and butter with homemade jam and cake, together with stewed plums from the orchard and junket and cream.

Amy loved the junket. Bessie told her she would show her how to make it. All that was needed was to fill a bowl with a pint of warm fresh milk straight from the cow and stir in the junket powder which contained rennet and came in flavours like strawberry and banana. It would set as soon as it was cold.

As soon as the meal was over, Bessie brought the washing-up bowl to the table, put the pots they'd used in and tipped hot water from the kettle over them. The washed dishes were lifted out one by one on to a tin tray and Amy dried them.

Bessie refilled the kettle, banked up the fire and said, 'Time for afternoon milking now. Come and help me look for the cows.'

'I know where they'll be,' Amy said. 'I passed them on my way home from school.'

'Yes, if you could bring the cows up with you tomorrow, it

would be a great help,' she said. 'It would save me having to walk down to look for them straight after tea.'

'They're such big things.' Amy wasn't sure about the cows.

'Cows are gentle creatures, there's no need to be afraid of them,' Bessie told her. 'They wouldn't hurt anybody.'

'But will they come when I tell them to?'

'Of course they will. Here they are, look. You call *hobe* to them.'

'*Hobe hobe*,' Amy called weakly. Both cows looked up at her and then their heads went straight down again to tear at the grass.

'It'll be easier tomorrow because you'll be below them. Just give them a tap and push them up. If you're calling them you need to shout,' Bessie said. 'You have to show them you are the boss.'

Amy tried again. They took a couple of paces towards her and paused for more grass.

Bessie let out a growl of irritation and waved her walking stick at them. Slowly they started to lumber up the steep sideland, taking the back way into the farmyard.

'They move for you because you have a stick,' Amy told her. 'I might feel braver if I had one.'

'Here,' she said, 'take this. You follow them. You'll need to open the back gate to the farmyard to let them in and be sure to shut it behind you. I'll go back the way we've come and open up the cowshed.'

Amy thought it a very risky thing she was about to do. She didn't think her sister June would want to do it and she wasn't scared of the dark or of crossing busy roads. Feeling very daring, Amy went up close to Grumpy and gave her a tap on the back. It made her quicken her pace and lift up her tail to let several steaming pats of manure burst out, just as she had for Uncle Jack.

Amy didn't feel so brave when it was time to open the gate to the farmyard. She had to pass them to reach it and climbed round in a big circle to do it. By then Bessie had opened the back door to the cowshed and Sunshine led the way straight into her own stall. Grumpy lumbered into hers.

'There,' Auntie Bessie said as Amy hovered at the door. 'That was excellent. Now come on in and I'll show you how I tie them up.'

Amy nodded grimly and flattened herself against the cowshed wall to keep as far away as possible from Grumpy's swishing tail. She watched Bessie pick up the heavy chain and fearlessly put both arms round Grumpy's neck to clip the ends together. Grumpy stood still and let her do it.

'They're used to it, you see. Now let's see you tie up Sunshine.'

They went to the next stall. Amy swallowed hard and made herself stretch her arms round the cow's thick neck to do it. It seemed absolutely enormous and her cheek rubbed against Sunshine's curly hide. Her tongue came out to lick the back of Amy's hand; it felt like sandpaper and her breath smelled of new milk.

'There, we'll make a country girl of you yet.' Auntie Bessie beamed at her as she turned to push a stool in position near Grumpy's udder. 'Would you like to learn to milk?'

'No thank you.' Amy fled back to the house. She was well pleased with what she'd achieved but couldn't cope with more just yet. Not even Marmaduke meowing for milk could make her stay.

Amy became aware that Grumpy was acting strangely and Auntie Bessie and Jack were concerned.

'What's the matter with her?' she asked but they just shook their heads. One afternoon, Jack came home from work and told them he'd made arrangements for Grumpy to see the bull and asked Amy if she would like to help him and Fly walk the cow up to Llanhafod farm for this. It would be her job to run ahead and open gates.

A premium bull was kept at Llanhafod, the big farm near the school, and his services were provided to the local farmers for a modest sum as a means of improving the breeding quality of the local cattle. On the road just below the farm, Amy had noticed an almost new telephone kiosk, and she thought she might be able to use it to speak to her family.

'We have a phone at home,' she told Jack, 'and Mum has one at the shop. I know how to use them, but this one is different. I lifted it up on the way home from school the other day but the operator didn't ask for my number. It has buttons and things inside to make it work. Can you show me what to do?'

Uncle Jack opened the door of the kiosk as they came level with it to see what she was talking about. 'No.' He let the door swing back. 'I know nothing about phones.'

'I think I'll have to put money in it, won't I?'

'I've never used one, I don't know. Nobody has a phone here.'

The farmer came to greet Jack as soon they drove Grumpy

into his farmyard. He let the bull out of its stall to join Grumpy while Amy was closing the gates behind them. She was entranced with what Grumpy was doing when the farmer's wife came out to join them.

She took Amy by the hand. 'Come indoors and have a glass of lemonade,' she invited. 'Better, Jack, if I take her away. No point in her losing her innocence.'

'Yes,' he said. 'She was asking me how the telephone works, can you tell her?'

Amy could see the recently erected sub-post office built of red zinc sheets against the side of the farmhouse, and was reminded that the farmer's wife was also the postmistress.

'We have a phone at home,' Amy said, 'and if I'm there Pa expects me to answer it when it rings, so I know how it works.'

'Yes, bach, it would be nice for you to talk to your family.' She took her into the sub-post office and picked up the phone.

'It's the one in the kiosk I want to know about.'

'I can put you through from here.'

'But I want to know how to use that one, so I can ring my Mum on the way home from school. She's got a phone at her shop. It's those buttons I want to know about and how to put the money in.'

'Come on then and I'll show you.' They walked the fifty yards down the road to the kiosk. 'You need two pennies to make it work.'

'I haven't brought any money with me,' Amy said, embarrassed. 'I thought perhaps tomorrow . . .'

'No matter.' The postmistress took a purse from her pocket and gave her twopence. 'You can pay me back tomorrow when you come to school.'

'I will,' Amy said eager to try it now. She watched carefully as the postmistress demonstrated how to operate the telephone and then did it under her supervision.

'That's right, bach.'

Amy felt excited as she heard the phone ringing in the hall at home.

'Amy!' Her mother was laughing with excitement and pleasure. 'You've found a phone! Lovely to hear you like this. How are you?' Amy laughed with her. 'Everybody is well here and missing you. Pat and her mother came into the shop today. She's going to be a bridesmaid to her cousin. I'm to make her a dress in lavender satin. Pat's fine, she asked about you.'

The sound of her mother's voice made the distance disappear. 'No, everything is fine here. No, no bombs, no gas attack and not a German in sight.'

Amy heard the pips denoting that her the time was up. 'Goodbye,' she said as the line went dead. She was left alone in the kiosk feeling homesick, and wishing she had more pennies to ring her mother again and tell her how much she wanted to come back to her family and friends.

Autumn was advancing and everybody was trying to help the war effort. At school, the children were told the Germans would stop the ships bringing any more oranges to Britain. They were taken out of school and along the lanes to pick rose hips from the hedges.

'Rose hips are full of vitamin C,' Miss Cosgrove told them. 'They will be made into rose-hip syrup for babies.' She also encouraged them to take sixpence to school on Fridays to buy a National Savings stamp. Two pupils walked to the sub-post office at the farm to buy them. These they stuck into the book provided, until they had the fifteen shillings needed to buy a Savings Certificate. Amy understood they were doing their bit, lending their money to the government to spend on tanks and guns to fight the enemy.

In the following weeks, the population was issued with ration books and identity cards, but everybody was amazed there were so few practical signs that Britain was at war. People had been told they must always carry their gas masks with them because a gas attack could come at any moment, but they soon gave up.

Amy's classmates began to drift back to Merseyside because it was just as quiet there. Miss Cosgrove packed up and went and the evacuees that were left were absorbed into the body of the school.

Amy wrote to her mother and told her all this, and put it to her that she should return too. '*I would like to,*' she wrote. '*Here I have nobody to play with once I leave school. The farms and cottages are too spread out.*'

She waited for a reply, fully expecting to be home and playing with Pat before much longer. It took Mum longer than usual to reply and when she did the answer was no.

We miss you very much and would love to have you back. But Pa and I think it would be wiser for you to stay where you are now you have settled in. We are thinking of your safety Amy. Auntie Bessie and Uncle Jack are very good to take you into their home and you should do your best to show you appreciate their kindness.

Amy felt pangs of disappointment but she got over it and began to settle down. Soon she was the only evacuee left and was put into the main class at school, with boys and girls ranging in age from seven to fourteen. They left to start work once they turned fourteen.

Amy sat at a well-scarred desk that accommodated four pupils. There were two open fires in the classroom that were lit from October to April. The boys were responsible for collecting morning sticks from the woods behind the chapel and also for bringing in the coal.

She was being taught now by Mrs Myfanwy Roberts, the schoolmistress in charge, who had her desk directly in front of one fire. She was well past middle age, a widow with two grown-up children who no longer lived at home. She wore printed smocks over dresses that Mum would consider smart. She was a good-looking woman with strong features and iron-grey hair drawn into a bun at the back of her neck. Behind her rimless glasses her dark eyes were as sharp as needles and missed nothing.

A position close to the other fire in the corner was highly prized by the girls who were grouped together on that side of the room. The best places went to the oldest and strongest, but they all put their sauce bottles full of milk close to the fire to warm by mid-morning.

Mrs Roberts was a disciplinarian, she bustled rather than walked and her Cuban heels beat a loud tattoo on the wooden floor. She had zero tolerance for talking in class, passing notes, or eating sweets. A biblical picture hung over her fireplace and she kept a cane tucked behind it with the handle in full view. Any sign of restlessness in class and the cane would be taken out in readiness and the slightest whisper after that would cause Mrs Roberts to rap it impatiently on her desk. It took very little more for the perpetrator to be called forward to receive punishment. One slap across each hand was considered the lighter sentence; it could be several strokes across the legs.

There wasn't a child in the school who wasn't in awe of her. Amy was terrified of her. As one of the youngest, her place in class was in the front row very near to Mrs Roberts and to avoid her wrath Amy concentrated hard and jumped to follow all her instructions. Bessie said Mrs Roberts had the reputation of being a good teacher and of being very caring of her pupils.

Some of the children in the class lived on the other side of the hill and had a long way to walk, as there was no proper road and no taxi on that route. If it rained and they arrived in wet clothes, Mrs Roberts would take them next door to School House and have them take off their sodden garments. She dressed them from a box of clothing she kept for the purpose. Wet shoes and socks would be dried off in her airing cupboard and returned at the end of the day.

She also made sure that every child had a mug of hot soup at lunchtime to augment their sandwiches. She bought bones in town and grew vegetables in her garden. The older girls were responsible for making soup in a fish kettle that covered two burners on a paraffin oil stove in the girls' cloakroom. Like the other young ones, Amy was pressed into service to peel onions and carrots.

She soon saw that the oil stove frequently gave off clouds of black smoke that could fill the cloakroom and snake under the door into the classroom. It was a question of getting the wicks adjusted to burn off the paraffin correctly. On days when the stove was acting up, they left the door to the cloakroom open so that Mrs Roberts could keep an eye on it from her desk. If for some reason the stove had gone out, and the soup wasn't ready, they were given a cup of hot cocoa instead. They each took twopence a week to pay for this nourishment.

Both Auntie Bessie and Uncle Jack had attended that school, though back then they'd had a different teacher. Bessie said the leaving age had been twelve in her day and she'd gone straight into service on a big farm on the other side of town. She was only allowed home one Sunday a month. But Jack had been kept home so often to help his family on their farm that he'd never learned to read and write. Even now, at harvest time, the number of children attending school fell away because they were needed to help at home.

Amy was pleased to be getting more letters. Milo wrote her a long letter about being a soldier and said he didn't like it. She knew he was in France but he said he wasn't allowed to tell her how the fighting was going. He enclosed a five shilling postal order. Amy felt quite rich.

June wrote too about her new life as a nurse, telling her she had to get up early and have breakfast with the rest of the nursing staff and then go to a ward for old men to make their beds, help serve their breakfast and get them washed. She thought that was more like domestic work than nursing, but she had a very nice uniform and everybody called her Nurse. At nine o'clock she went to the nursing school and spent the rest of the day in class there.

Amy's friend Pat sent her a postcard with a picture of Thurstaston cliffs and beach. She was back at school now but she'd again spent two weeks in a holiday cabin there and they'd had a lovely time. That made Amy homesick again because last year Pat's family had taken her and June with them. She bought a postcard in town for Pat with a view of the valley and asked her to send her telephone number because she might be able to ring her.

The following week she had Pat's reply and was able to make contact. Amy thought it was marvellous to tell her all her news and wished Pat had come with her, but she was making friends with the local children.

When school was over for the day she walked down the road with them rather than wait for the taxi to return. Glenys had a fairy cycle and sometimes came to school on that. She would walk home with them and let them take turns to ride her bike. Amy longed for one just like it. She remembered being with Pat and peering into a bike shop on the New Chester Road. They had both admired a fairy cycle they'd seen there.

CHAPTER SIXTEEN

CHRISTMAS WAS DRAWING CLOSER, and Leonie received a letter from Amy asking if she might come home to spend it with them. She was filled with sorrow and guilt as she told her daughter it wouldn't be possible.

All Leonie's children had left home that year, and although June was near enough to pay them occasional visits, the house seemed very quiet and dull without them.

When Leonie received a note from Amy's old school telling her that a coach would run on alternate Sundays into Wales so that parents might visit their evacuated children, she was delighted. She'd thought of making her own way there but Sunday was the only day she was free to go, and the trains ran a Sunday service which made it almost impossible.

Leonie longed to meet the people looking after Amy and see for herself where she was living. When June came home on her day off, she asked her if she'd like to go with her.

'Yes,' June said. 'In her letters poor Amy seems a bit lost, but it'll have to be soon. While I'm in preliminary nursing school I have every Sunday off, but once I start working on the wards I won't.'

Leonie arranged it for the last full Sunday that June would have free, which also happened to be the last Sunday before

Christmas. She wrote to Amy and her hostess to tell them.

Amy was thrilled at the news and so was Bessie, they reread her letters several times. '*The coach will drop us in town and we'll have to get a taxi to bring us the rest of the way*,' Mum had written.

Bessie dictated a letter to Amy telling Leonie they were three miles out of town and advising which garage could provide a taxi and where they must ask to be taken. Amy wrote on the bottom, '*Please Mum would you bring me a pair of hobnailed boots like all the other children wear to school? They call my lace-ups town shoes. Auntie Bessie says boots are very practical for the winter.*'

'What am I going to give your family to eat?' Bessie worried.

'Sunday dinner,' Jack said. 'They'll be here at dinnertime, won't they?'

'Mum writes that she doesn't know what time exactly,' Amy said.

'It'll be dinnertime near enough,' Jack said. 'The visitors will want their dinner.'

Amy had been excited since she'd read Mum's letter and when at last the day came, she went down through the cwm alone to meet them. Uncle Jack had stopped her going twice, telling her it was too early, but even so she sat on the five-bar gate at the roadside for a long time before she saw, further down the valley, the big black car snaking towards her.

She couldn't stand still when it pulled up in front of her. She was pulled into bear hugs and kisses but Mum and June seemed almost like strangers because she hadn't seen them for nearly four months. They unloaded bags and parcels and asked countless questions. Amy was able to explain everything and was proud to lead them up to the house.

Fly barked a welcome long before they could see him and

Bessie and Jack were waiting to receive them outside on the terrace. Amy wanted to see what they'd brought in the bags but Bessie said dinner was ready and they sat down at the big table to eat it straight away.

'It's very kind of you to share your rations with us,' Leonie said. They ate roast beef and roast potatoes with swede and cabbage. Amy's favourite bun loaf pudding, stewed pears and cream followed, and a very good dinner it was.

Leonie complimented Bessie on her cooking and said, 'It goes without saying that we're very grateful for all you're doing for Amy. She looks the picture of health, country life suits her.' She had made a fancy apron and some pot holders for Bessie who was more than pleased with them.

Amy couldn't wait to see what they'd brought for her and cooed with pleasure when she saw the plaid kilt and white blouse her mother had made for her to wear for best, with a warm cardigan to go over it.

'We've bought you that pair of boots you asked for,' June said. 'I chose them and I think they're lovely. I hope you like them too.'

'We couldn't get them in black,' Mum said. 'I hope you can wear them for school.'

'They don't mind what we wear at this school.'

'They'll be nice and warm for you over the winter months. We got them half a size bigger for you. You'd better try them on now to make sure they fit.'

Amy was surprised when she saw them. They were of soft pale tan leather and had a scalloped cuff round the ankle and fur inside. They were not at all what she'd asked for but they were pretty and comfortable.

Amy was very pleased with everything, but when there was only one more bag to open, she said, 'Is that my teddy bear?'

'No, I'm sorry, pet.' Mum looked guilty.

June said, 'I'm afraid Pa thought you didn't want it any more. He put it in an auction sale.'

'What?' Amy wailed. 'He's never sold it?'

'Yes, and he was pleased because it made three times what it cost new. There aren't any teddies in the shops now.'

'But I wanted it. It always sat on my bed.'

'We know,' June said sympathetically. 'We only found out when I started looking for it but I've brought you my Pekinese dog to take its place. You always fancied Goo Goo Ching, didn't you?'

'It appeals to older girls,' Mum told her. The Pekinese wasn't just a toy, it had a zip along its tummy and the compartment was lined with blue silk. 'You can keep your pyjamas inside and it can sit on your pillow.'

'Yes.' Amy was mollified and stroked the soft imitation fur. 'I've always liked your dog. Thank you.' They'd also brought several other packages wrapped up in colourful paper that they said she must not open until Christmas Day.

Amy couldn't wait to get June outside to see Fly and to find Marmaduke. She walked her across the field to see the hens and the calves and the pigs. June had brought her Box Brownie camera with her and took photographs of them all.

The time flew and Mum was saying she'd asked the taxi to meet them down on the road at half past three because the coach was due to pick them up in town at four. Bessie insisted on making them a cup of tea before they left and they all walked down to the road to see them off.

'You've been here no time at all.' Amy swung on her mother's arm, feeling full of resentment that she was leaving so soon. 'I don't want you to go.'

'We have to, pet. We'll come again.'

Amy couldn't stop her eyes filling with tears when the taxi came.

'Hello, Amy,' the driver called as he turned it round. She knew him because he drove the school taxi but that was a much bigger car than this.

She could see June was blinking hard and Mum had that straight determined face, which meant she was doing something she didn't like. Amy swallowed hard and waved until the car went round the corner and she could no longer see June waving through the back window.

'You've got a lovely family,' Jack said. 'They've brought you lots of presents. They want you back but think you'll be safer here with us just now, and you'll have a nice time here over Christmas.'

'Everybody else has gone back,' Amy complained. 'If it's safe for them, it's safe for me. It's hardly worth Mum and June coming when they only stay for a couple of hours.'

'Your mam said they'd started out before eight o'clock this morning,' Bessie said. 'And they won't be home before eight tonight. It's a long way, bach. Anyway, it's not all that bad here. I thought you liked being with us?'

'I do, but I'd rather be back at home.' Amy was glad they had to walk in single file up the cwm. Jack couldn't see her crying. By the time they reached the bridge she had her tears under control.

* * *

Amy's life was settling into a routine. Bessie offered her three pence a week if she would run across the sideland every morning before school to let the hens out for the day and take them a small helping of cracked Indian corn. They were free-range hens and expected to forage in the field and get most of their food that way.

For that sum, she was also expected to collect the eggs and shut the hens in at night, and bring the cows up to the cowshed when she came home from school and separate the milk afterwards.

Another frequent job was to carry water from the well. At first Amy had not recognised the well for what it was because it was nothing like the wells she'd seen in picture books. This was a spring which filled a shallow pool in the side of a bank. It was kept covered with a zinc roofing sheet held down with big stones so the animals couldn't push it off to drink. They were expected to drink from the stream at the bottom of the sideland.

Amy was soon enjoying all that. She pleaded to be allowed to take Fly out for walks but Jack said no, she mustn't untie him. However, Marmaduke was not like a city cat, spending his time curled up by the fire. He would purr and brush against her legs whenever he saw her and follow her across the fields when she saw to the hens, and see her off when she left for school. Every evening at milking time she went out to the cowshed to give him his sardine tin of milk.

'Just creep closer to Sunshine and see if you can fill it yourself,' Bessie said as she milked Grumpy. 'She won't kick you.'

Amy finally brought herself to try, but the first time she couldn't get any milk to spurt out. The next evening, Jack said,

'I learned to milk when I was seven, wouldn't you like to try? I could show you how.'

Amy stood trying to pluck up her courage, while Marmaduke meowed and rushed back and forth to his sardine tin. Jack found another bucket and stool for her and set them down in the right position. Amy thought it was very close indeed to those clumsy hooves and well within reach of her tail, but she was persuaded to sit on the stool.

'Use both hands and squeeze gently from the top of the teat like this.' He held out Marmaduke's tin and this time she managed to get a small squirt into it and then another.

He put it down for the cat and Amy was persuaded to carry on. He fetched some nuts and emptied them into Sunshine's manger and although she turned her head to look at Amy as she milked, she chewed contentedly on the nuts.

For a while, Amy was filled with jubilation – she could do it, she could milk – but then the thought of filling the bucket seemed an enormous task she'd never manage. She'd covered the bottom and was flagging when Jack said, 'Have you had enough? Shall I take over now?'

Amy was glad to give it up but was overjoyed that she'd at last screwed up her nerve to try it.

'You've done very well for a first time. Have another go tomorrow, and you'll soon get the hang of it.'

The spring weather came and although there was little sign of active conflict in Britain, the news Leonie listened to on the wireless was dire. She was worried about Milo who was now serving with the British Expeditionary Force in northern France, a fighting force of a quarter of a million men.

She knew he'd found it difficult to settle to army life, and the only thing that made it bearable was that his friend Duggie Jenkins had been posted to the same unit so he had a friend to keep him company. He counted that a miracle. He wrote that he couldn't believe how quickly they had advanced from being raw recruits to being fully trained infantry. Their formal training had passed in a flash.

On 10 May Hitler's forces suddenly swung into action and invaded Holland, Belgium and northern France with breathtaking ease. The French government swiftly capitulated and Leonie was horrified to hear that the British lines of supply and of retreat were being cut off by the enemy.

All England realised that the British Army had been encircled and was in a perilous situation. Leonie and Steve went through hell knowing Milo could be trapped on the wrong side of the Channel, and not knowing exactly where he was or what was happening to him made it worse. They read every newspaper they could and listened to every news broadcast. It really frightened Leonie to think of Milo being caught up in the fighting.

The news bulletins turned a rout into a victory for the British Army when the news broke that so many of its soldiers were being rescued in heroic fashion by a fleet of small, privately owned boats. Fishing boats and pleasure craft had made their way independently over to Dunkirk to augment the ships sent by the navy to bring the men home.

They heard of the chaos on the beaches but the days were passing, and those rescued were returning home and being counted. Still there was no news of Milo.

Leonie was preparing herself for the worst. For the last few nights she'd been unable to sleep and had wept in Steve's arms. She was exhausted. She spent hours sitting in Milo's bedroom, thinking of him as he'd been: a longed-for baby, a beautiful toddler, a child and then a grown man. She thought of all the love he'd shown her and that she might never see him again. Would she even know where his grave was?

After his training with dummy bullets, Milo found it frightening to be in a war zone and fighting with live ammunition. Now it was all in deadly earnest, the enemy meant to kill him and as many of his comrades as it could.

He'd hardly had time to get used to that before Hitler's lightning advance across the Low Countries took everybody by surprise. The first Milo knew of it was that they were ordered to abandon their positions and fall back. The withdrawal began in a disciplined and orderly fashion but the enemy was close on their heels.

Ground troops in panzer tanks with powerful 37 mm guns chased them. At the same time they endured attack from above, bombs exploded all around them and they were strafed by bullets from Stuka dive bombers.

Milo and Duggie were riding in the back of a lorry that had a canvas roof, squashed in with twenty other fleeing soldiers. Their lorry was one of a long line of army vehicles snaking back for miles, but the roads were already choked with civilian refugees trying to escape the German advance and progress was almost impossible.

Gradually the number of military vehicles was reduced as one by one they broke down, ran out of fuel or were blown up. The last order they received was to head for the Channel port of Dunkirk and by then it seemed it was every man for himself. It was no longer a matter of falling back, or of evacuation; they were fleeing for their lives.

It went on day after day, and night after night. There wasn't enough room for them to lie down in the lorry; they slept on their hard seats slumped against each other. Milo felt dirty, hungry and exhausted, but so far they'd been lucky, they'd been able to siphon fuel from vehicles that had broken down.

They were relying on each other and forging stronger links as they all sought survival. Two of their group were killed by bullets from a Stuka and had to be left behind, but it drew those remaining even closer.

On the fifth day they stopped by a canal, stripped off their clothes for the first time in almost a week, and swam. They came across a herd of cows and John, who had been a farm worker, milked them. The drink and the swim revived them all for a time, but fuel for the lorry finally gave out. They blew it up so the enemy wouldn't benefit from it and continued on foot.

They were too large a group to stay together. Not all could agree on the best route and some could move more quickly than others. Milo cricked his ankle jumping into a ditch to take cover from yet another Stuka attack and was reduced to hobbling, but one of their companions broke his leg. Some received gunshot wounds and were wounded by shrapnel, and many were too weary to keep going. Milo, Duggie and two others, John and Derek, continued on their way but found their route barred by the many canals on the outskirts of Dunkirk.

They were afraid the bridges would be manned by German troops so the only way to cross was to wade waist deep and if necessary swim. They fastened what ammunition they had left on their heads and held their rifles high.

Milo's relief at arriving at Dunkirk was short-lived. His first sight of the port horrified him. There were legions of Allied troops swarming across the beach; some were wading out into the sea, attempting to reach the small boats bobbing there. The sky was filled with planes that were dropping bombs on some larger ships that were berthed in the docks. As he watched, one that was half loaded received a direct hit and went up in flames.

There was no shelter for the troops on the beach. Bullets were whistling into the sand all around them, but to leave might mean they'd not get a passage home on a boat.

A group from a Welsh regiment was singing hymns and that reminded Milo of a last stand on a sinking ship and frightened him more than anything else. He was shocked into action when another Stuka dived across the beach and Derek dropped dead at his feet with a series of bullet holes in his chest.

The three remaining men turned and sprinted towards some bombed buildings that offered shelter. As Milo ran he felt a huge blow to his left side, which lifted him off his feet and flung him to the ground. An agonising pain shot through him.

Duggie and John turned back to pull him into what was left of a building, where they felt safer.

'Don't black out.' Duggie's voice sounded a long way away.

'What are we going to do?' John asked.

'I'm not leaving him.'

'He's bleeding like a stuck pig.'

'Didn't we see a first-aid post on the edge of the beach?'

'But will it still be manned?'

'I'll go and see,' Duggie said. 'You stay with him.'

The next thing Milo knew he was being half carried, half dragged. Somehow they managed to avoid the gunfire and flying bullets. He couldn't stand and he couldn't sit. He knew they'd reached the first-aid post when he was at last allowed to collapse and lie down.

'You'll be all right now,' Duggie said.

'No, I'm done for,' he gasped. Another pain made him wince. 'I've had it. You go while you still can.'

CHAPTER SEVENTEEN

ON FRIDAYS, AMY LOOKED FORWARD to ringing Pat as well her mother on her way home from school. She missed her a lot, and when Amy heard her voice, it always transported her back to her old life. She had a lot to tell Pat about the school she went to now. 'I'm ink monitor this week and I have to mix the ink powder and water and fill all the inkwells.'

There was no sign of Pat's familiar giggle, she sounded oddly strained. 'I thought you'd be worried.'

'What about?'

'Dunkirk, haven't you heard? It's on the wireless. They've been going on about it for days. Don't you have a wireless there?'

'Yes, I have *Children's Hour* on sometimes, but people don't listen to the news like they do back home.'

'Everybody's biting their nails about Dunkirk.'

'What's happened there?'

'All our soldiers are trapped in France. They've been caught by the Germans and they won't let them come home. Your Milo was sent to France, wasn't he?'

Amy suddenly realised what Pat was trying to tell her. She shivered. 'Yes, but I think he's all right, I had a letter from him last week.'

'I don't think he is. My mum says your family's worried stiff because he's missing.'

'What d'you mean, missing?' Amy was suddenly afraid and had a vision of German soldiers firing machine guns at her brother.

'Well, some of the soldiers have managed to escape and come home but there's no sign of Milo.'

'Then where is he?'

She heard Pat say, 'I thought you might know,' but the pips were sounding to indicate that time was up. The phone went dead and Amy burst into tears.

If the Germans had caught Milo, that meant he was a prisoner. What if they'd shot him already? Her heart was thumping like a machine as she groped in her pocket for more pennies to phone her mother's shop.

It was Elaine's voice that answered. 'I want my mum,' Amy wailed urgently. She could hear the sounds of the shop, the doorbell pinged and then Mum said, 'Amy love, is something the matter?'

'Pat says the Germans have trapped the British Army and might have caught Milo. Is this true?'

'We don't really know, darling. Not for sure.'

'He's missing, that's what she said. He's not come home with the other soldiers.'

'We don't know. They're not all home yet. Probably more will come.' She heard the anguish in her mother's voice and knew just how upset she was. 'Of course we're all worried because we don't know what is happening.'

Amy choked out, 'Milo could be hurt and not able to get home.'

'We haven't given up hope and you mustn't. He could still come back safe and sound. Perhaps all he needs is more time. We must be patient and hope that all is well.'

'Mum,' Amy said, desperate now, 'I want to come home to be with you. I want to be there when Milo comes. I never get to know anything here.'

'Darling, you will. I will let you know. Have you any more pennies?'

'No, I only brought four.'

'Is there a number on the phone in front of you? Tell me quickly what it is.'

Amy managed to choke it out.

'Right.' The pips were sounding and almost drowned out Mum's voice. 'Put the phone down and wait. I'll ring you back.'

Leonie silently berated Pat for telling Amy that Milo was missing. Why hadn't she foreseen that something like this might happen? She'd thought it a good idea for them to talk but it wasn't. She rang Amy back and did her best to comfort her, but it was hard when they were far apart like this. She could only say that they must wait and hope that Milo would get home.

Leonie's big fear was that Milo would come home with some dreadful injury that would ruin his life before he'd had time to enjoy any of it. She dreaded him ending up like his father.

She could feel tears stinging her eyes. When she finally put the phone down, she rushed upstairs to Elaine who did her best to comfort her, making her a cup of tea and repeating almost exactly the same words of comfort she'd used to Amy.

* * *

Amy was glad to find the other girls had walked on without her. She wanted to be alone because she couldn't stop the tears running down her cheeks.

If Mum was worried about Milo, and clearly she was, then he was in grave danger. Mum had been trying to comfort her but Amy doubted there was much hope left.

Poor Milo, sometimes he'd teased her and when he had his own friends he hadn't wanted her near him but most of the time he'd been very good to her. She would miss him if he didn't come back.

She told Bessie about Milo being missing when she got home, and she said, 'We'll put the wireless on at six o'clock to hear what is happening at Dunkirk.' Today there were stewed pears with banana junket and cream for tea.

'We have a pear tree at the top of the garden at home,' Amy told Bessie. 'But they're yellow pears not green like yours. Milo fixed a swing on it for me. It's a very tall tree with a main branch sticking out high up. He got some chains and a piece of thin rope and attached one end of the rope to the chain and a stone to the other. Then he threw the stone over the branch and pulled on the rope and that dragged the chain over the branch after it.'

'Your brother is clever,' Bessie said. 'He'd make a good farmer.'

'Yes, my swing has a red seat and much longer chains than the swings in the park, so it goes much higher. It's the best swing in the world. Sometimes Milo pushed me, but even if he didn't I can swing it high myself. It isn't a swing for babies; both he and June like to have a go on it.'

'How do you like these pears? I bottled them in the autumn

but I think I should have stewed them for longer.'

'They're lovely. We don't stew our pears, just eat them raw. When I left, I could see them turning yellow amongst the leaves. I used to stand on the seat and jump hard to bring them down. There were always a lot and when they were ripe they'd come raining down and sometimes hit me. Milo liked to make the pears fall down so he could eat them too.' Amy was almost blinded by tears again.

'Come on, bach,' Bessie said. 'It's time for milking and the cows don't like waiting. You come and help me. Sunshine is getting used to you milking her.'

Leonie was in the kitchen fighting her tears as she made cauliflower cheese for supper. She knew her eyes were red and wasn't pleased to hear the doorbell ring as Steve would wait for her to answer it. She wiped her face on a tea towel and was still wiping her hands as she went to the door.

'Good evening Mrs Dransfield.' She didn't at first recognise the man on her doorstep.

'Henry Jenkins,' he said. 'Duggie's father.'

'Oh yes!' Her heart somersaulted. 'Duggie was with Milo in France, have you heard from him?'

'Yes, he rang to tell me he's in Southampton.' Mr Jenkins was smiling. 'He and Milo came back in a fishing smack.'

'He did? Thank God for that. I've been so worried. Come in, come and tell us what you know.' She led him down the passage towards their living room, then stopped to throw open Steve's study door.

'Whatever is the matter?' Steve lowered his evening paper. 'Who is this?'

Leone laughed outright. 'Good news at last. This is Henry Jenkins – you know, Duggie's father.'

He stared at them irritably.

'He and Milo were in the same unit. He came to tell us they're both safely back in Southampton. Have a seat, Mr Jenkins.' She ushered him towards the only other chair in the room. 'How is Milo?'

'He's not very well, that's what I've come to tell you. I expect you're wondering why Milo hasn't phoned you himself. Duggie said they've taken him to the military hospital and he needs an operation. He's got a piece of shrapnel in his side, in his abdomen, and there's also a bullet lodged in his thigh.'

Leonie felt her head spinning. Was this really good news? His injuries sounded very like those Steve had suffered.

Steve said, 'But he's going to be all right?'

'They hope so.'

Leonie swallowed hard. It didn't seem all that hopeful. 'What happened to him? How was he hurt?'

'You've heard that it wasn't an orderly retreat through France? It took them a week and when they finally reached the beach at Dunkirk they were hungry, exhausted and had run out of ammunition for their rifles. There were plenty of soldiers left on the beach but very few boats to take them off and the evacuation was running out of time. The enemy was bombing and strafing the boats and the beach, and that was where Milo copped it. Those left were fighting for survival as well as for places on the few boats that remained. You've heard Milo mention John, another man from the same unit?'

Leonie shook her head. She felt sick.

'They took Milo to a first-aid post on the beach where they

bandaged him up and put him to lie on a stretcher. But then they heard they wouldn't take any more stretcher cases on the boats because a stretcher takes up enough space for two or three men. So Duggie and John half carried Milo between them, waded out into the sea, heaved him on board, and bagged the last few places on this fishing smack. I understand it was chaotic.'

'It sounds it,' Steve said. 'So Milo must thank his friends for getting him back.'

Leonie was afraid for her son. She tried to pull herself together. 'How is Duggie?'

'He can't believe his luck. He has no injuries and expects to be home on leave in a few days, but he says he hasn't slept properly for a week, he's exhausted. He was going to have a meal and go to bed and have his sleep out. John has a problem with his eyes. He's in the hospital with Milo.' Henry Jenkins took a piece of paper from his pocket. 'This is the name and address of the hospital, also the ward Milo is on and the phone number. It's a big military hospital and has all the expertise of dealing with war wounds. It's the best place for him.'

Leonie felt limp with relief. Milo was alive, she must be positive. It could so easily have been much worse for him. 'I'm so grateful to Duggie and his other friend.'

'We're both delighted and relieved,' Steve said. 'Thank you for coming round to tell us like this.' Steve got up and shook his hand. 'We're very grateful. Will you join us in a celebratory drink?'

He ushered them into the living room where the table was already set for an everyday supper for two. 'We have no champagne I'm afraid, but there's whisky or sherry.'

Henry Jenkins no longer seemed at ease. Leonie sipped her sherry and hoped the news about Milo was as good as Steve was assuming. She had a cold feeling in her stomach that his injuries might alter his life in the way Steve's injuries had altered his.

After supper, she put in a long-distance call to Netley Hospital to inquire how Milo was. She thought it was the ward sister who picked up the phone. 'He's had a large piece of shrapnel removed from his abdomen and damage to both his large and small bowel repaired.'

'And there's no damage to his other organs?' Leonie asked.

'Erm . . . Let me see.' Leonie could hear pages being turned. 'A little minor damage perhaps, but that is expected to heal naturally. The operation went well but he hasn't yet come round from the anaesthetic.'

Leonie put the phone down feeling that Milo wasn't out of the woods yet. Nevertheless, she made herself write a long comforting letter to Amy letting her know he was back in England.

CHAPTER EIGHTEEN

J UNE WAS GETTING USED to being called Nurse Dransfield but she didn't care much for the job. The bedpan round was absolutely disgusting but there were compensations. She'd got away from Pa and Mum and all that fuss every time she wanted an evening out and it was fun living with a lot of girls.

They were quite envious that she had a boyfriend with a home of his own where she could go at any time, and where she could be alone with him. They thought him handsome and very much a man of the world and were envious, too, that he kept taking her to such lovely places. Well, perhaps she had bragged about Ralph but they counted it quite a feather in her cap to have him waiting for her outside in his smart two-seater.

June worked long hours but she enjoyed her days off in the middle of the week when everybody else was either at school or at work. Today, she was going to the shop because Mum had promised to make her a party dress and June knew her mother wouldn't expect to be paid for it. She was hoping to persuade her to use one of Elaine's patterns. She wanted a dress that made her look a little older and more sophisticated than she was. She wanted something new to wear to the smart restaurants to which Ralph took her. He was always happy to buy dresses for her, but clothes rationing had become a perennial problem. A dress length took fewer coupons and Mum might give up some of her own, or persuade Pa to give up his.

'Come early,' Mum had said, 'before we get busy.'

Last evening, June had gone out with Ralph and spent the rest of the night with him in his house. He had brought her a cup of tea in bed before going to work and she'd snoozed on for another hour.

The shop was busy when she got there and Ida's sewing machine was positively racing while Mum dealt with customers. June picked up the folder containing Elaine's patterns and sat down to make her choice.

Mum looked tired, but then she always did. Putting up with Pa would take a lot out of anybody. He expected to be waited on hand and foot. She shouldn't let him get away with sitting about and doing nothing all day.

Mum pushed a pattern book into her hands and said before turning to another customer, 'These would be more suitable for your age group, pet. Go up to the flat and make us all a cup of tea, I'm dying for a drink.'

June did so and her mother joined her there ten minutes later. 'I've seen a pattern that I like,' June told her. It was one of Elaine's.

'That would look good on me,' Mum was pursing her lips, 'or any middle-aged woman. I don't think for you . . .'

'Mum, I adore this bodice.'

'Well, I could do you the bodice on a full skirt. That one is all swathed round the hips, it wouldn't suit you at all and there's a lot of work in it.'

'All right,' June grudgingly agreed. 'I saw some green satin downstairs that I like.'

'It would make up well in wool and you'd get more wear out of it. I've got a nice blue material. I'll show it to you when we go down.'

June said nothing. That was the best thing to do with her parents. They offered her choices but it was all a façade, they always wanted to choose everything for her.

'Why don't you pop in and see Pa while you're this close?' her mother suggested. 'He talks about you a lot, wondering how you're getting on. How do you like nursing?'

'It's all right, though it's mostly domestic work so far. They don't allow me near medicines or wounds yet.'

'That'll come. You could stay and have supper with us tonight. I've made a casserole.'

'I'm sorry, Mum, I've planned to go out with some of the girls tonight. We're going to the pictures to see Margaret Lockwood in *The Lady Vanishes*.' She'd seen that on the placards as the bus had passed the Plaza. 'I can only do that on my nights off.'

'Of course, pet. So you're making friends with the other girls in your group?'

'Yes, they're very nice. There's one I really like called Mary O'Leary. She has the next bedroom to mine. I'm going out with her tonight.'

June found it a struggle to get away and she had to agree to her dress being made up in that blue wool which Mum said would be warmer for her. As if being warm was more important than looking smart. She took the bus to the top of Grange Road and went round the big shops looking at the goods on offer. Not that she had any money, so she couldn't buy anything, and it didn't look as though she'd have much in the future. Her salary for the first year was £3.10/- a month, plus her keep and her uniform, but she had to buy her textbooks and her shoes and stockings out of that.

When it started to rain she went to Ralph's rooms. She loved being here on her own, it was almost like having her own place. It was well past lunchtime and she was hungry, so she made a pot of tea and a sandwich from what she found in the larder. He knew she'd be here and had promised to leave work as soon as he could.

The wind howled round the house during the afternoon and it was raining more heavily when he came home just after five, bringing a gorgeous chocolate cake. More than anything else, June enjoyed the time she spent with him in his rooms.

By eight in the evening they were getting hungry again. It was stormy by then and they could see the big trees in the park tossing furiously but that didn't stop Ralph taking her to New Brighton for dinner. After all, he could drive them from door to door so they needn't get wet, though the canvas roof was saturated and June felt an occasional cold drop fall on her head.

They were soon seated at a table in the restaurant window. The rain was gusting against it and blotting out any view but it didn't matter, Ralph was on good form, laughing and joking. He was so much fun. They shared a bottle of wine and the food was much better than that in the hospital.

When they left, the storm was at its height and in the blackout June couldn't even see the sea as they drove along the promenade, though she could hear the full tide thundering against the sea wall and the boom and suck as torrents of water crashed over on to the road.

The windscreen wipers couldn't cope with the downpour. 'I can barely see the road through this.' Ralph was peering nervously out and his unease put June on edge. 'A good job there's not much traffic about.'

June shivered, it was a wild night to be out. After they'd crossed Poulton Bridge and were coming into Birkenhead's dockland, Ralph spoke again. 'That big pub looks closed. The customers must have gone home early.'

'What time is it?' June tried to see her watch in the light from the dashboard. She usually aimed to be back at the nurses' home before they locked the front door but she wasn't too worried because her room was on the ground floor and she always took the catch off the window and left it fractionally open so she could squeeze her fingers in and push it up. As they neared the St James's roundabout, they could hear the piercing shriek of police sirens over the noise of the storm.

Ralph turned the car carefully into Laird Street and June felt panic streak through her as she saw multiple headlights racing towards them, one set on their side of the road.

As she felt Ralph try to swerve to avoid it she let out a scream and her heart bounced into her throat. A split second later came a violent jerk as their car was rammed and then the ear-splitting scrape and tear of metal and splintering glass. June felt as though she was being twisted and her head wrenched from her body. An almighty force catapulted her through the air. She felt a searing pain before she blacked out.

CHAPTER NINETEEN

THE FOLLOWING MORNING, THE telephone disturbed Steve as it rang in the hall outside his study. He stirred and stretched on his bed, knowing he'd fallen asleep again after Leonie had brought him his morning tea. 'Damn,' he swore.

By now she'd have gone to work. He couldn't rush to answer it, he still felt half asleep. It would surely stop ringing before he reached it. He let his head fall back on the pillow and waited for the annoying noise to stop. It took a long time. Probably it was somebody wanting to speak to Leonie.

About an hour later it started ringing again. Steve had his false leg strapped on and was almost dressed but he'd heard Mrs Killen come in and start to Hoover. He knew she'd answer it.

He heard her call, 'Mr Dransfield, somebody from the hospital wants to speak to you.'

He sighed, that must be June, but what could she want this early in the morning? Perhaps she was ringing to say she'd come and have supper with them tonight.

He'd got to his feet but Mrs Killen was hammering on his bedroom door. 'They say it's important and can I get you to the phone.'

'All right, I'm coming.' It made him irritable to be rushed.

June knew he couldn't cope with that. He snatched up the phone, 'Hello, June,' he said.

A brisk authoritative voice answered. 'I'm Sister Jackson, speaking from the General Hospital. Is that Mr Dransfield, father of Nurse June Dransfield?'

'Yes.' He was abrupt. 'Who else is likely to be here?'

'Oh!' Her shocked gasp told him she wasn't pleased at being spoken to like that. 'I'm afraid I have some bad news for you, Mr Dransfield. Your daughter has had an accident.'

'What sort of an accident?' he demanded. This woman was upsetting him.

'She was a passenger in a car involved in a crash, and was brought in here shortly after eleven o'clock last night.'

He took a deep breath. That didn't seem likely. 'Is this a joke?'

'Of course not, Mr Dransfield.' The woman was affronted. 'Nobody would joke about a thing like this.'

It sounded a serious accident. 'Well, I don't think it can be my daughter. Was it a man driving the car?'

'Yes, I believe so.'

'June doesn't know anybody who has a car, and she's one of your nurses, surely she'd have been in bed by that time.'

'Mr Dransfield,' she sounded as though she was drawing on the patience of Job, 'it is your daughter. There is no doubt about that and I must ask you please to come to the hospital to see us. As she's under age we need a parent to sign a consent form. She might need an operation.'

Steve could feel himself shaking, 'But I don't understand. What's happened to her? Is she badly hurt?'

'She has multiple cuts and concussion, together with a deep gash on the head.'

'But what was that you said about an operation?'

'Mr Dransfield, if you could come in and speak to her doctor, he will explain your daughter's condition to you. Speaking generally, after trauma the brain can swell and surgical intervention may be required. Please come in and sign a consent form so that we can treat your daughter if, in her case, it proves to be necessary.'

Steve couldn't get his breath, he couldn't cope with this. Not June! How could this terrible thing have happened to her? 'I'll ring her mother and let her know,' he choked out eventually. 'She'll come and see you.'

There was no way he could go out on the bus this morning. He definitely wasn't up to it. He was shaking all over and his brain had turned to mush. He couldn't even think of the number of Leonie's shop.

'Are you all right?' Mrs Killen pulled a chair behind him and pushed him on to it.

'No, I feel terrible. Something's happened to June. Can you get Leonie on the phone for me? She'll have to go to the hospital to see her.'

Leonie was equally shocked. She blurted out something of the problem to Ida and asked her to hold the fort until she got back. She grabbed her coat and ran the twenty yards along the road to the bus stop. Some distance away, she could see a bus lumbering towards her.

She was worried, not only about June but about Steve too, he could hardly get the words out to tell her what had happened and he couldn't remember of the name of the sister who had rung him.

She, too, found it hard to believe June had been out in a car with a man. June didn't know any men and she hadn't been at the hospital long enough to get to know a man well enough to go out with him. And last night had been so stormy. A tree had blown down in next door's garden.

Leonie didn't like hospitals. The smell of disinfectant brought back searing memories of visiting Steve when he'd been injured. She was directed to the nurses' sick bay – a side room on Ward 3. She found Sister Jackson sympathetic when she told her Steve was an invalid. She was efficient, too, and the consent form was produced for Leonie's signature.

'This might not be needed,' she said, 'but we should have it ready because we don't want any hold-up if it is.'

'How is she?'

'She has quite a deep cut on her head. She's had seventeen stitches in it.'

Leonie gasped, that sounded horrific. 'Seventeen stitches?'

'Yes, and I'm afraid they had to shave off her hair on that side.'

'Oh dear! She's very proud of her hair, she won't like that.'

'The good news is that when her hair grows again any scaring won't show.'

'I hadn't thought of that.'

'She's been unconscious for most of the time and hasn't been able to say much so far, but she's drifting in and out of consciousness this morning.'

'But she will get better?'

'We have every reason to suppose she will, but the outcome is never certain. We have to hope, Mrs Dransfield.'

'I don't understand how she came to be out with a man in a car in that awful storm.'

'We understand it was her boyfriend.'

'But she doesn't have a boyfriend. Do you know this man's name?'

Sister was looking through the file she'd made for June. 'He was brought here too, of course. You'll find him on Ward One. His name, yes, I made a note of it. His name's Ralph Harvey.'

'I've never heard of him,' Leonie burst out, but then paused. 'Hold on, Ralph . . . ?'

'Harvey.'

That could be Elaine's brother, couldn't it? Leonie was frowning, 'Yes, I think I know who he is.'

'I'll take you in to see her then. I arranged for somebody to sit with her so we'd know when she came round.'

Leonie followed her into a side ward. It contained two beds but only one was occupied. A nurse was sitting by June.

'Thank you, Nurse Coates. Nurse Dransfield's mother is here now and will stay with her for a while.'

Leonie sat down on the chair she vacated. June was lying flat without pillows and her eyes were closed. Her skin was the colour of tallow, with numerous red grazes. Her arm was attached to a drip, her fingers were bandaged and she had a large pad of cotton wool taped to one side of her head. What made June recognisable was her long golden hair spread out across the sheets.

Leonie couldn't stop her sharp intake of breath. Her daughter looked really ill.

The sister checked her drip. 'This is just to keep her hydrated while she's unconscious.'

Leonie reached for her daughter's free hand. It felt cold.

'Speak to her, it might help to bring her round.'

She nodded but once she was alone with June she was overcome with anger. Elaine liked to throw a party once in a while and Leonie had met Ralph Harvey on several occasions at her house. She remembered him now, he was usually the life and soul of the party but surely too old for her daughter. Leonie was ready to blame him for causing June's injuries and present suffering. And how did she come to be out in his car in last night's storm?

She tried to talk to her daughter. 'June, you told me you were going to the cinema last night with the nurse who has the next bedroom to yours.' June was breathing deeply but not even the smallest muscle on her face moved. 'Why did you change your mind?'

Leonie felt frustrated. There was so much she didn't know about what had happened. The only way she'd get to the bottom of this was to have a word with Elaine's brother. She went back to the sister's office to thank her and tell her she was leaving.

She asked to be directed to Ward One and found it without difficulty. The ward sister was a woman well past middle age, with a firm manner that brooked no argument, developed over many years of coping with patients drawn mostly from Birkenhead's tough dock workers. She seemed rushed.

'Mr Harvey already has visitors. Our official visiting hours are Wednesday and Sunday afternoons between two and four. Can you not come back then?'

Leonie felt like crying. She explained who she was and why she wanted to speak so urgently to him. The ward sister relented and patted Leonie's arm. 'Nurse Dransfield's mother? All right, but please don't stay long. That's Mr Harvey's bed over there, with the screens round it. The police are interviewing him.'

'What about?'

'The accident. You'd better take a seat outside the office until they go.'

Sitting still and waiting frustrated Leonie even more, but at last the two uniformed police officers walked out. A nurse removed the screens and beckoned Leonie forward. Elaine's brother looked very sorry for himself. He'd lost the look of self-assured debonair confidence she remembered and was propped up on pillows with his arm in a sling.

'Do you remember me? I'm June Dransfield's mother,' she said briskly, pulling out the chair near his bed. 'We met at Elaine's house. I didn't realise you knew my daughter. I want to know how she came to be in your car last night.'

'I took her out for a meal. I'm very sorry.' He paused. 'How is she?'

'Unconscious.'

'You haven't spoken to her?'

'She isn't capable of speech. I told you, she's unconscious.'

'Oh dear, I was hoping . . . They told me she had lots of grazes, I hope they aren't on her face. June will hate anything like that.'

'They're all over her.' Leonie didn't intend to make things easy for him. 'She told me she was going to the pictures with another nurse. Why did she change her mind? Did you persuade her?' Leonie swallowed hard, she'd failed to persuade June to share the casserole with her and Steve and that hurt now. 'Where did you take her?'

'We had dinner at the Queen's Hotel in New Brighton.'

Leonie gasped. He'd taken June out to New Brighton for dinner? 'You must have known it was dangerous to drive in a storm like that.'

She could see he was getting angry too. 'The accident wasn't my fault. You saw the police officers here. They told me there was an attempted robbery at the Midland Bank last night. The bank had had a new security alarm fitted and the police knew there were intruders on the premises. They disturbed them and they might have got away if they hadn't crashed into me. It seems the police were chasing them. So you see I'd have got June back safely but for that and nobody would have been any the wiser.'

Time stood still for Leonie as her mind flashed back to something Elaine had told her ages ago. She'd been confiding her worries about Steve when Elaine had confessed that her brother worried her. His marriage had failed and he'd become a rather wild bachelor about town.

Leonie could hardly spit the words out. 'How long has this been going on? It isn't the first time June's been out with you, is it?'

He sighed heavily. 'Well, you'll have to know now. Not only have those wretched robbers put us both in hospital but they're going to cause us no end of other problems. No, it isn't the first time. I've been taking her out for the last couple of years, possibly more.'

That took Leonie's breath away. That must mean June had been keeping him a secret for all that time. She'd thought her a normal happy teenager but she'd been secretive, devious and telling lies. She felt sick. 'What exactly has been going on?'

He shrugged and then winced. 'I'm very sorry. I should not have allowed her to keep secrets from you and her father. You must blame me.'

'I do,' Leonie said through clenched teeth.

'I love June. She loves me. We want to get married, but as she's under age, she'll need your permission.'

'Over my dead body,' Leonie retorted. 'You're saying you took up with June when she was only sixteen? And you encouraged her to keep it secret?'

He had the grace to look embarrassed. 'Yes, I'm sorry.'

'It's a bit late to apologise, isn't it? You look much older than her. How old are you?'

'Thirty-three.'

'Old enough to know better.'

'I don't know why it always comes down to age. People can fall in love at any age.'

'I'm horrified. I can't believe it. Elaine said you'd been married.'

'Yes, I was married for seven years but I was divorced long before I met June.'

'Have you been sleeping with her?'

He looked ashamed. 'I'm sorry you had to find out this way. As I said, we want to get married.'

Leonie stood up so suddenly the chair crashed back behind her. She stormed out of the ward, almost bumping into a nurse. She fumed at the bus stop, unable to keep still, unable to think clearly. What should she do about this? She was angry with June and absolutely furious with Ralph Harvey. She wanted to tell Steve but she ought to check on the shop first. She virtually had to pass it to go home.

Ida was pulling on her coat and told her what she'd done and who had come in during the morning. 'I've got to rush,' she said. 'The kids are coming home from school for their dinner today.'

To be back in familiar surroundings cleared Leonie's head. She was reaching for the phone to talk to Steve when she realised it was lunchtime and she could go home and see him. The sooner she brought him up to date the better because he'd be worried about June.

Mrs Killen was just leaving as she went in. 'Is June all right? I hear she's been in a car crash.'

'Yes, last night. She's not all right, she hasn't regained consciousness yet.'

'Poor June, but she'll be getting the right treatment in hospital, they'll bring her round, won't they?' Mrs Killen said. 'I'm glad you've come home, Mrs Dransfield, I wanted a word with you. I've been thinking for some time that I ought to do more to help the war effort. The munitions factory is working full out and is always advertising for more workers.'

Leonie felt her spirits plummet. 'You're not thinking of leaving me?'

'I don't like doing this, you've been very kind to me but they pay more money.'

Leonie sighed. 'And there is a war on. I don't know what I'll do without you.'

'Well, you don't need me to look after Amy in her school holidays now, so I'd like to give you a week's notice.'

'Oh dear, I'll be very sorry to see you go.'

'Mr Dransfield's just starting his lunch. I made a pan of vegetable broth this morning, there's plenty left if you want some.'

'Thanks, I will.' Leonie took off her coat, feeling very down. Mrs Killen was a good worker. She kept the house clean and tidy, laid the fire every morning and even did a bit of washing. Without her, she'd have a lot more to do.

She knew she'd find Steve tucking into his broth sitting in solitary splendour at the dining table. He wouldn't eat anywhere else. 'How is June?' he asked.

'The sister says she has concussion but she doesn't seem to have broken any bones.' Leonie pulled out a chair and sat down at the table with him. 'She's still unconscious so I couldn't talk to her.'

'But how did she come to be out in a car in that storm last night?'

'She's got a boyfriend, Steve, a long-term boyfriend.'

His soup spoon clanked back in the bowl. 'I can't believe that, she's never mentioned a boyfriend to me! What d'you mean, long term?'

'I went up to the male ward and asked to see the man she was with.'

'Good for you, I hope he's in a worse state than she is.'

'He had a dislocated shoulder, four broken ribs and he's cricked his ankle, but he's sitting up and looking in better shape. They've been seeing each other regularly for two years.'

'Seeing each other? You mean he's been taking her to the pictures?'

'He's been taking her to bars and restaurants while she's been telling us she's going to the pictures with her girlfriends.' Leonie felt hurt that her own daughter wasn't able to tell her the truth.

'She's been telling lies? June wouldn't, not to me.'

'He's got a flat close to the hospital. She goes there to spend time with him. I've been wondering if that was why she wanted to train there.'

Leonie saw the tide of anger rush up his cheeks. 'Good God! Are you saying they've been having sex? For the last two years?'

'I understand so. He says he wants to marry her.'

'A fine husband he'd make. It would be over my dead body.'

'That's exactly what I told him.'

'He's violated our daughter. This isn't a man, it's an animal. Did you get his name?'

'Ralph Harvey, he's Elaine's younger brother.'

'For God's sake, I never did like that woman. You've spent far too much time with her. I knew no good would come of it.' Steve was furious.

'It's no good going on about Elaine. This has nothing to do with her.'

'But it has, they must have met at her house. You must have taken her there.'

'I don't think so.'

'How else could she have met him?'

'I've no idea.'

He was outraged. 'Then you should have. You're her mother. You've let her run wild.'

'How many times have you said, "Leave June to me, I'll look after her?" You're her father and you're here all day. You said she was your favourite and you saw more of her than I did.'

His expression changed. 'You know I'm ill. I give all I can. I do my best but you expect too much from me.'

Leonie saw red. 'Believe you me I don't expect anything

from you because time and time again you fail to give it. I'm sick of the way you keep playing the wounded soldier, pretending to feel too ill to do anything.' She leapt to her feet. 'I just wish you'd accept some responsibility and help me when we have a problem.' She was heaving with fury as she went to the kitchen to get herself some soup, but it was the worry about June that was making them both jittery. Really, she was in no position to judge June. After all, she had done much the same thing with Nick. Falling in love could drive all reason from the mind.

Leonie was glad she could say with all honesty that she had to go back to the shop because she had two clients who were coming for fittings. But it didn't stop her feeling weighed down by the problem.

During the afternoon Elaine came in and Leonie could see she was embarrassed. 'I had a phone call telling me Ralph was in hospital,' she told Leonie. 'And I've just been to see him. I don't know what to say to you.'

Leonie felt tears prickling her eyes. 'I'm very worried about June. As soon as I heard about the crash, I was afraid it was something like this. She isn't the first girl he's been involved with, is she?'

'No, I told you all about him some time ago.'

'I know he's been married and had a string of girlfriends, all very young.' Leonie shuddered and blew her nose. 'I haven't told Steve about that yet and he's already dancing with rage. He feels he was close to June but she managed to keep all this from us. She knew we wouldn't let her go out with a man of his age. It was going on right under my eyes and it makes me feel guilty that I didn't even know about it.'

'Let's go upstairs and I'll make us a cup of tea. You mustn't blame yourself, Leonie.'

'But I do. So does Steve, he said this wouldn't have happened if I'd been a normal wife and stayed at home.'

'I hope you told him that if he'd been a normal husband who earned the family living you wouldn't have had to work.'

Leonie shook her head.

'No, of course you didn't. That's not the sort of thing you'd ever say. Don't let this come between you and me, Leonie. If this was what Ralph and June chose to do, neither you nor I could have stopped it. June must have known you wouldn't approve, otherwise why would she have kept it quiet?'

'But she's so young! I want her to be happy and have a better life than I've had but I'm afraid she's made a mess of it already.'

'That's up to her, Leonie, it was her choice.'

'But what are we going to do now? It's a bit late in the day to forbid her to see him. And now she's left home we'd have no control over that anyway.'

'It's still up to them what they do,' Elaine said. 'Tom says, let them get on with it, I'm not my brother's keeper.'

'But I have a duty to care for June. She thinks she's grown up but she's only eighteen.'

'I suppose so,' Elaine said sadly. 'While I was at the hospital I tried to see her, but the sister gave me a list of visiting times and refused to let me in. She did say June was floating in and out of consciousness and that she needed to rest.'

June was coming round and at first couldn't make out where she was. She felt fuzzy and ached all over and she had a thumping headache. She remembered the crash, the sound of tearing metal and the way she'd been thrown about and realised now she was lying in a hospital bed.

Oh God! Her family would surely have been told about the accident and that meant they must also know about Ralph. Pa would go berserk and Mum would look pained and say she was disappointed in her. She should have told her.

June saw the bell push placed conveniently close and jabbed her finger against it. A nurse appeared immediately. 'Oh good, you're awake at last. How d'you feel?'

'Awful. What happened to Ralph? How is he?'

'Is that your boyfriend?'

'Is he all right?'

'I understand he was admitted to Ward One. He has some broken ribs and a dislocated shoulder.'

The nurse took her blood pressure, washed her face and redressed her cuts and grazes, and all the time June tried to keep her wandering mind on how she was going to explain this to her parents.

The sister came to see her and said, 'Your mother has just rung to ask how you are. I told her you were fully conscious again and she said she'd come in and see you later on.'

June sank back against her pillows. She wasn't looking forward to that. What lousy luck to be found out in this way.

CHAPTER TWENTY

AMY WORE HER NEW boots to school and was somewhat offended when the girls laughed at them and called them bootees. She had wanted to wear hobnailed boots to be like them but Glenys told her that hers were much nicer and she wished she could have a similar pair.

She was delighted when her mother's letter about Milo came. She gave it to Bessie to read. 'There you are,' she said. 'He's home safe and sound. He's in hospital but they'll get him well again. You don't need to worry any more.'

Amy was getting used to her new school. Morning classes finished at midday, and after eating their sandwiches and soup at their desks, the children were free to go out. The other girls took her with them up into the woods that grew all round the hamlet. The trees were youngish oak trees with a lot of shrubbery-like undergrowth.

When they tired of playing hide and seek the girls would often make a den. They would collect bits of broken china from around the hamlet and lay it out in patterns on the moss round the roots of the trees. The most prized pieces were decorated with coloured patterns and gold paint and were so old that the edges no longer felt sharp. They'd make the surroundings pretty, find a log or two to sit on and sit round and talk. They called it their 'house'.

A bell was rung at two o'clock and woe betide anybody who was not back and ready to settle down at their desk. Afternoon school started with writing nature notes into an exercise book kept for that purpose. Amy wasn't over her fear of Mrs Roberts and she required at least one full page to be written.

Every day they all started with the same words. The west wind blows, because usually it did. The schoolroom windows were high so there was little to be seen through them but the tops of the trees and the sky, though Amy had learned to check the wind direction by looking to see which way the leaves were blowing. Then she would say whether it was warm and sunny or wet and cold.

That got her started but then she felt she needed a real insight into nature to fill the remaining three-quarters of a page. All round her she could see the farm children scribbling hard about birds and squirrels and voles, while she was sucking the end of her pen hoping for inspiration.

She thought country people noticed much more than those brought up in towns. Uncle Jack could look at wheel marks in a muddy lane and bits of straw caught in the hedge and tell her that the next farm had bought a cartload of straw and it had just been delivered.

Amy regretted that she saw very little on the way to school, she was always in a hurry to catch the taxi. She feared that if she didn't fill the required page she would attract Mrs Roberts' displeasure. Every week she demonstrated her prowess with the cane, though usually a caning was given for bad behaviour not poor schoolwork.

It took Amy a little while but eventually she realised that

Mrs Roberts would not know whether her nature notes were true facts or not. Once she turned to fiction Amy could easily fill much more than one page.

She wrote about watching red squirrels collecting nuts in the cwm, rabbits eating lettuce in the garden, crows pulling worms from the soil, and even a magpie picking up a gold-coloured button that had dropped from Aunt Bessie's dress. Bessie didn't have gold buttons on a dress but Mrs Roberts wouldn't know that either.

She was thrilled to receive a letter from Mum saying she would come to see her again and this time she would bring Pat with her. Amy had a lovely day, walking Pat and Mum round every part of Coed Cae Bach and showing them the animals. She boasted that she could milk Sunshine and allowed Pat to do her job of collecting eggs from the nesting boxes. Pat was envious of her good fortune and wished she could be evacuated. She brought Amy a lot books that her family had finished with.

Mum brought her new clothes that she'd made for her. Amy told her she'd very much like to have a bike for Christmas so she could cycle to school instead of having to rush for the taxi every morning. A fairy cycle like Glenys had.

Amy learned that June had been in a car accident driven by a friend but she was getting better and it was nothing to worry about. Milo was getting better too and would soon be brought by ambulance to a hospital nearer home so that Mum and Pa could visit him.

Steve hated the days when Leonie went to visit Amy in Wales. Sunday was the best day of the week when Leonie was home with him all day. He felt lonely all on his own and it was no good going to the pub because at the weekends Alfred Williams and Walter Duggan were at home with their families.

'Come with me,' Leonie had urged. 'It'll do you good to have a change of scene and they'll welcome you there.'

But Steve couldn't bring himself to go. Amy was another man's love child and though he'd grown attached in one way, he didn't feel the same about her as he did about Miles and June. He'd tried hard to treat her as he did the others, he could see she was a beguiling little girl, but there was some knot inside him he couldn't undo.

And he was worried about the other two. June had seemed to be avoiding him and Miles . . . It had really shocked him to hear Miles had an abdominal injury very similar to what he'd suffered. It had depressed him. He'd not always seen eye to eye with Miles but he wouldn't wish that on his worst enemy.

These days the doctors explained everything more explicitly and Leonie had passed on what they'd told her. Miles had had a piece of shrapnel embedded in his abdomen that had caused considerable trauma. They'd been able to repair small internal wounds to other organs but they'd had to cut a length of some eighteen inches from his small intestine because it was too damaged to repair. They'd joined the ends up again and told him it might cause some constriction but they were hopeful it would not affect him unduly.

Steve mused that these days they could do so much more. Surgery had been in its infancy in his day, but as he saw it, Leonie would have two invalids to take care of in future. At least Miles still had two legs and looked whole.

* * *

Leonie felt exhausted. She'd enjoyed her visit to Amy, she wanted to see for herself how she was getting on, but it meant she missed a more restful Sunday at home and it took extra time and effort to keep up with the chores she'd have done then.

It was a cruel turn of events that all her children had left home and she only had Steve left. She was desperately worried about Milo. It seemed like history repeating itself that he was going to be sent to a hospital near Chester.

But Steve had been in a convalescent home – just a big country house temporarily taken over for that purpose, and he'd been nursed by VADs who were volunteers. Leonie told herself a hundred times that Milo would be in a proper military hospital and today's nurses were properly trained. There had been huge medical advances in the last twenty years and much more could be done for the injured.

She was also worried about June. She was afraid that if she married Ralph, it would not turn out well. He had one broken marriage behind him and although Elaine was being determinedly optimistic about their future, earlier she'd talked about him as if she thought he'd always be off chasing another young girl.

Leonie was afraid he wouldn't make June happy and she knew only too well what a burden an unhappy marriage could be. She visited June several times in hospital and found she was reluctant to talk about Ralph.

'Please, Mum,' she said with the same pained attitude her father used, 'I don't feel well enough to talk about Ralph and it won't help anyway.'

When Leonie recounted that to Steve, he said, 'I wouldn't

put up with that. Next time, I'll come with you, she'll talk to me.'

They went the following day. Elaine had bought some grapes for her on the black market and they took them in. June smiled. 'That's very kind of her. They look lovely. Thank her, Mum, when you see her and tell her I'm very grateful.'

'June,' Steve began. 'You must stop seeing this fellow. You know without being told that he isn't the sort of person you should get involved with. No respectable man would carry on with a sixteen-year-old child and encourage her to hide it from her parents.'

Leonie saw the pink flush run up June's cheeks. She said with some dignity, 'I'm sorry I didn't tell you about him but I knew you and Mum wouldn't understand.'

'We understand only too well, my girl. You've been telling lies to me and your mother for the last two years. That is not acceptable behaviour. In future, you'll do what you are told.'

'Steve,' Leonie protested, 'we need to—'

'You'll not find happiness with him. I insist you send him packing.'

June was holding up her hands as though to fend him off. 'I love him, Pa,' she choked out. 'I don't like going against your wishes but I'm sorry, I'm not going to give him up. I want to marry him.'

'Marry him? The man's a bounder. Don't expect me to give my blessing for that.'

She said with dignity, 'If you won't give me your permission to marry then we'll have to wait until I'm twenty-one.'

'Grow up, can't you?' His face flushed with anger. 'You'll have changed your mind about him long before then, my girl.'

Leonie could see tears welling in June's eyes. She was about to suggest that Steve go because he was causing her distress but she didn't need to. He gave a gasp of irritation and stood up. 'I'm not staying to listen to this nonsense. I'm your father and I only want what is best for you. If you want to come back to my house, you'll do what I say.' The door of the side ward slammed behind him and June dissolved in tears.

Leonie put her arms round her daughter and did her best to comfort her. Although she had the same opinion about Ralph, she thought Steve had been unnecessarily heavy-handed with her. She stayed for another hour, but June hadn't recovered even then.

At eight o'clock every evening, the ward sisters and the day staff went off duty to be replaced by the night sister in charge of the hospital, and a nurse in her third year of training in charge of each ward. The formality of hospital life relaxed a little.

That evening, shortly after eight, June was delighted to see Ralph creep into her side ward and close the door quietly behind him.

When he turned to look at her, he said, 'Darling! What have I done to you? You're all grazes and bandages. I am sorry, love. How d'you feel?'

'Awful. In despair that we've been found out like this. Pa came in and gave me a very hard time.'

'He brought you grapes though.' The last few were on a plate on her locker.

'No he didn't. They were a gift from Elaine.'

'She didn't bring me any grapes.' He kissed her cheek and pulled up a chair near her bed.

'You've come off worse than me, you're all cuts and bruises.'

'They'll heal.'

'They won't leave scars I hope.'

'I have no cuts on my face, thank goodness. The worst thing is they've shaved half my head and put seventeen stitches in my scalp. I'm going to look awful for months until it grows. It could be years before my hair is all this length again.'

'You'll always look beautiful to me. Does your head hurt?'

'Yes, I can't rest it on the pillow on that side. The stitches are like wire and dig in to me. How are you?'

'I was lucky, only a dislocated shoulder which they put right straight away, and apart from that I've got a few cracked ribs that hurt when I laugh or yawn, and a sprained ankle. But I've got some bad news. I had a visit this morning from a friend who has rooms upstairs in the same house. He brought in my post. I've got my call-up papers. They want to put me in uniform in ten days' time.'

'Oh no!' June sank back against her pillows; this was the news she'd been dreading. 'I hate the thought of you leaving me. On top of all this trouble too. What are we going to do?'

Ralph was biting his lip. 'I spent this afternoon composing a letter to the War Office. I've told them that at the moment I'm in hospital recovering from a car crash and I made out my injuries were worse than they are. I understand it's likely they'll change the date on which I'm expected to report in.'

'Yes, but only to give you time to recover. In a week or so you'll still have to go. What good will that do?'

'It will give us time.' He felt for her hand. 'I'm as brassed off about this as you are. Now it's all out in the open, why don't we try to get married? It's what we always planned, isn't it? And you'd feel better about me going if you were my next of kin – my wife – wouldn't you?'

'Of course I would, but my family are dead against it. Pa ordered me to ditch you this afternoon. He thinks you're a rotter.'

'But you don't.'

'No.' It was a cry from her heart.

'I know I've made mistakes in the past but I promise you, June, come what may, I won't let you down. I'm older and wiser now. What I want is to make you happy and I believe I can. Maybe I won't be the best husband in the world but—'

'You will. Nobody else will do for me. I love you. You know I want to marry you more than anything else.'

She felt him try to gather her up in his arms to kiss her, but the pain made her cry out.

'Darling, I'm so sorry. I didn't mean to hurt you. What a mess I've made of everything.'

June shook her head. 'I'm all right.' She gave him a quavering smile. 'Just not well enough to be kissed yet.'

Ralph sighed. 'I think we should aim to get married before I have to go. I'd feel I had something to look forward to if I knew you were waiting here for me.'

'But Pa can be as obstinate as a mule. He won't give his permission.'

'There's always Gretna Green, have you thought of that?'

June's heart turned over. 'Elope, you mean? What a marvellous idea.'

'Well, it's not as easy as it's made out to be. I understand there's a legal requirement to live there for three weeks before we can be married.'

'But it could be done?'

'Yes, provided the War Office gives me time. I think I'm going to be discharged from here tomorrow. Elaine says she'll collect me and take me home to convalesce but I'd prefer to go to my place and think about this.'

'A day or so at Elaine's won't stop you thinking,' June said.

'I want to do it. It sounds romantic.'

'It might be the only way.'

The strong hospital smell made Leonie hold her breath. She associated hospitals with disasters and family troubles. She had been informed officially that Milo had been injured at Dunkirk and was in hospital at Netley near Southampton, but that relatives were not encouraged to travel to that area to visit at the present time. Milo would be sent nearer home when he was well enough.

Milo had written to her and told her not to worry, that all was well and he was recovering, but she knew he always put the best possible gloss on everything and didn't quite believe him. She'd had another letter from him yesterday letting her know that he'd been brought by ambulance to this hospital near Chester, and today she'd taken a day off work to come and see him.

She'd had to ask for directions half a dozen times but at last she'd found her way to the ward he was on. Leonie could feel her heart racing as she saw a male nurse coming towards her.

'Corporal Miles Dransfield?' he said. 'Yes, but I don't think he's in bed at the moment. You'll find him in the day room just down the corridor.'

It all seemed very different to the hospital June was in, there were no male nurses there and these young men hardly looked like nurses. She heard Milo's voice before she reached the open door. He was in the centre of a group all wearing army-issue dressing gowns and pyjamas, smoking, chattering and lolling on the sofas. He saw her almost immediately.

'Mum!' he called with real pleasure in his voice, but she noticed he found it a struggle to get to his feet and cross the room to her, but he gave her an enthusiastic hug when he managed it.

'Lovely to see you. Thanks for coming.'

He was walking her very slowly along the passage to a visitors' room where they could be alone. He needed a walking stick to lean on. 'I've given up the crutches,' he smiled.

It almost broke her heart to have to slow her steps to his. It was only a few months since she'd last seen him but Milo looked drawn and ill and was considerably thinner.

'How are you?' she asked.

'I'm getting on fine. My wounds are healing well, I've been having only fluids by mouth since my operation but I'm about to start on solids now. If I go on like this I think I'll be able to come home soon.'

'What about your leg?'

'That's OK too. They took the bullet out of my thigh. It missed the bone, thank goodness, and there's not too much damage to muscle and nerves. I'm having physiotherapy to get me moving again.'

'That's marvellous.' Leonie felt better. Milo hadn't really changed; he was still his cheery self, interested in everything and everybody. He told her a little of what he'd gone through and she brought him up to date with the family news, mostly about June's troubles.

Two weeks later, Leonie was very pleased to hear that Milo and June would both be brought home by hospital transport on the same day. She made up their beds, cleaned their rooms and although rationing and shortages were beginning to bite, she planned as good a dinner as she could to welcome them home. Then, as usual, she went to the shop.

CHAPTER TWENTY-ONE

Matron did a daily ward round accompanied by Sister Jackson and told June, 'The doctors have decided you are fit to be discharged. You will be allowed two weeks at home to recuperate and must then come back to the ward to see the doctor again. If all is well, you will then return to work.'

June didn't want to go home, she would have much preferred to go to Ralph's rooms. He had been home for nearly a week. He'd been to see her and rung her on the ward telephone when he knew Sister Jackson would be off duty, and she knew they'd have a lovely and relaxing time.

But Sister Jackson had ordered the transport to take her home, and June could see no way of changing its destination She was not looking forward to being at home with Pa while Mum was at work. It cheered her to learn she'd have Milo for company and at least it would be easier for Ralph to get in touch with her by phone.

On the day she was going home, Sister Jackson took out the seventeen stitches on her head and six more on her arm. It hurt as she pushed the scissors under the catgut and she seemed to be tugging at her hair. It took effort on June's part to keep silent and still.

'Your cuts have healed well,' she was told.

'My head still hurts,' June said; in fact, she still felt generally stiff and sore. Also, Sister Jackson painted some red antiseptic along the wound on her scalp that made it twice as noticeable. June objected to that.

'Don't wash your hair for another two or three days but when you do, this colour will go.'

'My hair has been hacked to ribbons,' June wailed. 'It's going to look a mess for ages.'

'You've been lucky,' the sister told her briskly. 'You don't have to worry about scarring; your hair will cover all that. This cut runs just to the top of your forehead and if it does leave a little scar there, you can comb your hair forward over it.'

June didn't feel lucky as she tried to comb what was left of her hair so that the damage didn't show. It wasn't possible. When she arrived home in the middle of the afternoon she had butterflies in her stomach but Milo was already there and greeted her with open arms.

Pa was dour, as she'd expected, 'I hope you've learned your lesson and that you'll give us no more problems,' he said and went back to his study.

Milo was sympathetic but he'd known about Ralph for some time. Now he sat on her bed, wanting to hear about the latest developments as she unpacked her case.

'I want to ring Ralph,' she said an hour later, when she'd caught up with his news too. 'But the phone's right outside Pa's study door. If he hears me lift it, he'll come rushing out and snatch it away.'

'Let's go to the kitchen and make a cup of tea,' Milo suggested. 'I'll take a cup to Pa and stay and chat to him.

Hopefully then he won't hear you use the phone.'

'Be sure to shut the door carefully behind you.'

'Don't stay on the phone too long.'

'Ten minutes,' June said.

'Oh dear.' Milo dithered. 'What can I talk to Pa about that'll keep him pegged down for ten minutes?'

'The war – it's the only thing that really interests him. Or ask him how he is.'

June was nervous and snatched a few mouthfuls of tea before following Milo to Pa's door. As soon as she heard the catch click shut, she was speaking to the operator. When she heard Ralph answer, she said, 'I'm home. What's your news?'

'I've heard from the War Office. I told you I had to send them a doctor's note to prove I'd really been hurt in a traffic accident. Well, they've given me a new date to report in. It's three months off.'

'I'm pleased,' June said. 'It's a help, though three months won't seem long.'

'It's long enough for us to get married. You still want to?'

'Of course I do, but I don't know how we're going to manage it.'

'Here's what I'll do. I'll come round tonight and see if I can talk to your parents. What would be the best time? I don't want to come while you're eating.'

'Not before quarter past eight.'

'I'll leave it till half past to make sure. I'm going to ask them formally for their permission to marry you.'

June sighed. 'I've already done that, they'll say no.'

'Then I'll say we'll elope to Gretna Green.'

'No! Pa will blow a fuse. He'll throw you out. I don't see—'

'I'll point out quietly that we don't really want to do that because we'll have to stay there for three weeks before we can be married, and as you have to report back to the hospital in two weeks, that will give you another problem.'

'I don't care about that.'

'Yes you do. You might be thrown off the course and then you'd have to look for another job.'

'That's true.'

'June, just think for a moment. They can't watch us all the time. I could meet you and we could be miles away before they find you've gone. Your father will understand that.'

'Well, if he doesn't, Mum will.'

'I hope they'll see we're really determined to get married and that they can't stop us. It's worth a try, isn't it?'

'But I don't know if Pa . . .'

June heard Milo making as much noise as he reasonably could as a warning that he was about to open the door.

'Yes,' she whispered urgently. 'I'll see you at half eight.' She slid the receiver gently back on its stand, hoping it wouldn't ping, and skipped back to the kitchen before Milo got there.

When she told him Ralph was planning to come and see Pa tonight, he said, 'I'm going to keep well out of the way while he's here.'

Leonie locked up her shop for the night and hurried home. She knew her children would be there and apart from Amy her family would be together again. She too had found it difficult to come to terms with what the accident had revealed of her daughter's life. She'd been devious and sly to keep it hidden from them for so long. She'd thought June was confiding in her when she'd shared little grumbles about Steve, but clearly that was not the case. But June was her daughter and she loved her, always had, she couldn't let this come between them.

Milo and June would both bring their temporary ration cards with them but that didn't help provide a meal to welcome them home. Yesterday, she'd rushed to the market in her lunch hour to try and get something that wasn't rationed. Liver was her first choice, but there was none to be had. Fish was her second choice, but she'd had to choose between kippers or cod's roe. She'd bought a pound of cod's roe and boiled it last night. Now it was cold and firm, all she'd have to do was cut it in slices and fry it. She could make mashed potatoes and perhaps open a tin of peas to go with it.

Milo met her at the door before she could get her key in the lock, and it comforted her to have one of his bear hugs. When she went to the kitchen, June hung back, which made it only too obvious she was expecting trouble. Both helped to get the meal on the table, but while Milo was in a happy mood and said he was delighted to be home, June seemed jittery and very much on edge.

Leonie had asked Steve to make a special effort not to lose his temper with June on her first night home. He had lit the fire in the living room and the meal passed very pleasantly. Milo made them all tea as coffee was impossible to get, and Leonie took hers to an armchair by the fire. She was weary and could feel herself drifting off.

Suddenly she realised June was at the living-room door and bringing a visitor in. She pulled herself up in the chair and was shocked to see it was Ralph Harvey.

'And who might this be?' Steve demanded.

'Pa, you know it's Ralph Harvey,' June gulped, 'my boy-friend.' Leonie could see she was shaking. 'He'd like to speak to you and Mum.'

Steve pulled himself to his feet with unusual speed and looked Ralph in the eye. 'Get out of my house,' he thundered. 'It's no good creeping in here to tell us you want to marry June. The answer is no, and we have nothing more to say to you.'

'Pa!' June cried.

Leonie was appalled. 'Steve, there's no harm in hearing what he has to say. Let's be reasonable.'

'I'm not going to change my mind. The man's a cad. He'll pull June down. The last thing she needs is a husband like that.'

June was suddenly steely-eyed and determined. 'That's it then, Pa, I'm going to pack my things and leave with Ralph. I didn't want to come here anyway, I'd much rather stay with him. Tomorrow, we'll set off for Greta Green and get married there. He's received his call-up papers, we'll not have much more time together and I'm not going to let you spoil it.'

With that they were gone. The door slammed with such force as they left that the noise reverberated round the room.

Leonie turned to Steve, in agony. 'Can't you see she'll never come back if we let her leave like this?'

'It'll do her no good to marry a man like that.'

'Ralph isn't all bad.'

'She's out of her mind.'

'She's in love. She's seeing things differently. They're going to get married anyway. What is the point of letting them go chasing up to Scotland? June only came out of hospital today, she can't be feeling well.'

'If it weren't for that man, she'd be in prime health.'

Leonie got to her feet slowly. 'Steve, I'm going to overrule you and give my permission. I'd rather they married here and we all remain on friendly terms.' She went out, closing the door quietly behind her.

In June's bedroom, she found Ralph and Milo sitting on Amy's bed, while June was feverishly throwing clothes into an open suitcase.

'I won't let you leave like this,' Leonie said, throwing her arms round her daughter. 'I'll give my permission for you to marry.' She held June until her sobs died down.

'Thank you, Mum. Ralph is everything to me, my whole life.'

The next morning, Leonie was unpicking a backless red velvet evening gown to make a party dress for a twelve-year-old when she saw June bring Ralph into the shop. She'd known they intended to go to the register office to see if they could arrange a date and time for their wedding. 'How did you get on?' she asked.

June was despondent. 'I have to have Pa's permission too,' she faltered. 'It has to be both parents not just one. What am I going to do?'

Leonie felt exhausted, she wanted to scream, nothing was working out as she expected. It seemed one problem after another was being piled on her back, but if June was going to marry her boyfriend before he joined the army, the push would have to come from her. June had already tried and failed. 'I'll try and persuade him tonight,' Leonie said quietly.

She picked up her scissors and turned back to the evening gown. She was getting more and more jobs like this – making new clothes from old. Cloth was scarce, and the quality just wasn't there, all fabric was stamped with the utility mark now. This was beautiful silk velvet with a luxurious pile, but it all had to lie in the same direction. She must get it right, the girl was big for twelve years and there was barely enough material to make the dress. She'd have to leave it for the moment, she couldn't concentrate this morning.

All day she tried to think of words that would persuade Steve to change his mind, but her head felt addled. June said she'd be eating out tonight, so at lunchtime Leonie used the temporary ration cards to buy three lamb chops for tonight's supper, and because it was easier if she planned ahead, she bought some stewing steak for tomorrow.

When she went home that evening, she found Milo had peeled some potatoes in readiness, bless him, and picked some spinach from the garden.

'Pa had another go at June,' he told her. 'She went off in a huff. She said she won't be in for supper tonight.'

'She came to the shop and told me.' Leonie sighed. 'She wants me to talk to Pa tonight. Get him to change his mind.'

'Not a hope,' Milo predicted. 'Once his mind's made up, he never changes it. He's more obstinate than a mule.'

'I'll have to try.' Leonie didn't know where she was going to find the energy. 'Did you see any mint growing in the garden?'

'Yes, I brought some in. Shall I make mint sauce?'

'Please, that would be a help.'

'Did you know Ralph has another car?' Milo went on. 'He says his insurance company arranged for him to use it until his own car is repaired.' He chuckled. 'He's complaining it's only a Morris twelve. Goodness knows how he manages to get petrol for it. I wish I could learn to drive. I'd love to have a car.'

'Not a hope now,' Leonie said. 'Don't you know there's a war on?'

'I had noticed.' He smiled wryly. 'Is there anything else to go on the table?'

'Just that mint sauce. Will you find Pa and tell him we're about ready?' Leonie carried on dishing up and took the first two plates to the table.

Milo came back with flushed cheeks. 'He said to tell you to hold up supper for ten minutes. He's listening to an interesting programme on the wireless.'

'Oh!' Leonie said. 'I'd better light the oven to keep the plates warm.' She needed Steve to be in a pliable mood when he came to the table.

Milo stopped her. 'I told him the meal would spoil if it was kept waiting,' he said angrily. 'I'll fetch his plate in.'

'Milo, you'll upset him before I start to plead June's case.'

'Sit down Mum, let's start without him.'

Leonie no longer had the energy to fight anyone. She sank down and started to eat. Steve came to the table before they'd finished.

'Oh, you've started without me.' He was put out.

'I'm sorry.'

'This is rather rude of you, Leonie. You've forgotten your manners. Nobody in this house shows respect for others any more.' He glowered at his plate. 'You haven't been strict enough bringing these children up. June behaved disgracefully this morning. She's totally out of control.'

Leonie wanted to groan. She wasn't going to stand a chance

with him when he was in a mood like this, but she'd promised June she'd try. 'About June . . .'

'Don't you start asking me to change my mind. I'm not going to give June my permission to marry and that's final. She needs to grow up before she marries anyone. She's behaving like a spoilt child.'

Leonie put down her knife and fork. She should have known it was no good trying. She'd have to tell June it was hopeless.

Milo asked, 'Pa, are you going to eat that chop?'

'No. I need peace and quiet to enjoy my food and I'm not hungry after all this. Anyway, one lamb chop is a very meagre meal and it's gone cold.' He pushed his plate away.

Milo picked it up, slid the chop on to his own plate and quietly began to eat it. 'It's too good to waste,' he said.

Leonie took a deep, calming breath. 'There's some rhubarb crumble left from last night,' she said. 'But no custard.'

Steve grunted impatiently. 'I'll have cheese and biscuits first.'

'Sorry, there's no cheese,' Leonie said.

He turned on her furiously. 'Isn't there anything else to eat in this house?'

'There's a couple of cream crackers and bread and jam.'

He brought his fists down on the table with a thump, making the crockery jump. 'This is ridiculous!'

Milo had cleaned his plate again. He laid down his knife and fork and said cheekily, 'Don't you know about rationing, Pa? There's a war on.'

He sat up stiffly. 'Don't you dare speak to me like that!'

'Well, I do dare. Somebody needs to tell you a few home

truths. Pa, I realise you grew up in this house when there was a cook and a housekeeper to run it, but now there's only Mum doing everything. And in addition she's the one going out to earn the money that pays for everything while you sit around like a lord all day.' He took a shuddering breath. 'And you have the nerve to tell her to hold supper up because you're interested in a wireless programme and must hear the end. You must be the most selfish person in the world.' He glowered at his father. 'I want you to know you're an absolute shit of a husband. You let Mum wait on you hand and foot, you don't appreciate what she does, you don't even notice when she's tired out.'

Steve's mouth sagged open in shock. 'I won't listen to any more of this. Go to your room.'

Milo's lips straightened into a hard line. 'Oh, I haven't finished, not by a long chalk. You're a shit of a father too.'

'Stop swearing at me! I won't have it!' Steve's face was scarlet with rage.

'Pa, believe me, you'd make a saint swear. You treat June and me as though we're still dependent on you for everything. You sit in your study reading newspapers all day, ordering your family about like slaves, but you take no responsibility for anything. Oh no, that's another job for Mum. She has to sort out the problems you cause. June is pleading to get married but you refuse to give your permission. You have such set ideas—'

'She's still a child, for God's sake!' Steve was blustering. 'Only eighteen. The man's a rotter, she doesn't know what she's letting herself in for.'

'Eighteen is considered old enough to fight for one's country

220

and die for it too,' Milo said slowly. 'I've seen lots of lads do it and I've come pretty close to doing it myself. June thinks eighteen is old enough to decide who she wants to marry.'

'Well, I don't.'

Milo was on his feet. 'Pa, you've made your opinion abundantly clear, but it is driving June away not only from you but from me and Mum too. You're pushing June to do exactly what you say you're trying to prevent.' He was angry and couldn't stop himself. 'I really can't understand why Mum stays here to be treated like this. I don't think many women would. You think you have the power and the right to create havoc in our lives.' Milo could feel sweat breaking out on his forehead but he wasn't going to stop until he'd had his say. 'No doubt it makes you feel important that you can, but you aren't living in the real world any more. Things are changing. You've been left behind but you don't think that matters. You've shut yourself off. You did your bit in the First World War and you think that's all you'll ever need to do.'

Steve pushed his chair back so violently that it rocked on its feet and he set off towards his bedroom, moving more speedily than usual. 'I need to lie down. I'm not staying to listen to any more of your ranting.'

'I could do with a lie-down too.' Milo raised his voice so that Steve would hear. 'But the dishes need washing and the kitchen needs clearing up. I don't feel I should rest while Mum does yet more work.'

Leonie gasped. 'Milo! You've gone too far this time.'

'It's high time somebody did. No, Mum, don't you go after him to try and soothe him. It would be better to let him stew in his own juice for a bit.' Milo began piling the plates together to carry them out to the kitchen. 'Come on, let's get the washing-up done and make some tea.'

Leonie couldn't believe how quickly the dishes were done when two of them worked together. Milo's understanding of her situation had surprised her and it told her that the last thing she need worry about was Milo turning out like his father.

'I'd have loved to train for a career at sea on the *Conway*,' he said, 'but Pa wouldn't hear of it. He wanted me to work in the business. Now with the coming of war, neither of us got what we wanted,' he ended with a gasp.

When Leonie turned to look at him he was holding on to the draining board and doubling up with pain. 'What is it?' she said.

'A touch of bellyache,' he said through clenched teeth. 'Perhaps I shouldn't have eaten Pa's chop too.'

'You're tired.'

'I'm spent.' He smiled wearily. 'Letting fly at Pa has taken the stuffing out of me.'

'Dunkirk did that. It's knocked you for six.'

'I'm getting better. A few days pottering about here and I'll get my strength back, but I'll take my cup of tea to bed and have an early night.'

'Yes, get into bed. You'll feel better in the morning.' Leonie was getting out cups and saucers for the tea.

'Mum, why three cups?' He put one back in the cupboard. 'Pa can come to the kitchen and get his own if he wants it. You spoil him.'

'He'll be upset.'

'I hope he is. Come on, bring your tea and sit by the fire in the living room. Give Pa time to calm down and think things

222

over.' Milo was recovering. In the living room he poked the fire into a blaze and put some more coal on.

'Go easy,' she said. 'Coal is hard to get, there's talk of it being rationed.'

Milo patted her arm and said goodnight. Leonie drank her tea. She was afraid Milo was far from well. She stared into the dancing flames, glad to have a few minutes to herself to relax before bedtime.

CHAPTER TWENTY-TWO

STEVE LAY ON HIS bed agonising over Milo's outburst. It was a terrible feeling to know his children hated him. He'd seen that on June's face and now on Milo's. They despised him. He couldn't get his breath when he recalled how Milo had told him to his face that he was a shit of a father. He would never have dared say such a thing to his own father. He'd probably have been whipped if he had.

Steve lay back studying the cracks in the ceiling. He couldn't get Milo's face out of his mind, crimson cheeks with beads of sweat across his nose and his eyes burning with fury and hate. Milo loathed him.

And June had been no better, she'd screamed at him like a fishwife. He'd always loved June. He was trying to protect her, it was for her own good. Neither of them understood how a father worried about them, tried to do his best for them always.

He turned over angrily, he'd eaten nothing since that biscuit at teatime and he was hungry. Leonie would bring him something on a tray soon. Milo had no business to wolf down his chop like that. He'd only done it to shame him.

He heard Leonie's voice, then Milo's. The kitchen door closed with a click, so they were going back to the living room. He thought of them sitting companionably by the fire – they got on very well together. But no, Milo was coming out again, 'Goodnight,' Milo said. He went to the bathroom and there was the sound of running water, so he must be going to bed.

Surely Leonie wouldn't forget that he'd had nothing to eat. Steve lifted his head from the pillow to listen but there was silence now, except for a ship hooting on the river.

He let himself fall back, engulfed in resentment. Leonie didn't love him any more, she'd made that clear before she'd borne her love child, but she'd never stopped looking after him. She must know he was hungry.

Milo had said he was a shit of a husband too; Steve hated him for saying that, but perhaps he was right, he hadn't been a good husband.

An hour later, Leonie woke to find the fire had died back to a few glowing coals. She was cross with herself, what sense was there in sleeping by the fire? She pulled herself stiffly to her feet and made her way to bed.

She opened her bedroom door quietly. All was dark within. In the light from the hall, she could just make out the curled-up mound that was Steve on his side of the bed. She hoped he was asleep. She crept to her bedside table and before switching on her lamp draped her cardigan over it to dim the light.

She got undressed quickly and slid into bed. With the room in darkness she was settling down to sleep when she felt Steve turn over. He said in a penitent whisper, 'I'll give June my permission to marry. It's pointless making them drive up to Gretna Green if they're determined to do it.'

Leonie was taken by surprise at his sudden change of mind. 'It is,' she agreed. 'They'll soon be parted and I think then it'll be a comfort to her to be his wife. She's afraid Ralph will be killed.'

'Yes, I'm sorry.' He sighed. 'I've been a fool, haven't I? My children loathe and hate me. I expect you do too.'

She knew she had to deny that. 'No, I don't hate you, Steve, but you always make things more difficult than they need be.'

'I know. Milo was right about that. Please don't leave me.' She heard the sob in his voice. 'I'll try to improve, do more to help in the house. Life has been hard for you, and I know I shouldn't make it harder. I'll get up with you in the morning and you must show me how to make the porridge.'

Leonie pulled him into her arms. 'That would be a great help,' she whispered and for the first time for ages, Steve gave her a real kiss.

The next day, when Leonie got home from work she found June and Ralph already there. 'I've invited him to have supper with us,' June said. 'We want to tell you about the arrangements we are making for our wedding, and I want you and Pa to get to know Ralph.'

'It's stew,' Leonie said, 'but it'll have to be small helpings.'

'We've brought a bottle of sherry and a cake for afters,' Ralph said.

'We want a very quiet wedding, absolutely no fuss,' June said. 'Just the family at the register office, and Elaine has offered to lay on the wedding breakfast afterwards. Wear your best clothes, there's no need to get anything new.'

'Except for you,' Leonie said. 'There's still time for me to make you a dress.'

'No, Mum, I've decided to wear the blue wool, the last dress you made for me. That will be fine. Unfortunately, we have to give twenty-one days' notice before we can be married, that's the law, and by then I'll be back at work. I'm hoping against hope I'll be able to get the day off.'

'What about you?' Milo asked Ralph.

'I'm back working in the bank now,' he said. 'We've chosen to be married on the Saturday because that makes it easier for me, but it means we won't be able to have a honeymoon.'

'Less to arrange,' Milo smiled, 'and less expense.'

'I'm worried about Amy,' June said. 'What are we going to do about her?'

'She'll expect to be your bridesmaid.'

'It's not going to be that sort of a wedding,' June said, 'but she's going to be mad at missing it.'

'It wouldn't be easy to get her here and back again.' Leonie had already pondered the problem.

'You've got a car,' Milo said to Ralph. 'Couldn't you fetch her?'

'We've talked about it,' June said. 'But it isn't really on. Ralph has to go to work and he'd have to buy the petrol on the black market.'

'Don't forget we could have an air raid while she's here,' her mother reminded them. Bombing had started on Merseyside with small attacks at the end of July 1940. To start with, they had exploded harmlessly in open fields but the raids were gradually building up. One night the planes might drop bombs over Liverpool, damaging infrastructure like the overhead railway and the next night it could be the turn of Birkenhead or Wallasey. People were being killed and injured, and everybody had grown fearful of the air raids.

'I'll write to her so she knows all about my wedding,' June said.

'And you could send her photographs and some wedding cake afterwards,' Leonie told her.

'If we have a wedding cake.'

'I'll make you one. I stocked up with dried fruit and icing sugar before the war started.'

'That's hoarding, Mum.' Milo smiled.

Leonie frowned. 'A pity it won't have long enough to mature.'

Amy always rushed home from school on Tuesday afternoons because she knew Mum wrote to her on Sundays and it would be delivered on Tuesday. Today was no exception; she found the expected letter waiting for her but was surprised to find it was from June.

Dear Amy,

I have some splendid news for you, so I'm writing to you this week instead of Mum. I'm very excited because I'm going to get married on October the twentieth. My husband-to-be is Elaine's younger brother and his name is Ralph Harvey. He'll be your brother-in-law and I hope you'll like him as much as I do.

It's all being done in a bit of a hurry because he's got his call-up papers and will have to go away to fight before long. You and I talked about weddings once and I said you could be my bridesmaid, but I'm not going to have a long white dress and veil, or any of the frills we talked about and no bridesmaids either. It isn't going to be that sort of wedding.

We are being bombed quite often at night and that is really terrifying, so Pa and Mum think it would be safer for you to stay where you are. I'm really sorry that you won't be beside me when I make my vows, I'd have loved to have had a dream wedding with you holding up my train, but with this war raging, it just can't be done. When it's all over, Amy, we'll have a wonderful party to make up for all this.

Milo is getting better all the time, and I'm getting over my car crash. My hair looks a terrible mess because they shaved it off where I had a cut on my head. It won't have time to grow back before I get married either, I'm mad about that, but I'm hoping to find a hat that covers the mess.

Don't be upset about missing my wedding. This war is stopping us all having a good time. I'm hoarding two films for the occasion so I'll be able to send you some photographs. We all send you lots of love, Mum especially, and she says she'll write to you next week.

Love,
June

Amy pushed the letter back into the envelope and couldn't stop her tears. Ages ago, she'd picked up a book in Mum's sewing room full of patterns for bridal wear and she and June had studied the designs and talked about the dream wedding they'd each have one day. She'd made June promise she could be her bridesmaid as she was likely to be married first. But now she wouldn't even be there.

She showed the letter to Bessie who said, 'It can't be helped in wartime, bach. People can no longer do what they want.' But that didn't cheer Amy up.

They were tying up the cows for milking when Bessie said, 'Jack is thinking of bringing the sheep down from the hill soon for tupping and perhaps he'll take you along to help. It won't be as exciting as a wedding but it will be a nice outing for you, wouldn't it?'

'What is tupping?' Amy asked. It was a word she hadn't heard before but Bessie didn't seem to know how to explain it.

Over supper that night, Jack said, 'Shall we bring the sheep down from the hill on Saturday afternoon?'

'Oh yes,' Amy agreed and that morning she helped Bessie make a pan of thick broth for their lunch and cut some sandwiches to take with them. Bessie went off to catch the bus into town to do the weekly shop, and Amy read her book and watched the pan simmer slowly on the trivet over the fire until Jack came home from work.

He brought his bike with him. Usually he left it in a shed on a nearby farm where they had a lane going down to the road. The path up the cwm and through the fields was impossible for bikes. His work was planting trees on Forestry Commission land which had once been an upland hill farm and was some twelve or so miles distant. Jack used his bike every day to get to a meeting point where they were picked up by lorry.

First they ate as much of the broth as they could and Jack fished out a slice of flitch bacon for each of them to eat with their bread.

'Why are you bringing the sheep home?' Amy wanted to know.

'I always do in the autumn once we've got the harvest in. They have to come to be tupped by the rams.'

'What's that?'

'Unless that happens there won't be any lambs. You'll see them doing it in the fields. We'll take them back in a few weeks to spend the winter up there, then I'll bring them down again for their lambs to be born here in the spring, where we can care for them.'

While Amy put on her coat and wellingtons, Jack wrapped some sacking round the cross bar of his bicycle to make it more comfortable for her to sit on, and tied a shallow wooden box to the carrier over the back wheel for Fly.

'Even the dog rides up,' he said, 'to save his energy for rounding up the sheep.' Fly was untied and they all set off walking across two fields to reach the top road that wound up to the hill.

There Amy was lifted on to the cross bar and Jack started to peddle. When he had the bike going he whistled to Fly who took a running jump into the box. Amy felt the bike wobble as he landed and felt anything but secure on her perch.

The top road was little more than a lane and just wide enough for a car but they didn't see even one all day. There were banks on both sides with hedges growing on top, so Amy couldn't see into the fields and very soon it became so steep that they all had to dismount and walk up it. This was repeated several times until they'd covered the six miles up to the sheepwalk.

Long before then the banks and hedges had given way to wire fencing. It was windy here and Amy could see for miles across rough heather-covered moorland and was amazed. It felt like being on top of the world. The lane came to an abrupt end with a five-bar gate across it. On the other side was Jack's thirty-acre sheepwalk. He called it hill land but to Amy it looked like moorland. The wind seemed near gale force. She put on the pixie hood that Jack had advised her to bring.

Fly was sent running in one direction to round up the sheep

and Amy was sent in the other. Jack directed the round-up with shouts and whistles. Amy had to jump from one rough tussock to another and more often than not splash into water in between.

It took a long time before Jack was satisfied that he'd rounded up all his flock, then one or two sheep were separated out as having the markings of another farmer. Amy was told to open the gate and the flock was pushed out on to the lane. The sheep immediately put their heads down to nibble at the fresh green grass on the verges, and Fly lay down to rest but kept his eye on his master.

'Time for bait,' Jack said, retrieving the packet of sandwiches from his saddle bag and offering them to Amy. She was hungry, but when he threw his crusts to the dog, she did the same. Fly received them with enthusiasm.

Going home was easier as it was downhill all the way. Fly ran loose so he could control the flock and kept them moving at a brisk pace. Jack and Amy followed on the bike. When they were nearing the fields above Coed Cae Bach, Jack hung back and whistled for Fly to halt the flock. When he'd achieved that, Amy was sent to creep along the bank to pass them while the dog stood guard and Jack prevented any retreat. She opened wide the gate to the first field and propped it open. Then she stood back to block the sheep from going further down the road.

Another whistle from Jack and Fly had them swooping into the field. Amy was sent to run alongside them to keep them near the hedge while Jack shut the gate behind them. Then there was the last gate to open into the little field and the flock was safely back at home.

Amy had much preferred the trip up to the sheepwalk to going shopping. She had seen half Wales laid out below her and felt full of fresh air, but she was exhausted and so was Fly. Bessie had returned from town, the Saturday sausages and Sunday joint were beginning to fill the kitchen with savoury scents and she was now out milking.

Jack said, 'I'd better go and give her a hand. Why don't you go and get Fly's dinner for him? He's had to work very hard today and he's tired. And I'd be grateful if you'd shut the hens in for me before you take your wellies off.'

Amy gave Fly an extra handful of food to reward him and found he'd already gone to sleep before she reached his kennel, but he was fully awake in an instant and excited to have it. She patted him and decided she'd had a lovely day. After shutting the hens in she found Jack in the house separating the milk while Bessie organised supper.

'Uncle Jack,' Amy said, 'can I help you take the sheep back up to the hill when they've been tupped?'

'Of course you can,' he said. 'I'll be very glad of your help. I couldn't have managed without you today.'

CHAPTER TWENTY-THREE

JUNE WAS BACK AT the hospital and helping to nurse the sick and injured. She blessed the fact that her nurse's uniform included a white cap, because it hid her shaved hair. Life suddenly seemed unreal. She found the raids terrifying, and the injuries flooding in afterwards made her see the full horror of war at first hand. It made her realise that Ralph might soon be in a worse position. She clung to him, glad that she could run across the park to be with him whenever he was at home and she was off duty.

She longed to stay all night with him, but when the air-raid sirens sounded all the nurses were ordered to the shelters. A stand-by rota was set up in case the small number of night staff couldn't cope with the casualties. Some were on first call and some on second, depending on the number of injured needing attention, but all would be called if the hospital was hit and needed to be evacuated. June had done enough drill to know that in the event of a raid, she'd be missed if she wasn't where she was expected to be.

She had asked to have her weekly day off on 20 October, and that had been agreed. Her only worry then was that she'd been told all leave would be cancelled and staff called in if the hospital was in difficulties because there were many bedridden patients who would need help.

On the night before her wedding, June went home to spend some time with her family. Ralph was invited for supper and Mum managed to put on a celebratory meal. He went home afterwards in his own car which had been returned to him looking like new.

That night it was Bootle that received the attention of the Luftwaffe, and though they had a warning, nothing fell nearby, so June felt she'd had a good night's sleep. In the morning, her mother came to her room bringing her a cup of tea. 'Stay in bed a little longer and rest,' she told her. But June wanted to enjoy every minute of this special day. It was a lovely morning, with the sun just breaking through the autumn mist.

'I'll get up,' she said, 'and pick some roses from the garden to make buttonholes. I want us to look like a wedding party when we go to the register office.'

'I've already picked every remaining flower,' Leonie said. 'I've had to pull off the odd brown petal from the outside of some, but it's been a good year for the roses.' She smiled. 'It's such a treat not to rush to open the shop, Ida will be in charge of the business today. I've made small buttonholes for the men and larger ones for the ladies. I've made a special one for you with two roses, one cream and one white, with some maidenhair fern to set them off. It looks surprisingly glamorous.'

June could hear the family collecting in the kitchen so she put on her dressing gown and went to join them. 'We're all going to have breakfast together,' Mum told her. 'I have four eggs, so as a treat it's going to be boiled eggs and toast.' The ration was one egg per person per week.

June was surprised to see Pa already up and trying to help.

He seemed a different person. 'I'll time them,' he said. 'Four minutes, isn't it? I'm fussy about my eggs.'

As the ceremony was due to take place at eleven that morning, it gave June time to have a leisurely bath and put on her blue wool dress and small hat of matching blue feathers. As her mother pinned her roses in place for her, June leaned closer and kissed her. 'Thank you,' she whispered, 'for talking Pa round. You made him change his mind.'

Leonie smiled. 'There's a happy family atmosphere this morning,' she said, 'but it's Milo you must thank for that.'

Tom and Elaine arrived to drive Pa, Mum and Milo to the register office. The twins were with them, looking like bridal attendants. Dulcie wore a pale blue satin dress with a skirt of many frills while Lucas was in navy velvet trousers and a white satin shirt.

'You both look beautiful,' June told them and made a mental note not to send Amy any photograph that showed them. She'd weep that they could be here and she could not.

Ralph arrived wearing his best suit. June pinned his button-hole in place and, hand in hand, they walked out to his car.

The Birkenhead register office had a large hall for weddings but as the wedding party numbered only seven and two children, they were guided towards a small room panelled in light oak. Leonie had a lump in her throat as she heard her daughter make her vows. This wasn't the wedding she had envisaged for her and she was afraid it had come much too soon, but June's groom was gazing at her with such love in his eyes that she felt heartened.

He was slipping the ring on her finger when the sound they

all feared and dreaded shredded the peaceful atmosphere. It was the siren sounding an alert. There was an involuntary pause and then the ceremony carried on as though nothing had happened. Dulcie started to cry and Elaine put an arm round her to comfort her.

Leonie shivered, she was glad now that she'd decided Amy should be evacuated and that she hadn't given in to temptation and brought her home today.

For June, the signing of the register came quickly. She'd sensed the rising tension as their guests listened for the sounds of explosion or gunfire outside, and now there was relief that the ceremony was over and the bombs hadn't come.

Ralph put down the pen and felt for her hand. The alert had frightened them and been a distraction. 'Daylight raids never amount to much,' he whispered to her, and sure enough it was still quiet when they went out.

The registrar advised them to take shelter but they decided to keep to their plans. Tom lined them up on the steps outside to be photographed, and as Ralph was escorting her back to his car, June heard the all-clear sounding its note of safety through the streets.

They were all in heightened good spirits when they reached Elaine's house, laughing with relief that the marriage had taken place despite Hitler's attempt to stop it. Tom had persuaded his wine merchant to allow him to buy two bottles of champagne for the occasion. He removed the cork with a resounding plop and filled the glasses. June felt the bubbles going up her nose as she sipped and felt her wedding was now going with a swing.

Elaine was good at entertaining at home but had had to turn to the black market to obtain two chickens, and rely on her home help to roast them. June felt they couldn't have had a better wedding breakfast anywhere. Pa praised it and thanked Elaine; he called it lunch though it was clearly more than that.

The afternoon was gone in a flash and at five o'clock Elaine made them a cup of tea and brought out the wedding cake. From the start, Mum had said regretfully she'd only be able to make one tier. It looked very festive, with a touch of pre-war richness.

June could see her mother wasn't so pleased when she cut into it. 'It's turned out to be a lighter fruit cake than I intended. I had the icing sugar put by but I couldn't get any almonds or almond paste to go under it.'

'There's almond paste here, Mum,' June said.

Her mother smiled. 'Elaine found me a recipe for a wartime substitute and provided the almond flavouring.'

'It looks a very good cake, Leonie,' Pa said, 'and we all know how hard it is to get anything these days.'

Leonie laughed as she cut slices. 'Ida let me borrow the wedding cake ornaments that came from a relative's wedding cake.'

'It tastes beautiful,' Ralph assured her. 'I've never tasted better cake,' and they all agreed.

Leonie put what was left back in its tin and gave it to June when they were leaving. 'You have it,' she said, 'and eat it. This is wartime wedding cake and won't keep.'

'I'm taking my bride home,' Ralph said as the family were kissing her goodbye. 'We're going to have a quiet evening because June has to go to work early tomorrow morning.'

* * *

Amy was waiting eagerly for the photographs of June's wedding, but it was Mum who wrote to her the following week. She ripped open the envelope to read, '*I'm going to tell you all about June's wedding,*' but almost the only thing Mum did tell her was that there had been an air-raid warning in the middle of it, and how everybody had said they were glad Amy was in a safe place.

She knew about the bombing in Liverpool and on the Wirral because another group of five evacuees arrived from Birkenhead. They were not from her school and she didn't know them. They came without a teacher, were immediately settled into Mrs Robert's class and seemed to think she was a local girl.

The next week, June did write to her and sent her three postcard-sized photographs taken at her wedding but she looked nothing like a bride. She was wearing a funny hat stuck on the side of her head and Mum was wearing a hat and coat Amy had seen many times before. She wasn't sure about the bridegroom either. He looked almost as old as Pa, but June wrote that he was being called up soon and she dreaded to see him go, so she must love him.

She also said that Elaine had given her a little box that had been left over from somebody else's wedding to send her a piece of her wedding cake. It arrived two days later and was very pretty with silver wedding bells and ribbons printed all over it, so even the postman knew she'd had a wedding in the family.

Amy opened it carefully and was disappointed to find it held just a sliver of cake. It looked pretty much like the fruit cake Auntie Bessie made except this had a tiny bit of icing on top.

She cut it into three pieces so Bessie and Jack could taste it too. They both said it was an excellent wedding cake and Jack said, 'A mouthful of wedding cake like this is said to bring you luck.'

Amy felt a little sorry for June; it was surely not the wedding her sister had expected and hoped for.

June couldn't bear to think of Ralph going away to fight. But yesterday, as instructed, he'd reported to a local army call-up centre and after a lot of form-filling he had been given a medical examination. He'd been passed as A1 medically fit, been given a warrant to travel by train and told to report to the army barracks at Catterick for basic training in four days' time. She was shocked; she'd not expected him to be spirited away so quickly.

'Catterick isn't far,' he told her. 'I'll be able to come back and see you when I get leave. It's probably safer there than it is here. They aren't getting air raids like we are.'

Ralph had already decided he would have to give up renting his rooms. 'I doubt I'll be able to afford them and anyway, what is the point? You'll have to live in the hospital and on your day off you'd be better going home than staying in those rooms by yourself. I'm glad I've got a few days to put my affairs in order.'

'Five more nights and four more days,' June mourned, but on only one would she be off duty and be able to spend it with him.

Ralph discovered he was obliged to give a month's notice on his flat, so it gave him time to pack and give some thought about what he would do with his furniture and belongings. Leonie told him she'd be happy to keep his bedroom furniture at her shop until he needed it again as she had an empty bedroom and there would be room for anything else to be stored in the unused cellar rooms at Mersey Reach. Pa offered to dispose of anything he didn't want to keep at auction and Elaine arranged for a van to move his things.

Ralph couldn't make up his mind what to do with his car. 'I'd like to take it up to Catterick to use there but petrol is almost impossible to get nowadays.' In the end decided to use his travel warrant and go up by train.

June had her day off on his last precious day at home, but he needed to drive his car to Mersey Reach where Milo helped him to disconnect the battery and put it up on blocks in one of the sheds. June went with him and they spent a lot of time with Milo but June wanted to savour her last day with Ralph and this wasn't how she'd have chosen to spend it. She couldn't go to see him off on the train the next day as she had to work.

As student nurses were forbidden to marry during their training, she had told nobody at the hospital that she had. There she was still Nurse Dransfield. Ralph had already bought her a gold chain on which to thread her engagement ring, so she added her wedding ring to it and wore them together, hidden under her uniform.

She thought of him all the time and the days seemed endless. She was really missing him, she'd spent so much time in his company recently that she'd let everything else in her life drop. It seemed her world was coming to an end.

That evening, when she came off duty at eight o'clock, she went up to his rooms. She had intended to do some more packing, there was still plenty to do, but she was overcome with misery and didn't achieve much. An hour later, she was surprised to hear a knock on the door. One of the other residents had come to tell her there was a phone call for her. She raced down the hall to the public pay phone and was delighted to find it was Ralph.

'I rang the nurses' home and was told you'd gone out, so I guessed where you'd be,' he said. 'I feel really down in the dumps at having to leave you. I'm here with a crowd of other men I don't know, all of whom would rather be somewhere else.'

He was on a pay phone too, but he had his small change lined up and was able to talk for a long time. She heard his first impressions of army life and he didn't like it. The army food was stodgy and they didn't give him time to eat it. He was to sleep in a hard and narrow bed, jammed in a hut with thirty others, and he'd spent most of the afternoon out on the parade ground in heavy drizzle, learning to march wearing boots that weighed a ton. He didn't know how he was going to cope with it.

June walked back across the park in the pitch dark of the blackout, had a hot bath and went to bed. She was in tears for a long time and was just settling down to sleep when the air-raid warning sounded and she had to go to the shelter.

Milo was getting plenty of sleep and couldn't remember when he'd last had so much leisure time in which to please himself. He felt well enough to go out and about and went to Ralph's rooms to help his sister pack up. On June's day off, he took her and Mum to the pictures. He went to see Duggie Jenkins' family and they seemed pleased to see him.

He knew Duggie had a sister called Floris but he'd had little to do with her in the past. Now she was working as a secretary for a company in Birkenhead making life jackets and other air-sea rescue equipment. She made him welcome and produced a cup of tea.

'Where is Duggie now?' Milo asked. 'I feel I owe my life to him. Once I was injured, if he hadn't dragged me out to the boat and heaved me on, I'd have succumbed on that Dunkirk beach.'

'Duggie would always do his best for his friends,' Henry Jenkins told him. 'They've sent him to the Far East. Singapore.'

'He wasn't given much time to recover from Dunkirk then?'

'He had a month at home,' Floris said, 'and he likes Singapore. Duggie felt lucky to have come home unscathed.'

'How is he?'

'In fine fettle.'

Floris told him of two other friends who used to go to Milo's shed to pore over yachting magazines and work on his old sailing dinghy. Milo had been quite envious of Derek Brierley and Phil Jones who had wanted careers at sea and had joined the merchant navy.

'They haven't had your luck,' Floris said. 'Both lost their lives in separate incidents. Their ships were sunk trying to bring essential supplies to English ports.'

Milo went home in a subdued frame of mind. It seemed he could have had less chance of survival if he'd joined the merchant navy. Seeing the Jenkins family had made him yearn to return to his old life. He wanted to shrug off being an invalid and get out on the river. The small dinghy, a pram really, that he'd used to get out to the *Vera May*, his fishing boat, was upturned in the back garden.

Mum came down the garden and he said, 'Help me roll it over, I want to see if it's all right.'

'You aren't strong enough to go out on the river yet,' she said. 'Leave it until you're passed as fit.'

'I'd like to take a look at the *Vera May*.' He pushed his hair back. 'Perhaps I'll ask somebody to come with me the first time I take her out.'

He went inside to the sitting-room window and put the binoculars on *Vera May*. She was bobbing about in permanent deep water where he'd left her and had been all the time he'd been away.

'Tomorrow I'll ask Mr Jenkins to come with me to have a closer look,' he told his mother. So far he'd been unable to make contact with any of his old friends; all his generation had been caught up in the war.

Henry Jenkins was balding and looking older, he said he was exhausted with his day job at Camell Laird's and his work as a warden at night, and Floris said she knew nothing about boats. But they kept him talking for an hour or so and when he asked Floris if she'd come to the pictures with him, her father said, 'I think I'd better mention right away that our Floris is spoken for. She writing almost daily to a merchant naval officer and she's expecting him home within the next few weeks.'

'Right,' Milo said. 'That's understood, but it's no reason not to come to the pictures with me, is it?'

'No, she spends too much time at home on her own.'

'I'd love to come.' Floris was all smiles.

Before he left, Henry Jenkins said, 'I can put you in touch with Oswald Hemmings if you like. You remember him? He taught you and Duggie to sail in that boat we did up. *Dido*, wasn't it?'

'Of course I remember him. He was Gerald's father and taught a lot of our friends to sail. Where is Gerald these days, d'you know?'

'He joined the Royal Navy and he's serving on the aircraft carrier, *Ark Royal*. We built it in Cammell Laird's and his father says it makes him feel he's never far from home because of the connection. Oswald might like a trip out in the *Vera May*.'

'Thank you. Tell him I'd be delighted if he'd come with me.'

That weekend, Mr Hemmings who still had his athletic build, brought a trailer to the garden and together they pushed the dinghy down to the beach. The tide was in and Mr Hemmings was happy to scull out to the *Vera May*. 'She looks scruffy.'

'Bound to,' Milo said, 'she's been neglected. Nobody has been near her for ages. Let's get on board and see if she's still watertight.'

'She is,' said Mr Hemmings once he'd checked her over. 'Dry as a drum inside. She needs cleaning up, perhaps a coat of paint, but that's all.'

CHAPTER TWENTY-FOUR

AIR RAIDS WERE BECOMING more frequent and Elaine said, 'You did the right thing by choosing to have Amy evacuated. It terrifies the twins to hear the air-raid warnings and they can't sleep even when the raids are over.'

'It worried me stiff at the time,' Leonie said. 'Amy could have ended up anywhere, but she was lucky. She has an excellent home. Couldn't be better, the people are kind to her. She's settled down and she's enjoying country life.'

'I didn't have the courage to do that but now Olive, Tom's unmarried sister, has offered to look after the twins so we took them to his family home last weekend. On Monday morning I entered them in the village school there.'

'That's Chester, isn't it?'

'Guilden Sutton, just outside Chester. It seems far enough away to ensure they have quiet nights. It was bliss going to bed knowing I could stay undisturbed until morning. I'd have loved to have stayed with the children but Tom has to be here to work and my little business is thriving so I decided my place was to stay here and look after it.'

'I'm glad you aren't deserting me,' Leonie told her.

'I'm not going to do that. Tom and I plan to go and see the

children most weekends, that'll give us a few peaceful nights to catch up with our sleep.'

'Lucky you, I wish we had relatives living in a quiet spot not very far away.'

'It's ideal for that but Tom's mother and sister moved to an old cottage when his father died and they have only two bedrooms so they don't have enough room to put us up as well as the twins. The twins think it's fun to sleep on two camp beds in Olive's room but she has to look after her mother who is eighty-six and not very well. It's marvellous that she's willing to take the twins in but we don't feel we can put on her to do any more. But as you know, Nick lives in Chester and has said we must feel free to stay at his house at weekends. We can collect the twins and all sleep at his place, and if we can't get enough petrol we can go by public transport.'

Leonie tried not to think of Nick. 'Without the children, you and Tom are going to have much more freedom during the week.'

'We are. Leonie, why don't we take it in turns to open up the shop in the mornings? I can deal with any of your customers that come in, and it won't be on my conscience if I have Friday afternoons off to get ready to go to Chester.'

'That sounds a great idea and then sometimes I could sleep in after a night of heavy raids.'

In the weeks running up to Christmas, the nights were often very noisy with exploding bombs, screaming fire engines and the thunder of ack-ack guns on a nearby emplacement as they tried to shoot the enemy planes down. When she heard the warning siren, Leonie would get up and wake Milo to go down to the cellar.

'I'm not going down there,' Steve said. 'I'd catch my death of cold. Anyway, I'll be all right in my bed.'

'Unless we get a direct hit,' Milo said.

'In that case you wouldn't survive in the cellar,' he retorted.

The raids became so frequent that Leonie and Milo almost gave up using their bedrooms. It wasn't pleasant to be woken up in the middle of the night to get out of a warm bed and go down those outside steps to the cellar. It was easier to go down at bedtime with a hot-water bottle and spend the whole night down there.

'With proper beds, we've got a more comfortable shelter than most,' Milo said. Leonie was glad to have his company. He slept near her in the room she'd intended to share with Steve.

Milo told everybody he was continuing to improve, though Leonie knew he was still having bouts of acute abdominal pain, but he was always cheerful and he helped her about the house. Every few weeks he returned to the hospital for a few days to have further check-ups and then he'd come back home for another month of convalescence.

June hated being parted from Ralph and dreaded taking the keys of his flat back to the landlord at the end of the month. It was somewhere to go when she was off duty, she could think about him there, and feel his presence all round her and be soothed. It helped to settle her and made her realise she'd she have to knuckle down and give more of her attention to nursing. She'd been to lectures and scribbled a few notes and never opened the book again until she was in the next lecture. She'd bought textbooks from the list she'd been given but had not opened them either.

She was growing a little stubble along her scar and had taken to wearing a beret when she wanted to go out and was not in uniform.

She'd found it time-consuming to put her long hair up into a bun before she had breakfast. She was more used to the French pleat but that didn't fit well under her cap. So after much heart-searching because she thought her hair was her best feature, she decided to have her long hair cut really short and found it much easier to run a comb through that in the mornings.

She wrote and received long daily letters from Ralph and if he rang her at the nurses' home it made her day. Her working hours were long and she had to attend lectures and study as well; she felt she was lucky to have plenty of new friends to provide companionship in what spare time she had. When she had a day off she went home and spent it with Milo and Mum.

It was several weeks before Ralph was given leave, but eventually he phoned to say he had a forty-eight-hour pass and would be staying with Elaine and could she join him there. Ralph had the weekend off, and hadn't given June enough notice to ask for her day off to coincide. Also a day off on a Saturday was popular with the nurses, but the girl who had been given that agreed to swap so June might be off.

When June put it to the ward sister she pulled a face. 'Nurse Halligan is a second-year nurse,' she said severely, 'and you are very much her junior and lack her experience. I have to balance the skills of the staff on duty at all times.'

June was afraid she wasn't going to get it and wished she could say Ralph was her husband and not her fiancé, but in the end the sister capitulated, and as the new week started on

Sunday, she gave her a half-day then as well. It was the most she could ever get and she was pleased and excited at the thought of seeing Ralph again.

He had two nights away from his barracks, but June could only spend one with him. Elaine and Tom put off going to Chester to see the twins until Saturday morning, so they could see something of Ralph. They were sociable and made her feel welcome. Elaine was a good hostess and took pleasure in providing meals for guests but with rationing, it was no longer easy. Also, her house was modern and her guest room next to her own. Not wanting to be overheard, they both felt inhibited. They spent the night in whispered conversation and neither felt they'd had much sleep but the next morning Elaine and Tom were away early and they had the house to themselves.

They didn't want to go out and preferred to sit around all day until the evening. 'We'll have to go to a restaurant,' Ralph said, 'there's hardly anything to eat in the house.'

He drove her back to the hospital by ten o'clock and promised to be outside waiting for her when she came off duty at lunchtime the next day.

On Sunday afternoon, they went for a long cold walk along the beach as far as Bromborough. That evening, she saw Ralph off on the train, caught the bus back to the hospital and was in bed by eight o'clock.

After that Ralph was given regular days off twice a month and June was then able to ask for her days off before the sister drew up the off-duty list. They were getting used to staying at Elaine's house, and Ralph took her out to restaurants and theatres, though when they had the house to themselves they preferred stay in on their own. It seemed that they had given up almost everything that mattered to them to help the war effort.

A few days after she'd last seen Ralph, she'd come off duty at eight o'clock with the rest of the day staff, had a hot bath and got ready for bed. They all did that and then congregated in the sitting room in their dressing gowns, drinking tea, gossiping and listening to the war news on the wireless. June hoped Ralph would ring her for a chat and answered the pay phone when it rang in the hall. The second time she did that it was Ralph's voice she heard.

'How are you, love? I've got some news.' She could hear the excitement in his voice and knew it was good news. 'Guess what? I've been selected for officer training. It will be a short-service commission.'

'Marvellous,' June sang out. 'Then I shall be an officer's wife!' She looked round guiltily hoping that no one had heard her say that, because she'd told nobody that she was married.

'I've got a pass out for ninety-six hours next week.'

'But I'll only be able to have one day off,' she mourned.

'We'll manage something. After that I'm to report to the college which is just outside Chester, so we won't be so far apart and I won't have to waste so much of my leave on the train.'

June was delighted. 'And it'll keep you here in England for longer, where you'll be safe.' Nothing could have pleased her more. Ralph would be paid more and perhaps be less likely to be killed; she hoped so anyway.

'Once I'm on that course I'll get regular time off,' he crowed. 'Things are looking better, aren't they?'

When at last Ralph hung up, June was so full of joy that she went back to the sitting room to recount all he'd said, though she was careful to describe him as her fiancé.

When she went home for her next day off, she told the family while they were sitting round the table having supper. Milo was impressed. 'Good for him!'

Pa looked down his nose at her. 'I don't understand how they come to pick Ralph out for officer training while Miles is left in the ranks. Ralph is no gentleman.'

'Perhaps they want brains these days, Pa,' Milo said. 'Perhaps he has more of those.'

'If you aren't rated as officer material with your private schooling, I can't see why Ralph should be.' Steve was adamant.

'He's older,' June smiled diplomatically, 'and perhaps wiser than most.'

Steve had felt wary and resentful towards Milo since the day he'd shown how much he despised him. Since then Milo had apologised for swearing at him and treated him as though it hadn't happened. Steve had watched him recover from his injuries and was surprised at the progress he was making.

Steve had been out in the garden picking purple sprouting broccoli for supper tonight because Leonie had asked him to. It was dark when she came home and it was impossible to pick vegetables without showing a light. Milo was in the kitchen when Steve took the broccoli in.

He looked much better than he had when he'd first come home, every inch a Dransfield, tall and slim but with broad shoulders. Milo had a handsome face that reminded Steve of his older brother who had been killed in the Battle of Arras, he even had his reddish-brown hair.

To start with he'd kept telling him, 'You shouldn't do too much. It'll be better for you in the long run if you take things easy at this stage.'

'I'm all right, Pa,' he'd always said. 'I think that the more I do, the better I feel. I need to find out what I'm capable of doing.'

Now he said, 'Would you like a cup of tea?'

'Your mother will be home soon, she'll make us one.'

'Mum will be tired. I don't feel I can ask her to do things I can manage for myself.'

That brought Steve up short and he left Miles to it. He brought a cup of tea to his study for his father and Steve felt that showed him up as unwilling to help himself. Miles immediately went off to do something else in the kitchen, no doubt start their evening meal.

Leonie came home some time later and put her head breezily round his door to say hello but went straight to the kitchen. He could hear her talking to Miles and though he couldn't catch what they were saying, their chatter sounded bright and cheerful. It made Steve feel lonely and isolated.

He even felt a little envious that Miles could do so much. He was going out and about with other people, going out on the river in that stupid boat that had been such a mistake to buy. He'd even taken a girl to the pictures.

Steve felt that in the long run Miles would suffer by rushing his convalescence. He thought it unlikely the army would require his services in future and that would come as an almighty shock to him.

Working in the hospital, June felt the terror all around her as bombs exploded nearby. It took a huge effort to push fear to the back of her mind and concentrate on what needed to be done, but that was the only way she could make herself useful in the team helping those who had been hurt.

She was short of sleep and looked forward to the two weeks' holiday she was entitled to now that she'd completed six months' training. Ralph was at Eaton Hall, on the Duke of Westminster's estate, which had been taken over as a college to provide officer training for short-service commissions. He was in the middle of his course and said it would be impossible for him to have time off.

'I'd like to book you into a hotel near the college,' he said. 'So I can see more of you. I have most evenings off and quite a lot of time at weekends though I'm afraid you'll be alone a good deal.'

'That's what I want to do,' June said. 'I'll be able to amuse myself going round the shops and I'll get away from the air raids.'

'We have had a couple of warnings since I've been here but they've come to nothing.'

June packed her case and was relieved to get away from Birkenhead where the bomb damage was spreading in all directions. She found Ralph had booked her into a small boarding house only a few hundred yards or so from the main gate of the college. The other three guests were also relatives of military personnel.

Ralph came and took her out to dinner on the nights he was free. He came every night and spent some of it in her double bed. She was wakened when his alarm went off early in the morning and heard him pull on his clothes before creeping out. She luxuriated in being able to go back to sleep until the gong signalled it was breakfast time. Sometimes she'd eaten so much at night that she didn't bother to get up then.

She found there was a frequent bus service into the main shopping area, but though Ralph gave her money to spend on herself the shops were a disappointment because there was little to buy. Cosmetics were in short supply and she had to try several shops before she could buy a lipstick. Clothes now carried the utility mark, and were all much the same in plain styles showing a military influence. Fashion had ceased to exist and her mother could make better clothes for her. Her hair was growing; she had it restyled in curls round her face which made her feel better.

Chester was a lovely city, and there was plenty for her to see and do. She walked the walls with one of her fellow guests, but to really enjoy herself she needed Ralph with her all the time. She went back to the hospital feeling rested and refreshed.

When Ralph's course finished, he passed out as a second lieutenant and was given a forty-eight-hour pass. He came to spend it at Elaine's house and June managed to get time off in order to spend one night there with him.

He met her outside the hospital in his new uniform. She felt very proud as she took his arm and walked with him to the bus stop but she had a sinking feeling in her stomach because she knew when this leave was over, it could be a very long time before she saw him again.

The time they shared passed in a flash. June went to see him off on the train to Aldershot. The station was crowded with other military personnel catching the same train. Woodside was the terminus and the train was standing at the platform. June had to take a firm grip on her emotions; she didn't want him to remember her in tears. 'I'll be preparing a big welcome for when you come back. We'll really have something to celebrate then.'

'To think of you waiting at home for me gives me something to keep me sane,' he told her, 'something to look forward to.' He turned to open the door of a carriage, tossed his newspaper on the vacant window seat, pushed his bag up on the luggage rack, and jumped down to put his arms round her and kiss her goodbye. June tried to smile and not look miserable.

'I'm afraid I may be sent abroad now,' he murmured in her ear.

That made June cling more tightly to him, she knew that was almost a certainty. 'I know . . .'

'If I don't come back—'

'Don't say that!'

'If the worst happens—'

She pulled her face away from his. 'There's no reason to suppose it will. We must both stay positive. Milo came back when we'd almost given up hope.'

'Yes, I know. Darling, I don't want you to grieve. Not like Queen Victoria did. I want you to pick yourself up and get on with your life. You're still very young and very pretty; sooner or later, you'll find somebody else.'

'No, I couldn't possibly do that.' The tears were flooding down her face now, she couldn't stop them. She heard the guard blow his whistle, saw Ralph climb back on the train through her tears and then he was gone.

CHAPTER TWENTY-FIVE

TWO WEEKS BEFORE CHRISTMAS 1940, Amy came home from school one day and Auntie Bessie said, 'I had a letter from your mother this morning. She says she'd like to come and see you again and bring your brother Milo.'

Amy was thrilled. 'I haven't seen Milo for ages.' When she sat down to have her tea, the letter was laid out on the table beside the bowl of strawberry junket for her to read.

She let out a scream of delight. 'They're bringing me a bike for Christmas. I'll be able to go to school on it. I won't have to get up early to catch the taxi.'

'And sometimes miss it,' Bessie added.

'Even if I do,' Amy laughed, 'I can still get to school before nine o'clock if I run part of the way.'

Her mother had written, '*I'm sorry for Amy's sake that we can't keep it a secret until Christmas Day, but I can see no way of doing that. She'll have time to look forward to it now.*'

'Isn't that marvellous?' Amy was excited. 'It isn't as if I still believed in Father Christmas. I've wanted a bike for ages.'

On the Sunday they were due, Amy was down on the road waiting for them for more than half an hour before they came. As the taxi pulled up at the bottom of the cwm, the first thing she saw was the bike strapped to the back with a scarlet ribbon fluttering from the seat. Between seeing that and Milo stepping out to swing her up into a hug in the way he always had, Amy was too intoxicated to speak.

'Amy.' He laughed with her. 'You're tons heavier than you used to be, I can hardly lift you.'

She felt a pang when she took a second look at her bike. 'It's not a fairy cycle like Glenys's.'

'You've grown too big for a fairy cycle,' Milo scoffed.

Her mother hugged her. 'This is just one size smaller than an adult bike,' she told her, 'and we've had a hard time getting a bike of any sort. June tried to buy one in the bike shop after our first visit, but they had no children's bikes in stock. Pa has been looking out for one in the auction rooms, but I put a firm order in at the bike shop and eventually they got a few in.'

Amy and Milo carried it up the *cwm*, walking one behind the other on the narrow path, while Leonie carried the suitcase they'd brought. Jack and Bessie met them at the gate and took them in to have a Sunday lunch of roast pork and the first of Bessie's Christmas puddings.

Afterwards, Amy watched her mother bring out gift-wrapped packages for her as well as for Bessie and Jack. They gave her eggs and butter to fill the suitcase, as well as a boiling fowl already cleaned and plucked.

Leonie beamed. 'That's a huge treat. It will make us a couple of excellent meals and I'm very grateful for all this food. You're very kind to me as well as to Amy.'

While her mother helped with the washing-up, Amy pulled Milo out to see the farm. They stroked Fly and went round the henhouses collecting eggs.

'D'you know,' Milo said, 'there's no reason why we shouldn't keep a few hens at home. The ration is one egg a week per person and if we forgo that we can buy poultry food instead.'

When they went back indoors he asked Jack's advice on keeping poultry. 'Amy does most of it for us,' he said. 'You'll need to make some sort of a shelter for them in your garden, with a perch and a couple of nesting boxes. They'll need an outside pen to provide fresh air and ground for them to scratch in. Then it's just a matter of giving them food and water.'

'They'll eat kitchen scraps of any sort,' Bessie added, 'potato peelings and carrot tops.'

'We could give you a couple of pullets,' Jack said, 'if you could take them home on the bus.'

Amy saw her mother draw back at the thought.

'Why not?' Milo was enthusiastic. 'Would it be possible?'

'I don't see why not. A cardboard box with air holes in, we might have one somewhere. We buy day-old chicks sometimes and they come that way. But your best bet would be to take a hen that's gone broody with a clutch of eggs and see if you can hatch your own.'

'I'd like to try,' Milo said.

Leonie looked alarmed. 'You'd have to make a pen first.'

'Yes,' Jack said, 'and right now we don't have a young broody hen. Not one that's worth taking all that way.'

When Amy had seen her family off she came back feeling very low but Jack picked up her bike. 'Come on,' he said, and took her down to their nearest neighbouring farm. 'We need to ask if you can keep your bike in their shed where I keep mine.'

It was a little further for her to cycle along the road to and from school, but there was an unmade lane she could ride down even if it would be a bit steep to come up. It cut out the cwm and the very steep sideland.

That agreed, they looked in the shed and Jack was about to roll her bike alongside his when Amy said, 'I want to try it out before I go to school on it tomorrow.'

'You'll be all right? You've ridden a bike before?'

'A fairy cycle, yes.'

'Then you'll have no trouble with this. Go down the lane to the road, there's nowhere else you could try it out. I'll see you back home when you've had enough. Be careful now.'

Amy wheeled it into the lane. This was a bit scary but she preferred to do it on her own. The bike felt big and awkward and the lane was steep with an uneven surface of small stones and dusty earth because it hadn't rained recently.

She wobbled but regained balance and with the brakes firmly on rolled down to the road. She had to get off to open and close the gate at the bottom but once on the tarmacked road it felt wonderful. She rode through a hamlet and on to Glenys's house. Glenys was delighted to see her and wanted her to stay and play, but her father said, 'It's getting dark. I think, Amy, you'd better go back. Bessie will be worried about you.'

He was right about that. It was pitch dark when she wheeled her bike into the shed and she had to walk up two fields after that. Bessie was scolding Jack for letting her go when he did. 'There isn't a light showing anywhere, I was afraid you wouldn't find your way back in this blackout.'

'But I did,' she said, and felt triumphant at having succeeded in managing her bike. It had been marvellous to feel the wind in her hair as she sped along. 'I love it,' she told Jack. 'It's the best Christmas present I've ever had.'

'And it isn't even Christmas yet,' Bessie pointed out. 'By rights you shouldn't ride that bike until it is.'

She had ordered a goose for Christmas. Many of the nearby farms kept a flock of geese to fatten, though Bessie and Jack did not. The week beforehand, she was out helping her relatives pluck feathers as the birds were made ready for the oven.

'I'm glad those geese have gone,' Amy said. She found the big flocks of geese frightening, more frightening than the big carthorse at the farm below, whose field she had to cross to reach the bike shed. The geese squawked and screeched and hissed when they heard her coming and as she crossed their farmyard, they'd put their necks straight out and come rushing at her.

'Take a stick,' Bessie advised and continued to send her on errands to her relatives. 'Wear your wellingtons so they can't nip your legs.'

Amy had a lovely time over the holiday. Bessie entertained her relatives and Amy went with them when they were invited back. They had big dinners with Christmas puddings, cakes, mince pies and trifles to follow. There was no shortage of food on the farms. Once the dishes had been cleared away, they played cards round the table.

Amy still had presents to open on Christmas morning. Mum had made her a new coat for best and she had books from June and chocolate from Milo.

June felt terrible having said goodbye to Ralph, knowing he'd be sent to fight in some war zone. He'd told her he'd been issued with tropical kit but that was his only clue as to his destination. But soon she had a letter from him giving his postal address as Middle East Forces. He told her he wasn't allowed to let her know exactly where, and letters could be censored. Milo guessed immediately that it was Egypt and a good posting for him to have.

Pa said, 'I'm happy to say it's the one area of this war where the allies are proving successful. Once Mussolini joined in the fight on Hitler's side, he ordered his troops to march on Egypt. The Suez Canal is a vital route and it would have been a feather in his cap to capture that, but our troops have got the Italians on the run.'

'That will please Ralph.'

'It pleases all England,' Pa said proudly.

Ralph told her he was working in battalion headquarters so she knew he would be some distance from the front line. He said his office had once been a big hotel and when work was over for the day he would walk to another luxury hotel and swim in their pool. He wrote of palm trees and gardens and told her that troops were removed from the front line and sent to his area for rest and relaxation. Milo thought he could be in Cairo or Alexandria, and if so he was very lucky.

June took a greater interest in the fighting in that area. It seemed that once Italy joined the war, it launched an attack on Egypt and the Italians were repulsed by British and Australian forces under General Wavell. She was greatly heartened. Ralph wrote almost daily and told her more than once that he thought she was in a more dangerous place than he was and she mustn't worry about him. She began to believe him and was able to relax.

She settled down at the hospital and now she wasn't rushing out to spend time with Ralph she found her fellow nurses friendly and ready to include her in their outings. She also gave more time and attention to her lectures and became interested. Like everybody else she was frightened during air raids but she'd been drilled in what she must do if the hospital received a direct hit or was badly damaged and began to feel she could enjoy her new career. She was glad it was considered vital war work.

In January the air raids grew worse and Milo wanted, above everything else, to be fit and well again. He wanted to return to army life and catch up with his friends in the unit. He hoped that in another month when he next went back to the hospital to be assessed, he'd be passed fit to return to active service.

In the meantime, he busied himself about the house doing some of the cooking. He and Mum had looked round the garden and they'd decided that the small shed built on to the end of the house for storing bikes and prams could easily be turned into a henhouse. He fixed an old broom handle across it to make a perch and found a couple of wooden boxes for them to lay their eggs in. The difficult part was how to fence off a few yards of garden to make an outside pen for them. He asked in the two hardware shops if they had chicken wire but the answer was no.

He managed to get some diesel and one day when it wasn't too cold he took Oswald Hemmings out fishing in the *Vera May*. They brought back a good catch of dabs, small flat fish which were a bit bony but the flesh was delicious. He and Pa feasted on them late at night when he got home. Mum was already asleep.

The next morning he took some of the remaining dabs

round to Beechwood and gave them to Colleen Greenway who was delighted. Alison, one of Pat's older sisters, happened to be at home that day and was called down from upstairs to admire them. He hadn't seen Alison for years and rather liked the look of her.

He told them about his plans to keep hens to provide them with eggs, and the need to build a pen for them.

'There's a trellis in our garden you could take,' Mrs Greenway said. 'It used to cut off our vegetable patch from the lawn near the house. Last year the vegetable patch was put down to potatoes and carrots and part of the lawn dug up to grow salad vegetables.'

Alison took him out to the back garden to show him. 'Once this trellis supported a prolific honeysuckle hedge,' she said, 'but the hedge was getting old.'

'It was planted twenty-five years ago,' her mother called from the back door, 'and it was dying off so we dug it up.'

'We had to renew the trellis a few years earlier so you might get a bit more use from it.'

Milo was enthusiastic. 'It's sound, in very good condition and just what I need. If you can spare it I'd be very grateful.'

Alison helped him dismantle it there and then, and they balanced it on a wheelbarrow and made several trips to take it round to Mersey Reach.

He'd taken Floris Jenkins to the pictures several times and knew she and Henry would both be at work that afternoon, so he left another parcel of dabs at their back door and put a note through the front to tell them the fish were there. He then called to see his mother at the shop and asked for advice on how to make a fish pie for supper tonight.

It was lunchtime when he got home and he and Pa ate two dabs each with bread and margarine and spent some of the afternoon making the last of the fish into a fish pie. The next morning, he was surprised when Pa offered to come out and help him erect the trellis to make the hen pen.

'We can use the garden wall for one side,' Milo said, 'and then there'll be enough trellis to do the job.'

'Is six feet high enough? Can hens fly?'

'I don't know. I'll write to Amy and get her to find out.'

'I reckon you'll still need wire netting,' his father pointed out. 'The holes in the trellis are big enough for chicks to escape through. You could plant a hedge on the outside but it would take time to grow.'

Milo was happy enough pottering round doing things to fill his day and he thought it helped him both feel better and recover from his injuries. Floris came round the following evening to thank him for the fish and happened to mention that her father was absolutely exhausted because he was out fire-watching every time there was an air raid and was also putting in a fifty-hour working week at Camell Laird's.

'I could fire-watch,' Milo said. 'I feel I ought to be doing something to help instead of enjoying this endless leisure.'

'You're on sick leave.' Floris smiled. 'You should concentrate on getting well.'

But he went home with Floris and spoke to her father about fire-watching. 'Take him round to see Alfred Beale,' he told his daughter. 'He organises the fire-watching rota and lives at the end of our road.'

'We're glad of any help we can get,' Mr Beale assured Milo. 'We're all tired out because the moon is full and we're having a spell of good clear nights and Jerry is making the most of them.'

At that moment, the ominous sound they knew so well rose and fell, wailing out its warning.

'Nine fifteen, they're early tonight.' Alfred Beale rose wearily to his feet. 'Come on, lad. If you're willing, I'll show you what we'll need you to do and you can tell me when the all-clear sounds whether you'll do a regular stint.'

'I'll be glad to.' Milo gulped.

'Do you need to let your family know what you're doing?'

'Yes. Should I wear warmer clothes? I could run home.'

'No time for that, use my phone and I'll find you a warm coat. You run home, Floris, and tell your dad to take a night off and try to get some sleep in the Anderson. I'll show Milo what's needed and he can take his place.'

Milo heard his father pick up the phone at home. 'I'm going to learn about fire-watching, Pa,' he told him. 'Tell Mum I won't be home till this raid is over and possibly not then. Tell her she's not to worry.'

CHAPTER TWENTY-SIX

STEVE SLID THE PHONE back on its rest, feeling shocked. He was ashamed that he'd made no effort to do what his son had done. He'd sat back and let everybody else fight this war to keep him safe. He'd felt it was his right, he'd done his bit. But Miles had already done his bit too and he was ready to do more.

Milo came home at breakfast time covered with thick grey dust. He paused at the back door to shake it off the cap and coat he'd borrowed from Alfred Beale. 'This must be the dust of ages,' he said. 'Everything near a bombed building is coated with it.'

Steve was stirring the porridge pan on the stove. 'They say it's old plaster and brick dust.' He'd read about it in the newspapers.

'It smells horrible, stinks, and gets into everything.' Milo slumped on to a chair at the kitchen table, his face greyish white with fatigue.

'Should you be doing this?' Leonie asked, sliding a cup of tea in front of him. 'You're tired out.'

'I'm dog tired, but yes, I should.'

His father asked, 'You've been fire-watching?'

'Yes, but once the all-clear sounded, that wasn't needed, so

I followed Alfred Beale who went to help the civil defence workers and ARP wardens. It wasn't all over for them.'

'What did you have to do?'

'Dig into the wreckage for bodies.'

'What? What had happened?'

'It was behind the market. When the bombs started dropping last night, a double-decker bus stopped in front of the public shelter there, and the passengers all ran inside. Half an hour later, it got a direct hit.'

'Were they killed?' Leonie asked horrified. 'How many?'

'They had fourteen bodies out when I left, but they're still digging. They sent me home, said I was past it but everybody else was exhausted too. I can go to bed now, Mum, most them have to turn round and do a day's work.'

'Oh my God!'

'I must wash my hands and face before I eat.' Milo got shakily to his feet and went off towards the bathroom.

When he came back, Steve said, 'I want you to take me with you next time you go fire-watching.'

He saw the surprise on their faces as they both turned to look at him. 'I think it's about time I gave a hand,' he said. 'In a war like this, it's all hands to the pump, isn't it?'

Since the New Year, Amy had been phoning her mother every Friday afternoon on the way home from school. Mum was always at the shop at that time of day and always had plenty of news about the family. Quite often she rang Pat too, she was always bubbling with things to tell her.

She wished Pat could sometimes phone her. If occasionally Amy didn't ring, it was because it cost twopence to make a call and that would buy her a bar of chocolate or some sweets in town the next day. There was one shopkeeper who saved sweets under the counter for her.

She also liked to buy *The Girls' Crystal*. When June had been her age, she'd loved a magazine called *The Schoolgirl* and bought it every week and then she bound them together to make two huge volumes. She'd handed them on to Amy, and once she'd started to read those she'd decided she'd grown out of Enid Blyton's Sunny Stories.

In *The Schoolgirl* most of the stories were written by Frank Richards, a prolific writer of stories set in both boys' and girls' boarding schools. Amy knew there was no chance of her going to a school like that but she was sure she would have enjoyed it, it sounded as though the girls had great fun.

The Schoolgirl was no longer being published and *The Girls' Crystal* was the nearest Amy could buy to that, but paper shortages meant it was miserably thin and the main picture covered only half the front page to make room for some of the story. The stories were no longer by Frank Richards and Amy thought them not nearly so good.

Auntie Bessie had only a large Welsh bible and a cookery book, but when her friends and relatives heard that Amy liked to read, they brought her their books and allowed her to keep them for as long as she needed. That way she came by many of the classics like *Alice in Wonderland* and *The Wind in the Willows*.

At school, reading practice was occasionally undertaken as a group and everybody dreaded it. As book monitor, Amy handed out the reading books. The pupils lined up against the wall and each had to read aloud in turn a paragraph from the same story, while the rest followed with their fingers on the written page. Amy had never got over her fear of Mrs Roberts and always did what was expected of her as quickly and as well as she could, hoping to avoid being noticed.

Some of her fellow pupils found reading aloud hard and she knew that having Mrs Roberts' full attention made them very uncomfortable. It was a long drawn out procedure and Mrs Roberts' impatience seemed to build up, making even adequate readers quake in their shoes.

'Come along, Gwilym. You're mumbling. Open your mouth when you read or I can't hear. Now sound out the first letter. Yes, it is F. Do concentrate. You could read this word at the beginning of term with no trouble.'

Amy felt for him as he stumbled and mumbled and hoped against hope that when her turn came she wouldn't be made to feel stupid by Mrs Roberts. But she knew what it was to be tongue-tied in these circumstances and she was afraid her brain would be addled. Well before it was her turn to read she counted out the paragraphs to find which one would be hers. Closing her mind against the struggling efforts of others, she read it through carefully. Worryingly, it had only three lines. Would Mrs Roberts want her to read more? Most of the paragraphs were twice that length.

To be on the safe side, she went through the next paragraph too, to make sure she could read the whole thing smoothly.

Amy's heart was thudding when her turn came. She held her book well away from her and spoke up as clearly as she could. She managed her first three lines without a fault, and then because she knew she could, she swept straight into the next paragraph.

'Stop!' Mrs Roberts called impatiently. 'Stop, that's enough.'
Thankfully Amy did, she'd come through unscathed.

Leonie walked home from her shop one evening to find both
Steve and Milo in the kitchen and the meal well in hand. She
knew as soon as she went in that they had good news to impart.

'It's Amy,' Milo said. 'Her teacher has written to us.'

'What has she done?'

Steve smiled. 'It seems she's brighter than our other two.'
He pushed the opened letter across the table to Leonie. It was
addressed to both her and Steve.

*Amy's reading ability is above average for her age, and I believe she
shows grammar school capability. If you are agreeable, please
complete the enclosed form and I will enter her for the scholarship
examination and prepare her for it.*

*Should she be successful, she would be awarded a grammar
school place next September.*

'That's marvellous.' Leonie was delighted. 'I was afraid changing schools and leaving home would upset her schoolwork.'

'Little Amy's all there,' Milo said, 'as bright as a button.'

'Yes.' Steve beamed at her. 'It's a good idea, it means we
won't have to pay school fees for her.'

Soon after that, Amy was working at the sums the whole class
had been set when Mrs Roberts summoned her to her desk.
She jerked to her feet, shocked to be singled out. A summons to
come forward and stand in front of Mrs Roberts was dreaded
by them all. It usually meant a punishment.

'Amy,' she said. 'Recently I wrote to your parents saying I thought you might be capable of passing the scholarship exam and going to the grammar school. I've received a reply from your mother saying she is pleased and very much wants you to try.'

Amy could feel her cheeks burning. She didn't want any more changes, she was getting used to this school now.

'I shall set homework for you to do every night to prepare you for this examination. It means you'll have to work hard. Are you willing to do this?'

'Yes, Mrs Roberts.' If Mum wanted it, what else could she say? She was about to turn away.

'Right, well, you might as well start straight away.' Two notebooks were pushed in front of her. 'These are your homework books. One is for arithmetic and the other for English. Write your name on them, and this is the work I want you to do tonight.' Two examination papers from previous years were put on top. 'Do questions four, five, and six on the arithmetic paper and questions one and three on the English.'

Amy stared at them in shock. 'Yes, Mrs Roberts.'

'I'll go through your answers with you tomorrow.'

'Yes, Mrs Roberts. Thank you.'

Amy felt there was no end to the schoolwork she was given and found she had very little time to herself in the evenings after that.

Ralph was a good letter writer and June received letters from him regularly. They were love letters and she thought them quite romantic. He told her how much she meant to him and how much he longed for traditional married life. 'I stayed a bachelor for far too long,' he wrote. 'I didn't realise what I was missing.'

He also wrote about the plans he was making for the end of the war. They'd buy a house and set up home together; they'd have children and he wanted nothing more than to go back to his job in the bank and be a good husband and father.

The nurses collected their letters from behind webbing on a board in the corridor outside the dining room. Sometimes the post was sorted into alphabetical order and available by the mid-morning coffee break, but often June had to wait until she went into dinner – they had their main meal in the middle of the day. She had developed the habit of checking every time she passed the board and her air letters were easy to pick out. Today, on her way into first dinner, she pulled out another letter.

She had no time to read it and anyway Ralph's letters were something to savour and dream over. She pushed it into her pocket with a warm feeling that all was well in her world. Dinner was bangers and mash with onion gravy and she laughed with Mary O'Leary about a disaster she'd had in the sluice that morning.

As she was leaving the dining room, her eye scanned the letters board and she noticed an orange envelope where her letters were usually displayed. She pulled it out and was shocked to find it was a telegram addressed to her. She knew what this could mean and could hardly breathe as she ripped it open.

We regret to inform you that Lieutenant Ralph Harvey has been killed in action. Please accept our sincere condolences.

June felt her head swimming in disbelief and everything was going black.

'June, what's the matter?' She felt Doreen Brown catch at her and try to hold her.

When she came round she was lying on a bed in the nurses' sick bay and the full horror of what had happened hit her. She couldn't stop the tears coursing down her face and in her agony she showed Sister Jackson the telegram and the wedding ring she wore round her neck. She admitted that she'd secretly married Ralph. He was her husband. Sister was sympathetic but asked one of the doctors to prescribe a sedative and June slept for most of the afternoon.

She felt no better when she woke up. Matron came to see her and told her she should never have married secretly but she gave her two days off duty for this week. June got up and went back to the nurses' home where she washed her face and changed out of her uniform. She caught the bus and went to her mother's shop. She knew she'd be in time to catch both her and Elaine before they went home.

She put her arms round Elaine and told her about her brother, and they wept together. Mum was both sympathetic and supportive but for June it didn't seem to help. If Ralph was dead nothing could help. Her future couldn't be as she'd expected, everything was ruined forever.

CHAPTER TWENTY-SEVEN

J UNE KNEW HER FAMILY and friends had done their best to comfort her but she felt bereft. Nothing could possibly help her now. She couldn't understand what had caused Ralph's death when he'd told her he was in a safer place than she was. It had come with savage suddenness.

She went back on duty when her two days' leave was up, determined not to weep any more. She almost broke down when she found her friends offering words of sympathy and was only able to keep going by keeping her mind set on the next task she had to do. She couldn't sleep and hardly knew what day it was, she felt like a zombie.

It was a week later that she received a letter from Ralph's commanding officer. She stuffed it into her pocket to read later when she was alone, but all afternoon she was torn with curiosity about what it would tell her. She tore it open in the sluice to peep at it.

Your husband was a valuable member of my team and very popular with his fellow officers.

When another nurse came in she slid it back into her pocket, it appeared to be no more than a letter of condolence, but that evening in her bedroom she found she was wrong. He told her how Ralph had died.

It seemed a lone plane had flown over the city and without warning it had strafed the military establishments with machine-gun fire. It had never happened before and had not been thought to be a danger, but in times of war such attacks did happen.

Lieutenant Ralph Harvey and another officer were unfortunately crossing the open compound that divided the buildings making up battalion headquarters at the time, and had been unable to find cover. Lieutenant Ralph Harvey had been hit by two bullets, one in his leg and another in his head and was killed instantly. He had not suffered.

June lay back on her bed and thought of Ralph. She was glad to know exactly what had happened but it seemed such a waste of his life. He hadn't helped to win the war, he'd done nothing heroic. He'd just been unlucky enough to be in the wrong place at the wrong time. It was only six weeks since she'd said goodbye to him.

A few days later she received two more letters, one was from the battalion padre who sent his sincere condolences and said Ralph would be sadly missed. The other was from a fellow officer who described himself as Ralph's friend, and told her again of the circumstances in which he'd been killed.

I'm totally gutted. We counted ourselves lucky, we were enjoying ourselves here, doing something useful to help the war effort in what we thought was a safe and pleasant backwater. However, at the back of our minds we all realised that in wartime the worst could happen. We both felt we had to write letters to our loved ones in case it did. I'm so sorry Ralph copped it and I'm enclosing the letter he asked me to send to you.

It was sealed in its envelope and her name was written in Ralph's handwriting. With shaking fingers she slit it open and drew out the letter. It was dated six weeks earlier.

My darling darling June,

Today, one of the men I came out with was killed and it has driven home that it could just as easily have been me. If it had been, I know you'd be devastated so I'm writing this just in case. But I hope with all my heart that you and I can open it together when this war is over.

You have given me reason to live. I was making a mess of my life until I met you and you turned it all round for me. It took me a long time to find you and I want you to know I've never loved anyone as I have you. You are everything to me and to leave you standing on that railway platform was the most painful thing that's happened to me.

We've made plans for our future. We want only what other couples want, a home and children of our own, and if we could have those I know we would be happy for the rest of our lives.

If this is not to be, I want you to try and forget me. You are still very young. I want you to live your life to the full and find happiness elsewhere and enjoy the best the world has to offer. If the worst does happen to me, don't look back and mourn your loss. Try to think of me watching over you from the next world, wishing you well, loving you and urging you on. If it's possible I certainly will be.

Darling June, I wish I could be with you now to comfort you. I would be if I could.
   All my love always,
      Ralph.

Ralph's death was a shock to Milo and his parents, too, were deeply upset. June had spent two days at home weeping and her eyes were red and swollen. It upset them all to see her like that.

'Why did we make a scene about them marrying?' his mother sighed. 'It must be a comfort to her now that she was his wife.'

His father was very much on edge. 'As Ralph has been killed I can't see it makes any difference to her now,' he said grumpily, but Milo knew he very much regretted standing out against him. He admitted as much. 'I was wrong about him,' he said. 'I think he would have stood by June.'

The next time Milo was about to report for fire-watching, Pa set out with him. He was surprised to hear that Pa had joined the Civil Defence Service and had undergone some training so he could be fitted into the team.

Milo had been given a regular fire-watching position at the top of the church tower which gave a wide view across Merseyside, but the stone steps to get up there were narrow, steep, uneven, and there was no handrail. Many found them difficult but for Pa they were impossible.

Instead, Pa's training enabled him to take charge of the telephones in the ARP post and direct the wardens to help where it was most needed. It was his job to summon ambulances and police as required. Milo was impressed and in the days that followed he found the team welcomed Pa.

Milo was due to return to the hospital in Chester to be assessed and had been doing regular exercises to improve his fitness, knowing he'd be put through his paces in the gym. He expected to be found fit for work. His unit was now fighting in the desert in North Africa and he hoped to be sent to join them.

He was familiar with the hospital, its routine and staff, and was relaxed when he reported in. He was not alone, there were nine of them recalled for assessment and he'd met most of them on previous visits. To see them again was a pleasure, though he could see some were nervous of the outcome. It didn't bother him to strip and be examined by the doctors. He enjoyed the session in the gym with the physiotherapists. He hadn't managed to do all he'd been asked but he thought he'd done reasonably well.

The next morning when he presented himself to the senior doctors to hear the outcome, he was looking forward to being told he was fit and fully recovered. When it was his turn to enter the room, he saluted and stood to attention. Only when he was told to stand at ease did he notice that the atmosphere was sombre. The proceedings were very formal and Milo was soon filled with foreboding.

'We are sorry,' he was told. 'We find you are no longer fit enough to serve.'

It took him a moment to take in what they meant. 'But I feel quite well again. I'm over my injuries. I've been fire-watching four nights a week.' The worst he'd been expecting was being told he needed to take another month's convalescence and return for further assessment.

'You've certainly recovered to that point, but the army expects serving soldiers to be super fit. They have to be able to cope with modern warfare. We feel it would not be fair to you to expect more of you than you can give.'

Milo felt confused. He was being put out of the army! Discharged! He found that hard to believe. He was told to present himself somewhere else to start the process. Somewhere along the way, he was told he'd be given a pension. Pa had been given a pension when this had happened to him. But Pa had lost a leg, while he was perfectly all right.

Leonie was at the shop treadling hard on a long straight seam when her phone rang. She only had to hear one word to recognise Steve's voice. 'They were queuing at the fish shop for cod,' he told her, 'but half an hour later when my turn came, it had all gone. I had to use the ration book and get some mince for tonight.'

'Thank you for doing the shopping, at least we've got something for Milo to eat when he comes home from the hospital.'

'Tell me what I have to do,' he said, 'and I can get the meal started.'

She was delighted that Steve seemed to have turned over a new leaf. He no longer expected her to wait on him. He was helping with the housework and getting up to help make the breakfast porridge. He'd even enrolled in the Civil Defence Service.

When she got home from work that evening, Steve was in the kitchen, a pan simmering on the stove.

'Will you taste the stew, Leonie?' he said. 'It doesn't taste like the stews you make. Have I done it right?' He was washing cabbage at the sink and had the potatoes ready peeled.

'Perhaps a little more salt,' she suggested. 'But it's fine. You're a marvellous help to me.'

'I saw this queue at the off-licence and joined it. I was able to get a bottle of sherry. Let's have a glass now.'

Leonie got out the glasses. 'You've really changed. I do appreciate your help with the chores.'

He poured a glass of sherry for her and said, 'There's a war on. I have to do my bit like everybody else, don't I?'

Leone smiled. 'Being more active seems to be doing you good.' He was no longer depressed and angry. As soon as he heard the wail of the air-raid siren, he was off out, whether he was supposed to be on duty or not.

'It's what most of the men do,' he told Leonie. 'We're all volunteers. We want to help all we can. I wish I'd been able to get something more exciting than mince. Milo will want to celebrate if he's been passed as fully recovered.'

'He'll have been well fed at the hospital over the last day or so, but . . .' she broke off. 'Here he is.' A blast of cold air followed him into the kitchen.

Steve knew at first glance that things had not gone as Milo had hoped. He looked thoroughly miserable.

'What's happened, love?' Leonie asked.

Slowly he took off his coat and turned to face them. 'I'm to be invalided out of the army, pensioned off.'

Steve was shocked. 'Discharged on grounds of ill health?'

Milo pulled a face. 'They said I had recovered from my injuries but they were afraid I'd never achieve the super fitness required in today's fighting forces, that it wouldn't be fair to send me into battle.'

'I was afraid you were being over-optimistic,' Steve said

dourly. 'The wardens sent you home when you were digging the injured out, didn't they? Said you were spent, hadn't the energy left to lift the spade.' He could see the pain on his son's face.

'The point is, Pa, what am I going to do now?'

'George will find you a slot in the firm. We've been ordered to give our staff their jobs back when the war's over.'

'No, Pa, that's not what I want. I shall look for something else, something that interests me more – something to help the war effort.'

'Well there's plenty of work like that about.' Steve reflected that his son was coping with the problems his serious injury had caused far better than he'd ever done himself.

He spent some time reading in bed that night, and when Leonie put out the light she said, 'Milo's taken it very well. I was very afraid he'd . . .'

Steve heard his own voice grate. 'Expect you to wait on him hand and foot as I did?'

'Well, not exactly, but . . .'

'It was a humbling experience to see him take up his life again exactly where he'd left off. He fully expected nothing to change, but if he's not fit enough to serve in the army, then obviously his capabilities are different now.'

'He's doing his best,' Leonie said softly. 'He's not going to let it limit what he does. Not if he can help it.'

'I wish I'd been as strong as him.' Steve couldn't hold back a heavy sigh. 'All these years I've been wallowing in self-pity.'

'The doctors were treating you for depression.'

'They were, but why did I always look on the black side of

everything? I saw myself as a physical wreck and never even tried. Miles pointed out that I was a selfish shit who thought only of himself and that you all had to fight for anything that wasn't my idea.'

'I know, but—'

'I took it badly but it was the shake-up I needed. It brought me to my senses, that and the fact that he set me an example by getting back on his feet and going out to live his life. He showed me what I should have done.'

'Well, you're trying now,' Leonie said and turned towards him. 'Suddenly you're much more like the man I married.'

Steve was so relieved that he took her in his arms and kissed her in the way he used to when he was young.

It was weeks since Milo had first written to Duggie Jenkins and he'd posted off some boating magazines and another note since, but he'd heard nothing from him. Floris had told him they often didn't hear from him for weeks and he knew from hard experience that it wasn't always possible to write. But when Milo came home from the hospital he found a letter from Duggie propped up on his dressing table. Mum said it had arrived yesterday. He threw himself on the bed to read it and Duggie's words leapt off the paper. He hadn't changed a bit, he was still his old cheerful self.

Later, Milo went round to the Jenkins' house when he knew they'd be home from work. Floris danced to the door when he rang the bell.

'We each got a letter from him this morning. Dad's took a month to get here, but mine only a few days. At least we know he's alive and well.'

Milo offered them his letter from Duggie to read. 'There's quite a lot about his life there.'

When Floris handed it back, she said, 'He was obviously delighted to hear from you.'

'How are you?' her father said. 'How did you get on at the hospital?'

'They discharged me, but I've also been discharged from the army. I'm no longer fit enough to fight.'

Floris looked shocked. 'But you always seem so well to us.'

'Yes.' He admitted it had come as a shock to him and told them how it had happened. 'It's left me feeling at a bit of a loss. I can't make up my mind what to do next.'

'You were working in your family business, weren't you?'

'Yes, but I didn't enjoy it. I've told Pa I don't want to go back. With the war, it's losing ground anyway.'

'Then give yourself a day or two to think about it,' Henry Jenkins advised. 'It's a new career you're looking for. Think about what you like doing, what you enjoy. There are jobs everywhere. Right now, you can have your pick.'

'I wanted to go to sea, but now . . .' Milo hesitated. 'Something to do with ships perhaps.'

Floris laughed. 'I work for Beauforte Air Sea Rescue. That's to do with ships and Dad works for Cammell Laird's.'

'We're desperate for more staff,' Henry said, 'and I suspect Beauforte's in the same position. We're building ships as fast as we can to replace those being sunk in the Atlantic by U-boats.'

'And they all need full safety equipment before they put to sea.' Floris smiled. 'Both are considered vital for the war effort.'

'What exactly do you do?' Milo asked Henry.

'I'm a ship's architect. There are vacancies in the drawing office if you fancy something like that.'

'I do, I think that would suit me.'

'Think about it first,' Henry said. 'Don't rush into the first thing that sounds halfway suitable. Find out what else there is available to you. Look in the newspapers, go to the library, talk to people. Think about doing the job hour after hour, day after day for years on end. Come back next week and we'll mull it over. Perhaps I can help.'

When Floris showed him out, she said, 'Don't mind, Dad, Milo. He treats you like he does Duggie. He's missing him.'

Milo had found him a helpful support. 'He talks a lot of sense.'

While working on the ward, June had little time to dwell on her loss and that went for the time she spent in the classroom too. She needed to keep her mind on what she was doing to survive. It was when she was off duty that she missed Ralph most. She had plenty of company from her fellow nurses and that helped. She knew they all tried to include her in trips to the cinema or to a dance hall. 'You need to get out and about more,' they told her, 'not mope here in your room.'

June didn't feel ready to go out dancing yet. She didn't want to talk to other men. She knew several of her fellow student nurses were older than her and were still seeking boyfriends. But marrying Ralph had changed her, made her grow up in a hurry. She still wore Ralph's wedding ring on a gold chain round her neck under her uniform.

Only rarely now did she have a storm of tears. When she needed comfort, she took out Ralph's letter to read again. It was becoming creased but it eased her mind. For June it was enough to feel she would survive and that she was doing her bit at the hospital to help the war effort.

As usual, Nick Bailey was expecting Tom and Elaine to come and stay for the weekend. He enjoyed their company; he was envious of their stable marriage and their twins.

When he'd told them he'd proposed to Heather, Tom had said straight away, 'She's a stunning looking girl but she's too young for you. She'll not want to stay at home every evening listening to the wireless. Do you have the energy to keep up with her?'

Nick thought he had and he was tired of being on his own. 'I'm in a rut. I need to get out and about more.' He'd felt ready to have another try at marriage. 'Heather will be good for me.'

She was equally keen to be married and it seemed pointless to delay it at his age. It took place only two months later in the register office.

Heather had boundless energy, she enjoyed dancing, racing, rowing on the river, she wanted him to take her to theatres, cinemas and for meals out. Nick couldn't concentrate in the office; he felt tired and grew less enthusiastic about going out. There was no let-up for him at the weekends. Tom and Elaine bored Heather; they came too often, and as for those twins . . .

'Everything revolves round those tiresome children,' she complained. 'They climb all over me and I'm sick of playing Snap, Ludo and Snakes and Ladders.'

After six months of marriage, Nick was afraid Tom had been right because they were growing tetchy with each other.

He suggested that being together at work as well as at home was perhaps too much.

'Would you like to look for a different job?' he'd asked. Women without young children were required to work in wartime and employers were in need of extra staff of every sort. She found a new job the following week.

'I'm to be secretary to the manager of a luxurious hotel, the Cavanagh. I'm looking forward to it. I think it should be fun.'

In the following weeks, Nick thought Heather was happier, she said she was enjoying her new job. But it left him short-handed in the office and he couldn't get a reasonable replacement for her. Heather chatted about making friends with the people she was working with and started going out in the evenings with the girls – to a dancing class, she said, and she was enjoying that too.

He missed her company. He thought he was letting her down. 'You don't have to go with other girls,' he told her. 'I'll take you anywhere you want to go.'

He'd expected Heather to take him up on that but she didn't. 'I'm quite happy to go with my friends,' she'd said coldly.

It had occurred to Nick that he could take her out to dinner on Friday nights, together with Tom and Elaine. He thought Heather would be pleased and it would help to repay Elaine for all the times he'd eaten at her house and would also help to stretch the rations. The problem was, the twins would have to remain with Olive and Aunt Bernie until Saturday morning.

He discussed it with Tom and booked a table at Heather's favourite restaurant but the arrangement didn't please either her or the twins and they did it only once. The tiffs he had with Heather became more serious rows and they were having them more often. He did his best to keep the peace but it wasn't always possible.

Nick knew he was failing yet again to achieve a happy marriage. He didn't want to return to the loneliness of his widowed years. He found himself thinking more often of Leonie and Amy. When in the evenings he was left at home alone, he got out Leonie's letters and the photographs of Amy and read them all through again, regretting what couldn't be.

One Saturday evening, Heather had an argument with Elaine as they were preparing dinner and flounced to their bedroom and started to pack. 'Where are you going?' Nick asked, alarmed.

'Do you care?' she spat between her teeth.

'Of course I care, you're my wife.'

'But you care more about your so-called brother and his wife.'

'You can't just walk out on me like this.'

'Watch me,' she snapped, tossing a satin nightdress into her case. 'I've had enough of your friends. I don't like them, especially their kids. I'm going to the Cavanagh. I can share a friend's room for the night.' He knew many of the hotel staff lived in.

'But you'll come back?' Nick could feel sweat breaking out on his forehead.

'When they've gone,' she said and the door slammed behind her as she flounced out. He had a miserable time trying to explain it to Tom and Elaine.

'We're coming too often,' Elaine said sadly. 'We're putting on you, taking advantage. I'm sorry.'

'Blast this war,' Tom said. 'It makes life very difficult.'

That weekend, the Cliffords were relying on public transport to get home. This was happening more often and usually they left late on Sunday afternoon. Nick would go with the twins to the railway station to see Tom and Elaine off and then take the children back to Olive and Aunt Bernie. They always invited him to have his evening meal with them – he was, after all, one of the family. That Sunday they were surprised to find Heather wasn't with him and he had to give the painful explanation over again.

When he got home she was already curled up in bed. 'Your friends impose on us. Surely you can see there are things I'd rather do at the weekend than run round after them? I can't do what I want in my own home.'

Nick tried to explain about the bombing raids, about the help and support he'd received from Tom. But after that, she refused to stay at home if Tom and his family were coming. Tom didn't feel he could continue to come every weekend.

Nick began to fear that Heather might leave him. She was spending more time with people he'd never met than she was with him. He began to lose hope.

One Sunday night Heather returned with an empty case and started to pull her clothes from the wardrobe.

'I've made up my mind to go,' she said angrily. 'I've had enough of living with you. I'm sick and tired of it. I want a divorce. You know how to go about getting it, don't you?'

Nick had half expected that she'd ask for a separation, but a divorce, straight off like that? He'd dealt with a few couples seeking divorce and he knew it was deeply shaming and carried a stigma ever after. He was so shocked that it took him a moment to get his words out. 'You can't get a divorce on the spur of the moment. It's difficult and takes a long time. You need to think hard about it.'

'What d'you think I've been doing these last months?'

'We should talk—'

'I'm not going to let you talk me out of it. You're an old has-been. You never want to do anything except read and entertain your boring friends.'

He moistened his lips. 'Have you got—'

'Of course I've got another man.' Her beautiful eyes blazed defiance. He'd suspected for some time that she might have. 'I want to live with him, he's a lot more fun than you. He's got more go in him.'

Nick felt as though he'd been kicked. 'I see.'

'You'd have to be half blind not to. I haven't exactly kept him hidden.'

He was sorry and shocked that it was to end like this. Heather was not the woman he'd believed she was.

'It was a mistake,' she said. 'We both know that, don't we?'

His hands were trembling. He put them in his pockets. 'There have to be specific grounds on which a divorce can be granted.'

'I don't care about the grounds, desertion, adultery – anything. Whatever is easiest. You know more about that sort of thing than I do. I'll plead guilty to anything short of murder. I just want to be free of you.'

Nick felt he couldn't argue against that. At this stage he didn't want to, it would be futile. Nevertheless, his sense of loss was raw and painful. He felt he was touching bottom again.

Chapter Twenty-Eight

I T WAS THURSDAY, ELAINE HAD worked hard all day and was tired. She heard the phone ring and Tom pick it up while she was in the kitchen making a frugal supper from the leftover scraps from last night. They ate in the kitchen these days where it was warm and also saved the trouble of setting the dining-room table.

When the meal was ready, she went to the living-room door to call Tom in, and found he was still talking on the phone and signalling that he couldn't come just yet.

'Who is it?' she mouthed.

'Nick.'

Tom would usually tell him they were about to sit down to eat and he'd ring back later. Elaine could see from her husband's face that they were talking about something important and stayed to listen.

'If you feel like coming over for a bit of company, don't hesitate.'

Elaine pulled a face; she and Tom had already agreed that they wanted an early night.

'No, all right then. Yes, I know you might get caught in an air raid. I'm very sorry to hear this, Nick . . . yes, we'll come tomorrow for the weekend.' At last the phone went down.

'What's happened?' Elaine wanted to know.

'Heather's left him. She wants a divorce.'

'Well I'm not surprised, are you? We know things have been a bit sour between them for some time.'

'She's told him she admits adultery and desertion. She's given him names and dates and told him to file for it.'

'He'll be upset.'

'He's very upset, he was almost in tears. It seems Heather has gone off and left him to get the divorce started.'

'It should help to speed things up if she's ready to admit adultery.'

'It's going to take a long time, and it will cost him a pretty penny.'

'Poor old Nick, he doesn't have much luck with his women.'

'He was in Liverpool waiting for a train and sounded very down. That's why I asked him over. He doesn't want to handle the divorce himself, he'd been to ask William Lomax, his old boss, to take care of it.'

'I hope she isn't going to demand maintenance and all that. Come and eat. Our dinner's getting cold.'

'It seems Heather's got another boyfriend. A younger man, the manager of that hotel where she works.'

'Oh dear, you always said she was too young for him.'

'Too young and too flighty. Leonie is more his type.'

'But she wouldn't leave Steve.'

'We'll have to cheer him up over the weekend. What's this we're eating?'

'I thought I'd fry up these few slices of cold pork with the leftover mashed potato and add a few sprouts. A pity it's gone cold.'

Tom's fork prodded it without enthusiasm. 'What won't fatten will fill.'

Steve felt more alive than he had done in years. He no longer felt he'd been tossed on the scrap heap. He wore his uniform with pride and was building up a camaraderie with his fellow ARP wardens. He felt useful, part of a group helping the injured and the homeless.

During air raids, on three or four nights each week, he manned the telephones in the ARP post. He answered the calls for help, directed the other wardens to where they were needed and called out the ambulance and fire services as required. It had taken him a time to get on top of the job, but now he always knew where the bombs had fallen and exactly where his fellow wardens were working at any one time. Having only one leg was no disadvantage when it came to doing this.

In order to concentrate on his job he had to ignore the cacophony of noise outside, the explosions, the ambulance sirens and the big guns firing into the sky, and he felt relatively safe surrounded by sandbags in the cellar that was the ARP post. Steve only realised the full horror of what was happening when he listened to the agonised tales the other wardens told and saw the growing devastation, the craters and the rubble in the streets.

December had been a bad month, but they all thought the bombing was easing off in January, and in Birkenhead there were no deaths or serious injuries during February. Although the raids hadn't stopped, they began to hope that the worst was over. But in the bright moonlit nights of early March they realised how wrong they were. More enemy planes were coming with larger bomb loads. They were creating mayhem. One Saturday night, Steve had just sat down for supper when the air-raid warning sounded.

'Oh dear,' Leonie said. 'Why did I bother to make toad in the hole? Please eat it, both of you, before you go.'

Steve could see Miles shovelling his helping down as fast as he could. He tried to do the same, but as it would probably give him indigestion he slid what was left between two slices of bread to take with him. They were both still eating when they left home.

Steve knew he couldn't keep up with Miles, 'Don't wait for me,' he told him.

Miles slowed down though he had further to go. 'No sign of enemy planes yet,' he said easily.

'Don't get too blasé about it.'

They were approaching the ARP post. 'Bet you're the first here,' his son said and he was right. Steve noticed that Miles broke into a jog as he carried on towards the church.

This time, they had a longer than usual warning of the enemy's approach but it turned out to be the worst night Steve had ever experienced. One minute the wardens were all sitting around waiting and drinking tea, and in the next, bombs seemed to be exploding in the street outside. Steve found himself ducking involuntarily, his heart pounding like an engine. A string of bombs had fallen very close.

The calls for help came almost immediately and never stopped. Before long, he found himself alone in the cellar, all the wardens had been deployed. The only help he could offer then was to call out other services and give advice.

The wardens dribbled back in ones and twos as they dealt

with the problems and Steve sent them on to another call. The all-clear sounded about one in the morning and, heaving a sigh of relief, he put on the kettle to make tea. He had a moment then to wonder how Miles had fared and whether Leonie had been afraid to be on her own in a raid like that. He'd been really scared, feeling the next explosion could not miss the ARP post.

He knew his fellow wardens would not be back until they'd freed the last of those trapped by falling masonry, until the last of the injured were despatched to hospital and the last of those made homeless were found temporary shelter. He sat back to wait for them and sipped his tea, feeling he'd earned a rest.

Twenty minutes later, he was horrified to hear the warning wailing out again and within minutes it sounded as though all hell had broken loose. The phone never stopped ringing and people came banging on his door seeking help and first aid for others. Before long, he lost the electricity supply, but that was not uncommon. He lit the hurricane lamp and carried on handing out their store of spades, stretchers and other equipment. The phone went dead half an hour later but still the bombs rained down.

It was almost five o'clock when the all-clear sounded again and Steve was exhausted. He knew by then that just a hundred or so yards away on the border of Rock Ferry, the corner of Jubilee Street and Nelson Street had received a string of bombs early in the night.

The damage was extensive and there had been a considerable number of injuries as well as loss of life. Nelson Street had a row of suburban shops, the sort where the owner lived in the flat above. Jubilee Street jutted at right angles from it and consisted of two facing terraces of moderately sized Victorian parlour houses. All had cellars beneath them that were being used as air-raid shelters.

Steve had redirected exhausted civil defence workers to go there. He'd repeatedly heard ambulance sirens zoning in on it. Now he perfunctorily cleared up the ARP post and went to see the area for himself on his way home.

Milo had spent that same night feeling half paralysed with horror on the top of the church tower. It was a cold, frosty, moonlit night and he could see the parish laid out below almost as clearly as in daylight. Even worse, the Mersey glittered in the silver light, confirming to the Luftwaffe navigators that they were on target.

Above him, Milo could hear the throbbing engines of enemy planes; the sound was quite different from their own. He shivered, it was scary to think of being so close with nothing but a few barrage balloons in between. He could pick out the roof of his own home.

The Germans would be able to see the church and its tower; perhaps they could even see him. Having grown up in this area he didn't need to consult the street maps laid out below in the bell room.

When the bombs started to rain down, the deafening noise made him jerk with shock, and the huge flashes of light when they hit the ground and exploded half blinded him. He was frightened for the Jenkins family who he knew lived close by. The bombs had fallen close together which increased the danger of a fire. He half crouched behind the stone coping, trying to see in every direction, afraid he might miss a fire if he lifted his gaze from the ground. It was his job to watch for an outbreak and alert the local fire station, so they could reach it as soon as possible. The problem was the night was alive with explosions and flashes of light. He could hear masonry crashing to the ground but could see no fire.

Then, in the Birkenhead docks, he saw flames. A warehouse perhaps? He was reaching for the fixed line that connected him to the fire station when he saw a shower of incendiary bombs descending into the flames. An instant later an incandescent fireball burst into the sky, but he was already talking to a fire officer at the station. The docks were a raging inferno in minutes. Horrified, he watched a barrage balloon catch fire and drift lower over the town. He had to concentrate hard to decide where it would come down, and there were other fires taking hold.

Milo was kept on his toes until the all-clear came at one o'clock. He stayed for ten more minutes, reporting on where the flames appeared brightest and still growing and where fires he'd reported earlier were dying back.

There was still plenty of activity down at ground level. The church hall was open and being used as a temporary shelter for those made homeless. A WVS van was stationed outside providing hot tea and sandwiches for both workers and victims.

Milo warmed his hands on a welcome mug of tea and felt an overpowering sense of relief that it was all over for the time being. He felt very tired, but too tense and strung up to think of sleep. He was worried about his friends, for all he knew, Floris Jenkins could have been alone in the house when those bombs

CHAPTER TWENTY-NINE

MILO SWORE UNDER HIS BREATH, but there was nothing else he could do but turn and run back to the church. Before he'd reached the top of the tower the bombs were falling again. This time the bombardment went on hour after hour until he was totally exhausted and his eyes were smarting. By the time somebody came to relieve him, there was a pall of black smoke over the docks and it was drifting across the streets.

Milo almost felt his way down the steep stairs and as he stumbled outside, the all-clear went again. The crowd round the church had grown, the church hall was almost full to capacity and there were others busy dealing with the problems.

He felt he couldn't cope with much more, he needed sleep above everything else, but he decided to deviate from his route home to see if the Jenkins family was all right.

He'd been giving Henry Jenkins' advice about choosing a job a good deal of thought and he'd decided he would like to work in the drawing office at Laird's, and if possible learn to be a ship's architect.

He was relieved to find the Jenkins' house in Connaught Street in total darkness and so far as he could see in the blackout it was undamaged. He assumed the family had not been harmed though the noise at the top of the road would have kept them awake in their cellar. He could hear it now.

He was appalled when he turned the corner into Nelson Street. Rescue work was being carried out with dimmed hurricane lamps and torches. It was still too dark to see clearly but the sky was getting lighter in the east, and reaching up against it were outlined bare black spars of roof timbers. Of the row of eight shops along Nelson Street stretching from Connaught Street to Jubilee Street, six had been reduced to a bank of rubble. The two nearest him had walls still standing but had lost most of their roofs and windows.

Numerous civil defence workers were gathered here, as well as police officers and a lot of civilians who were desperately digging in the rubble, some using their bare hands. He felt so sorry for the people who'd lived here, they had lost both their homes and their businesses.

'Round here we all use our cellars as air-raid shelters,' an old man standing next to him volunteered. 'They've got ten people out alive so far, but also fourteen dead.'

Milo recoiled with horror. 'There could be more?'

'Probably will be. They're working along the row, trying to be methodical, but they had to stop because they came across an unexploded bomb and had to wait for the bomb disposal team to come and make it safe. You should see Jubilee Street, a lot of houses have gone there but they've got everybody out now.'

An ambulance was standing by and a WVS van was dispensing hot drinks. A mug was put into Milo's hand. It was a comfort to sip hot tea.

'Here, have some chocolate to go with that.' The old man

picked up a twopenny bar with its wrapper soiled but still complete. 'They won't be able to sell it now, will they?' There was broken glass and sweets strewn everywhere, and those that were wrapped were being picked up and eaten. Milo knew the end shop had been a newsagent and tobacconist's and the one next to it a greengrocers. He was crunching potatoes and carrots under his feet.

Milo had seen the notice many times, *If found guilty, the penalty for looting is death.* It seemed very harsh, particularly now when it was beginning to rain and if these scarce sweets were soaked they'd be wasted. Milo bit into the chocolate bar, he was hungry.

The old man next to him was doing the same. 'They tell us that a cellar is the safest place, but are they right? The residents here won't believe that in future, not now they've had their whole building collapse on top of them.' A few more slates slid to the ground and shattered. 'It's not safe now.'

Milo suddenly remembered that his mother had spent the night alone in their cellar, unless Pa had been relieved and sent home earlier. 'I'll have to go . . .'

A small cheer went up from the crowd digging into the greengrocer's cellar on the other side of the road. 'Good, they've found somebody else alive,' the old man said.

An ambulance man was running back to his vehicle to bring out a stretcher but there was a cry of warning from the diggers as one wall of the cellar began to collapse and they had to leap out of the way.

'Nothing's safe here,' Milo gasped. His eye was caught by a couple of police officers cordoning off the sweet and tobacconist's shop on the corner, and he found himself staring at his father.

It had to be Pa. Even in this half-light he'd recognise his uneven gait. He was leaning on his walking stick and listening to a woman nursing a baby on one arm. She was imploring Pa to do something and struggling to control a toddler with her free hand. Milo crossed the road, pushing through the crowd towards him.

'You can't go inside,' the police officer was telling Pa when he reached him. 'This building is likely to collapse at any moment.'

The woman screamed, 'My lads are inside.'

'Madam, there's nobody inside,' the policeman told her. 'We've spoken to the owners, they're safe and say there was nobody else in these premises.'

'I've just seen our Billy dodge inside.'

'Our Roddy's gone with him,' said a young girl swinging on the woman's skirts. 'It's true.'

'Get them out, please,' the woman screamed, panic-stricken. 'Get them out before they're hurt.'

'Nobody can go inside,' the constable said. 'It isn't safe.'

'You'd better let me take a look,' Milo heard his father say, and he began to limp determinedly towards what had been the shop door. He pulled himself inside and disappeared from view.

Milo went to follow him but the policeman caught his arm. 'No, my orders are to stop people putting themselves in danger, I can't allow it. There was nobody inside, I tell you.'

The next moment Pa was back, half dragging a lad of about twelve. 'Billy,' his mother shouted with relief. 'You stupid fool, what did you go in there for?'

'They sell model Spitfires in there,' his sister said, 'and ciggies. They wanted to get some.'

'Thank you, sir.' The woman was hugging her son and reaching out to Pa. 'Thank God our Billy's safe.'

'But what about our Roddy?' his sister was jumping up and down. 'They both went in, I saw them.'

'Sir, I cannot allow—'

Pa pushed past him. His eyes glittered with fatigue. 'Let me in, there's no time to waste,' he said firmly.

Milo could hardly believe it. He waited, holding his breath; he could feel the crowd round him doing the same. He heard a rumble and then, in the growing light, he saw the wall actually move. Beside him, the woman screamed and so did her children.

Suddenly, there was a thundering crash, the ground beneath Milo's feet seemed to shudder and what had remained of the row of shops collapsed into a pile of bricks, mortar and shattered woodwork. A cloud of thick cloying dust rose from it.

Like everybody else in the crowd, Milo was stunned.

'My Roddy,' the woman's cried. 'Save my little Roddy. Oh my God.'

Within moments Milo was heaving the bricks away from the mound where the doorway had been. Soon he had many willing helpers. They all had an opinion about Pa. Milo heard many say he was a brave man, a hero, but a few thought he'd been a fool to take such a risk with his life for feral street children like the Lewises. The odds had been against him from the start. Several said Billy Lewis had no business to lead his younger brother into bombed premises to loot toys, sweets and cigarettes. He was to blame for what had happened. He owed his life to Mr Dransfield, his mother had absolutely no control over him.

Mrs Lewis stood weeping, watching and hearing most of this with her baby crying and her remaining children huddling close, until a police officer suggested she took her children home.

'We're bombed out,' Billy shouted back defiantly. 'We haven't got a home. We've lost everything, even our dog Spot.'

Only then did someone mention that his father, Alfred Lewis, was away at sea, defying German U-boats to bring essential food and war supplies into British ports. The WVS was summoned to take charge of the family, find emergency accommodation for them and milk for the baby. Milo could have wept for their plight.

It took an hour and a half to get both the bodies out. Roddy Lewis aged ten and Steven Dransfield aged fifty-eight.

Milo felt absolutely drained as he identified his father's body and watched the police officer label it. 'He was a very brave man,' he said, 'he deserves a medal for going back into that building.'

He went on to ask question after question about him, his address, his date of birth, his next of kin. Milo struggled with the answers and watched the policeman fill in the form. He was too tired to think. He ached with fatigue.

'He will be taken to lie in the church,' the officer told him. 'Do you need help to find and inform relatives?

'No,' Milo said, and tried to tell him how he'd spent the night. A list of local funeral directors was put in his hand, together with several other documents.

'Your father will be released for burial tomorrow. It would

be a help if you can make arrangements as soon as possible. Where do you live?'

Milo knew at this time of the morning his mother would be at work in her shop and he was put in the back of a police car and told he'd be dropped off there. His head was in turmoil. Pa had been killed and the nature of his death shocked him to the core.

Never in a month of Sundays would he have believed Pa capable of saving a child's life. Pa didn't even like children. Milo was afraid he'd misjudged his father. He'd resented him. And now it was too late.

It was a relief to find his mother's shop undamaged and to see it open and her head bent over her sewing machine. After such a night, he'd been worried that something might have happened to her. Her face lit up when she saw him.

'It was a dreadful night. I was afraid . . .'

'I'm all right, Mum.' His lip trembled. 'Let's go upstairs.' He locked the shop door and turned the sign to read *Closed*. 'I've something to tell you.'

He saw the colour drain from her face. 'Is it about Pa?' she asked.

Leonie wept for her husband, but Milo couldn't stay awake any longer. He curled up in the corner of the sofa and his eyes were closing. 'Go to sleep,' she said and covered him with the car rug she kept under the cushion for that purpose. 'You're exhausted.'

'Just for an hour. Wake me.'

'No, you need longer than that.'

'I have things to . . .' His voice was drifting away on his breath.

Leonie went back to the shop but it was a very quiet morning, with few people out and about. Like Milo, they needed to catch up on their sleep. The noise in the night had not only kept Leonie awake but rigid with fear. After a bad night, June usually phoned to make sure she was all right, but this morning the phones were not working.

Steve was dead. She'd been on edge every hour of every night in a fever of terror that one or more members of her family might be killed. The hospital where June was training was very close to the Birkenhead docks.

Poor Steve! His life ended like that. Leonie felt totally drained; she hadn't expected to be overflowing with grief like this, but recently Steve had been making a huge effort. He'd been less selfish, he'd been thinking of her needs and the needs of others. He'd taken a greater part in the life of the family and she had found herself relying on him more and more. She was able to relax and enjoy her evenings spent in his company.

For a long time, she'd thought their marriage was dead, but somehow after all these years it had fluttered into life again. They'd talked about it, laughed about it and had agreed they felt happier. Miraculously, they both felt they'd turned over a new leaf and their marriage had been revived. Leonie no longer thought of it as a duty to stay with him, it was what she wanted to do. She'd had real hope for the future.

It seemed a very long morning. The customers stayed away, even the two who had arranged to come for fittings. She'd brought a sandwich for her lunch but she couldn't eat. Elaine came in and Leonie poured out all her agony on her shoulder.

An hour later June came down on the bus to see if they were all right. Leonie pulled her into her arms and started to explain what had happened to her father.

'Pa's been killed? Oh no! It was such an awful night, I've been dreading . . . I felt so afraid for you all. And Milo? Is he . . . ?'

'He's asleep upstairs. He's all right.'

It was terrible for Leonie seeing June's distress. For her, it was the second death of a loved one that the war had dealt her. They wept together. 'How did it happen?' June sniffed.

'You can be proud of Pa,' Leonie told her. June's eyes opened in astonishment as she heard the details of what he had done.

Later, Elaine crept upstairs to make a pot of tea for them and reported that Milo was still fast asleep on the sofa. There was an air-raid warning in the middle of the afternoon, but the siren didn't wake him and no bombs fell nearby.

Leonie slipped out to the shops to buy a loaf but there was no fish or offal to be had so late in the day. When it was time to close the shop, she woke Milo and they walked home together. Leonie used her key to let them in and the first thing she saw was a letter from Amy lying on the mat. Leonie left Milo to pick it up and worried about how she was going to tell her daughter that Pa had been killed.

The house seemed cold and unwelcoming. The living room grate was full of ash and cinders. Steve had always been here; only very rarely had she been in this house without him.

She retreated to the kitchen where Milo was sitting at the table staring at the envelope. 'It won't be easy,' he said, 'to tell Amy about Pa on the phone. She'll feel nothing will ever be the same, and she's not with us. Poor kid.'

Leonie sighed. 'Quite apart from any grief she feels, it'll bring home to her that it could happen to the rest of us and she could end up an orphan.'

'That's not very likely,' Milo told her drily.

'But that's how Amy will see it. You know what she's like.' Leonie tore open the letter and sat down to read it. 'Auntie Bessie's got a broody hen she thinks would suit us. Amy wants to know if we can come soon to collect it.'

'We could do both,' Milo said. 'It would be better to tell her face to face than by letter or phone. Is it this Sunday the coach goes?'

'We've got to bury Pa.' Leonie couldn't see beyond that.

'I'll try and make arrangements tomorrow,' Milo said. 'Don't worry about that now.'

'What are we going to eat? It won't be much of a dinner tonight,' she said. 'I have potatoes and there's cabbage in the garden but not much else.'

She got up to look in the larder. 'The choice is between a tin of Spam or I have a large tin of mackerel here. I suppose that would be all right.'

'Spam,' Milo decided, 'and I can see a tin of baked beans there too. Could we have that instead of the cabbage? It would make a change.'

Wearily, Leonie lifted both tins out. It would save her having to go out to look for a cabbage. They ate at the kitchen table and as soon as they'd finished they put all the lights out and went down to the cellar and went to bed down there.

Milo slept all through the night but Leonie lay awake listening to the frightening sounds of yet another raid.

Chapter Thirty

WITHIN THE NEXT FEW days, accounts of Steven Dransfield's courageous death appeared in the *Echo*, the *Liverpool Post* and the *Birkenhead News*. There were photos of the Lewis brothers, Billy whose life he'd saved and little Roddy who had died. Leonie felt proud of her husband and wished he was here with her to see all this. It would have given him back his self-esteem. Elaine said he deserved a medal.

Leonie had felt in a mental fog since Steve's death, though she did write to Auntie Bessie to tell her what had happened, saying she and Milo would like to visit so they could tell Amy personally. She worried she was leaving Milo to handle most of the funeral arrangements and do all the other tasks associated with death, and was afraid she was pushing too much on him.

'I want to help where I can, Mum,' he told her.

'I want Pa to lie in the Dransfield family grave. Well, it's what he'd want.'

'Yes, that's in hand. All coffins are being made of cardboard at the moment, so there are no decisions to be made there.'

Leonie was not surprised to find all the local undertakers were very busy and it would be nearly two weeks before Steve could be buried. She booked the coach trip for her and Milo on what turned out to be a dark, wet Sunday. Rain hurled against the coach windows for most of the way. Leonie was wearing her galoshes – rubber over-shoes as protection against the wet grass – but the rain had stopped before they got there.

'Amy will run down to meet us on her own,' she told Milo. 'Bessie will be seeing to the dinner.'

'So we'll tell her straight away?'

'Yes, if we can. Better to get it over with at the beginning of the visit. It'll give us time to comfort her.'

When their taxi pulled up at the bottom of the cwm, Amy snatched the door open. She was bubbling with excitement as she kissed Leonie and flung herself at Milo and tried to hug them both at the same time. She couldn't bear to walk in single file on the narrow path and almost towed Leonie up the incline. She chatted nineteen to the dozen about the broody hen they were to take home with them.

'I've called her Hetty,' Amy announced. 'She's speckled black and white. I hope you like her.'

'We will,' they told her. Leonie couldn't bring herself to dampen such exuberance. 'Later,' she mouthed to Milo.

Uncle Jack and Auntie Bessie met them at the door and gave her knowing looks. Leonie shook her head as they were invited indoors and then they were sitting down to eat Sunday lunch. Amy was in such high spirits that it was quite a jolly meal. She dragged Milo out to see Hetty while Leonie helped Bessie clear away and wash up.

'Go after them,' Bessie urged. 'That's more important now. This won't take me and Jack five minutes.'

Leonie had to put on her mac as it was drizzling again. She heard Amy laugh as she crossed the farmyard and that guided her to the building where the hens were kept.

'Hetty isn't a very big hen,' Amy was saying. 'This is Hetty, Mum.' The speckled hen she was pointing to was stalking around making strange clucking sounds. 'Jack says that means she wants chicks to look after and she'll sit on a nest to hatch them out. He thinks ten eggs will be as many as she can manage. He's picked out the eggs he thinks most likely to hatch out but she hasn't started to sit on them yet.'

Leonie couldn't stem her tide of enthusiasm.

'Bessie thought it better if you took the eggs with you and settled her on them as soon as you get home.'

'I've got everything ready for her.' Milo told her how he'd turned the shed against the house where she used to keep her tricycle and doll's pram into a henhouse, and how Pat's sister Alison had helped him build a pen for them.

Leonie had a moment of panic, at this rate it would be time to go before she'd got the bad news out. She had to do it now.

'Amy love, there's something we have to tell you.'

Her daughter's dancing blue eyes fastened on hers. 'Something exciting?'

'Something sad, very sad.' She paused, there was no easy way to say it. 'I'm afraid Pa has been killed.'

She watched the light fade from Amy's face. 'Killed? You mean he'd dead? How?'

Leonie went on to tell her and pulled out the bundle of newspaper cuttings she'd brought in her pocket. 'He was very brave. A hero in fact, he saved one boy's life and was trying to save another.'

Amy couldn't see to read, her eyes were full of tears. 'But if Pa's dead I'll never see him again, will I?'

'I'm afraid not.' Leonie gave her a handkerchief and sat

down on a wooden crate to pull her on to her knee in a hug. Milo read out the articles to her.

'He didn't say goodbye to me,' Amy whimpered.

'He wasn't able to say goodbye to any of us,' Leonie wasn't far from tears herself.

'He could have written to say goodbye,' she sobbed. 'He's never ever written to me, not even once, though I've written to him.'

'You know Pa,' Milo said. 'He often feels quite poorly.'

'Yes, I know.'

They went for a walk then although it was raining more heavily. Leonie held one of her hands and Milo the other. She took them across the field to see again what a commercially made henhouse looked like and then to fetch the cows up from the sideland ready for milking.

When they got back, Jack was in the farmyard packing Hetty into a box for the journey. 'I've decided Hetty ought to have another hen to keep her company,' he said. 'This Rhode Island Red has just begun to lay, she should do well for you.'

'That's Polly,' Amy said. 'Her feathers are the same colour as your hair, Milo.'

Leonie was pleased Jack had managed to distract Amy's thoughts but she was embarrassed at his generosity and wanted to pay for the hens and the eggs, but Jack refused to let her. They went indoors and Amy showed the newspaper cuttings to Bessie and she read them out to Jack.

'Your father was a very brave man,' Bessie told her. 'Not many men would risk their lives like that. You must be proud of what he did.'

'I am.' Amy was biting her lips. 'Can I come home with you

and Milo, Mum? I'd be able to look after Hetty and Polly and—'

'No love. You'd be frightened in the raids. You're safer here in the country.'

'Pat's there.'

'I bet she's scared stiff,' Milo said. 'When I spoke to her sister Aileen the other day, she said they were all terrified and that her mother was thinking of taking the family away from Merseyside.'

'It's dangerous there at the moment,' Jack added.

'It's just as dangerous for Mum and Milo,' Amy retorted. She paused for a moment. 'Mum, if you were killed in a raid, who would look after me?'

'That won't happen, love.'

'But it might. If Pa can be killed, then so can you.'

'Don't forget about me and June,' Milo put in quickly. 'It's lucky we're so much older, we could look after you if there was nobody else.'

Bessie threw her arms round her in a hug. 'If the worst does happen, you could stay here with us, couldn't you? Jack and I would bring you up, we'd be more than happy to do that.'

Amy seemed comforted though Leonie noticed that Milo had to blow his nose hard and Bessie's eyes were swimming.

'I'm going to make you a cup of tea before you have to go,' she said as she lowered the kettle into the flames.

When the time came for them to leave, Amy clung to her mother. 'Couldn't I come home with you for a little while? I don't want you and Milo to leave me.'

'It wouldn't be safe for you,' Milo said.

'No, love, I'm sorry.' Leonie hugged her. 'I hate leaving you like this, but it's much the wisest and the safest thing for you.'

'But I want to go to Pa's funeral.'

'Little girls don't go to funerals,' Jack said. 'You wouldn't like it.'

'I want to say goodbye to Pa.'

Leonie took a deep breath. 'I want you to be brave and stay here. Auntie Bessie and Uncle Jack will look after you.'

'Of course we will,' Bessie assured her. 'We'd be lost without you now.'

Usually when they walked down to the road to meet the taxi, Amy came alone to see them off, but today Bessie came too. Amy was in floods of tears and Leonie's last view of her daughter was of Bessie holding her tight and trying to comfort her. She hated leaving her when she was so upset.

When they boarded the coach, Milo said, 'Good job it isn't full.' He took one full seat and kept Hetty's box beside him. Leonie sat across the aisle and tried to soothe the Rhode Island Red that had been tied into a sack and kept moving about. Both were very audible. Their fellow passengers were in no doubt they were bringing hens home.

Leonie was in agony during the days that followed. She felt she couldn't feel better until Steve was finally laid to rest. It helped when a few days later she received a note from Auntie Bessie saying Amy had settled down once they'd gone and hadn't mentioned her father since.

Milo had put Hetty to sit on the eggs and Polly had joined her in the henhouse. She was spending the night alone on the perch and each morning produced a brown egg. Leonie exchanged their egg ration coupons for hen food, and though it was a fine meal and very different to the hen food Amy had shown her, both hens seemed happy to eat it mixed up with boiled potato peelings and household scraps.

Leonie knew Milo had arranged for his father to be brought to St Mark's Church where his funeral would be held. There was no longer a florist in the neighbourhood so she picked the best of the May flowers from the garden and tied them into bouquets.

The day of the funeral came at last. June had been given a half day of compassionate leave to come. She arrived after lunch looking white-faced and tired. The previous night had brought another heavy raid and she'd been roused from her bed at midnight to help. Neither she nor Leonie were able to control their tears. Leonie had expected the funeral to be very quiet, with only the family and a few of her friends, but because of the publicity about Steve's bravery, it was very well attended. Many of his fellow ARP members came, together with neighbours she rarely saw these days.

Elaine provided the funeral refreshments in her house but few went there. Leonie was relieved when it was all over.

Milo felt he had to take responsibility for his mother now that he was the man of the house. He was also trying to keep to his rota of fire-watching. And, on top of this, he had to remember to look after the hens. He was relieved to find that Hetty was as keen to sit on the eggs as Bessie had said she'd be, while Polly scratched happily in their outside enclosure.

He was mixing their food one evening when Alison

Greenway came round. 'Pat tells me Amy's sent you some hens. I'd like to see them.'

'You've come just at the right moment,' he told her. 'I'm about to feed them.' He led the way and put their feed down in their pen. Polly rushed in from the outside enclosure and Hetty heaved herself off her clutch of eggs. Alison stood with him at the open door watching them. The evening sun was dappling her hair, she was really pretty. Milo couldn't take his eyes from her.

He screwed up his courage. 'I'd like to ask you to come to the pictures with me,' he said slowly, 'but I'm shattered and might fall asleep. I need my spare time to catch up with my sleep, but it's a lovely fine evening, how about a walk along the Esplanade towards Rock Ferry instead? I'll still be able to have an early night after that.' It pleased him to see her face light up at the suggestion, and they set off straight away.

'I shall miss seeing the old *Conway* in the river,' she told him. 'The place won't seem the same without her. It's thought to be too dangerous to keep a training ship here with all the young men on board.'

There had been a training ship for officers of the merchant navy moored in the river since 1859. The present vessel had started life as HMS *Nile* and came into service in 1877, and was later renamed HMS *Conway*. 'Dad says he's heard she's about to be towed to the Menai Straights for safety,' Alison said.

Milo sighed, remembering the days when he'd hoped to train on the *Conway*. 'Once there were three old ships anchored here. Do you remember them?'

She nodded. 'I do. Everybody and everything is being evacuated. Dad is talking of finding somewhere safer for us as a family. The trouble is that everything in reach of work for him and school for my sisters has been snapped up long ago.'

Alison was in her last term at school and the examinations for Higher School Certificate would be on her soon. 'No point in evacuating me now.'

'What are you going to do?'

'Dad thinks I should try for a place at Liverpool University but with the war on . . .' She shrugged. 'Really I don't know what I want to do. I feel Mum is edging me towards teaching. She was a teacher, but I don't know . . . My older sister Charlotte is in the WRNS and likes it, so I think I'll do the same.'

Milo frowned. 'You'll be going away?'

'Yes. I'm eighteen now so once I leave school I'll be drafted into war work if I don't choose it for myself.' She looked up and smiled. 'Everybody tells us that choosing a career is a very important decision, but not having any particular bent or ambition makes it very hard.'

Milo understood exactly. 'And it's even worse if one's parents start pushing. Pa wanted me to work in the family business and I tried it for a year before war broke out but I always felt I was a round nut in a square hole. It was conscription that got me out of that.'

Alison sighed. 'In my case it's the war that's pushing me. I don't have time to think about it.'

'I should have refused to do what Pa wanted but I didn't have the guts to stand up to him.' He looked down at her tawny brown hair curling on her shoulders and her neatly pretty face with wide-spaced smiling eyes. His heart gave a lurch as he realised he wanted to get to know Alison better. 'Except that I hope you won't decide to join the WRNS. All my friends go away and I'm left here by myself.'

'You've fought for your country and done your share, so you're ahead of me there.'

'Do you want to fight for your country?'

Her forehead creased in thought. 'No, not particularly, but it's something we all think we should do.'

Milo remembered Henry Jenkins' words: 'Think again about what you really want,' he'd advised. 'Make up your own mind and don't let anybody change it for you.' Then, after a moment, smiling broadly Milo added, 'What d'you think about coming to the pictures with me on Saturday?'

She giggled. 'That's easy, the answer's yes. Basil Rathbone is on at the Lyceum in *The Hound of the Baskervilles*. I'd love to see that.'

'So would I. I like Sherlock Holmes. I'll call round and collect you on Saturday.'

They took their seats while the films to be shown in the coming weeks were being advertised. *Gone with the Wind* had pride of place though its showing was still some time off.

'I'd really love to see that too.' Alison sighed with longing. 'I've read some reviews and they all raved about it.'

'Then we mustn't miss it when it comes,' Milo said, taking her hand in his. 'We'll come together. Consider that a date.'

Milo went home feeling pleased that he'd found a girl who was interested in him. Floris was all very well and quite good company but she made it clear she preferred another. Alison was more openly responsive to him and he liked that. Her touch could make the back of his neck tingle. He couldn't get enough of her. Even so, he knew he wouldn't feel settled in civilian life until he had a job. He was tired of thinking about his future, he wanted to get on with it now.

The following night he called round to see Henry Jenkins. It was he who opened the front door and released a cloud of savoury scents. He was still chewing.

'I'm sorry,' Milo said, 'I'm disturbing your meal.'

'No matter but if you're thinking of taking Floris to the pictures, you're out of luck,' he told him. 'Her boyfriend's home on leave, he's taken her out.'

'It was you I wanted to see. Do you have time for a word with me, Mr Jenkins?' Milo had formulated the words to ask. 'I've taken your advice and thought hard about a career and I'd like to make some progress now.'

'Of course, lad, come on in.' He opened the door wider and led the way to the kitchen where the remains of his evening meal were on the table. 'There's a cup of tea in the pot and what about a slice of Floris's cake?' He gave Milo a mischievous smile. 'She made it to show off her baking skills to Barry and pretty good it is. So what are your thoughts about a career? Have you made up your mind?'

'I think I'd like to be a ship's architect like you, but would a job in your drawing office lead to that? I've been reading up about it and it seems I'd need a background in ship's engineering, wouldn't I?'

He nodded. 'I started as an apprentice engineer but I was sixteen and you're a bit beyond that now. It won't have done you any harm to knock about doing other work.'

'I'm twenty-four, is that too old to start?'

'That depends on you. You would need a job in our

engineering division and you'd have to keep your wits about you and consider yourself a trainee, but I reckon you'd pick it up. You'd be facing several years of hard study at night school to sit the qualifying exams of the Royal Institute of Naval Architects.'

'How long would it take me?'

'That again depends on you. You wouldn't be an official apprentice so it would be up to you to set your own pace. You'd have a lot to learn as it's not just preliminary design of the vessel.'

'I need something to get my teeth into. I want to end up with a decent job. Do you think I could do it?'

'Milo, I know you could. Didn't I see what you were capable of when we all worked on *Dido* in your garden? Of course you'd have to work at it, but yes, I'm sure you have the ability.'

Milo sat back with a sigh of satisfaction. 'Then that's what I'd like to do. But will I be able to get a job in Cammell Laird's?'

'There's no problem there, the war has given us as much work as we can cope with and like everybody else we're crying out for more staff.' He scribbled a name and address on a scrap of paper. 'Write your application to this fellow and we'll take it from there.'

Milo went home feeling better and did exactly what Mr Jenkins had suggested. He posted the letter the next day and went round to tell Alison that evening.

When she came to the door, she almost fell on him. 'You've come at just the right moment. Wait a sec while I get my coat.' She came back buttoning it up and took his hand. 'Let's go for a walk.' She led the way down the garden to the Esplanade.

'Has something happened? You look as though you need a long walk,' he pulled her arm through his.

'I've just had a dust-up with Dad and Mum, so things are a bit chilly in there at the moment. I told them I didn't want to go to university and I wasn't going to apply. I want to be a newspaper reporter and I understand the *Liverpool Echo* takes on beginners from time to time but they like them to be able to type, and to have a knowledge of shorthand would be a help too.'

Milo was pleased, it sounded as though Alison was planning to stay nearby. 'What's wrong with that? Is it because it won't help the war effort? They're afraid you'll be directed to a munitions factory?'

'I'll probably be left alone if I stay in full-time education. No, they think if I'm to be a reporter I'd do better to go to university first. Get properly educated, as Mum put it.'

'Nothing wrong with that either.'

'The real trouble is Charlotte went to commercial college and as soon as she'd got the certificates to prove she was capable, she joined the WRNS. According to Mum she didn't fulfil her potential – she's working beneath her ability and all that, but honestly she loves it. They think I'll do the same thing.'

'They're thinking of what would be best for you, Alison. Not like my father who was thinking of the family business, not of me. You should—'

'Hang on,' she held up her hand, 'your advice was that I should make up my own mind and not be persuaded otherwise. Well, I have thought about it, I've made up my mind and I want to be a reporter, so don't you turn against me.' Alison was agitated and had broken away from him.

'I'm not,' he said. 'I wouldn't. I'm all for it.' He slid an arm round her waist and drew her closer. 'I want you to stay here near me.'

'That's another thing. They think I'm too young to be thinking of boyfriends. I mean eighteen is eighteen, after all, and more than old enough to know what I want. They think you've talked me into staying near you.'

'I wanted to,' he admitted. 'But I didn't.'

'No, you didn't. It's Mum, she went to Edinburgh University and she'd like her daughters to follow in her footsteps.'

'Well, it doesn't have to be Edinburgh, Liverpool is on the doorstep.'

'It would take three years. I know she wants me to have what she had, but what good did all that studying do her? She taught for two years and then got married and had us five kids. She might as well not have bothered.'

'It must have made her a wiser person.'

'Absolutely not! She's bigoted, she thinks that without university education we'll get nowhere. I want to get on with my life but they think I'm in too much of a hurry to grow up. Don't let yourself be persuaded into marriage until you're older, they say.'

Milo pulled her to a halt. 'Has somebody asked you?'

'No.'

'Thank goodness for that. I don't want you whipped away from under my nose.' He bent over and kissed her cheek, then pulled her closer and his lips fastened on hers.

'We'll both have to buckle down and learn how to earn a living, especially me, but we'll have as much fun as we can while we do it.' Milo laughed. 'When it comes to marriage,

I want you to promise you'll give me first refusal.'

Alison doubled up with the giggles. 'I promise,' she said.

The following week, Milo received a reply to his job application to Cammell Laird's, inviting him to come for an interview in three days' time. He was nervous because such a lot was riding on this. He looked at his suits, he had three that he used to wear on a three-week rota to work in the family antique shop and he could still get into them. Mum had had one cleaned for him to wear to his father's funeral, so it would be that one.

He felt he was received in a friendly fashion and assured he'd be given every opportunity to learn to be a ship's architect, though he'd need to do a basic engineering course first. 'You'll have to attend night school classes from this autumn – and pass the relevant examinations, of course.'

'Of course.'

He was told that Henry Jenkins had given him an outstanding reference but that he'd need to get another. He thought perhaps he'd go straight over to Liverpool and see George at the shop. He'd probably be willing to provide one and it was arranged that he would start work next Monday.

Milo was thrilled, at last he was making a start on his career. Alison reported that her mother had agreed that she should apply for a place in the secretarial college Charlotte had attended for the autumn term. 'So we've both made a start,' she said.

The night the chicks were due to hatch was fine and clear, with the moon almost full. Everybody dreaded that combination because it meant that somewhere on Merseyside they were going to have another visit from enemy planes. Milo hoped it wasn't going to be their area tonight, but he had to stand by in case it was.

Milo and Alison were keeping a close eye on Hetty's nest. It all happened as they'd expected, but no sooner had the first chick emerged from its shell than the air-raid siren sounded. Milo was aghast. 'I'll have to go. It's my turn for fire-watching.'

'So will I,' Alison said. Milo knew she had strict instructions to return home whenever an air-raid warning sounded.

It fell to Leonie to look after the chicks and she was fascinated. Hetty pulled the skin from around each chick in turn and helped them out of their shells while Polly charged round the henhouse instead of going up on the perch, as though she wanted to help too.

One egg appeared addled and one chick somehow got trodden on and survived only one day, but within a week Milo had eight healthy chicks and Polly had taken over the mothering of two of them.

He went round to ask Alison if she'd like to come and see them, and all the Greenway sisters, Aileen, Joan and Pat, came with her and billed and cooed over the chicks for ages. Pat couldn't get over the fact that the hens had come from the farm where Amy was evacuated and she'd chosen their names.

'The next time Amy rings,' she said, 'I shall tell her that I've seen them and they're lovely. Milo, would you bring us a broody hen back next time you go?'

'No,' he said. 'I can't keep asking Auntie Bessie for her hens. She's very kind to Amy and to us, but her hens are her livelihood.'

'I'll ask Amy to do it when I speak to her.'

'No Pat,' Alison said firmly. 'Don't be a pest.'

'Dad will buy a hen for me, especially as it will lay—'

'No! Dad is trying to evacuate you all to somewhere safer. The last thing he'll need is to have chickens to evacuate as well.'

CHAPTER THIRTY-ONE

MARCH THE 15TH WAS Elaine and Tom's wedding anniversary and Milo was delighted when he and his mother were invited to have dinner at their home. June was expected too and so were the couple who lived next door. He was looking forward to getting to know Elaine and her husband better because he knew they were important to his mother and sister. He hoped fervently that the Luftwaffe would allow them peace to enjoy the evening.

If all went well, he and his family would walk home afterwards. If not, the Cliffords had an Anderson shelter in their back garden with four bunk beds in it so Mum and June could spend the rest of the night with them. It was his turn to fire-watch so if the air-raid warning sounded, he would have to leave them.

He fed the chicks and shut them up for the night before getting ready. His mother came home from work to wash and change into a red dress she'd made for herself recently. In case she had to spend the night in Elaine's shelter, she packed her siren suit in a bag to take with her. She never went anywhere without this warm, one-piece outfit of trousers and jacket with a zip up the front. It was proving very popular because it was so practical, even the Prime Minister Winston Churchill and his wife wore siren suits. Mum had made one for Milo as well as for countless customers.

He felt he was made very welcome. Tom had managed to get some wine and Elaine provided an excellent spread in the circumstances. His mother had contributed a pint of milk, four fresh eggs and a large tin of peaches she'd been hoarding for months. He understood the neighbours had done something similar. He liked them, they turned out to be good company and the first part of the evening was very jolly.

But it was a fine night and the moon was full, and they were all expecting another raid. The last two nights had been quiet, London and Birmingham had received the enemy's attention, and they couldn't believe they'd be left in peace for a third night.

In the event, the Luftwaffe came earlier than usual. Elaine was apologising for the drink she was about to make to finish off the meal. 'Sorry, we are reduced to Camp Coffee or tea,' when the air-raid warning blared across the town, sending shivers down Milo's spine.

'Oh, blast,' Elaine cried in frustration. 'I hoped they'd take a night off tonight. Why do they have to spoil everything?'

'It might be a false alarm,' Tom said, trying to soothe her. 'Or they may be heading somewhere else. Let's sit tight and carry on for a while. More dessert, June?'

Milo hurriedly scraped up the last of his trifle and stood up. 'Thank you for a lovely meal. It's been a great evening but I have to go.'

'You did warn us it was your turn to fire-watch,' Elaine said sadly.

He could see that the warning had put them all on edge. As

he pulled on his warm coat and the balaclava helmet June had knitted for him, they were listening for further ominous sounds.

'Goodnight,' he said. 'See you later, Mum.'

'Hope you have a quiet night,' she called after him.

Milo jogged up to the church and climbed to the top of the tower. Britain's newest radar system meant they were given earlier warnings that enemy aircraft were approaching. But tonight he barely had time to survey the river glistening in the moonlight with the barrage balloons floating in the sky and every ship clearly visible before the first bombs began to fall.

He was watching for the spurt of orange flames against the grey background and was thankful to see nothing like that but he was aware of bombs bursting all round him and was afraid that one had fallen very close to his home. He kept looking in that direction and from the distance of three-quarters of a mile or so he thought it looked different. It seemed hazier down there than it had, and had the roof changed?

Another wave of enemy planes was overhead and he saw a fire spring to life and gather strength. He leapt to the phone to report its position. Another fire was clearly visible on the docks. He could see as well as hear the anti-aircraft guns firing from the Shore Fields.

As soon as there was a lull, his gaze went towards his own home. There was more cloud about than there had been and when one passed in front of the moon it was quite dark. He wasn't sure but he had a heavy feeling in the pit of his stomach that their house had been damaged. It worried him and he had to fight the urge to rush home to find out, but his duty was to stay here in case another wave of bombers came over. He was glad nobody had been at home tonight.

At last the all-clear sounded and he was free to go. He ran most of the way home. When he reached the back garden he was so shocked he had to hold on to the gate until he got his breath back. Part of the roof had indeed gone. A road of terraced houses backed along the side wall of their garden and he thought that the two closest had also been damaged. He could hear the wail of an ambulance from that road but could see nothing.

Fortunately nobody had been here to get hurt. Their bungalow was L-shaped, and one gable end now seemed to be just a wall so their main living rooms were without a roof. He heard a few more slates slide down to crash and splinter in front of the house. All the windows and most of the frames had gone from the bedroom wing. He felt appalled, paralysed with horror. Where would they live?

His own shed, the old summer house by the back gate, was still intact, even the window glass was in place. He thought of the hens and baby chicks then and was relieved to find that shed intact too. He opened the door and heard Hetty's soft motherly clucks. There was a panic-stricken fluttering of feathers but he could make out that the other hen was all right. He blessed the fact that they had two acres of garden.

He walked round to the front, glass splintering under his feet. He could see roof timbers and slates scattered over the front garden and some down on the Esplanade and even on the shore. The tide was full in and lapping gently on the sand, sounding exactly as it always had. Suddenly, all his strength seemed to desert him and he felt absolutely whacked. He told himself this was not surprising since he'd worked all day and been on his feet for half the night. He felt a desperate need to lie down and sleep, but where was the best place?

He tried to get inside the house but the front door was in place and still locked. He went round to the back. They had beds in the cellar but it was very dark on this side of the building. Like everybody else he kept a small torch in his pocket with the glass half blanked out to limit the light. He shone it down the stone steps and saw the way down was almost blocked with glass, slates and general debris. Also, the roof had gone from this part of the building, what if there was no floor either? He couldn't see well enough to find out one way or the other.

A couple more slates crashed down inside the building. It wouldn't be safe to go in until daylight when he'd be able to see what the damage was. He went to the bedroom wing and walked through the ceiling-to-floor Victorian sash window straight into his bedroom. Half the heavily moulded ceiling was down and there was glass everywhere, sometimes quite big pieces because he'd glued paper in a criss-cross pattern to prevent it splintering.

He snatched the eiderdown from his bed. Glass from it tinkled down so he shook off all he could, grabbed his pillows and as many of his blankets as he could and retreated to his shed. By the dim light of his torch he made a nest of his bedding on the floor and took off his shoes and his heavy coat. He lay down and pulled his coat over him and nothing could have stopped him falling asleep.

Milo woke up in the grey of dawn feeling stiff and cold. He put on his shoes to take another look at the damage to his home. It confirmed his worst fears. It would not be possible to live in it now. Pots, pans and broken crockery he didn't recognise had been blown across their garden. All that must have come from the houses in the next road. The sight of such destruction made him feel sick but he knew now what he must do. He set off to walk to Elaine's house and break the news to his mother.

Tom was up in his dressing gown making morning tea. Milo felt depressed and near to tears as he blurted out the news. He was pushed towards a chair at the kitchen table and a cup of tea put in front of him. Within moments Mum was sitting opposite to him and then June and Elaine were pulling out chairs to join them. He tried to tell them what he'd seen but he couldn't stop the tears rolling down his face. 'Where are we going to live?' he wailed.

'There's the flat over the shop,' his mother said quietly. 'It's a roof over our heads, isn't it?' He was surprised at her stoic attitude. 'We need to salvage the beds because we have none there. Were the beds all right?'

He shook his head. 'I don't know.'

Tom said, 'I'll drive you down to see for yourselves.'

'Thank you,' Mum said. 'The sooner we sort this out, the better.' Milo stood up to go with them.

'Not you,' Leonie said. 'Milo, you're out on your feet. You need more sleep.'

'I'm coming,' he told her. 'I can't sleep now.'

Milo thought the damage looked worse than ever now the sun was getting up.

'It doesn't look safe to go inside,' Tom warned. 'That wall could collapse at any minute.'

'It's now or never,' his mother said grimly. 'We've got to have beds and bedding.'

'Yours first then,' Milo said. 'Let's get out what we can.'

331

'Mine's too big for the small rooms over the shop,' she said. 'Single beds would be better. We'll take them all, yours, June's and Amy's.'

Milo found himself in his bedroom shaking the dusk and dirt from a paperback he'd only half read, and picking up his alarm clock. He could see June was bringing out the same sorts of things from her room.

'We should concentrate on getting the valuables and essentials,' he told her.

'I want these.'

He found two suitcases and gave her one. 'Put your beads and other trinkets in here,' he advised.

They worked hard dragging out all they could into the garden and then had to collapse the beds while Elaine loaded whatever would fit into the car. Soon they were all covered with the grey dust that smelled so horrible.

Ida had opened up the shop by the time they got there and was surprised to see both them and the growing pile of domestic goods and utensils being unloaded on the pavement outside.

'I thought we got off quite lightly last night,' she said, aghast as she helped wipe everything down before it was carried upstairs.

'I'm afraid you'll have to stand in for me today,' Leonie told her.

'I'll be glad to. Everyone will understand if I tell them why. But I can't work all day, I'll have to leave in time to collect my grandchildren from school.'

'I know, I'll be grateful for any extra hours you can do.'

Milo telephoned his boss at Cammell Laird's to explain why

he hadn't shown up for work, and then he asked to speak to Henry Jenkins.

'Don't think of coming in today,' Mr Jenkins told him, 'and if you need any help, come round and see us tonight.'

Milo thought it amazing that the phone still worked and while his family's life had been savaged, so little seemed to have changed in the rest of the world.

Elaine wanted to move her desk out from the larger bedroom.

'No,' Leonie said. 'Milo's bed can go against the far wall and you can continue to work at this end.'

'After all,' Milo said, 'you only use it in the daytime.'

'Milo, are you sure you won't mind doubling up?' Elaine said.

'He won't,' his mother assured her. 'Milo can be pretty messy but no doubt you'll both manage once you get used to it.'

'I'll have to go to the office,' Tom said, 'but I'll run you back to Mersey Reach. Elaine will want to stay and help you sort things out.'

Before she left, Leonie rang George Courtney at the shop and asked him to come down to see if any antiques could be salvaged. Back on the Esplanade they found the wardens and police had taken charge and were telling them it was too dangerous to go inside the house again.

'We have to,' his mother insisted, 'if we are to salvage any more from our home of thirty years. We need the stuff, we can't buy replacements.'

Milo thought of what had happened to Pa when he'd ignored that advice. But he had to go in too, he couldn't leave that to the women of the family. They carried on.

'We have officially requested that gas, water and electricity supplies be cut off,' a warden told them, 'and what remains of the building be made safe.'

'You think it's a write-off?'

'Almost certainly,' he said.

'I've lived here all my married life.' Milo heard the agony in his mother's voice.

'I'm sorry, it's official policy. I understand there's government compensation you can apply for.'

'All the same, we'll salvage all we can now,' she said in her usual stoic manner.

Milo saw George Courtney and one of his assistants arrive in the firm's van to help. They, too, crunched through the broken glass to climb inside and assess what remained.

'Careful,' Milo warned. 'The floor isn't safe in the dining room, part of it has fallen in.' He carried out several of the heavy ship pictures of which his father had been so proud.

'I'll have them all cleaned up and sell them in the shop,' George said. 'A few of them need to have their frames repaired and at least two have scratch marks on the painting itself, but I think they'll sell.'

'Do your best with them, George.'

'I will.'

Milo helped him pick out the best of the antiques to go to the shop and George arranged for a considerable collection of household bric-a-brac to be sent to auction.

CHAPTER THIRTY-TWO

ON THAT SAME FRIDAY, AMY was also having a difficult time. Her examination was getting close and she was doing homework every night. She felt she had very little time to herself but in addition, last month Mrs Roberts had decided that all her pupils should learn a craft. 'Would you like to learn to knit, Amy? Or do embroidery?'

She didn't want to do either at the moment, she wanted to relax and read when she'd finished her homework. But June was good at knitting so she picked that.

Mrs Roberts had loaned her a simple pattern for gloves that would fit her, Auntie Bessie had provided her with some blue wool and she'd painstakingly begun to knit. Now every evening, in addition to homework, she had to knit enough for Mrs Roberts to appreciate that her glove was growing.

Yesterday, she'd reached the bottom of the fingers and Mrs Roberts had done the difficult part of casting on stitches for the first finger. She'd been told to finish that finger for today and had managed it. Mrs Roberts had smiled and said she was pleased to see her so enthusiastic about knitting. 'I'll cast on the stitches for the second finger so you can carry on over the weekend.'

Amy felt she'd been standing at Mrs Roberts' desk for ages.

She was shifting her weight from one foot to the other as she tried to concentrate on what she was being told. She'd been embarrassed to see her teacher marking two of her sums wrong and felt guilty because she'd rushed her homework last night so she could go out and milk with Uncle Jack.

'Do those two again for me tonight,' she said, and in addition Amy received a double ration of homework for the weekend.

She was looking forward to talking to her mother and also Pat on the way home. It was her Friday-night treat. She escaped from school as quickly as she could and rode her bike down to the phone box, leant it against the grassy bank and went inside. Mum was always at the shop on Friday afternoons.

She heard the phone ring. It seemed nobody was there, so she tried her home number. Nothing happened, it didn't even ring. Finally she tried Pat's number.

Pat's voice answered but she sounded rushed, excited and shocked and not really like her. 'Amy, is that you? We had a terrible night last night and your house got bombed. Half the roof has been blown off.'

Amy felt her heart jolt against her ribs. She was horrified. 'Where are Mum and Milo? Are they all right?'

'Me and Alison went along to look but we couldn't find either of them. The hens are all right though.'

'But Mum? Where is she?'

'I don't know, Amy. My mum went along to see for herself but she found nobody there. Everybody is panicking round here. My family is going to be evacuated this afternoon. Dad's found a house for us near Chirk. We're all going. Mum is going to stay with us but Dad and Alison will come back on Monday. We're going to go to new schools there. We're all frantically packing. Mum says she can't stand any more nights like last night. It was terrifying because it was so near.'

'But what about my mum?'

'Honestly, we don't know. We haven't seen any of your family. Dad forbade us to go to your house, he says it's dangerous and more of the roof could collapse on us.'

'Is my mum in hospital?'

'We know nothing. Dad's shouting for me to come. The car's packed and we're ready to start.'

'My mum isn't dead, is she? She can't be. And what about Milo?' Amy heard the pips telling her the money had run out. 'Ring me back.' She was reading off the number of the call box as Mum had taught her to do. She shouted, 'I've got to know what's happened.'

'I can't—' The line went dead.

Amy waited, her heart drumming, but it didn't ring again. Her head was reeling. What was she to do now?

Her eyes stung with unshed tears. If her home had been bombed and lost part of its roof then the explosion would have disconnected the phone but Mum and Milo could have been hurt and sent to hospital or, even worse, be dead.

She got on her bike and cycled down the road with a feeling of cold horror settling in her stomach.

Some of her school friends had walked past the phone box while she was inside. She rode straight past them to get home to Auntie Bessie. She left her bike in its usual place in an outbuilding at the nearby farm and jogged up two fields. She saw Bessie in the meadow doing something with one of the sheep she and Jack had brought down from the hill a few weeks ago. She ran towards her instead of going to the house.

'Bessie, I think my mum could be dead!'

Bessie's face contorted. 'No, bach, she won't be.'

'What's that you're doing?'

'Trying to get this lamb out. Has something happened?'

'Our house has been bombed, half the roof is missing.'

'Who told you that?'

'Pat did.'

'Pat? She's just a child, bach, how do you know it's true?'

'It is. I know it is. I'm afraid something dreadful has happened to Mum.'

'Well we don't know that for sure.'

'I'm worried. She's not at her shop and she always is. She waits for me to ring.'

'I know, but perhaps today – wait a moment. I have to do this first.'

'I've got to go home. I want my mum.'

'No, bach. Let me think about it. Look, here's the lamb coming now. It's quite a big one.' She put her finger in its mouth to clear its airway. 'It's breathing, a fine healthy ram lamb. Jack will be pleased with this. I must just check that it isn't a twin. Yes, I think – yes, it is. We're lucky, we'll have two. See how the mother is licking this first one? Amy? Amy, where are you going?'

She was running up the steep hill towards the house. 'Set the kettle to boil,' Bessie called after her. 'We'll have tea as soon as I come up. Everything is ready.'

Amy was panting when she reached the house. It was too early for Jack to be home from work and as usual the front door was propped open. The table was set for tea with a glass dish of strawberry junket and a jug of cream, her favourite, but she went straight upstairs to get her money from the pretty cardboard box on her dressing table that had been given to her by the postmistress.

She had a pound note that smelled of chocolate because the box had once held chocolates. She pushed it into the pocket of her coat, together with the several half-crowns and other silver and dumped her homework bag on her bed before scampering back down the stairs. She headed down the meadow towards the other farm and the outbuilding where she'd left her bike. Auntie Bessie was still in the field attending to that ewe, and calling to her.

'I've got to go home to find my mum,' she shouted back. She didn't stop. To go home now was much the best thing to do, she'd find out then about Mum and Milo.

She retrieved her bike and rode as hard as she could into town. Mum always came on a special coach when she visited, but Amy knew there were trains that would take her home. She rode straight to the station at the top of town and wheeled her bike inside. She knew about trains, that was how they travelled when Mum took them to the seaside for their summer holidays. But stations were busy places and she thought at first this one was deserted. Then she saw an elderly man in a peaked cap and navy serge uniform sitting behind a glass panel with gold lettering on it spelling out the word 'Tickets'.

'I want to go to Birkenhead,' she told him. 'Is there a train going there tonight?'

'Birkenhead? You could catch the down train to the junction. It'll be coming through in a few minutes, it's almost due. Then you need to change at both Gobowen and Oswestry to get on the main line into Birkenhead.'

Amy's head swam. 'That's a lot of changes. You're sure it's possible for me to do it?'

'Certainly, *bach*, it's possible. There's a big hospital at Gobowen and a small train shunts back and fore between there and Oswestry.'

'I'll have a ticket please.' She was getting out her money. 'A child's ticket, I'm under fourteen.'

'Single or return?'

For the first time it occurred to her that she mightn't have enough money for a train journey. 'Single. How much will that be?'

She heard the ping and saw the green ticket shoot up from the machine. It cost most of what she had. She said, 'I want to take my bike with me.'

'That'll have to go in the guard's van and you'll need a ticket for it too. That'll be . . . Hold on. I'll need to look that up.'

Amy nervously fingered the coins she had left. 'If I leave my bike here till I come back, will you look after it for me?'

'But you need a return ticket. It works out cheaper that way.'

'No,' she said. 'Perhaps I'll come back on the coach.'

'You're not running away, are you?' he asked suspiciously. 'You're not from these parts.'

'I'm from Birkenhead and I have to go home urgently.'

'Here's the train, the signal's dropped.'

'What about my bike?'

'All right, *bach*. It can stay in the lost property office. What's your name? I'll label it. You'll have to cross the bridge to the down line.'

'I'm Amy Dransfield. Thank you.'

Amy took to her heels and ran across the bridge as the train steamed into the station. Her heart was thumping but she felt victorious. There was nobody else getting on but one passenger got off and held the carriage door open for her. She shot inside, holding her breath until the guard slammed the door shut behind her. She heard him blow the whistle and felt the train jerk forward. She'd managed it, she was on her way home.

Bessie had been shocked to see Amy rush down to their neighbouring farm and though she'd called out to her she hadn't paused in her headlong flight. Bessie knew she couldn't possibly catch her up because Amy already had a head start. She found it hard to believe the child was setting off to go home to Merseyside. Bessie had no idea how to make the journey, so how could Amy possibly find her way?

When she was sure both the two newborn lambs were all right and the mother ewe was taking care of them, she hurried back to the house. Amy had come back here for something. She went upstairs to her bedroom to see if she'd left any clues. Her schoolbag had slid off the bed on to the floor.

It took her only a moment to realise she'd come to collect her money. The pretty chocolate box that Gwlithyn Jones the postmistress had given her to store her valuables was open on the dressing table, displaying its contents. There was only an embroidered handkerchief and a gold wire brooch spelling her name.

Bessie felt like crying. She'd been so involved with that dratted ewe that she'd not paid attention to Amy. She should have stopped her running off. Poor Amy had been in a frenzy when she'd called across the field to tell her she was afraid her mother was dead and that a bomb had blown the roof off her home. The child could get lost anywhere between here and Birkenhead. Nobody would even know where to look.

Bessie was distraught, she couldn't sit to her afternoon tea. She went out to get the cows in for milking. That would have to be done regardless of what was happening to Amy. She ran the separator and was out feeding the pigs when Jack came home. She unloaded all her worries on him.

'I noticed her bike wasn't in the shed.' Jack frowned. 'I thought she might have wheeled it up here because she had a puncture.'

'No.' Bessie shook her head. 'Let's have our tea and think about what we should do.'

Actually, she'd thought of nothing else since Amy had gone and had already made up her mind. 'I've written down Amy's full name and address and also that of her mother's shop and the phone numbers. We must let her know that Amy found out her home had been bombed and she was worried stiff about her. That we think she's gone to try and find her.'

'I can't,' Jack said. 'I don't know how to use the phone.'

'Neither does anyone else round here. Nobody's got one. You must see Gwlithyn Jones. She'll ring up for you, if you take her the money. She does it for everybody else. '

'Couldn't you go?'

'Better if you did that. I can't ride a bike, I haven't got one. I'll stay here and finish the evening work and then make supper.'

She watched him go striding back down the field. From the gate he called back to her, 'Keep an eye on this ewe.' He was jabbing his finger at it. 'I think she could be the next to lamb.'

Bessie stood watching the ewe for a few moments. Already it was dusk and would soon be dark; there was nothing else for it, she let Fly off his chain and opened the door to an outhouse. The ewe would have to come indoors for the night in case she needed help lambing. If she left her in the field they'd never catch her in the dark. Fly worked better for Jack than he ever did for her, but eventually they managed it.

With all the animals shut in for the night, Bessie retired to the house to build up the fire and make supper. She couldn't stop worrying about Amy. She couldn't remember what Amy had said exactly about not being able to speak to her mother. She wished she'd concentrated more at the time and hoped from the bottom of her heart that Leonie and Milo were all right.

She kept going outside to look down the dark fields to see if Jack was coming back. There wasn't a glimmer of light showing anywhere, that was the law, but there was enough moonlight for her see a figure coming up the meadow.

He was exhausted and slumped on to the settle. 'Gwlithyn Jones couldn't get through to either of those phone numbers,' he said. 'She thought the bombs might have put them out of order and the best thing for us to do was to let the police know that Amy had gone. She phoned for me and they said they'd try and contact her family.'

'Oh dear!' Bessie felt as though she had a block of ice in her stomach. 'That could mean the worst has happened.'

'No, the postmistress said it means the bombing has brought the phone lines down. It's no good worrying about what could have happened. We'll know soon enough.'

'I do feel I've let her mother down,' Bessie said sadly. 'She was relying on me to look after Amy. I do hope nothing happens to her.'

After Ralph's death, June had gone through a few weeks when she didn't care whether she lived or died. The bombs no longer frightened her. She did what she had to do and shut her mind to everything else. But when she saw that the home she'd been brought up in had had its roof blown off she was totally horrified. She felt she and her family were having a run of very bad luck. First she'd lost Ralph, then Pa and now this.

It was her day off, but instead of her usual day of rest she'd worked hard helping to salvage their belongings from their bombed house and sort out what Mum and Milo would need in the flat. More upsetting than carrying out beds was the sight of all their personal belongings broken and shattered across the floor. She couldn't help picking up things Amy might want in the future. She was tired and knew Mum and Milo were exhausted. For them it was equally bad, if not worse. She had seen her mother fighting tears several times today but she was quietly getting on with what had to be done.

There was a huge pile of clothes and household linen that would need washing or dry cleaning before it could be used again and they'd failed to find storage space in the tiny kitchen in the flat for all the domestic utensils they'd brought from home. Elaine was doing her best to help. 'We can store some of your things in our house,' she said. 'Tom can put them up in the loft until you need them.'

Tom arrived with the car to see how much headway they'd made. As he usually did on Fridays, he'd left work early so they could go to Chester. June saw Elaine take her husband aside and say, 'We can't leave Leonie to cope with this on her own. Do you think we should stay here tonight?'

'I was thinking that myself. When I get home I'll ring Olive and Nick and tell them we won't be coming.'

It was half past four and they were all hungry, dirty and tired, Elaine said, 'Come on, let's all go back to our house and have something to eat. We had nothing but a sandwich at lunchtime and I'm empty. Leonie, you must stay with us tonight, this flat is a chaotic shambles and the beds aren't made up.'

'Are you sure?' She looked bone weary. 'After all you've done today I feel we're imposing on you.'

'No you're not. Besides, what if there's an air raid? Do you have anywhere to shelter?'

'There's a public shelter in the park.' Milo looked deadbeat too.

'Yes, there is,' Elaine agreed. 'We've been there when we had a daylight raid, but I wouldn't care to get out of bed in the middle of the night and rush to sit in there with half the neighbourhood. Leonie, you and June stayed with us last night, so it's no trouble to us if you sleep in our guest room again.'

'I spent most of the night in your shelter.'

'Yes, and as June will have to go back to the hospital after we've had supper, there's room for you too, Milo.'

'Thank you,' Milo said. 'It's not my turn to fire-watch tonight, so I'd like to stay with you.'

June was glad to get into Tom's car for the journey, she was weary too. Milo said as they got out, 'I could forgo supper, Elaine. If you don't mind, I feel I really need a bath. I've got this horrible dust in my hair and then I'd like to curl up in your Anderson shelter. I can hardly keep awake.'

Elaine said, 'I put the immersion heater on at lunchtime, I thought we'd all need baths, so you'll find there's plenty of hot water, but you must have something to eat too. You go and have your bath now while I think about what we can eat.'

June followed Elaine into the kitchen. 'If I caught the bus back to the hospital now I'd be in time for supper and you'd have one less to feed.'

'No, June. Stay and eat with us then I'll run you back in the car.'

Tom went to the phone in the hall and they could hear him talking to his sister Olive. 'Sorry to muck you about but I don't think we can come tonight to collect the twins after all. Leonie, Elaine's partner, has been bombed out of house and home and needs all the help she can get.' Then he was talking to Dulcie, 'Sorry, love, yes I'm disappointed too, but we hope to come and see you tomorrow.'

June felt her mother was lucky to have friends like the Cliffords. 'What can I do to help with supper?' she asked Elaine.

'Set the table while I have a think about what we can eat.'

Tom came back. 'I can't get hold of Nick. He's left the office but he's not at home. I'll have to try again later.'

'Will two tins of soup be enough for five of us?' Elaine wondered.

'If two is all you have,' June said, 'it'll have to be. Add a little milk to stretch it.'

'I do have milk but I'll have to use water. I need the milk to make a pint of custard. I have some stewed apple left over and the remains of a plain cake and that will give us some sort of a pudding.'

'Are we going to have a main course?'

Elaine sighed. 'The best I can do is sardines on toast. What is the world coming to?'

'None of us will go to bed hungry,' June said, 'and it's good of you to feed us all in these difficult times.' She set the table and helped to open the tins.

Milo appeared at the table with his newly washed hair slicked back. 'I'm all ready for bed,' he said. He was wearing the siren suit Leonie had made for him. If they hadn't all been so tired, Elaine's scratch meal would have been quite a jolly occasion.

'I would never have believed mixing tomato soup with chicken soup would turn out to be so tasty,' June told her.

Milo thanked Elaine as soon as they'd finished eating and was on his way out to the Anderson shelter in the garden when he turned back.

'What a clot I am,' he said. 'I've forgotten to feed the hens. I'll walk down and do it now.'

'No,' Leonie said. 'You've hardly slept in the past twenty-four hours. Go and lie down, I'll see to it.'

They all protested that in the blackout she mustn't walk all that way alone. Tom offered to drive her down.

In the end, Elaine said, 'No need, I'm going to take June back to the hospital, we can run down there first and see to the chicks together.'

'Sorry, sorry, sorry,' Milo said. 'I salvaged the hen food and put it in the gardener's shed with all those other things we took out of the house. It's a dry meal and I've been adding a bit of water to it and any household scraps we had. And because they were turning off the water, I filled a bucket and some bottles and put them in the shed for the hens too. Will you top up their drinking water while you're at it?'

'We'll do everything,' June said and Elaine wrapped up a dry crust of bread she thought the hens might like.

'Looking after them isn't going to be easy now the water is shut off and we aren't living there,' Milo worried.

'Don't be long,' Tom said. 'Perhaps I should take June. I don't like to think of you driving about in a raid.'

'No,' Elaine said. 'We hardly ever get a raid before ten o'clock. Are you ready, June?'

'Goodnight, Mum.' She kissed Leonie's cheek. 'We'll get through this. Things can only get better.'

'Yes, at least I don't have to worry about Amy. It's a comfort to know she's being well looked after and in a safe place.'

It was another clear moonlit night, so they knew the Luftwaffe was more than likely to come again. June had no difficulty seeing her way round the garden and led the way to the big shed to find and mix the hen food. They'd all looked at the chicks earlier in the day and now when they opened the door of their shed they came scurrying out of the nest behind Hetty. Polly fluttered down from the perch to feed too. Elaine found two fresh eggs in the nesting boxes.

'That gives me four, we'll be able to have eggs for breakfast,' she said. 'All is well here, but there's that pile of clean bedlinen still here.'

'Yes, it's what I salvaged from Mum's blanket chest.'

'She's going to need it to make up the beds. Let's take it up now. We almost have to pass the shop and tomorrow Tom and I will probably go to Chester to see the twins so for your mother that would mean Shanks's pony and carrying it up. I do miss not having my car. This petrol shortage is a real pain.'

June helped her pack the boot and the back seat, and five minutes later they were up at the shop. Elaine unlocked the door while June carried all she could straight upstairs, so that when the shop opened in the morning, all would be ready to carry on the business.

Upstairs, she divided the bedding between the three beds. 'Good job we got the frames put together this afternoon,' she said. 'Are we going to make them up?'

'No, I'm shattered. That can be done tomorrow now we've got this far.' Elaine was passing the phone in the sitting room when it began to ring.

'Who could it be at this time of night?' she said as she picked the receiver up. June watched her. Elaine looked perplexed and answered in monosyllables.

'No,' she said at last. 'She isn't here but she's staying at my house. You can ring her there,' and she gave her own phone number.

'Who was that?' June asked.

'It was the police wanting your mother. They wouldn't tell me what it was about.'

'Probably about being bombed out.' June sighed.

'Yes, come on. Let's get you back to the hospital.'

When Elaine returned home, she was taken aback to find Leonie in tears and Tom pacing the sitting-room floor. 'What's happened?'

'It's Amy,' Tom said. 'The police have rung up; the people

349

she's billeted with have reported her missing. They think she's come here to find her mother.'

'Oh my God!'

'It seems Amy spoke to her friend Pat on the phone this afternoon. Pat told her about the house being bombed.'

Elaine shivered. Leonie's tearful eyes looked up to meet hers. 'That's the only place she'd be likely to go. I hoped you'd find her down there. She wasn't . . . ?'

'No, there was no sign of her.'

'The police said she'll almost certainly make for her home.'

'If she'd been there . . . Well, we'd have seen her and she'd have seen us.'

'Perhaps she went inside the house,' Leonie said faintly. 'Perhaps she fell through the floor. Perhaps . . .'

'I don't think so,' Elaine said firmly. 'She would have heard us and called out. We spent some time there seeing to the hens and we heard nothing, and nothing seemed to have changed since we left there earlier on. We took some more of your stuff up to the shop. She wasn't there either.'

'She wouldn't be there.' Leonie dabbed at her eyes. 'She wouldn't be able to get in, she doesn't have a key.'

'Well, it seems she hasn't reached home yet,' Elaine said. 'Unless she went to her friend's house, the one that lives a few doors further along the Esplanade.'

'I thought of that,' Leonie said. 'And as the phones are working again I tried to phone Colleen Greenway. There was no answer but I heard it ring and ring. I seem to remember her saying they'd at last found a cottage to rent so the whole family could get away from here. I think they were going today.'

'Would Amy be able to find her way back home?' Elaine asked.

'I don't think she would.' Leonie couldn't stop the tears running down her cheeks. 'She's never travelled on her own. She knows nothing about trains and buses. It frightens me to think of it. Amy could be anywhere.'

CHAPTER THIRTY-THREE

LEONIE HAD NEVER FELT so low, she was exhausted mentally and physically. After seeing what had happened to her home it had taken all her strength to keep her mind on practicalities – what she urgently needed to do. Everybody had rallied round to help and she was just beginning to believe she could survive when the police had informed her that Amy was missing.

She felt she could take no more and couldn't stop her tears. Elaine wanted her to go to bed, but she'd not be able to sleep until she knew Amy was safe. Almost anybody out in a raid would be scared stiff, and Amy hadn't experienced one before. If they had a raid tonight she'd be absolutely terrified.

'She could be there by now,' Leonie sobbed. 'She could have got home after you and June left. There's nowhere else she's likely to go.'

Tom was looking at her sympathetically. 'I'll go down and take another look in case she's there.'

'Thank you. Tom, I'll come with you, I want to see for myself.'

'All right,' he said and waited while she pulled a coat on over her siren suit.

When they got to Mersey Reach the moon had disappeared

behind a heavy cloud and it seemed ominously dark. Everything should have been familiar, she'd lived here for nearly thirty years, but it wasn't. She could just make out the change in the shape of the roof, and the smell was alarmingly different. Now there was the stench of old plaster and soot instead of the fresh scent of the river.

'Amy,' she called. 'Amy, are you here?'

Tom echoed her words in a louder voice. 'Amy?'

They listened but the only sound came from the front where the full Mersey tide was hurling waves against the Esplanade.

'If Amy has come, where would she be? Where would we be likely to find her?' Tom asked.

Leonie had to think. 'She'd find the hens. They are what she knows.' She led the way with glass splintering beneath her feet. She opened the henhouse door and shone the torch inside – they all carried on these days. It caused Polly to flutter down from her perch and cackle a welcome. Leonie had hoped to find Amy curled up inside with them.

'She's not here,' she said sadly, backing out and only just managing to close the door before Polly escaped. She was close against the house here and it was darker than ever. She stubbed her toe against something but couldn't see what. Supporting herself against the rough brick wall of the house, she felt round with her foot. One flash from Tom's dimmed torch showed debris of every sort had blown to clutter the path.

He switched his torch off, the public were advised not to show a light outside, it was against blackout regulations. 'It's dangerous to try and walk down here in the dark,' he said. 'Amy? Amy, are you here?' When there was no answer, he said, 'Let's go back.'

'I hope she didn't try to get in the house.' Leonie was striding up the garden to check inside the other sheds.

'She isn't here.' Tom was heading back to his car. 'I think we should go home and try to get some sleep.'

Leonie was agonised. 'But the police think she's on her way here, she could reach here as soon as we've gone.'

'Amy won't be able to get here in the middle of the night. The buses stop running shortly after ten, and it has gone that.'

'I hate to think of her being here by herself.' Leonie tried to see her watch and failed. 'To come all this way and find the place deserted. She'd be terrified, especially if we have a raid.'

'It doesn't bear thinking about.'

As soon as Leonie entered Elaine's kitchen, she was given a hot drink and urged to go to bed. 'I'll go straight to the shelter,' she said. 'Then I don't have to get up if there's a raid.'

For Nick, Friday had been busy but it was now half three and he liked to leave early when he was expecting Tom and Elaine to come for the weekend. He was in his office with a client who was involved in a complicated case, when fifteen-year-old Maisie Beggs, Heather's replacement, rang through to tell him there was a policeman asking to see him about a personal matter.

'Does he have an appointment?'

'No, he's says he's prepared to wait but he must see you today.'

'All right.' Nick assumed he was a new client and he was taken aback when twenty minutes later Miss Beggs ushered in a uniformed police constable who stood by the door riffling through his notebook.

Nick felt his heart begin to race. He didn't look like a client and if it was a personal matter surely he wouldn't have come in full uniform? For the first time Nick wondered if the matter was personal to him. 'Have a seat,' he said. 'Has something happened?'

The police officer remained standing. 'Yes, sir, I'm afraid it has. We believe your wife . . .' He began to read from his notebook. 'Mrs Heather Mary Bailey was a passenger on the train bound for London that was derailed outside Birmingham last night. You heard about that?'

Nick's mouth felt suddenly dry. He'd heard a passing reference to it on the BBC's eight o'clock news while he'd been eating his breakfast, but he hadn't known Heather intended to visit London. 'No, no. Tell me please.'

'Well, last night there was an air raid in the Birmingham area that damaged the railway tracks. The Great Western overnight sleeper via Crewe was travelling on the line at the time and four of its front carriages were derailed. There have been fatalities, sir, and I'm afraid it's my duty to inform you that . . .'

'Fatalities?' Nick shuddered with icy anticipation. 'You've come to tell me Heather has been killed?'

'We believe, sir, that it's possible she has. Ration cards, identity card etcetera were found in a handbag we believe to be hers.'

'I see.'

'I'm sorry.' The police officer scribbled in his book. 'I have to ask if you would be willing to identify the body. We could arrange for it to be brought to the morgue in Chester.'

'Yes,' Nick said. The room was beginning to eddy round

him. Heather, so full of life and energy, always full of new plans, it didn't seem possible that she was dead.

'There appears to have been a gentleman with her. We think it could be a Mr Charles Brody. Would you also be prepared to identify him?'

'No, I can't do that. You'll have to get someone from the Cavanagh Hotel.'

'Yes, that was the address on his papers.'

Nick made himself ask. 'How many were killed?'

'Six on the train but many more injured, some badly.'

'Thank you.'

'We'll let you know when we have it arranged.'

When he left, Nick threw himself back into his chair and stared into space. He'd had such high hopes when he'd married Heather. She was . . . She had been, a very beautiful girl and once he'd felt love for her and been close, but it had all gone wrong. All the same, he hated to think she'd suffered such a violent death.

He felt cold with the shock. He couldn't think straight, his mind was whirling; he'd not be able to do any more work this afternoon, there was no point in trying. He put on his mac and trilby and told his senior clerk he was leaving. Usually he caught a bus at ten past five to carry him the three stops to his home but he had no idea of its timetable. He walked, hoping it would clear his head and stop him shaking.

He needed to call in at the local shops. He was a good customer and the fishmonger there had promised to keep him three trout if at all possible. He fetched them from a back room, holding them out for him to see, plump and gleaming with freshness.

'Lovely,' Nick said. He'd also asked him to keep a small piece of cod for the twins.

'I couldn't get much cod this morning,' the fishmonger said. 'It'll have to be whiting.'

'Thank you. That will do very nicely.' Olive had always bought whiting for her cat, but the twins wouldn't know the difference. He was relieved to have tonight's dinner organised and bought a loaf at the baker's shop before going on.

His house was cold but clean and tidy, he was glad Lily Bales who cleaned for him had been today to tidy up before Elaine and Tom arrived. He poured himself a whisky and sat down, feeling low, to meditate on the premature end that had been Heather's lot.

He must have dozed in his armchair because it was getting dark now and felt colder than ever. He'd been a fool not to light his fire when he'd first come home to have the room warm for when the twins arrived. It had been laid ready so he put a match to it and watched the flames flare greedily through the newspaper. He was hungry and looking forward to his dinner. He couldn't get Heather out of his mind and shuddered. Thank goodness Tom and Elaine would be here tonight. He needed company.

The phone rang and it amazed him to hear Tom's voice just when he'd been thinking of him. He told him about Heather because it was in the forefront of his mind.

'I'm sorry, Nick. But it's going to make things easier for you, isn't it? You won't have to worry about a divorce.'

'No, I won't.' He'd realised that, but what was the matter with him that he hadn't got round to ringing William Lomax about it? 'I'm a widower now but—'

'Nick, we've got big problems here,' Tom cut in. 'I don't think Elaine and I will be able to come tonight. Leonie's house has been badly damaged by the bombs, half the roof has gone and she and Milo won't be able to go on living there.'

Nick shivered as icy fingers seemed to clutch his stomach. 'Was Leonie hurt? It must have been terrifying for her. Has she lost everything?'

'Not everything. Elaine has been helping her all day to salvage what she can. But there's—'

'Where will she live now?' Why had he been worrying about Heather when this had happened to Leonie? It would turn her world upside down. 'She's got the shop premises, hasn't she? Will there be room for her and her son to live there? Was Milo hurt?'

'Nick, listen to me, will you? The bombing isn't her only problem, there's worse.'

'What could be worse than having no roof over your head?'

'Amy has run away.'

He couldn't get his breath and the pause dragged on.

'Nick, are you there?'

'Yes . . . What do you mean, run away? From Wales where she was evacuated? I thought she was happy there.' He couldn't get the words out quickly enough. 'Leonie wrote that she was glad she'd made the decision to let her go.'

'Apparently Amy just upped and left. She ran off before they could stop her. She spoke to her friend Pat on the phone and they think she told her about her home being bombed and the roof caving in, that Pat frightened her. They understood that Amy meant to come home to her mother but Elaine and

June went to Mersey Reach to feed the hens and they found no sign of her.'

Nick cleared his throat. 'She'd be worried about her mother and brother, wouldn't she? Leonie wasn't hurt?'

'No, she stayed with us last night. She was in our shelter and Milo was out fire-watching, so neither were anywhere near at the time of the raid. They're fine except that Leonie's worried stiff about Amy. She's left Wales but she hasn't come home and nobody knows where she is.'

'What can I do to help?' he asked.

'Nothing. Elaine and I think we should stay here tonight to give Leonie some support.'

'Of course.'

'We'll come tomorrow, if Amy's all right. The police have her classed as a missing person and hopefully are making inquiries.'

'If you have news of her you'll let me know?'

'Yes, of course. I tried to phone you earlier. Have you been out?'

'I left work early. Heather – you know.'

'Yes, sorry about her.'

Nick collapsed back on his armchair. He ought to eat but he was no longer hungry. In fact he felt sick. He hoped the fish would keep until tomorrow. But poor Leonie, he wished he was there to comfort her.

A little later he got up to make himself some tea and had another thought. He rang Tom.

'What time was it when Elaine fed the hens? Should you go down to take another look before you go to bed, in case—'

'Elaine thinks Leonie won't go to bed unless we do.'

'When you've been, will you ring me again to let me know?'

'If that's what you want.'

'It is, I'm her father, damn it. I don't care how late it is.'

'All right, Nick.'

He tried to read, he tried to listen to the wireless, but he could think only of Amy lost in all those miles between Wales and Merseyside. The wait until Tom rang again seemed endless.

'Amy isn't there, Nick. Leonie couldn't settle without a last look round so I took her with me, but here was no sign of the child.'

'There must be something we can do.' He felt agonised.

'Go to bed, Nick. Milo is asleep in our Anderson shelter and Elaine and Leonie are just going down – and, oh heavens, there's another raid beginning now as I speak.'

Nick heard the air-raid warning through the phone. His legs felt suddenly weak. Amy could be in real danger and even if she wasn't, she'd be alone and petrified. His heart went out to her.

'There's nothing more any of us can do but wait. Perhaps by morning . . .'

Amy looked round the empty railway carriage as it gathered speed and she got her breath back. She was very worried about her home being bombed and losing its roof and terrified about what could have happened to Mum and Milo. She'd been shocked when Pat had told her but now she began to panic.

The pounding of the engine and the sight of fields flashing past the window seemed very alien as she'd rarely been on a train before. It drove home that she'd run away from Auntie

Bessie and Uncle Jack and although she'd caught the train to Birkenhead, she wasn't at all sure she'd ever get there.

She'd been told to change trains three times but she wasn't at all clear in her mind how this was to be done. She got out her ticket to study it but there was no advice on that. She sank back in the velvet cushions, scared and shivering and wishing she'd stayed where she was, where everything was familiar and she'd felt safe.

Then as the train drew up in a country station and stopped opposite a uniformed porter she managed to get the window down and call out that she was worried about where she must change trains.

'Everybody must change at the junction,' he said. 'That's next stop. This train goes back.'

Amy sank back in her seat, relieved to have learned that but still scared about what she was doing.

'All change,' she heard the porters calling at the next station and got out to ask about the new train she must board.

She had to go to a different platform for the Oswestry train but though sick with foreboding, she managed that too. This time three ladies got into the carriage with her. Amy looked out of the window knowing she must not miss the station where she had to make the next change but was fearful she might. One of the elderly ladies started to talk to her and Amy was very relieved to hear that Oswestry was still an hour or so away and that she was going there too.

'I'll tell you when you have to get off,' she told her before she closed her eyes and settled back for a nap.

Amy sat back too and wished she had something to read. She was hungry and would have liked something to eat too.

Gradually the train filled up with passengers. When the old lady told her that Oswestry would be the next station, Amy buttoned up her coat in readiness. 'Will you be met here?' the woman asked.

'No, I'm just changing trains to go to Birkenhead.'

'Then you need to catch the Gobowen train and change again there. It'll be waiting in the station. I live here so I know about the local trains. It'll only take ten or fifteen minutes and shunts backwards and forwards.'

Amy was full of gratitude as she was put on the train. 'You'll have no trouble knowing where to get off,' she was told, 'because everybody will.'

This was a different sort of train, it was full and the passengers were sitting in long rows instead of in carriages. When it pulled up in Gobowen, they all surged out and the porters were shouting directions to catch onward trains.

She felt better when she boarded the train going into Birkenhead Woodside. She knew where that was. In fact, she thought the line went through Rock Ferry Station and that was nearer home than going to Woodside. If it stopped there, she'd get out and know exactly where she was because Mum and June took her that way when they caught the underground into Liverpool.

She sat by the window and watched carefully as the small stations flew by. It had been getting dark for some time and now night was upon them and it wasn't always possible to read the names of the stations unless the train stopped. The lights were dimmed everywhere and Amy was not used to the blackout. In the country, blackout was quite different because there was no man-made light anywhere.

With relief, she began to recognise the names of the stations and knew she was right, this was the line that went through Rock Ferry. Her fear now was that it might not stop, but yes, she could feel it slowing. It was going to stop.

She got out and followed other passengers to the exit. The air felt heavy and smelled of soot and of fire. She'd travelled this way several times with Mum and so found the bus stop without difficulty. A bus drew up in front of her within moments.

It was packed and she had to stand but she didn't mind, she was filled with exultation. She'd managed it! She'd soon be with her family again, and wouldn't they be surprised to see her?

She got off the bus at the stop in New Chester Road which was only a hundred yards from her mother's shop. She couldn't remember ever being out on a night as dark as this. Always before there'd been lights streaming out from the shops and other buildings, now there were no street lamps and even the traffic was driving on dimmed headlights. But the lie of the land was reassuringly familiar. The first thing she did was to run along to the front door of the shop. So far as she could see it hadn't changed and that was reassuring too.

It looked deserted, but at this time of night it would be. She knew there was a doorbell that rang upstairs in the flat. It was fixed unobtrusively on the door frame up in the left-hand corner. Amy reached up and pressed it hard. She heard it ring but there was no response. She rang it again, keeping her finger on it for longer, but again there was no response.

In normal circumstances, that was what she'd expect. They would all be at home. Perhaps Pat was wrong. Perhaps the damage wasn't all that bad. The thing to do now was to go and see. She felt she was on the last lap of the journey and would soon find out what had happened to her family.

She ran but had only gone a few yards when the screaming wail of the air-raid siren scared the living daylights out of her and made her clutch at somebody's front gate.

The sound died away and nothing seemed to have changed. She'd never heard it before, they didn't have such things in the country. She looked up nervously and could see silvery barrage balloons bobbing over her head. She went on again more slowly but her heart was hammering away. She wanted her mum.

The fact that the bombers had blown the roof off her house last night didn't mean they wouldn't come again tonight. She should have known that. Pat and her family had gone away at four o'clock so they wouldn't have to spend another night here. Everybody was terrified of the German bombers.

She started to run again and fear put wings on her feet. At last she came to her own back gate and its familiarity made her feel safer until she turned down the garden path and felt the glass splinter beneath her shoes. She looked up and saw the bare gable wall of her home standing up stark against the sky and the roof sagging down into the living room and entirely missing over the hall.

She was shaking with shock. Pat had been right! 'Mum,' she called. 'Mummy, where are you?' She wiped the tears from her face with her hands. 'Mum? Mum?' She'd never wanted her more. She shouldn't have come. Mum and Milo had told her it wouldn't be safe for her. After all, the bombs had killed Pa. They could kill her.

She couldn't hold back the sharp intake of breath when she

saw the devastation of the bedroom wing. What was she to do now? She walked round to the front garden where the destruction seemed worse. In the distance she heard the crump crump of falling bombs, and saw yellow flames take hold on the Liverpool bank, flutter and grow, dancing ever higher.

She turned and ran back through the gardens to Pat's house because Pat had said Alison and her father would be coming back. She hammered on their back door, wanting their company more than she had ever wanted it before, but nobody came. Slowly, she went back to her own garden. She heard the gurgle of a hen as she neared the henhouse shed so she opened the door.

Polly cackled and fluttered down from her perch and here was Hetty with her chicks. They were like old friends though she could barely make them out in the dark. The very smell of the henhouse was comforting. They had fresh water, so somebody was looking after them. Milo and Mum were surely not far away. They would come tomorrow to feed them. Carefully, she closed the door again and looked about her.

Milo's summer house seemed untouched. She let herself in, feeling too tired to think. June was living at the hospital and that was miles away. Where would Mum go if she couldn't live here? Auntie Elaine's house perhaps but that was a long way away too. Milo had lots of friends but she hardly knew them.

A shaft of silvery moonlight shining through the window showed up a heap of pillows and blankets in the corner of the shed and she sensed that Milo had been here recently. She pulled them into the shadows under the wooden workbench than ran under the window. It felt safer and more private here.

CHAPTER THIRTY-FOUR

NICK WAS SHAKING AS he put the phone down. The thought of Amy being lost and alone in an air raid was making him sweat. He'd known fear himself in a raid, though like every other adult he'd tried to hide it. His own daughter and he hardly knew her. He'd never been able to help her in any way, he'd had to leave all that to Leonie, but it seemed she'd be spending tonight alone and in a strange place. She must be very frightened now.

He wanted to help her if he could, but what could anybody do but go to her home and wait for her to come? Leonie and Tom were much nearer and he knew they'd do that. He couldn't rest, he had to do something. He could go to Mersey Reach and see for himself, he had enough petrol in his car to get there and back.

But Tom thought Amy wouldn't be able to get there tonight. Would it be wiser to wait till first light? He could go to bed and set his alarm for five o'clock. That would give him plenty of time to dress and make a flask of tea. If it was still dark when he got there he could wait. He'd never been inside Leonie's house, but he'd driven her home from the shop several times so he knew where to go.

But he couldn't sleep, he tossed and turned and finally got

up an hour earlier than he'd intended. The roads were empty and it took him less time than he'd supposed to get there. He parked outside the big double gates, wide enough to get a furniture van in or a boat out. When he tried the latch he thought at first they must be locked, but no the gate had dropped and was dragging on the ground.

The sky was getting lighter in the east and he could see the shape of the house outlined against it, the roof partly gone and reduced to broken and sagging timbers. The sight made him suck in his breath in dismay. It was a scene of devastation, the house had been destroyed. He ached to comfort Leonie. He knew how she must feel about this. He shuddered, this place was enough to scare anybody.

After a moment he called, 'Amy, Amy, are you there?'

He listened for an answer but all he heard was a soft cackle he couldn't place. It came again. Of course! Elaine had told him about Milo's poultry. He found the shed and unaccountably it was undamaged. He went inside, pulling the door shut behind him and that caused a lot more cackling and fluttering. He found his torch and shone the thin beam round. The hens were all right, they'd been shut in for the night, so presumably Milo would return in daylight to let them out again.

He retraced his steps and saw other sheds that seemed undamaged. He'd passed one by the gate, Leonie had told him about Milo taking a shed over as a club room when he was a boy, and guessed that was it. He opened the door and let in the cold dawn air and sensed immediately that he was not alone.

'Amy,' he said softly. 'Amy, are you here?' He shone his torch round and thought at first he was mistaken, but then he heard a rustle from under the workbench. He shone the light in that direction and saw the girl shrink away from him. His heart turned over with relief, with joy that he'd found her. He directed his torch at the roof and went down on his haunches.

'Amy,' he said softly. 'Don't be afraid, I've come to help you.'

She pushed her face forward, wide-set eyes peered doubtfully at him. 'Who are you? I don't know you, do I?'

He had to bite back the words, I am your father. 'Nick,' he said. 'My name's Nick. I'm a friend of Elaine's, you know her, don't you? And Tom is almost my brother. Your mother is staying with them. She can't live here any more, the roof has gone.'

'I know.' The girl was crawling out of the blankets and he could see something of her now. 'Was my mum hurt when the house got bombed?'

'No, she was at Elaine's house the night it happened. She's fine and so are Milo and June.' She hung back, suspicion on her face. 'Don't be afraid, my car's outside. I'll take you to them.'

Slowly she put on her shoes. Her hair hadn't been cut for months, she had one thin pigtail little more than shoulder length but its partner had come undone and her hair on that side swung in a limp curtain. She looked frightened. He had to stop himself throwing his arms round her in a gesture of comfort. That might frighten her more.

'Everybody's been worried stiff about you.'

'I'm all right,' her smile quivered, 'but I'm glad you found me.'

'I'm glad too,' he said. He was feeling for her hand, about to lead her out to his car, when she stiffened.

'There's somebody outside.' It was a horrified whisper and she was shrinking away from him, but he'd heard a footfall too. Somebody else was creeping about. Looters? If so, they were certainly trespassing.

His heart was hammering as he opened the door, determined to defend his young daughter and keep her safe from whoever it was. Somebody was trying to come into the shed! Nick found he was clutching at a soft woollen coat, while flailing arms brushed his head and shoulders. He tried to restrain them.

A soft voice he immediately recognised said, 'Nick, is it you?'

He wanted to laugh. His spirits soared, he felt hysterical. 'It's me.' He wrapped his arms round her in a welcoming hug. 'Amy, here's your mother.'

With a gurgle of joy, Leonie swept her daughter into her arms. 'Darling, thank goodness you got here safely. I've been so worried about you.' Still hugging Amy, she looked up and said, 'Thank you, Nick. Oh, it's lovely to see you both again.'

Smiles didn't leave their faces. They kept hugging each other. Leonie kissed them both. Nick felt he'd found at last what he'd spent his life hoping for. He wanted to stop the world at this moment. After a while he said, 'I'd better get you to Tom's house.' He ushered them to his car. 'They're worried about you too, Amy.'

Leonie felt up on cloud nine. She couldn't bear to let her daughter out of her arms and shared the front seat of the car with her. She was delighted and relieved to have Amy restored to her unhurt, but bemused as well to have found Nick looking for Amy too. That must mean she still meant a lot to him.

Leonie studied what she could see of Nick's profile as he drove and said, 'I couldn't sleep, I decided the only thing to do was to walk down and check again whether Amy had reached home.'

'Mum, did you walk all that way in the blackout to find me? You must have been worried.'

'I was out of my mind. But Nick, how did you come to be looking for her?'

'I couldn't sleep either.' In the dim light from the dashboard she saw him flash a smile in her direction. 'After Tom told me Amy was missing I tossed and turned for hours. I had to do something so I came to look for her.'

'I shouldn't have left Auntie Bessie's, should I?'

'No,' her mother said firmly. 'You shouldn't have.'

'I'm sorry.' Amy's voice shook. 'I've caused you all a lot of trouble.'

'And anxiety,' Nick said. 'For Auntie Bessie too.'

When he pulled up on Tom's drive, the house was still and silent. 'It's not really light yet,' Leonie said. 'They're probably still asleep in their air-raid shelter but they leave the back door open so we can get in.'

She led the way round the back, but in the dark she could hear Tom and Elaine coming across the garden towards them. 'Here they are.'

'You've found Amy! Thank goodness for that. And Nick too!' They were both trying to hug and kiss Amy at the same time. Milo was the last to come running up and he swung her off her feet in the way he always did. Leonie was drawn into the kitchen surrounded by her friends and family all laughing and talking at once.

Elaine put on the kettle for tea and they all helped to make toast. The scent filled the kitchen. 'I'm hungry,' Amy said. 'I had no tea and no supper last night.'

They all fussed round her, wanting to hear about her journey. Elaine boiled an egg for her and Leonie cut soldiers to go with it. Tom brought out the honey jar with just the last inch remaining and set it in front of her. Milo had to rush to get ready for work. Tom went to pack a few things and ring his sister to tell her he'd collect the twins this morning.

Nick said, 'You've got a key to my place, haven't you? Eat the fish for lunch while it's still fresh.'

'Before I go to work I need to go home to let the hens out,' Milo said.

'I should have thought of that while I was down there,' Amy spoke with her mouth full.

'You go to work,' Tom said. 'There's no hurry for that. I'll pop down to do that when I'm leaving for Chester.'

Elaine said, 'I'll open the shop for you first, Leonie, you'll want to see to Amy. Tom, can you stop and collect me on the way?'

'Yes, all right, I'll only be an hour at the most.'

'Ida should be there by ten.'

The house emptied and the stampede subsided. Nick couldn't take his eyes off Leonie and Amy and was delighted to be left with them. He'd spent a lot of time in this house and felt at home here. He settled down with another cup of tea and began to daydream of what might be possible if Leonie wanted it too.

It was Leonie who said, 'I must send a telegram to Auntie

Bessie to tell her you're safe and thank her for letting us know so promptly. It was very wrong of you to leave like that, Amy.'

Nick came to the support of his daughter. 'She was afraid you and Milo had been hurt – or even worse.' He was rewarded with a nod of agreement from her.

Leonie went on, 'You've caused a great deal of trouble for a lot of people. Do you realise Uncle Jack called out the Welsh police to help find you?'

'And now we have to get you back to Wales,' Nick said.

'Do I have to go?' she wheedled, comfortable in her mother's arms.

'Yes,' he and her mother chorused. Leonie laughed and reminded her, 'Next Thursday you are sitting your scholarship exam. We want you to do well so you need to be settled back there as soon as possible.'

'You went there to get away from the air raids,' Nick explained. 'You didn't like being in one last night, did you?'

Amy shivered. 'That noise they make to warn you the bombers are coming, I didn't like that. It was scary.'

'Last night the bombers weren't aiming their bombs on us,' her mother said. 'We had the alert and we heard them go over but it sounded as though they were over Bootle way, so for us it was a good night. We want to get you back to Wales before they come here again.'

Nick looked from one to the other and knew he wanted to stay close to them. He felt a frisson of excitement run through him. If Leonie wanted that, there was no reason now why they couldn't.

'I don't have enough petrol coupons to drive there and

back,' he lamented. 'It'll have to be the train. I'll see if I can find out what time they run.' He went to the phone. Everywhere posters were plastered asking, *Is Your Journey Really Necessary?* And trains were notorious for being late since the heavy raids had started.

'Amy, you look as though you need a bath and a hair wash. Elaine's put the immersion on so we'll do that next, but we've no clean clothes for you here.' Leonie took her up and started the bath running. 'I'll help you wash your hair and then you can bath yourself. Elaine's left out some of Dulcie's knickers and socks, which she fears will be too small, and a pair of her own which will probably be too big. You'll have to choose between them or put on your dirty ones.'

Nick followed them up to the bathroom door and listened to the sounds of family life within. He didn't feel he could go in, Amy mightn't like it. He called, 'Leonie, it is possible to get there and back by train today if we catch one leaving Woodside at ten o'clock. Well, according to the timetable it is. I'll take Amy back for you.'

'I could do that.' Leonie sounded at a loss.

'I can go by myself,' Amy piped up indignantly. 'I got here without any help, didn't I?'

'You certainly did,' Nick said, 'but you won't be going back on your own. No, absolutely not. We all need to know that you've got there safely. I will take you.'

'I'd like to come too,' Leonie said.

'Yes please, Mum.'

'We'd both like you to come,' Nick said, 'but it will be a long day for your mother, Amy, and she already looks exhausted. Besides, she has still got a lot of straightening out to do in the shop before she can live there and she must order a Morrison shelter today if she can.'

'Yes,' she said. 'I've got to do that. Nick, it's very kind of you to offer. I have to be sensible, Amy love, and let him do it.'

Nick was already running down to the phone, to dictate a telegram to Auntie Bessie telling her Amy was safe and he was bringing her back this afternoon. Then he rang his chief clerk and told him that he didn't intend to come in today and asked him to help Miss Beggs cancel all his appointments and reschedule them for next week.

They were about to go when Nick said, 'I'm going to drive to the station and leave my car there. If you're ready, why don't you come with us and I'll drop you off at your shop?'

'Yes please. I don't have to get ready, all my things are there so I needn't hold you up.'

'I wish my mum could come with us.'

'In this world Amy, we all wish for a lot of things we can't have, especially now there's a war on. Your mum can't do everything though she tries. She's had a lot of extra work and worry with the house being bombed, and she said she couldn't sleep at all last night when she knew you were missing. So I'm afraid you'll have to put up with me escorting you back.'

She sniffed hard. 'I know I shouldn't have come.'

'No, but you did well. You had to keep your wits about you to find your way home and you were brave. But please don't try it again, there's a good girl.'

As Nick stopped his car outside the shop and Leonie kissed Amy goodbye, he said, 'Elaine and Tom can settle into my house without me. I'll come back here to see you, shall I?'

CHAPTER THIRTY-FIVE

LEONIE STOOD ON THE pavement waving goodbye to Amy as Nick's car pulled away. The utter relief she'd felt at finding Amy unharmed and the shock of seeing Nick after eleven years had left her spinning with pleasure. She'd been dead dog weary when she'd walked down to Mersey Reach before dawn, but she no longer felt tired. She was filled with zest to face the day.

Ida was machining hard in the shop window. She'd heard from Elaine that Amy had turned up unharmed and Leonie stopped for a moment to share some of her joy about that. Then she went upstairs to the phone in the sitting room to enquire if it was possible to get a Morrison shelter. It seemed that it was. 'But we won't be able to deliver it today,' she was told. 'It'll be Monday at the earliest.'

Pleased with that, Leonie ran back downstairs to size up the room behind the shop where their customers were measured and fitted. Elaine was just finishing with a customer and showing her out.

'This is the only possible place to have the shelter installed,' she said to Ida who had finished the garment she'd been working on. 'But it will make things tight.'

'We'll be able to use it as another cutting-out table.'

Elaine came rushing back. 'Tom's outside, I'll have to go. Will you come with Nick when he gets back?'

'I don't know. I don't know what Nick intends to do. In fact I don't know whether I'm on my head or my heels, but I'm so happy everything has come right.'

'So am I.'

'I've even managed to order a Morrison shelter though they aren't sure when they can deliver it.'

'You must both stay at my place until you've got it erected. I'll see you when I do then.' Leonie followed her through the shop. 'Sorry I can't stay to help you organise things here, it's a real mess upstairs. Goodbye.' The shop doorbell rang as she opened it.

'Goodbye,' Leonie said. Nothing could dent her happiness this morning.

Ida said, 'I heard that, you won't be able to put your mind to sewing until your flat is straight. The sewing is well in hand at the moment. Let me help you to make up those beds for a start. It's an easier job if there are two.'

When they'd made up the beds, Leonie set about trying to organise her clothes and belongings to make it possible to sleep in the smaller bedroom in reasonable comfort. Ida dusted and Hoovered. Leonie had far too much stuff for the one wardrobe and small space. She and Ida packed the rest into boxes and bags and put them up in the loft out of the way.

She almost danced to the tiny kitchen and did the same there. It was harder because many more things had been salvaged from Mersey Reach. When it came to the sitting room it was quite impossible, they had an enormous number of ornaments. She gave a mantel clock to Ida and put some Dresden china shepherdesses on one side to give to Elaine. 'At least I've got the loft to store the surplus,' she said as they put that up too.

'You're very brave,' Ida said. 'You lost the house you've lived in for years and you're still cheerful.'

'None of my children have been hurt,' she said, 'and everybody has been so generous with their help. I've salvaged a lot of my things and I'll be able to claim compensation for the house from the government. I've a lot to be thankful for.' She mused that she had much more to make her happy than that.

Together they started to tidy up the living room and remove the dust and grime from all over the flat brought in with her salvaged belongings.

Nick had been equally relieved to find Amy. She'd seen deep concern for the child on his face. She didn't need to be told that Nick loved her and felt responsibility for her as her father. There was still more, she'd come face to face with Nick and found the pull of attraction to him was as strong as ever. It was over a decade since she'd sent him away and of course he'd changed. There was silver in the dark hair over his temples, the laughter lines round his eyes were deeper and he'd put on a little weight. But she would have aged too. She glanced in the mirror and decided she looked a complete mess, tired, dirty, unkempt and definitely older. She'd never had a bath in this flat but it was time to start.

She went to the bathroom and ran water into the small bath to rinse it out. There was an ancient gas appliance to heat the water that looked positively dangerous but thankfully a stained and dusty leaflet of advice on how to light it was tucked behind the pipework. She found a box of matches and set about following the instructions.

Nick had known she had more work to do than she was likely to accomplish today. Yes, she would have liked to take Amy back to Wales but she'd always found the journey very tiring. Nick wanted to get to know Amy and what better than a long journey in which to do it. And he'd said he'd come back and see her. She mustn't bank on him staying with her, though she hoped he would. They hadn't had time to discuss anything.

'You've nothing much to eat here and you'll need a meal tonight,' Ida said. 'Shall I go out to see if I can find something that isn't rationed, sausages or offal for something?'

'Yes please.' Leonie handed over her pages of ration points with some money. 'Bring some biscuits if you see any.'

'Shall I bring some fish and chips back with me? I'm getting hungry.'

Milo rang. 'Have you been able to make any progress with the flat?'

'Yes,' she said. 'It's all cleaned up and your bed is ready. I had no trouble ordering an air-raid shelter but it won't be delivered for a day or two.'

He laughed. 'A bit ambitious, wasn't it, to think it could be by tonight? Are you going to spend the night there?'

'I'm not sure. Nick's taken Amy to Wales and he'll be coming back here.'

'If there's a raid tonight, it's my turn to fire-watch. I've left my sleeping bag in Elaine's shelter and it would be nearer for me to go there.'

'That's fine. She said we must all feel free to use it if we wanted to. If you want to get into the house, Elaine's keys are under the flower pot by the back door.'

'She told me. Mum, Alison is going to meet me from work with a picnic lunch and we're going to take the bus to Eastham and have a walk through the woods. She says the bluebells are out now. Then she's invited me to eat at her place tonight.'

'Well, I won't be seeing much of you today. Be sure to lock Elaine's house up if you go in.'

'Yes. Goodnight, Mum, see you tomorrow.'

At one o'clock, Leonie closed the shop and had a bath and washed her hair. She was in her dressing gown when Ida returned with packages that smelled delicious. 'I've got us a pennyworth of chips each,' she said. 'I couldn't get fish or fishcakes, they'd all gone, but these will keep us going, won't they?'

She'd also brought two lamb's hearts and a packet of stuffing mix, together with potatoes and a loaf. 'Sorry, I queued for biscuits but they'd sold out before I reached the counter.'

'Doesn't matter.' They ate their chips together and drank tea before Ida went home. 'Thanks for everything,' Leonie said. 'You've worked overtime today.'

Leonie went to get dressed. The clothes she'd had in her wardrobe and her chest of drawers had not been harmed. She took out her newest white blouse and grey skirt, wanting to look her best when Nick returned. She was filled with hopeful anticipation but also apprehension. Would Nick see her just as Amy's mother? He might not want to take up with her again. Why should he when she'd sent him away all those years ago? She was afraid he might not want what she wanted.

The afternoon seemed to drag. She'd expected him back before four o'clock but that time came and went. She prepared the lamb's hearts for the oven. Ida had intended the second one for Milo and she was glad he wouldn't need it tonight. She'd do roast potatoes and there were good cabbages in the garden at Mersey Reach but she couldn't face going down to fetch one now. She'd salvaged a few tins from the kitchen there, one of which contained peas. That would have to do.

Five o'clock and still no sign of Nick. She ought to finish off a dress Elaine had designed and make it ready for a valued customer to have a fitting on Monday morning, but her energy had gone, she was tired and her mind was still on Nick. Suddenly, the heart-stopping wail of an air-raid warning blared out, making her jump. She thought it would never stop. It was the last thing they needed now.

So far, few bombs had been dropped in daylight hours, but all the same it increased her tension. She listened anxiously. There was hardly anybody about and little traffic on the main road outside. She decided she'd shelter under the stairs if she heard enemy aircraft overhead and pulled the bedding intended for furnishing the Morrison shelter into what she hoped was the safest position. She tried to do a bit of sewing but she was too tired now to do anything more.

When Nick finally came, Leonie leapt to her feet to greet him. 'Let me take your coat. How did you get on?'

'All right, except I almost dozed off on the train and nearly missed one of the connections.'

He looked round a little self-consciously.

'There's nobody else here,' she said.

'Auntie Bessie seems fond of Amy and she's a very kind person.'

'She is.' She'd been looking forward to having his company all day and now she was stiff and awkward with him.

'I take it Elaine and Tom went to my place for the weekend?'

'Yes.' She made herself ask, 'Will you stay here with me?'

He smiled and nodded. 'I was afraid you wouldn't want me to.'

'I do, of course I do.'

'Let's go upstairs. I want to hear how you got on.'

Seated on the opposite end of the sofa, he seemed more relaxed. 'I'm glad you let me take Amy back. It gave me a chance to talk to her, to get to know her, and I wanted to see where she was living. I can picture her now in the coming weeks.'

'The countryside there is beautiful.'

'Yes, Amy was fascinated by the lambs. There were lots of them running about in the fields as we went along. We collected her bike from the lost property office at the station and she rode it round to the garage to order the taxi and they strapped it on the back.'

'She wasn't upset because I didn't take her?'

'She soon got over that. She knew she shouldn't have come. I asked the taxi driver to wait half an hour for me so I could catch the next train back.'

Leonie nodded, how sensible he was.

'Auntie Bessie wanted to make me a cup of tea and when I said I hadn't time, she gave me a glass of milk and wrapped up a couple of slices of cake for me to take away with me.'

'Were there refreshment carriages on the train?'

'No, not on any of the trains we travelled on so I was glad to have it. I was still hungry and managed to buy a bun in the station at Oswestry.'

'Then you'll be starving by now. I'll start supper. I've done all the preparation, it's just a matter of cooking it.'

He followed her into the kitchen and stood watching her light the gas. She felt his arms go round her. He turned her round and kissed her full on the mouth. 'I've been aching to do that since the moment I set eyes on you last night,' he whispered. 'I want us to be married.'

'So do I,' Leonie said shyly.

'Soon,' he added. 'We've already waited for over a decade.'

'As soon as possible,' she agreed. 'We can't have a big wedding and a lot of fuss and I had that the first time round anyway, I don't need it.'

'What about next month then?'

Leonie stretched up to return his kiss and knew he loved her as much as she loved him. Their daughter had brought them together again.

That Saturday June had her off-duty in the morning, which was when most of the other girls that were off went shopping. She'd had such a busy time the day before that she went back to the nurses' home and curled up on the sofa to read, but it was quiet and she dozed off and slept until nearly midday.

At lunch, there was much talk about the terrible bomb damage in the town. June, still full of agony, told them her home had been so badly damaged it was no longer possible to live in it. As she worked on the ward she worried about how her mother was getting on sorting out the flat. It had been a chaotic mess when she'd last seen it and they'd all been exhausted.

The evening were lighter now and when she came off duty at eight o'clock, she decided to collect her suitcase of personal belongings. In her haste yesterday she'd pushed it inside one of the garden sheds, but she was afraid to leave it there for long because there were so many rumours about looting. After that, she'd call in and see Mum and perhaps give her a hand with straightening things out.

The dusk was thickening when she reached the garden gate and as soon as it closed behind her she could see the glimmer of a shaded flashlight. She stopped in her tracks, her heart pounding; her first thought was that she'd caught looters red handed. Then she heard a cackle and the door to the henhouse close. Full of relief she called, 'Milo, is that you?'

'Hello, yes, I'm just shutting the chicks in for the night. You missed all the excitement yesterday.'

He was bursting to tell her the news about Amy coming home from Wales, and how worried they'd all been about her.

'Amy's here then?'

'I'm not sure.' He told her how kind Elaine and Tom had been and how their friend, Nicholas Bailey, had come from Chester and had found Amy bedded down in the clubhouse he'd made from the old summer house. 'Mum wanted her to go back and Nick was planning to take her. I thought I'd look in on Mum now.'

'So did I,' June said.

'Let's get a move on then. If we get another raid, I'll have to rush off to fire-watch again.'

June had to ring the shop doorbell twice before she heard

footsteps coming. Mum ushered them inside quickly. Once upstairs in the light, June could see that her mother's cheeks were pink and she looked radiant. 'Is Amy still here?' June asked.

'No, Nick took her back to Wales. He's here. Come and say hello. This is Nicholas Bailey, I don't think you know him, do you June?'

'We have met,' he said, coming towards her with his hand outstretched. 'But you won't remember me, it was a long time ago.'

'I've heard Elaine mention your name,' she told him, and was surprised when, as well as clasping her hand, he bent to kiss her cheek.

He grinned broadly at her. 'Your mother has told me a great deal about you.'

June sensed his joyful mood and felt an air of pleasure and happiness sparking in the atmosphere, but it was Milo who asked, 'Has something happened?'

'Yes,' her mother laughed. 'I'm going to tell them, Nick. I want us to have everything out in the open from now on. Nick and I are going to be married.'

'What?' June couldn't believe it.

'And it's going to be quite soon.'

'A bit sudden, isn't it Mum?' Milo asked, looking from Nick to his mother.'

She sat down on the sofa and pulled June down on one side of her and Milo on the other. Clasping their hands, she said, 'It isn't at all sudden. Quite the opposite in fact. Nick is Amy's father.'

It took June some time to digest this information. Her mother had had a love affair that she'd kept secret while she and Milo had been growing up. She understood then why Mum had been so ready to help her and Ralph. It all made perfect sense.

'I'm so happy for you,' she breathed. 'I wish both of you all the very best in the world. You deserve it.'

When Amy returned to Coed Cae Bach she found Auntie Bessie gently reproachful. Nick had reminded her to apologise for the trouble she'd caused her and Uncle Jack. She felt ashamed now of taking off as she had. She did that as soon as Nick left but she was unable to hold back her tears and Bessie ended up trying to comfort her.

On Sunday she did the homework she should have done on Thursday night, but she knew she'd have been given a good deal more to do over the weekend if she'd been at school. She was afraid Mrs Roberts would be cross with her and Mum really wanted her to do well in the exam.

As she'd missed school on Friday, Bessie said, 'I'll write a note for you to take to Mrs Roberts tomorrow.'

'Could you say you kept me home because I had a cold?' Amy asked. She didn't want her to know she'd run home.

'No,' Uncle Jack said. 'She'll already know what happened and why. News travels fast in the country. Don't you worry about it. Come on out now and help me with the afternoon milking.'

On Monday, Amy was surprised to find Mrs Roberts quite sympathetic. She received more homework but not as much as usual. 'You've worked very hard, Amy, and I think you'll do well. Perhaps you should do a little less homework this week. We don't want you to be overtired on Thursday.'

Amy was to sit the examination in the grammar school in town and she wasn't looking forward to it. 'You must be there in plenty of time,' Mrs Roberts told her. 'The exam starts at ten o'clock and you must be there at least fifteen minutes before that. Do you have a watch?'

'Yes.' Amy rolled up the cuff of her jersey to show her. 'My mum gave it to me for Christmas.'

'Good. Can you find your way to the grammar school?'

'Yes, I met Glenys in town one Saturday. She was coming out from her piano lesson and I asked her to show me where it was. We walked down to see it. It's a bit out of town.'

'Yes, it is. You can take the school taxi back into town after it has dropped the children off here and you may be able to catch it to come back in the afternoon if you hurry to the garage as soon as the afternoon exam finishes. Shall I have a word with the driver?'

'I'd rather go on my bike,' Amy said. 'They've got bike sheds there, I saw them.'

'Of course, if you prefer. You've got a lock for your bike?'

'Yes, thank you.'

'It could be needed. Take your usual sandwich and bottle of milk with you for your lunch. You will sit a maths paper in the morning and English and Welsh in the afternoon, with an hour and a half break between them.'

On Wednesday, Mrs Roberts marked her homework and wished her well in the exam. 'Do your best and I'm sure you'll be fine. You're well up to the required standard.'

The thought of the exam hung heavily over her. But the next morning, Amy found once she settled down and looked at the questions that they weren't too bad. It was just like doing the homework that Mrs Roberts had been setting her for the last eight weeks.

Despite all the wartime difficulties, Leonie felt life had suddenly taken a turn for the better. She couldn't forget Steve, she never would, she'd shared too much of her life with him, and the fact that he'd died a hero made her put the bad times to the back of her mind. It was getting back with Nick that was making all the difference.

That first weekend they spent together they didn't go out and they didn't speak to anybody else. They had so much to catch up with but Nick had to return to Chester on Sunday night. Elaine came to work on Monday morning and swept her into a big bear hug. She'd already heard the news from Nick.

'Congratulations,' she said. 'At last you've both seen sense. You'll be good for each other. I know you will.'

'It'll mean big changes.' Leonie had been giving them some thought.

'Of course it will,' Elaine enthused. 'Marriage usually does, but think of what you had to do to move your home to the flat upstairs. You achieved that in no time at all, didn't you?'

'That job isn't finished, the hens are still down there. I've walked down this morning to feed them and let them into their outside pen. Milo's going to ask his friends to help him bring them up.'

'Oh gosh, what a job. Are you going to put them in the yard here?'

'Where else? We've got to make looking after them more convenient than it is now.'

Leonie looked out of the window at the courtyard effect they'd made in the backyard. It was a quite a pleasant place to sit out on fine days and it had improved the view from the back windows.

'We'll have to find a henhouse from somewhere first. We can't move their present shed, it's built on to the side of the house. I'm afraid it'll spoil the courtyard.'

'Oh dear,' Elaine was frowning. The window of her office looked over the back of the premises. 'I was wondering whether they'd be better in our garden, but with the Anderson shelter and Tom's attempt at digging for victory, there isn't much space left. He's put most of it down to growing vegetables.'

'I'll ask Nick what sort of a garden he has and whether he'd be willing to have them.'

'He has a big garden with apple trees. He's growing vegetables too, but I reckon he has space for a henhouse at the bottom end.'

'I'll ask if he's willing.'

'Where are you going to live, Leonie? I mean, if you're going to marry him, you'll be going there, won't you?'

'Yes, but I've got this business and travelling from Chester every day would reduce the time I'd have here. Unravelling my life after all this time is very complicated.'

'I know, Tom and I have talked about it and wondered what you'll do.'

'Nick and I have talked about it too but we've not made much progress on that.'

'Leonie, I would be willing to buy you out if that's what you want. I'm getting better at sewing but a long way off you yet. But Ida is settled here and she's a reliable worker. I'd need to take on another full-time seamstress and then I could handle pretty much what goes through the business now. I'd aim to expand my side, provide high-class designs and fit. It's a good time to do it, there's nothing but utility clothes in the shops and very little choice in styles.'

'That would solve my main difficulty. Let me think about it because there's Milo too, he has nowhere else to live and he needs to stay near his job.'

'We've already talked about that, haven't we? I won't want to live in the flat.'

'Unless you get bombed out of your house.'

'Heaven forbid, but I'm not even going to consider that. I'd be willing to rent it to Milo, I know him well enough to trust him. I couldn't rent it to a complete stranger because there's no way I can lock away any of the stuff in the shop.'

'If you explain that you don't want him to touch your property, I know he'd respect your wishes.'

Elaine smiled. 'I'd want his bed out of my office but he'd only need one bedroom.'

It was Leonie's turn to deliberate.

'Milo is twenty-four now, isn't he?' Elaine asked

'Nearly twenty-five.'

'He's more than old enough to take care of himself, and he'll have everything he needs, use of kitchen and bathroom and a decent size bedroom to himself. He'll probably enjoy it.'

'He's not terribly tidy, Elaine. You'll have to lay down the law about that and about keeping the place clean.'

'He'll be on his own in the evenings and at weekends because I'll be using it only for business. With so many families bombed out he won't get a better deal than that.'

'He'll be over the moon and with the bus stop only fifty yards from the front door, it'll be easier for him to get to work.'

'What's that lorry doing outside?'

'Oh! I'm expecting a Morrison shelter to be delivered. Is it that? Yes, I do believe it is.'

The front door pinged and Leonie rushed down to find a burly workman in the shop. 'We've brought your shelter,' he said. 'Where d'you want it erected?'

'In here.' She ushered him into the back room where their customers were fitted.

'You're not going to be left with all that much space.' He stamped on the floor. 'You've no cellar under here?'

'No, it's solid.' Leonie went back upstairs to see Elaine. 'Milo will even have his own shelter,' she said.

CHAPTER THIRTY-SIX

THE WORKMEN WERE LEAVING. They had slid the mattress she'd kept under the stairs inside the shelter for her. She was tossing in the pillows and blankets on top of it as Elaine prepared to go. Leonie thanked her for her offer. 'Think about it,' Elaine urged. 'Talk it over with Nick.'

Leonie sat down to scribble a note to Milo, reminding him to feed the hens and bring up a lettuce from the garden at Mersey Reach. '*Sorry*,' she wrote, '*I'm going to Chester, you'll have to make your own supper tonight. Help yourself to anything you can find. There are tins and oddments we brought up earlier.*'

Then she rang Nick at his office and told him she was about to leave. Feeling on top of the world, she ran out to catch the Chester bus that ran along the main road outside.

Nick had asked her to come and said he'd run her back in the car later. She was excited at the thought of spending the evening with him and looking forward to seeing his house. She laughed to herself that she'd agreed to share it with him without even seeing it. Nick was about to turn her life upside down. She felt he was giving her back her youth.

When the bus drew to the stop in the centre of the city, she could see him waiting, his gaze sweeping through the passengers. A smile lit up his face when he saw her. His kiss on her cheek was as light as a butterfly's but he pulled her close and threaded her arm through his as they walked to his car.

As he drove out to the suburbs, all his attention was on the road but Leonie couldn't take her eyes off him. His well-groomed hands moved expertly on the wheel, his profile was calm and handsome.

'We have so much to decide,' he said, 'that I've asked Lily Bales, who cleans up for me, to make us a meal. It's easier to think calmly at home and talk things through, so I thought it better not to go to a restaurant tonight.'

Leonie's heart was racing as he pulled into the drive of a modest modern house. 'This is it.' He took her into his arms as soon as the front door closed behind them. 'Come and see.' He took her by the hand and led her from room to room. Leonie couldn't take it all in. 'Really, it's nothing special. I was looking for bachelor's accommodation when I chose this. Will it be big enough for us?'

'Of course, Nick.'

'There are three bedrooms but it's a bit tight when Tom and Elaine come with their twins.'

'I like it. It's very smart.'

'That's Elaine's influence. She helped me furnish it.'

'You've made it very comfortable. It's lovely.'

'It's easy to keep warm and clean – at least that's what she tells me.'

'Elaine will be right about that.'

'If you want to change anything, I'll be quite happy to—'

'No, I can't improve on this, especially not now. Elaine's better at this sort of thing than I am.' Leonie told him of her offer to buy her business and also rent the flat to Milo.

'That solves our problems for us.' He laughed. 'I hope you jumped at it.'

'I told her I'd think it over. Goodness! Where was my head?'

He gave her a hug. 'You've had a lot to think about. Ring her now and tell her it's exactly what you want.' He pushed her towards the phone. 'Tell her it's what I want too. It'll make everything possible for us and take you away from the air raids.'

Leonie was heading towards the phone when he caught her hand. 'Am I being selfish? Do you want to keep your business? You've worked hard at building it up.'

'No, what I want is to be here with you.'

'You could start another business here, if that's what you want.'

Leonie nodded and picked up the phone. 'Perhaps, but right now I'm too excited about getting married to think about that.'

Elaine sounded over the moon. 'It's exactly what I want too,' she said. 'I've already had a word with Ida. She met a woman in Woolworths who once worked with her. She's local and she's looking for a job. On Monday, I'll ask Ida to get in touch and tell her to come and see me.'

Nick gave her another delighted hug. 'All you need to do now is to agree a price and I'll do the rest.'

'Since it's going to Elaine I don't much mind.'

'We'll have it independently valued,' he said. 'That's what she'd want. Leonie, let's fix the soonest possible wedding date. We don't need to wait for months. I want us to be together, we've waited long enough.'

It was what Leonie wanted too. 'But we need to think of Amy. She missed June's wedding and Steve's funeral. I don't want her to feel excluded from . . .'

Nick kissed her forehead. 'We must have her here for our wedding. That's important for me too, I want her to accept me as her father.'

'Of course we must.' Leonie gave a little hiccup of joy as she had another thought. 'Amy could stay on here. Live with us from now on, I mean. You've seen very little of the Luftwaffe in Chester. She'd be safe enough here.'

'That's true, but don't you think it would be wiser to wait until we get her exam results? She'll reach secondary school age next September and whether she gets a scholarship or she doesn't, she'll need to start a new school then. I suggest she goes back to Wales after our wedding and has the summer term at her present school.'

'Of course,' Leonie agreed rather reluctantly. 'That would be the best thing for her. She's happy there with Auntie Bessie, and there's no sense in snatching her away when she'd have to go to a strange primary school here for a couple of months.'

Leonie stayed with Nick that night. 'I don't approve of the young doing this before marriage,' she said. 'But we are well on in life and we've already had a child.'

'And been parted for eleven years,' Nick said. 'You're very sensible. There is no point in waiting any longer.'

Leonie returned to the shop early on Tuesday morning feeling rested and settled in her mind. She was going to stay for a few days to wind things up and pack her personal possessions.

She had a lot of preparations and arrangements to make for her wedding.

Nick came to spend the evening with her. 'I can't bear us to be parted,' he said. He, too, had been making arrangements. 'To be married on a Saturday is the most convenient day for us all and Saturdays are pretty well booked up, but the curate of my local church has agreed to marry us at ten on a Saturday just over six weeks from now.'

Leonie smiled. 'Six weeks, that's great. We can wait that long can't we?'

'Yes. We have to allow three weeks for the banns to be called first.'

'Once I'm sorted here, I'll move in with you.'

'I'm going to borrow and beg petrol coupons from everybody I know so we can bring Amy home for the occasion on the Friday evening and take her back on the Sunday afternoon.'

Leonie wrote to Auntie Bessie to let her know what she was planning and when Amy rang her at the shop a few days later she told her all about it. She was fizzing with excitement. 'I want to be your bridesmaid and wear a long frock and flowers in my hair.'

'It's not going to be that sort of a wedding, sweetheart. I'm not going to wear a long white bridal gown.'

'Why not?'

'Because I've been married before and there's a war on. It's going to be a very quiet wedding, just the family and Nick's family, but you can be my bridesmaid in a short dress.'

Amy hesitated. 'Then it'll have to be a very special dress, won't it?'

'Yes, I'll make you a special dress,' Leonie immediately bit her lip. Amy had been noticeably taller when she'd last seen her and she had no up-to-date measurements for her. 'How did you get on in your exam?'

'All right, I think. I'm glad it's over and I don't have to do homework any more.'

Leonie was kept very busy. She'd decided to make her own dress for the wedding, and was choosing some pretty blue shantung from amongst the fabrics her business allowed her to keep in the shop when Elaine said, 'Let me design something special for you. It'll be my wedding present to you. And I'll make a dress for Amy from the same material. She'd like that, wouldn't she?'

'Elaine! You've done so much for me already.'

'Nonsense, I want to. In fact, I insist.'

'Thank you, thank you. Do you think this shantung would be suitable for Amy?'

'Well, it isn't real shantung is it? It should be silk and this is a mixture of cotton and rayon, a wartime copy. Pure cotton would be more suitable for a young girl.'

'I thought it would be nice for her to have the same material as me but I don't want to be married in cotton and she's expecting a very special dress. It'll have to be something silky.'

'How about this then?' Elaine indicated another wartime copy of shantung but a better quality. It was much the same cornflower blue but with a white pattern of leaves on it.

Leonie fingered it. 'Yes, I like that.'

'I could make you an outfit using both plain and patterned material. Let me have a think and play around with some patterns.'

'Not too fancy. We both need dresses we'll be able to wear on more ordinary occasions.'

'Leonie, you're going to look smart on your wedding day, whether it's wartime or not. Leave this to me.'

She was glad to. She had more than enough to do. Nick had bought a second-hand henhouse and had it installed behind his garage in the back garden. He and Leonie built a secure outdoor run alongside it. Milo and Alison packed up the poultry at Mersey Reach and Tom collected them in his car and took them to Chester that weekend. Together they helped Leonie settle them into their new quarters.

Nick tried to reserve a table for a restaurant lunch after the wedding but was having difficulty. The wedding venues were booked up and when he tried the local restaurants they could offer only their usual Saturday midday lunch of sausage and mash or Spam and chips. Lily Bales worked part-time for a firm of local caterers and recommended them. Nick got in touch and they agreed to come to his house and prepare and serve a celebratory lunch for twelve people. They suggested fruit salad and trifle for dessert.

The problem for Nick now was that he would have to provide the food. He went round to his local fishmonger and asked if he could get him a whole salmon. That, with salad, would provide the main part of the menu.

'Because it's unrationed it'll be very expensive.' The fishmonger shook his dead doubtfully. 'And I can't guarantee I'll be able to get it.'

'I have to be sure,' Nick said. 'This is not an occasion when I want to open tins of fish at the last moment.'

He laughed. 'I'll do my best. How many is it to feed?'

'Nine adults and three children.'

'Twelve portions would be easier. I have more chance of doing that.'

'Good. If not, nine of salmon and three of something else, plaice or even cod would do.'

'Or if I can't get any salmon, twelve portions of any fish that can be served cold – party style.'

'That's right.' Nick smiled. 'Don't forget I'm relying on you to get something for me. This is for my wedding breakfast.'

'All right,' the fishmonger said with a smile, 'I'll guarantee your order of twelve portions of some luxury fish.'

Ida was going to make the cake, but it would not be a traditional wedding cake because icing sugar and dried fruit were unobtainable. She suggested a large chocolate cake which she could make with cocoa and cover with melted chocolate bars.

The build-up to the wedding was hectic, and the day arrived before Leonie felt ready for it. She was thrilled with her wedding outfit. It was a dress of the flowered material with a jacket of the plain material to wear over it. She bought a white hat to wear with it and Elaine fitted a matching hatband to it.

On the Friday before, she went with Nick to collect Amy and had a lovely day out; it was much less exhausting when they went both ways by car. They had to return via Elaine's house as Amy's dress wasn't quite finished. She needed to have a fitting before Elaine could be satisfied it would make Amy look her best. She would finish it off that night and bring it with her tomorrow when she came to the wedding.

Milo and June were staying with them that night and they all got up early, collected Alison on the way and arrived on the doorstep while Nick, Leonie and Amy were having breakfast in their dressing gowns. They dropped Milo, June and Alison and went off to collect the rest of the family for the wedding.

'Who are they?' Amy wanted to know.

'I was brought up by Tom's parents so his family is also my family,' Nick said. 'So the twins, Dulcie and Luke, will be coming, you know them, and my Aunt Bernice and their Auntie Olive.'

June and Alison had arrived in their wedding outfits so they washed up. Amy went out in her dressing gown to see Hetty and her chicks and returned with a brown egg from Polly.

Nick sent Leonie off to have a bath and change into her wedding finery, and took the girls into the garden to find flowers they could cut.

'We need flowers to make a posy for the bride and we all need a buttonhole,' he said. 'I'm afraid there aren't many. It's a bit early in the year for my garden.'

'No,' Alison said. 'That's a lovely rose hedge over there.'

'Rambling roses,' he said. 'Bigger flowers with lots of petals would be more suited for a wedding, especially for the bride.'

'If rambling roses are all you have, that's what we'll have to use.'

'They'll look very nice,' Alison said. The rose hedge was in full flower. Alison fashioned them into a posy for Leonie and pushed the stalks though the centre of a fancy paper doily.

'I want a bouquet to carry,' Amy said, so she made a smaller version for her.

'They look very professional.' Nick was impressed. They found blooms to make buttonholes for all the adults.

Milo was sent to collect the fish and brought back six

portions of salmon and six portions of plaice and the fish-monger's apologies, it was the best he could do. By that time the caterers had arrived. They'd given Nick a list of food he'd have to provide for them to complete the menu. He'd had to ask Lily Bales to buy salad vegetables yesterday, because he and Leonie had driven to Wales. Now he lifted the box on to the kitchen table and the caterers took over the kitchen and dining room.

Amy was tearing round and it was June who took charge of her, running a bath for her and helping her into her new dress which fitted her perfectly. Elaine had made a little bonnet from the plain cloth and plenty of stiffening and Leonie thought she looked both sweet and smart with her hair combed out and brushed back so it hung down beneath her bonnet. Amy was absolutely thrilled with her outfit.

They all squeezed into Nick's car for the short drive to the church, which was very old and big. Tom and Elaine and their family were already inside waiting for the ceremony to begin. Nick peeped in from the porch and whispered that Lily Bales and her daughter were there too and one or two other people he didn't know.

The curate, ready robed, came to greet them and led Nick and Tom, who was acting as his best man, forward. Nick turned to drop a gentle kiss on Leonie's forehead before leaving her. Milo led her down the aisle a minute or two later and Amy followed so closely she kept touching her.

Leonie felt bemused, this was nothing like her very formal first wedding and unlike any she'd ever been to. The marriage service began and she handed Amy her posy of flowers. She seemed to be juggling with the two posies. Leonie turned away to listen to the time-honoured words, but she was also conscious of Nick standing tall and upright on her right side and a rather overawed Amy edging forward on her left.

Today Leonie was wearing Steve's wedding ring on her right hand, so that Nick's could be slid on to her wedding finger. As she signed the register, she thought of how she'd longed for this moment when they'd first met and marvelled that Nick's love had survived all that time.

Elaine, Olive and Nick had brought their cameras and each had managed to hoard a little film and were prepared to use it lavishly today. They started with the traditional view of the bride and groom standing on the church steps, and had to press a member of the public into taking one or two pictures of all twelve of them together. Leonie tossed her bouquet into the air, aiming it at Alison. She caught it deftly but blushed as she realised the implication. Amy refused to part with hers.

They piled into the two cars to go home after that and found that Lily Bales and her daughter had arrived just before them. 'A very simple and dignified service,' Lily whispered to Leonie as she held out a tray of drinks to welcome the bridal party home.

Leonie relaxed and the rest of the party did too. Although Nick had initially decided a buffet would be the best he could do, the caterers had decided it would be possible to seat twelve by adding two smaller tables to the one in the dining room and covering them all with a sheet before laying two damask tablecloths cornerwise across that. The caterers had provided cutlery, china and glassware and with two small vases of rambling roses. It looked magnifient.

Nick had failed to get champagne but he'd managed a few

bottles of white wine. Leonie thought the caterers served an excellent meal with style and Ida's cake was magnificent. She was sorry she hadn't been able to invite Ida but Elaine needed her to open the shop. Saturday was one of their busiest days.

Under the control of the caterers the meal proceeded effortlessly at a dignified pace, and a party atmosphere began to develop. Leonie heard Amy laugh and was thankful the child was happy. Amy and the twins had slid down from the table and were unpacking a bag of toys Elaine had brought. All the adults heard her piping voice announce that she'd got a new daddy today, and suggest that they go to see the chickens because they were more interesting than toys.

Nick was being very attentive to his Aunt Bernice who was now approaching ninety and very frail. She seemed to be enjoying herself and her quavering voice was recounting some tale from Tom and Nick's childhood. Leonie looked round the table at her guests and felt very fortunate to have friends and family like them.

She felt proud of her older children. Milo had made every effort to recover as quickly as possible from his dreadful injuries and he'd not allowed his war experiences to cloud his future. He'd coped so much better than his father had, but Milo had a different personality, he was outgoing and set out to make friends wherever he could. She knew he was happy with his choice of work and she didn't doubt that he'd continue to make a success of his life.

June had been more changed by her experience than he had, but Leonie knew her torrents of grief over Ralph's death were easing, though she was by no means over her loss. June was wearing the blue wool dress Leonie had made for her two years ago which at the time hadn't seemed to please her much.

She was now a very serious twenty-year-old, but she had other things in her life – a growing interest in nursing and new friends. The knowledge that she was doing valuable war work was giving her confidence and she was beginning to develop an aura of calm serenity.

Leonie could hear Elaine telling Olive how thrilled she was to be running her own business at last, that it was an ambition realised after many years and that she'd learned a great deal from Leonie.

That made Leonie smile, throughout those years Elaine had been her main support and a firm friend, and it was owing to her generosity that she'd been able to come and live with Nick with so little fuss. She loved Elaine dearly.

Dulcie and Luke were wearing the same outfits they'd worn to June's wedding and they still looked smart though they'd been let out and let down to fit them.

She caught Nick's gaze and he gave her an intimate smile as though there was no one else in the room. Leonie knew she'd never loved anyone more and she'd be very happy with him.

It was almost four o'clock when they rose from the table and by then Aunt Bernice was tired. Tom drove her, his sister and the twins home, and he called back half an hour later to give June, Milo and Alison a lift back into Birkenhead.

Leonie was very content to be left alone with Nick and Amy. 'We're a new family,' she marvelled, 'together at last.'

Nick nodded. 'Amy, we have to wait a little longer until you can live with us permanently but it's guaranteed that you will.'

'When the school holidays start,' she said.

'Yes. Let's go for a walk to stretch our legs,' Leonie said.

Amy walked between them, holding on to one hand of each.

When, a few weeks later, Leonie heard that Amy had achieved a scholarship and would take it up at the Queen's School, Chester, in September, and her new family would be permanently together, she felt there was nothing more she could ask of life.

Liverpool Love Song

Anne Baker

When Helen Redwood is tragically widowed, she and her daughter, Chloe, move to Liverpool to be closer to her family. But it is tending her beautiful garden with her handsome young gardener, Rex Kenwright, that ultimately saves Helen from grief. No stranger to bereavement himself, Rex finds comfort in Helen's company although seventeen-year-old Chloe is the one who steals his heart.

Chloe has dreams of her own, however, and when she announces that she is pregnant and moving in with her boyfriend, Adam Livingstone, she has no idea of the effect this will have on those she loves. Nor does she anticipate the rocky road to happiness that lies ahead . . .

Praise for Anne Baker's gripping Merseyside sagas:

'Baker's understanding and compassion for very human dilemmas makes her one of romantic fiction's most popular authors' *Lancashire Evening Post*

'A stirring tale of romance and passion, poverty and ambition' *Liverpool Echo*

978 0 7553 7833 3

headline

Nancy's War

Anne Baker

As the Second World War looms, Nancy Seymour is told that her RAF pilot husband, Charles, has been killed. Devastated by her loss, she struggles to support their little girl, Caro, on her own. But, as bombs start to fall on Merseyside, Charles's father offers them sanctuary, in the form of a cottage in the countryside. Meanwhile, Charles's mother Henrietta is hell-bent on making Nancy's life a misery. For dark secrets lurk in the Seymour family and Henrietta will stop at nothing to keep them hidden. With the danger of war ever-present, Nancy is determined to protect her loved ones from harm, knowing that if she can survive the years of peril ahead, then perhaps one day she will find happiness again . . .

Praise for Anne Baker's touching Merseyside sagas:

'A stirring tale of romance and passion, poverty and ambition' *Liverpool Echo*

'Truly compelling . . . rich in language and descriptive prose' *Newcastle Upon Tyne Evening Chronicle*

'A heart-warming saga' *Woman's Weekly*

978 0 7553 5667 6

headline

Through Rose-Coloured Glasses

Anne Baker

Dinah Radcliffe doesn't have much money to spend on fine things, but she lives contentedly with her mother, Sarah, in their cosy house in Walton. Dinah and Sarah have seen their share of troubles since Dinah's father was killed in the Great War but the Radcliffes have always made the best of what they have.

When Dinah meets widowed businessman Richard Haldane at the races, her life changes beyond recognition. Richard sweeps Dinah off her feet, dazzling her with a glimpse of wealth and privilege beyond her wildest dreams, and their whirlwind romance leads to marriage in a matter of weeks. But is Richard the man she thought he was? Soon, Dinah learns that money can't buy you happiness, and that she's married to someone who takes far more dangerous risks than just betting on his horses . . .

Praise for Anne Baker's touching Merseyside sagas:

'A stirring tale of romance and passion, poverty and ambition' *Liverpool Echo*

'A heart-warming saga' *Woman's Weekly*

'With characters who are strong, warm and sincere, this is a joy to read' *Coventry Evening Telegraph*

978 0 7553 5665 2

headline